CONTENTS

"What just happened?" Shelby demanded.

"Dynamite."

She gave Barrett an incredulous look. "Dynamite? As in TNT?"

He nodded. "Plenty left around here from the mining days."

"Why would someone light up a stick and toss it at me? It has to be the guy who threatened me."

"Maybe, unless you've angered somebody else."

She folded her arms and skewered him with such a look of disdain it almost made him smile.

He didn't answer. Whatever she had or hadn't done, it wasn't his business. Yet once again, he found himself trying to extricate her from a pile of trouble.

"What makes you think it's not the man who threatened me?" she said.

"Doesn't seem like a rational thing for him to do."

"He threatened to kill me recently, if you remember."

"Words don't mean much. My father believes him to be an honorable man, deep down."

She met his eyes, her own glimmering with unreadable emotion. "I admire that kind of familial respect."

Something was under those words, something deep and painful and raw.

Dana Mentink is a nationally bestselling author. She has been honored to win two Carol Awards, a HOLT Medallion and an RT Reviewers' Choice Best Book Award. She's authored more than thirty novels to date for Love Inspired Suspense and Harlequin Heartwarming. Dana loves feedback from her readers. Contact her at danamentink.com.

Susan Sleeman is a bestselling author of inspirational and clean-read romantic suspense books and mysteries. She received an RT Reviewers' Choice Best Book Award for *Thread of Suspicion. No Way Out* and *The Christmas Witness* were finalists for the Daphne du Maurier Award for Excellence. She's had the pleasure of living in nine states and currently lives in Oregon. To learn more about Susan, visit her website at susansleeman.com.

Christmas Protector

USA TODAY Bestselling Author

Dana Mentink

&

Susan Sleeman

2 Thrilling Stories
Cowboy Christmas Guardian and *Holiday Secrets*

LOVE INSPIRED
INSPIRATIONAL ROMANCE

LOVE INSPIRED®
INSPIRATIONAL ROMANCE

ISBN-13: 978-1-335-42988-9

Christmas Protector

Copyright © 2022 by Harlequin Enterprises ULC

Cowboy Christmas Guardian
First published in 2017. This edition published in 2022.
Copyright © 2017 by Dana Mentink

Holiday Secrets
First published in 2017. This edition published in 2022.
Copyright © 2017 by Susan Sleeman

Recycling programs
for this product may
not exist in your area.

For questions and comments about the quality of this book, please contact us
at CustomerService@Harlequin.com.

Love Inspired
22 Adelaide St. West, 41st Floor
Toronto, Ontario M5H 4E3, Canada
www.LoveInspired.com

Printed in U.S.A.

COWBOY
CHRISTMAS GUARDIAN

Dana Mentink

This book is dedicated to Phil and Nancy Fay,
horse lovers, baseball fans and faithful servants.

And we know that all things work together for good to them that love God, to them who are the called according to his purpose.
—*Romans* 8:28

Chapter One

Barrett Thorn shouted to his younger brother between
the clashes of thunder that ripped through the winter
darkness. "Gonna go after her. See to the paddock."
Swanny, the runaway pregnant mare, was prone to pan-
icking during lightning storms and, true to form, she'd
broken through the paddock and bolted.

A flash of lightning illuminated Jack, sitting astride
his mare, shoulders hunched against the storm. Barrett
was relieved that it was not Jack's twin, Owen, out in
the treacherous night. Owen was not physically healed
yet, in spite of his bravado. The war had damaged him
inside and out. It would be his first Christmas back
home since his return from Afghanistan.

In his typical quiet way, Jack didn't answer, pulling
his horse into a fluid turn and trotting away through
the pouring rain. Their father, Tom, was back at the
house where Keegan and Owen were helping him check
on the other sixty horses in their care. The Gold Bar
Ranch, was the finest setup in the town of Gold Bar and
maybe in the entire region, in his humble opinion, but it
took all of them to keep it that way. Most of their herd

would be fine, Barrett figured, but the more recent arrivals they were boarding for clients over the Christmas holidays might not feel as comfortable in their newer surroundings. Horses could be almost as unpredictable as people. Almost.

From his vantage point on the bluff astride his rock-solid horse, Titan, Barrett had seen only the streak of Swanny's white flanks moving through the undulating branches of the wind-whipped pines. He held Titan still, listening, rain collecting on his close-cut beard and funneling off his hat.

With a section of fencing failing yet again on the western perimeter of the Gold Bar's thousand-acre ranch, the horse would have had easy access to the abutting land, a swath of ravine and hills cut through by a river swollen by yet another storm.

"Why couldn't you stay in the stable like all the other horses?" He was suddenly struck by a memory so strong it hitched up his breath.

"Swanny doesn't care about all your cowboy orders," Sabrina used to say. He could picture his wife, whom he'd nicknamed Bree, so clearly in his mind. Her fringe of blond bangs fell over eyes that saw through his macho facade and right into the most tender places in his soul. Bree was the woman God meant to be his partner, his love, his best friend, riding beside him through this life.

Except that she was gone in a moment of carelessness, lost in a crushing tangle of metal.

His stomach tensed with white-hot rage at the person who had taken her away and stripped him of any kind of a future.

Titan's uneasy shifting pulled him from the memory. He had to get to Swanny soon, before she broke a leg or got tangled up in barbed wire. He urged Titan through the gap in the busted fence and onto Joe Hatcher's property with only a small flicker of unease.

He wondered if the surly saddler had followed through on his threat to set booby traps to keep local kids from fooling around, searching for gold. If he had the time, he'd knock on Hatcher's door and ask permission, but Swanny was in danger. He wasn't about to let pleasantries get in the way of rescuing the poor beast.

"Hope we don't get shot," he muttered to Titan. They picked their way carefully over the flattest stretch of ground that sloped down to a densely wooded area. Not the greatest place to hang out during a lightning storm, but Swanny was scared, no doubt, and might have headed for the comfort of the overhanging branches.

Barrett rode closer, the noise of the rain mingling with the sound of the swollen river at the bottom of a crevasse just beyond the trees. Fingers to his lips, he let out a piercing whistle which usually alerted his horses that there would be a sugar cube or an apple for them if they presented themselves. It worked on some horses and not on others. Swanny never failed to come for her bit of dessert.

"A hopeless sweet tooth," Bree used to say.

Ducking as the wet branches slapped the back of his neck, he pushed on into the trees. Titan stopped short, as surprised as Barrett at what they saw.

A cream-colored compact car, foreign made, was parked under the bushes. It looked to be fairly new and sported out-of-state Nevada plates. Definitely not a vehicle he'd ever be caught dead in. He could not picture Joe Hatcher driving such a thing either, but who would trespass on his property and go so far as to park their car in such an isolated corner? And for what purpose?

A crackle of branches drew his attention.

"It's Barrett Thorn. I'm looking for my horse," he called out, figuring it was the best way not to get shot if Joe Hatcher was out patrolling his property. "Who's there?"

No answer, but neither did he hear the sound of a shotgun being cocked, so that was a plus.

The rain pounded harder. Titan shifted his weight to indicate that he did not understand his master's crazy choice to remain in the elements when there was a perfectly good barn back on the Gold Bar Ranch.

At the moment, Barrett was beginning to question his own actions, too. Swanny would wind up back at the barn sooner or later, and it would be a lot easier trying to find her after sunup. He might be risking his own safety and that of Titan by continuing the search mission. Was he going the extra mile to find the horse because she was his duty? Or because she had been Bree's favorite?

"You'd do it for any of the horses," he mumbled to himself. He patted Titan's neck, the storm howling around them.

No one emerged from the undergrowth. It must have been an animal or a storm-related noise he'd heard. Of course. What else would it have been? Swanny would have responded to his whistle long ago.

Still, he waited a minute longer. His cowboy hat was not enough to keep the driving rain from snaking down his neck, wetting his shirt under his jacket. His jeans were soaked from his belt to the top of his boots.

If Swanny was in the woods somewhere, she'd have

shown herself by now, he felt certain. It was time to search elsewhere. The car would remain a mystery for someone else to solve.

"We'll go check the east end again, in case your daffy girl changed her mind and started back home," he said. Titan twitched an ear, eager to be heading out of the storm, and began his about-face.

Thump.

Barrett pulled Titan to a stop. What he'd heard this time wasn't a twig snapping.

Thump, thump.

Cold prickles erupted on the back of his neck at the sound. Hopping from the saddle, he approached the car.

Another thump and a woman's cry.

Coming from inside the trunk.

Shelby Arroyo slammed her sneakers against the metal lid of the trunk and kicked for all she was worth. The effort sent pain shooting up her neck to her skull where her attacker had struck her from behind while she'd been fumbling in her trunk. She was scared, terrified even and angry at herself.

"How stupid you are," Shelby hissed. "Staying out until nightfall without even letting Uncle Ken know your route." Absorbed in the area geology as she usually was, completely oblivious, she'd not got even a glimpse of the person who had hit her over the head and pushed her in. And where was her cell phone? She stopped kicking long enough to grope again around the pitch-black space, encountering nothing but the bag of extra shoes she'd left there. The little pack she carried with her assaying tools, driver's license, phone, keys and wallet had fallen from her hand, probably taken by her attacker along with her soil samples.

Why? The samples were worthless, just a way for her to collect information about the area geology, and she had less than twenty dollars in her wallet.

Whoever had done it must have been watching her, biding their time. The thought froze her. Strange hands had lifted her up, dumped her in and left her there. She was fortunate the guy hadn't decided to kill her, unless he figured she'd die in the trunk before anyone found her. It would be a slow, unkind death, of hunger and thirst. A flood of panic stampeded inside. *Stop it, Shelby.*

She kicked again in frustration. "Let...me...out," she hollered to no one. Try as she might, she could find no internal trunk release. There had to be one somewhere, but her shaking fingers simply could not locate it and of course she'd never taken the time to read the owner's manual. *Who imagines they're going to get locked in their own trunk?* she thought bitterly.

The car jolted.

She almost screamed.

Someone was attempting to open the trunk from the outside. Her heart jumped to her throat. Was it help? But who would know where to find her except the man who had locked her there in the first place? No innocent bystander would be out strolling along in a downpour at ten o'clock at night.

He'd come back.

Her mind scrambled, trying to figure out some means of defense. She had nothing, no weapon, no phone. "God..." she started, but that wouldn't do any good. Prayers were fine and all, but she knew she had to rely on herself, as she'd told her mother so many times before the woman no longer knew who Shelby was.

Resolve hardened inside Shelby like hot lava hitting cold ocean water. She intended to use every shred of muscle she possessed to save herself. No divine intervention required. Tensing her legs, she poised to kick out, straining to hear over the whoosh of rain.

Was that footsteps now, heading away?

No. The car was lurching under a heavy onslaught at the front end, the metal shuddering around her. There was a sound of breaking glass. After a moment, the trunk release triggered and the lid slid open a couple of inches. She paused to give him just enough time to return to the back of the vehicle. Timing would be crucial.

One chance is all you get, Shelby, she thought.

She was blinded by the glare from a flashlight whoever it was must have been holding. Another half second. With an explosive effort, she bucked her feet out as hard as she could. The trunk lid made contact.

She heard a man's grunt of surprise and pain, but she did not stop long enough to assess the damage. Instead she was out and running as fast as she could over the open ground.

"Stop," a man's deep voice called.

No way, her mind shot back but her feet did not slow. Pain pounded through her neck and shoulders but the adrenaline kept it at bay. She had to get to a house or find a place to hole up until morning to buy herself time.

"Stop," the voice came again louder, closer. "There's a…"

She did not hear the last word. Running faster than she'd known she could, Shelby flew, feet slipping on wet rocks and tripping over the uneven patches of ground.

He was drawing nearer, moving surprisingly fast for a big man. A glance told her he was as wet as she was, a cowboy hat hiding his face.

She pressed harder and he yelled again, but she gave his words no heed.

A smell of sodden vegetation and the faraway sound of running water triggered an alarm bell in her mind. Cold air wafted up from somewhere far below. The ground suddenly gave way underneath her as she plunged into nothingness.

Chapter Two

Barrett skidded to a stop at the edge of the ravine, flopping down on his belly. Rain slashed at him and the almost-perfect darkness obliterated her from view. He shined his flashlight down into the ravine.

It took him several minutes to spot her, the gleam of one pale arm showing against the slick rock. She lay perfectly still on her back on a narrow ledge of rock, one leg dangling down into the abyss.

Dead? His blood went cold. *No, not dead, unconscious*, he told himself firmly.

It wasn't going to be easy logistically to get to her. Plus, if she awakened, she'd probably try to claw his eyes out or something and send them both to the bottom of the ravine. Rubbing his chin where the trunk lid had caught him, he tasted blood in his mouth.

He pulled his phone from his pocket, dialed Jack and explained the situation in twenty words or less. Jack would alert their father and brothers. There was no sense contacting the volunteer fire department since it might take upward of thirty minutes to an hour to assemble any kind of rescue group out here, especially on such a night.

Titan eased close at Barrett's whistle. Barrett retrieved a rope from the saddlebag, shoving his hat inside. He tied the rope to a sturdy trunk that overhung the ravine. If he'd stopped to think a minute, he might have considered the recklessness of his actions. Slippery slope, inadequate light, storm raging and a volatile woman at the bottom of it all.

Best to call in rescue and wait, or delay until his brothers showed up. But something in the way she lay there, body twisted, slender and vulnerable in the storm, would not let him delay a moment more.

Looping the other end of the rope around himself, he eased outward into the gap back first, beginning his rappel over the edge.

Titan shook his mane and stamped a hoof on the ground.

"I know, buddy," Barrett muttered. "This is just all kinds of crazy." His horse's brown eyes were the last thing he saw as he plunged into the darkness.

The series of storms had saturated the ground, washing away ribbons of soil and leaving behind a lattice of twisted roots. Bits of rock pattered down from above, striking his neck and shoulders. The rope scratched against his palms, reminding him that he should have had the good sense to retrieve his leather gloves from the saddlebag along with the rope. His boots scraped even more material away from the cliff wall as he navigated down to the ledge.

As far as he could tell, the woman had not moved. The fall hadn't covered a great distance, no more than fifteen feet, he figured, but who knew what kind of injuries she might have sustained if nothing had broken her fall? Again the cold, sick sensation gathered in his belly.

When he was about a yard from the ledge, he stopped, feet braced against the mud. "Ma'am?" he called. "My name is Barrett Thorn and I'm coming to help you."

She didn't answer. He hadn't figured she would, but it was worth a shot.

He settled gingerly onto the ledge, crouching next to her. A mass of wet hair covered her face and he reached out a finger to pull it away. Her profile was visible, nose small, chin narrow, face heart shaped. The delicacy of it struck him.

Without warning, he was plunged back in time some four years earlier, when he'd pulled Bree from the wrecked car. Her eyes had been shut, too, but they'd fluttered open for one precious moment before they'd closed for the last time. There was nothing in this world that could hurt worse than that, except being reminded every day in a million ways that he was alone. Strange the things he missed about Bree.

The pillow next to his with a satin case to "keep away the wrinkles" of which he'd never seen a hint on her face.

Her ready laughter.

The smell of the candles she always insisted on lighting for every evening meal.

Her horrendous cooking. He even missed that. What he wouldn't give for a chance to eat another plateful of tuna casserole, crunchy with half-cooked noodles. He swatted at a trail of water running down his cheek. *Business at hand, Barrett.*

Swallowing hard, he found the junction of the unconscious woman's chin and neck, and pressed his fingers there, seeking a pulse.

"Lord God," he prayed, but he could not finish. The last time he had prayed for the life of a young woman, his woman, his love, God's answer had been no. Gritted teeth, pounding heart, his soul quaked with fear that he would find no spark of life. Gone, like Bree, with him crouched there helpless. Rubbing his hands as dry as he could, he tried one more time. This time, the proof was dramatic.

She jerked to a sitting position with a scream and shot out a hand that nearly shoved him over the edge.

"Easy," he said, holding open palms up to show her he was not a threat. "I'm not going to hurt you."

Her eyes were wide as silver dollars, whole body trembling. Her breath came in short bursts as she scrabbled away as far as she could get from him. He attempted to reassure her that he wasn't some random killer who'd appeared on a ledge in a storm, but she moved backward and he lunged forward to catch her.

The rock ledge gave way beneath her feet. Her eyes were bright with fear as she disappeared before his eyes for the second time.

Shelby's senses cartwheeled through a dizzying cascade as her legs slithered over the side. Pitch-black night, cold rain, the sick sensation of no ground under her feet. The jagged edge of rocks cut into her belly as she clutched at anything that might keep her from falling the rest of the way.

"Help," she wanted to scream, but she could not manage a single syllable as she continued to slip down the slope.

Rocks ground against her hips and roots broke away

under her fingers. She felt a jerk and a painful pressure on her wrist. Looking up against the sheeting rain, she saw the man with the beard hanging on to her wrist with both hands. His full mouth was contorted with the effort.

No, no, her mind screamed. He'd come to finish what he'd started when he'd struck her and stuffed her in the trunk of her car. She braced her legs against the canyon wall to push away.

"Listen," he said between clenched teeth. "I am not the guy who hurt you. You're just gonna have to trust me on that because you're wiggling and I don't wanna drop you."

Trust him? She had no intention of doing any such thing, but the canyon below her did not give her much choice. Die on the rocks, or live long enough to get away from the bearded guy? Her forearms ached and her ribs burned with pain.

"Give me your other hand," he ordered.

Fighting her instincts, she heaved her other arm up and he clasped it tight. They both breathed hard for a few seconds before he began to haul her back up. She helped with her legs as much as she could. Inch by painful inch, she was pulled upward until she landed on her knees on the ledge. The man bent over at the waist, panting.

Their eyes locked, like two wild animals sizing each other up.

"Barrett," came a shout from above, making her jump.

"I got her," he hollered back. "Gonna need to pull us up."

There was some response that she could not decipher.

He puffed out a breath and straightened, rising to

something over six feet she guessed, plenty strong enough to have clobbered her and shoved her into the trunk. Then again, if his goal was to hurt her, why would he have kept her from falling into the ravine? Doubt clouded her thinking along with the cold that seemed to be freezing her one layer at a time.

"All right," he said. "My brothers are going to pull us up on the rope, so you have to hang on to me for a minute, okay?"

Not okay. The furthest thing from okay. To deliver herself into the hands of this stranger and now his brothers? Needing more time to think, she shook her head.

His expression went a little softer, or so she imagined. "I know you've been through a fright and you're scared, but I'm a good guy, mostly." He offered a wry smile. "At least, some folks might say so. I'm not here to hurt you, but there's really no way I can prove that to you under the present circumstances."

He could be telling the truth but her fear still ran rampant. She pressed herself to the cliff wall, staying far out of reach.

He tucked his hands onto his hips. "All right. If that's your choice, we'll honor it. I've never in my life forced a woman to do anything she didn't want to, but I for one am tired of being out here in the rain, and I've got a horse to find, so if you really want to stay down here by yourself, it's a long wait until sunrise."

She saw now there was a rope knotted around his waist. He looped an extra length around himself, grabbed hold above his head and shouted to his brothers to start pulling.

Below, the river water rushed wildly on past the rocky ground. The wind teased her wet skin, her body shivering uncontrollably. She recalled her mother's admonition, always gentle, too gentle. *So stubborn, Shell. It's not always you against the world.*

"Wait," she said.

Water ran down his crew-cut hair and wide chin. Slowly he held out a hand to her.

Just get out of the ravine, she told herself. *Then you can figure if this guy is the genial cowboy or the man who locked you up.* She reached out shaking fingers. His palms were rough and calloused, the hands of a working man, and he scooped her to his side in one strong movement.

His shoulders were solid, wide under the sodden jacket, his waist tapered and trim as she clung to him, gripping his leather belt.

"Keep holding on tight," he advised.

She did as the rope was pulled up from above. The journey threatened to spin them in circles, but the man she'd heard called Barrett kept them relatively steady by bracing his long legs against the canyon walls.

Foot by slippery foot, they gradually reached the top where she found herself surrounded by three more men and their horses. Their physical similarities marked them as brothers, except for the one who was more slender and lanky than the other three.

"I'll call for an ambulance when I can get a signal," said the brother who was still astride his horse. He peered down at her curiously.

Another handed her a blanket. Barrett helped wrap it around her shoulders.

"Mama's waiting at the house," one of the brothers said.

Barrett nodded, taking the reins to a big horse from

one and retrieving his wet hat from the saddlebag. "You can ride with me—" he hesitated "—unless you'd rather not."

She was miserable and shivering badly as she surveyed the men who stared at her. Something in their appearance took the edge off her suspicion, or maybe it was the reference to Mama. She'd always called her mother that, a sweet endearment that bridged the gap between angry daughter and desperate mother. *Mama.* Two syllables packed to the brim with feelings, and she would give anything to say it one more time and see understanding in her mother's eyes.

We're oil and water sometimes, Shelby, but I'll always be your Mama.

Oil and water. More like fire and ice.

Mama, I miss you.

Expelling a breath and straightening her shoulders, she nodded. Barrett got onto his horse in one fluid motion and offered her an arm.

After a moment of paralyzing doubt, she took it and he swung her up behind him.

"Where are we going?" she said into his ear.

"Home," he said, urging the horse through the pounding rain.

Chapter Three

Barrett was not too cold to feel uncomfortable at having a woman's arms wrapped around his waist. It had been four long years since any woman had touched him except his mother and assorted relatives. The lady was strong and soft at the same time, holding on to him tentatively, it seemed to him. Fortunately, Titan was eager to get back to the barn so his pace was brisk as they returned to the house.

The string of Christmas lights twined around the porch railing twinkled in the gloom. His father met them, taking the reins from Barrett as he helped the woman off the horse. Barrett tied the horses under the wide porch as a temporary measure until he could unsaddle them, dry them down and see to their feed.

His father tipped his wet hat to her and introduced himself. "Tom Thorn. Very sorry for your trouble, miss. Come inside and my wife, Evie, will help you feel comfortable."

"Thank you," she said.

"Got Swanny," he said to Barrett. "She's in the barn, looking plenty sorry."

"I'm sure." Barrett chuckled. More likely, she was pleased as could be now that she was back in a warm stable with a bucket of oats. It eased his mind to know that his wife's dotty horse was unhurt after her mad escape.

Barrett's mother stood in the doorway, gesturing. "Enough chatting, Barrett. Bring that poor girl in the house."

"Yes, ma'am." He followed her in where Evie looked the woman up and down. His mother was all of four feet eleven inches, hair graying but green eyes sparkling as brightly as they ever had.

"What's your name, honey?" she asked.

"Shelby," the woman replied, teeth chattering.

"Well, Miss Shelby, I am eager to hear how in the world you got halfway down a ravine on Joe Hatcher's property, but first things first. Everybody needs some dry clothes. I've got a pot of coffee on, so go change, boys, and we'll have a talk."

She put an arm around Shelby's shoulders. "Come with me. We'll get you a change of clothes and check out your bruises." She chuckled. "Don't worry. I was an RN before I traded it in for ranch life, so I'm not just a nosy mom to those four gorillas."

Barrett marched to his room, stripped off his wet clothes and pulled on a dry pair of jeans and a T-shirt, along with his less favored pair of boots. He tried not to rush, but he was dying to hear Shelby's story. It was an odd sensation. Since Bree died, he had been interested in nothing and no one, only his family and the workings of the Gold Bar Ranch where his life was 100 percent about the horses.

Forcing a slow pace, he ambled into the kitchen to

find twins, Jack and Owen, sitting at the table sipping coffee while their youngest brother, Keegan, leaned against the refrigerator, munching a cheese sandwich.

Keegan had a bottomless appetite and a head for mischief. He shook his dark hair from his face and grinned. "So, Barrett. For once it's not me that broke the rules. What's it feel like to be a trespasser?"

Owen laughed as their father joined them. "Good thing you didn't run across any of Joe Hatcher's booby traps."

"Those are rumors," their father said with a frown. He scrubbed a hand over a scalp of stubbly gray hair that had not thinned in spite of his seventy-three years. "Joe is a good man, or used to be. Top-notch saddler until his life took a turn."

"If you say so," Owen said.

"I do say so, son," he said quietly. "Everyone's life takes a turn now and then, doesn't it?"

"Yes, sir." Owen looked at the table, probably feeling again the enemy bullets that had carved a trail into his leg and left him scarred and limping. Keegan understood, too. He was adopted into the Thorn family at age sixteen when there was no one to care for him but Evie and Tom Thorn. In Barrett's case, one careless turn of a drunk driver's wheel had brought his life to a full stop.

Yes, he agreed. Life could take a sudden turn.

Owen and Jack stood as their mother ushered Shelby in and seated her in one of their vacated chairs.

At last he could get a good look at her. Trying not to stare, he drank in the details. She was slender and fine boned, probably somewhere close to five feet seven inches. Now he could see that her eyes were the green of forest moss, her hair brown. She'd pulled it into a wet ponytail that swept the flannel shirt his mom had loaned her. A navy blue pair of sweatpants, which his mother must have dug up from somewhere, engulfed her legs.

"I think she's going to be okay," Evie said. "But I would lobby for a hospital visit to be sure there isn't a concussion from where she was struck on the head."

Struck on the head? What kind of person would hit a woman? That notion made his stomach flip. And the fact that she thought he'd done it? He cleared his throat and introduced everyone properly.

Shelby nodded solemnly at each brother and his parents.

"Thank you," she said, her gaze finally landing on him. "Especially you, Barrett. I… I thought…" She twisted a finger in the hem of her borrowed shirt. "Well, anyway, thank you."

He nodded. "What were you doing on Hatcher's property?"

His mother shot him a scolding look. "Can you offer her a cup of coffee before you start the interrogation? Even cowboys should have good manners."

Ignoring the smiles from his brothers, he poured a cup of coffee and handed it to Shelby.

"Thank you," she said, the slight quirk of her lips indicating she was enjoying seeing him chastised. "I thought I was still on my uncle's property. I got caught up in my work and I didn't realize I'd strayed. Lost track of the time, too." She looked thoroughly embarrassed.

Her uncle? Which of their neighbors was her relation? He was about to ask when a loud pounding on the front door made her jump, spilling some of the coffee.

"Don't think that's the cops yet," Owen said. "I called them, but they're working an overturned lumber truck on the main road that has traffic stopped in and out of town." He opened the door.

Joe Hatcher stepped in, white hair plastered over his skull. His angry gaze swept the kitchen until it fastened on Shelby. "I was out checking my property. Saw Barrett pulling you out of the ravine. You got no business on my land, like I told you last week. You trespass again and you're gonna get hurt," he snarled.

All the brothers stepped a pace forward.

"You'll be civil," their father said, "or you'll leave."

"Civil?" Hatcher's eyes narrowed. "I gotta be civil when she can trespass on my land? Go poking around in my mine?"

"I wasn't anywhere near your mine and I didn't mean to stray onto your property. That was my mistake. I was taking some samples along the road and I got disoriented."

Samples? For what purpose? Barrett wondered.

"Fool thing to do. You deserve what you got," Hatcher said.

Shelby stood and lifted her chin. "So was it you who hit me from behind and locked me in the trunk of my car?"

"'Course not," he said. "If I'd known you were on my land, I'd have shot you."

Evie gasped and Barrett started to speak, but Shelby faced Hatcher, a glint of fire in her expression. "There is no need for threats. I apologize for trespassing. I was taking some surface samples and I didn't realize I was no longer on my uncle's property."

"But let's be clear," she continued. "That isn't your mine. I have every right to enter and collect samples and I will do that in the near future."

"You gonna tell me I don't own the property that's been in my family for a hundred years?" he snapped.

"Of course you own the land. That's why I came to see you last week, but you wouldn't talk to me. As I would have explained if you'd answered your phone or read your mail, you don't own the mineral rights. My uncle does, and he wants an assay of the ore. That's my job and you don't have the legal right to interfere."

Hatcher's mouth worked, brows drawn into a ferocious scowl. "I don't care what the law says. If you step on my property again, I'll kill you."

Barrett's pulse hammered as he grabbed Hatcher by the arm. "That's enough. You're leaving."

Hatcher shook away Barrett's grip but stalked to the front door with Barrett following. "Get your car off my property," he called to Shelby. Before he stepped outside, he poked Barrett in the chest. "You won't be so eager to help when you know who her kin is," he hissed.

Barrett stared him down. "Doesn't matter. You're not going to come into this home and threaten a woman's life."

Muttering, Hatcher stomped down the porch steps.

Barrett shut the door, Hatcher's words replaying in his mind. As he returned to the kitchen, a trickle of suspicion slithered through his belly. It couldn't be. "Shelby, who is your uncle?"

"Ken Arroyo," she said. "Do you know him?"

Barrett could feel the weight of his family staring at him. Time seemed to slow as if the hands of the old carriage clock were being held by some invisible force, his breaths ticking along in rhythm.

"Yes," he said finally. "I know him."

"You're neighbors," she said uncertainly, "even

though he's not here for part of the year. You must be friends, then?"

"No, not friends." *The furthest thing from friends.*

She cocked her head slightly, long tendrils that had escaped the ponytail curling around her face, her glance taking in the stricken looks around the table. "I can see that my uncle has no fans here. Do you want to tell me what's going on?"

No, he thought. *No, I don't.*

She watched Barrett exhale long and slow. He couldn't be older than his early thirties but there was a deep storehouse of grief and fatigue in his electric-blue eyes that made her wonder. He rubbed a hand over his chin as if to smooth away some painful thought.

"Not the time. If you're feeling better, I'll drive you to the hospital, or you're welcome to wait here for the police."

"I don't need a hospital. I need to get back. The police can talk to me at Uncle Ken's house." She stood. "I'm okay and I can find my own way to my car."

"Begging your pardon, but I'll escort you."

"Not necessary."

Barrett didn't answer.

Evie appeared to have recovered her composure. "We will bring you your clothes when they're dry."

"Thank you very much, but I can pick them up. You have all been extremely kind. I can't thank you enough."

Evie took her by the hand. There was something forced in her smile and it made Shelby sad. For a few minutes, it had been nice to feel like someone's daughter again. It pained her that somehow things had changed, though she didn't know why.

"That's what neighbors do," Evie said. "Barrett will see you back."

Barrett stood stiffly by the door.

"Hey," Owen said, moving close to his brother. Shelby noted he had a pronounced limp. "I can take her," he said quietly, but Shelby heard him anyway.

Barrett shook his head. "I got this."

What was it about her relationship with Uncle Ken that had instantaneously set up a wall between her and the Thorn family?

It's not your problem. You're here for Uncle Ken. The Thorns could put up walls for whatever reason and it was of no consequence to her. At the moment, her entire life goal was to get back to her uncle's place and enjoy the hottest shower she could stand.

Barrett led her outside. As she passed the foyer, she caught the scent of pine from a Christmas tree. It was standing in the corner of the room, festooned with ornaments. On the fireplace mantel, green branches were trimmed with tiny red glass balls. A framed photo graced the mantel, a grinning Barrett without the cowboy hat, his arm around a young woman, radiant in a wedding dress, her long hair pinned back with white roses. She was lovely. Barrett flicked her a glance, catching Shelby looking at the picture. She looked away and followed him outside.

The rain had slackened off to a weak sprinkle. The events of the day overwhelmed her as her mind spooled through the memories. A sudden blow to the head, the sensation of being hauled into her trunk, the awful sound of the lid slamming shut.

The attack had been from Joe Hatcher, she was sure of it, but why? Just to keep her away from the mine?

Out of greed? Anger at her perceived trespassing? Or perhaps he had some deep-seated resentment about her uncle, too?

"You ride?" Barrett said, pulling her back to the present.

"Since I was a kid," she said. That was probably overstating. She'd slacked off on her riding since her youth when she would visit her uncle in the summertime, but she found herself wanting to prove her worth to Barrett Thorn. Bad enough that he'd had to rescue her from a locked trunk and lug her out of a ravine. She couldn't leave him thinking she was some flimsy damsel-in-distress type.

He untied the horse that Jack had been riding. "Lady is a gentle ride."

She was right. He did think she was clueless. Ignoring his offered hand, she put her foot in the stirrup and climbed onto the saddle.

Barrett mounted his horse and clicked his tongue at the big animal.

Shelby was grateful that the rain had tapered off. Moonlight cast a weak glow over the landscape as they trailed back to where she'd parked her car. Her own stupid mistake made her groan inwardly. Some assayer. Hadn't even realized she'd strayed onto Hatcher's property.

Determined not to incur any more embarrassment for one evening, she slipped off Lady and handed the reins to Barrett. He was a giant astride the big horse, and as immovable as a cliff.

"Thank you again," she said. "I owe you a debt of gratitude."

"Don't owe me anything. I'll help you find your keys or maybe I can hot-wire it."

"No need for you to stay. I'll find them."

He ignored her, dismounting and beginning a search of the wet ground.

She hesitated, curiosity burning inside. "Barrett, what do you have against my uncle?"

He looked away. "Don't need to talk about that now."

"It's not likely we're going to do much chatting in the future." That got no reaction. "So tell me. If you have a beef against Uncle Ken, then I have a right to know. He's my only family."

Barrett's mouth tightened into a thin line. "No disrespect intended, ma'am, but you don't have a right to know."

She folded her arms, her pulse kicking up. "If Uncle Ken has an enemy right next door, then it is my business."

Barrett looked down at her, considering, shoulders a broad, tense wall against the night sky. He blew out a breath. "All right. You want to know so bad, I'll tell you."

She waited quietly.

"Ken's son killed my wife."

The words dropped like stones. *Killed my wife.* She found herself unable to speak. An endless moment passed between them but she could not think of a single response.

"Let's find those keys," he finally said.

Her thoughts ran rampant as they searched. Glass littered the ground from where Barrett had broken the window.

Her cousin Devon had killed Barrett Thorn's wife? She flashed back to the photo she'd seen, a radiant bride and her handsome groom. With a surge of guilt, she realized she hadn't been back to her uncle's ranch in so long that she had only known the barest hint about what was going on in the lives of Uncle Ken and Devon.

She'd known Devon had gone to prison for causing an accident that had killed a woman, but she did not know the particulars. The times she'd called, Uncle Ken had steadfastly refused to discuss it.

Still lost in thought, she found her pack under a nearby shrub. There was no sign of her samples, but everything else was there.

Barrett held the reins of the two horses in his hands. He looked somewhere over her head, anywhere but in her eyes.

"I'll wait until you get your car started," he said. "Good night, Miss Arroyo."

In his tone, she heard the bitterness. *Ken's son killed my wife.* She was anxious to get away, to sort it all out in her mind.

A noise behind her made her turn.

Barrett was staring at something in the distance. His attention was riveted to a spot under the trees, pitch-black except for a soft orange glow.

Her mind was slow to put it together. The orange glow was not an electric or battery light. It sparkled and fizzed like a firecracker on the Fourth of July.

No, not a firecracker.

A fuse.

"No," Barrett shouted.

Shelby could not see who was standing there under the trees. With a blur of movement, the stranger launched the dynamite through the air. It arced a golden trail through the night, speeding straight toward her.

Chapter Four

Barrett dropped the reins, grabbed Shelby's hand and yanked her after him. There wasn't time to do anything but dive behind a pile of boulders and put his bulk between her and whatever shrapnel was about to come their way.

The explosion was deafening. Shards of glass flew through the air, smashing on the rocks and cutting into his back as he tried to block Shelby from the falling debris. His eardrums rang with the percussive burst. The ground shuddered under them. He looked up in time to see Lady and Titan bolt, fleeing to the safety of the trees.

Shelby stirred in his arms but he caged her there with his body.

"Stay still until we know there's nothing else coming."

She probably wasn't thrilled about his command, but she acquiesced.

It was silent save for the wind in the branches and his own harsh breathing. Through the thin jacket his mother had insisted she wear, he felt her sides rising and falling in rapid rhythm. After a few moments, he poked his head up above the pile of rocks, watching for signs of movement. He saw nothing but a flicker of white as Titan led Lady away from the danger.

Barrett eased up and crawled from the hiding place, offering Shelby a hand. She took it, and together they surveyed the damage. He still kept a cautious eye on the trees.

The front of her car was blackened and twisted, smoke pouring out through the broken windshield. Her expression was hard to read in the scant moonlight. Fear? Outrage? Confusion? All of them would apply.

"What just happened?" she demanded, hands on hips.

"Dynamite."

She gave him an incredulous look. "So somebody actually ignited a stick of dynamite and lobbed it at me?"

He nodded. "Plenty left around here from the mining days. Easy to lay hands on it."

"I don't care where it came from. The bigger point here is why would someone light up a stick and toss it at me? It has to be Joe Hatcher."

"Maybe, unless you've angered somebody else."

She folded her arms and skewered him with such a look of disdain it almost made him smile.

"I haven't done anything to anyone in this town."

He didn't answer. Whatever she had or hadn't done wasn't his business. Yet once again, he found himself trying to extricate her from a pile of trouble.

"What makes you think it's not Joe Hatcher?" she said.

"Doesn't seem like a rational thing for him to do."

"He threatened to kill me recently, if you remember."

"And that was completely out of line, but he might

have been shooting his mouth off. My father believes him to be an honorable man, deep down."

"And you believe that, too?"

He cocked his head. "I don't know, but I trust my father. So for now, I'll reserve judgment."

She met his eyes, her own glimmering with unreadable emotion. "I admire that kind of familial respect."

Something was under those words, something deep and painful and raw.

Since he did not know what to say, he dialed his cell phone and told his family about the newest development.

"Road's still blocked to our ranch," Owen told him. "Cops said they'll circle around and meet you at Arroyo's place."

Arroyo's place. He'd rather crawl through a cactus field, but he could not think of any way out of it. "Okay," he said.

"Need backup?"

"Nah, thanks, though."

He pocketed the phone and joined Shelby, who was examining the remains of her car.

"As soon as I get the horses back, we'll go to your uncle's place. Cops will meet us there."

She stared gloomily at the wrecked vehicle. "My first new car."

He decided it was not the time to tell her a nice half-ton pickup might have held up better than her flimsy foreign-made tin can.

His mother's voice rang through his memory. *In the multitude of words there wanteth not sin: but he that refraineth his lips is wise.* He'd had to copy that proverb out as punishment a number of times when he was a kid. All the Thorn brothers had, except Jack, who was so quiet no one ever knew what he was thinking.

And then there was the youngest Thorn. Their mother would probably still be having Keegan write out Bible verses if she could get him to do it. Barrett didn't figure Keegan would ever master the art of restraint.

He heard no sign at all that the person who had tossed the dynamite was still around, so he figured it was okay to leave Shelby there while he went after the horses. Titan wouldn't have gone too far and Lady would stay with him. Horses weren't as smart as humans, but they knew the survival basics.

Retrieving his hat from the ground and shaking off a sprinkling of glass and dirt, he put it on and headed for the trees. He was surprised to find that Shelby was following him.

"I… I figured I'd help," she said.

Help? That surprised him. Maybe she was scared to be left alone, but she seemed like the kind who wasn't scared of much.

A memory came back to him so strong it cut his heart in two. His wife, Bree, was the bravest woman he'd known, but she'd been petrified of snakes. The day a little gopher snake wriggled into the kitchen, she'd leaped onto Barrett's back piggyback-style, hollering for him to get rid of it. He'd been laughing so hard tears had run down his face.

A drop of rain splatted his cheek and he realized he was standing still. Shelby was looking at him inquiringly.

"Are you okay?" she said softly.

"Just thinking." He turned away and she laid her hand very gently on his shoulder.

"Wait a minute. You're bleeding. I think you got cut by some flying glass."

He shrugged. "It's okay."

But she did not let go. Instead she lifted the bottom edge of his jacket. He felt her fingers graze over his back, the sting of the cool air against the cut at odds with the softness of her touch.

"It doesn't look deep, but it needs bandaging."

He was caught there, wanting to pull away, yet part of him wished to stay, to accept the comfort of her gentle fingers, a connection he had not experienced in a very long time. Blinking, he cleared his throat, moving just enough that she let go of his jacket.

"There," he said, relief pouring through him. "There's Titan." He whistled and the horse approached, with Lady following a pace behind. He took the reins and patted the horse. "It's all right, buddy. The dynamite scared all of us."

Lady was composed enough to allow Shelby to mount. When Barrett was astride Titan, they headed along the muddy trail toward Ken Arroyo's property.

He had not spoken to Ken since the trial when Devon was imprisoned for killing Bree. Ken had bought his son the fancy car and given him all the money he needed to enable his party-boy lifestyle. As far as Barrett was concerned, Ken might as well have bought his good-for-nothing son the liquor that he guzzled before getting behind the wheel.

Anger lit inside Barrett's gut like a burning coal, just as hot as it had been since his wife was taken from him.

Would he be able to keep his mouth shut to prevent the ire from spilling out like acid?

Just keep quiet, he told himself as they picked their way toward the house of his enemy.

Shelby was lost in thought as they followed the trail to her uncle's property. Who would want to throw her in the trunk of her car and then toss a stick of dynamite at her? It had to be Joe Hatcher. He had threatened to kill her, hadn't he? But what would he gain except to keep her out of the mine and buy himself a whole lot of unwanted attention?

As they neared the ranch, she could see Barrett straighten. His back must be hurting. Her fingers tingled at the memory of his strong muscles. The man despised her uncle, yet he'd twice bailed her out of a terrible situation. It must be that cowboy-honor thing.

She felt a deep-down ache in her temple behind her left eye. Migraine or a residual pain from her attack? No time to ponder that as the big ranch house loomed before them.

Uncle Ken had built the home thirty years before, as a summer place for him and his wife, Opal, but Opal had died in childbirth.

Uncle Ken lived most of the year on the east coast with Devon, tending to his commercial real estate business and summering at the California ranch until Devon was fifteen. Summers there had been idyllic. The three of them— Shelby, her sister, Erin, and Devon—rode horses, drank lemonade and caught frogs in the creek.

She'd envied Devon for his situation. It was so different from her own, as a child of a single mother who quaked with fear when the monthly bills came due. She wondered how Devon was faring now. State prison was a world removed from his comfortable home with Uncle Ken.

A police car was parked in front of the two-story house on the wide circular drive. Barrett looped the reins around a split rail fence. Uncle Ken was an equine fanatic and he kept three horses in the back pasture even though he rarely rode anymore, leaving their care to an employee, but she figured Barrett wasn't about to make himself or his own horses at home on Uncle Ken's ranch.

His son killed my wife.

She'd not seen Devon since his high school graduation, the happy kid with the wide smile. How differently Barrett must see him, the killer of his wife. She had no idea how the next few minutes would go as she reached the front door. Barrett followed her in, lingering a few paces behind.

The lamps in the front parlor illuminated a well-appointed front room with sleek leather furniture and richly hued area rugs, not a Christmas decoration to be seen anywhere. Uncle Ken was deep in conversation with a young police officer whose close-cropped hair and rain slicker were damp. Her uncle broke off and wrapped Shelby in a hug, his wide face flushed with emotion.

"I can't believe what's happened to you. Are you okay? Are you hurt at all?"

"No," she said, giving him a reassuring squeeze. "I'm okay, thanks to Mr. Thorn."

Barrett grimaced.

Uncle Ken's mouth twitched as he looked at Barrett. "Thank you," he said quietly, "for taking care of my niece."

Barrett shrugged, hands jammed into his pockets, avoiding eye contact. His jaw was tight, shoulders tense.

The police officer introduced himself to Shelby. "I'm Chris Larraby. I'll be handling your case. I spoke to Joe Hatcher. He was upset about the trespassing, but he says he had nothing to do with locking you in your trunk."

"Well, now we've got a stick of dynamite thrown into the mix," Shelby said. "You can ask him about that."

"Did either of you see who threw it?"

Barrett shook his head.

"I didn't see a thing either," Shelby added.

"It had to be Hatcher," Uncle Ken said. "He made threats."

"Doesn't prove anything," Barrett said.

"It's common sense. Why would you defend him?" Ken's eyes narrowed. "Is it because Shelby is my kin? You'd be happy to see her hurt to get back at me, is that it?"

Barrett's eyes blazed. "No, that's not it."

Larraby raised a palm. "Let's leave the past out of it."

Barrett's expression read, "How are we gonna do that?" But he kept quiet.

Shelby went over the details again while Larraby jotted notes on a small pad of paper. He tucked it into his front pocket. "We'll photograph and give it a once over when the storm's through. In the meantime, Miss Arroyo, I'd advise that you don't go poking around Gold Bar by yourself until we figure out what's going on here."

He paused at the door. "And tell your family to keep their cool also, huh, Barrett?"

Barrett's chin went up. "I'm not telling them anything. We have nothing to do with any of this."

"Yeah?" Larraby's voice went so quiet Shelby almost didn't hear it. "If there's trouble around, Keegan's usually not far away."

Barrett's nostrils flared and the vein in his jaw jumped. "Do your job and solve the case, Larraby," he said. "I don't want anything to do with the Arroyos, and neither does my family."

Shelby watched Barrett stalk through the door. Her emotions clashed loudly inside her. So Barrett and his family wanted nothing to do with her? That was just fine, but if Barrett thought she was going to get run out of town on a rail, he had another think coming. She owed everything to her uncle, the man who had financed her college education, tried to help her mother when the creditors came calling. He was practically a parent to her since her mother had denied Shelby and Erin access to their real father, or so she'd believed until recently.

I'm not going to tuck my tail and run, Barrett, she thought. She would do the job her uncle had hired her to do and nothing, not Joe Hatcher or the Thorn family or anyone else, would stand in her way.

Chapter Five

A̲t his customary hour of 4:00 a.m., Barrett made it into the kitchen and grabbed a cup of coffee. The cuts on his back stung, but work would make him forget about the discomfort. Owen was already sitting at the table with a steaming mug. He immediately stopped massaging his upper thigh when Barrett arrived, but not quickly enough.

Barrett sat across from him. "Pain bad today?"

Owen shook off the question. "No."

It was not the truth, of course. Barrett could see by the slight sheen of perspiration on his brother's forehead that his leg was killing him. It also meant he was still steering clear of the pain meds that had been more destructive than the bullets. *Stay strong, brother.*

"Checking fences today with Jack. Can you and Keegan handle the feeding?"

"I can handle it myself," Owen said defiantly, challenging his brother to disagree. He did not. Barrett knew the power of work could heal a man; it had helped heal him after Bree's death. Ken Arroyo's words from the night before galled him afresh.

Is it because Shelby is my kin? You'd be happy to see her hurt to get back at me, is that it?

Barrett's bitterness was mixed with shame because, following the accident, he'd been in such anguish, steeped in rage unlike he'd ever experienced, that he'd wished every bad thing he could imagine on the Arroyo family. Years of prayer and penitence and God's grace had helped restore him, at least mostly. He had not found the strength to completely forgive Devon Arroyo yet, but at least the rage no longer completely consumed him from the inside out. Devon was a kid who'd made a tragic mistake. Barrett's feelings for Ken were another matter entirely.

Again the conversation circled through his mind.

I don't want anything to do with the Arroyos, and neither does my family.

Well, that part was true anyway. Shelby Arroyo could solve her own problems.

"That's it?" Owen said.

"That's what?"

"You're not going to talk about what happened last night with you and Shelby?"

"I already told you. It's all over."

Owen raised an eyebrow and chugged some coffee. "You two almost got blown up, and you're not worried about her?"

"She's not my problem, and she can take care of herself."

"Uh-huh. Locked in a trunk and almost blown up in the same day. Clearly she can take care of herself."

Barrett grabbed his jacket, unwilling to talk anymore about Shelby. "Mama wants mistletoe."

Owen laughed. "Of course she does. I'll give that job to Keegan. He climbs trees like a monkey."

Barrett and Jack met up in the stable. Jack had already saddled both Lady and Titan, who seemed to be suffering no ill effects from their frightening episode the evening before.

For a second, Barrett wondered if Shelby had any nightmares about what happened. Bree had periodic nightmares that would leave her trembling and crying. He would roll over and embrace her, kiss her hair and rub circles on her back until she fell asleep again. Funny, she could never recall the bad dreams upon waking.

"You make them go away," she would say, "so I can't remember."

Oh, how he'd loved her. Sometimes he wished he could forget the pain just as easily as she forgot the nightmares. But the pain was a part of the blessing God had given him in Bree, and he would not reject a single moment of it, anguish and all. Bree was with God and she knew no pain, that was his comfort.

He pulled himself back to the present. Jack was already leading Lady out, so he scrambled to catch up, wondering why his thoughts of Shelby and Bree were getting tangled together.

The fences were in better shape than he anticipated and by lunchtime they were heading back after a few minor fixes. The clouds promised more rain, but for now the sky was holding. He admired the wet gold of the grass which would not regain its brilliant emerald until the spring. The glistening oaks dripped down on them as they picked their way back to the house at just after eleven. His stomach rumbled and the horses were hungry, too, judging by the way they picked up their pace as they neared the barn.

Barrett handed Titan over to Ella Cahill, who beamed a bright smile from under her tangle of red hair. Though she was in her late twenties, she barely came up to the horses' withers. Ella was tiny but ferociously devoted to her disabled sister and to the Thorns, whom she treated as family. She and Owen had been inseparable as young children. She'd got into some trouble after Owen deployed, but Barrett didn't know the particulars.

"Hey, Barrett. You're late. Did you forget Titan is due for his pedicure?"

In spite of her young age, Ella was the best farrier that had ever worked at Gold Bar Ranch. She had a gift, a connection with the horses that defied description. "No way. Didn't forget."

"I'll get Titan some breakfast. He likes to munch while I work on him," she said.

Barrett caught sight of an older horse that gleamed almost white gold, narrow chested with a bright silky mane, delicate and powerful at the same time. He did a double take. "Isn't that Arroyo's Akhal Teke? Is Ken here?"

Ella shook her head, smile dimming. "No, his niece is, and I already got the third degree from Ms. Arroyo so it's your turn. She's in the house," she said, turning away to lead Titan into the barn.

"The third degree about what?" Barrett called to her, but she didn't answer.

He stared from the high-spirited horse, which was eyeing him suspiciously, to the house. What was Shelby Arroyo doing back at the Gold Bar? And what was she doing riding a hot-blooded horse like the Akhal Teke?

Jack fisted his hands on his hips. "You coming?"

Barrett suddenly felt unsure, reluctant to subject himself to Shelby's soft green eyes. He felt like bolting as Titan had done to escape the dynamite. Why the sudden onslaught of ridiculous emotion? What was the matter with him?

"Yeah, I'm coming," he said angrily, cramming his hat more firmly on his head as he strode past his brother.

Shelby held her chin up as she heard the noise from outside. Barrett's mother stood and went to the big simmering pot on the stove.

"Boys will want some soup on a cold day like this," Evie said. "They've been up since before sunrise checking fences."

Shelby had been hoping she'd somehow miss seeing one particular Thorn brother. All she'd needed was her pile of clothes and some information, which she'd been semisuccessful in prying out of the farrier. "I'll get out of your way. Thank you for laundering my clothes, Mrs. Thorn."

"Please call me Evie. Why don't you stay for lunch? I'm baking gingerbread men later and I'd love some help. The boys are terrible at decorating cookies. My gingerbread men all turn out looking like zombies after the boys are done."

The front door opened and Shelby heard the sound of jackets being hung up on the hall stand. Her stomach tightened. "No, thank you. That's very kind but I think, since my cousin caused Bree's accident, I shouldn't be here longer than necessary."

Evie's mouth tightened for a moment. "What happened to Bree was a tragedy, for everyone, but God can make good out of it."

Shelby sighed. "That's what my mother would have said."

"You don't believe her?"

"She wanted to believe in the happy, God-will-provide kind of thing, but that didn't play out in our lives when my sister and I were younger. It took me a long time to understand." Even when they were eating canned beans for dinner. Even when their father left after the divorce and her mother had refused to let the girls go live with him, the woman had clung to her stubborn, rose-colored view of life.

Now that Shelby wasn't a child anymore, she had grown to respect her mother for believing God's promises. After all, Shelby and her sister grew up just fine. She wished desperately that she could tell her mother she'd been right, to ask forgiveness for dismissing her mother's staunch, faith-grounded optimism. Pain licked at her insides.

"She's, um, disabled now," Shelby said flatly. "She had a stroke that affected her brain. My sister was caring for her until we had to move her into a place with full-time nursing."

"Is your father still around?"

"He lives in Canada. I haven't seen him in a long time. I recently discovered that, uh, he isn't interested in being a father, never was."

"I'm sorry." Evie took her hand, the skin of her palms warm and calloused and comforting.

"Me, too, but my mother did her best trying to be Mom and Dad to us." Yet another thing she should have said before it was too late.

Evie hesitated and then took a breath. "You know, we have a lot of holiday fun around here. We host a Christmas Eve dinner for the town. I want to invite you to hang out with the Thorn clan. I mean, if you don't have plans with your uncle."

Shelby understood. Uncle Ken was not welcome here, for all Evie Thorn's assurances about God making it all turn out okay. Even the matriarch of the Thorn family blamed Uncle Ken for his son's actions.

So much for grace and forgiveness. Fine, the Arroyos didn't need grace, especially not from this family. She detached herself from Evie's grasp. "Thank you again. I'd better go and let you get lunch served."

She hustled to the front door, thinking she would escape before the brothers arrived in the kitchen for lunch. Barrett met her just as she stepped outside.

"Hello," he said politely.

She could not help but marvel at the electric blue of his eyes, the most brilliant hue, like the sky on the first day of summer vacation. His gaze seemed to pierce right through her. There was something in his look, something accusatory? Suspicious?

Distrustful, she decided. Fine. She did not trust him either, even though he had crawled into a ravine to haul her out. Her face went hot at the memory.

She held up her bundle. "Just picking up my clothes."

"You riding the Teke?"

"Yes. My uncle doesn't ride much anymore and Diamond needs it."

"Spirited horse, even if she is older."

She raised an eyebrow. "Are you implying I can't handle her?"

He shrugged. "Just observing. I remember hearing

that your uncle bought her from Hatcher's wife a while back. Sold off a bunch of horses then."

"I didn't know who Uncle Ken bought her from, but I wonder why Hatcher or anybody would want to sell off a gorgeous horse like that."

"Wouldn't recommend asking him. You two haven't exactly hit it off."

She tossed her hair back. "He's going to be seeing more of me than he likes. I'm on my way to the police station later today. I'm going to ask Officer Larraby to come with me to force Hatcher to let me into that mine this afternoon."

"Oh."

"What?" She stared into the implacable blue gaze. "My uncle owns the mineral rights. Legally, Hatcher can't refuse me, and it's Larraby's job to uphold the law in this town, isn't it?"

No change of expression on his face. "Uh-huh."

"Would you care to elaborate on your 'uh-huh'?"

"Uh-uh."

She groaned. "You don't talk a whole lot, do you?"

"More than my brother Jack."

Now there was the tiny quirk to his mouth that indicated the hint of a smile.

Her annoyance ebbed. "Well, anyway, I'm going to do my job with or without Hatcher's consent." She reached for the door but he opened it first, ushering her outside.

"Even if it causes trouble?"

She shot him a look. "Would you stop caring for your horses if it meant trouble?"

"Never."

"Well, then, I guess we're on the same page." His

face did not indicate as much. "Are you, I mean, is your back okay?"

"Only scratches."

She had the feeling Barrett would say that even if he'd nearly been cut in half. She untied Diamond and climbed into the saddle.

Barrett looked at her. His eyes were contemplative, tense. "Be careful. It's dangerous," he said.

"What's dangerous? Diamond or tangling with Hatcher?"

"Take your pick," he said.

"I can take care of myself," she said, wishing at once that she hadn't. Still, she did not see disdain or ridicule in his expression, only a glimmer of some emotion she could not name, buried deep.

Guiding Diamond home, pain throbbed in her temple and she tried not to think about the burning dynamite arcing toward her. Hatcher? Someone else? Who might be in the dense cover of trees watching her?

Waiting?

Chapter Six

Barrett loaded two English saddles into the truck next to a case of homemade pickles and drove them to Hatcher's Saddlery to be oiled and tended before the next round of riding lessons started up after the holidays. The Gold Bar offered training in both Western-and-English-style riding. With Christmas Eve just a week away, the chores were piling up. He'd promised to start working on putting up the tables for the holiday dinner. He'd not felt much holiday cheer at all since Bree died, but at least he was now able to enjoy his mother's pleasure at the festivities hosted on the ranch.

Joe Hatcher operated his saddlery out of a small building set on his sprawling acreage. A thick cluster of oak trees and shrubs screened the workshop from the residence where Hatcher lived with his daughter, Emmaline.

Barrett did not know Hatcher's ex-wife, Cora, well. Their families hadn't socialized much and Hatcher's divorce happened when Barrett was too steeped in Bree's death to pay much attention to such things. He had to believe it was hard to raise a kid alone, especially a girl who would grow into a woman just as hard to figure out as any other of her kind. *Women*, Barrett mused. *Who could possibly understand them?*

Barrett was surprised to see another truck already parked in front, a familiar fully loaded model with shiny green paint.

Ken Arroyo's vehicle.

Barrett debated whether or not to put his truck in Reverse and return another time. Instead he sucked in a breath as he heard loud voices coming from inside the saddlery. One was Joe Hatcher's low rumble and the other a higher-pitched, feminine timbre, which made his breath catch. Shelby? She had not waited for the police to accompany her before she confronted Hatcher with her plan. Barrett groaned inwardly. Typical.

Chris Larraby pulled up in his police vehicle next to Barrett. He hastened from the car and entered the shop. Barrett hesitated only a moment longer before he followed Larraby in.

"You need to be reasonable," Shelby was saying. She did a double take when she saw Barrett, but she did not move away from her position across the counter from Hatcher.

Hatcher looked anything but reasonable. His nostrils flared like an enraged bull's. "Don't care what your fancy papers say."

"That's why I asked Officer Larraby to come," Shelby said, calmly.

"Sorry I was late," Larraby said. "Something came up."

"Gonna strong-arm me, Chris?" Hatcher said.

"Nothing like that, Joe, just calm down."

Shelby shook her head. "I have a legal right to go in that mine and he's here to see that you comply."

"That right?" Hatcher said, staring at Larraby. "You gonna force me?"

"Let her do her thing," Larraby said. "She's within the law."

"And if you interfere," Shelby said, "you're breaking it." Her expression softened a bit. "Look, I don't want to make this hard on you. I'm here to assess the mine. That's all. That's my job."

Hatcher's eyebrows drew together in a scowl. "And if you decide there's gold worth mining down there, I have to let your uncle dig up my place?"

"That's not my decision to make. I'm only a fact finder."

"Well, find your facts somewhere else," he snapped. "I'm not gonna let you snoop around my property."

Shelby crossed her arms. "Why not, Mr. Hatcher? What are you so afraid that I will see?"

Time seemed to stop for a moment as the two locked eyes. Then Hatcher slammed a hand down on the counter. "I ain't afraid. It's the principle."

But Barrett had seen the evidence and he knew Shelby had, too, the flash of emotion that darted across Joe Hatcher's face. Fear. What was the source, Barrett wondered.

He felt a presence at his elbow and looked down at the petite Emmaline. The blond-haired woman was probably in her early twenties, yet she had the appearance of a teen. She chewed her lip, arms folded protectively around her, brown eyes wide.

Barrett nodded at her. "A little disagreement. Going to be okay."

She gave him a grateful smile. "I hate yelling."

Probably heard a lot of that with Joe Hatcher for a father, Barrett figured.

Larraby's radio crackled and he listened to the dispatcher for a moment. "I have to go. Let the lady on your property."

"Now?" Hatcher demanded.

"Now."

"That an order?"

"I don't want to make it into one. Just do it."

Shelby and Barrett followed Larraby out to his car. Emmaline trailed behind.

"Thank you, Officer," Shelby said.

Larraby scowled. "Don't thank me. I don't like strangers coming into town and upsetting the locals. Personally, I would react the same way Joe is. Do what you need to do. Get in and get out."

Shelby's cheeks pinked, but she did not reply.

"Aren't you going to stay in case things go bad?" Barrett said.

"Joe's not going to do anything." Larraby yanked open his car door. "And I'm a cop, not a babysitter."

"This isn't safe, with everything that's happened," Barrett growled.

"If you're so concerned, you go with her." He slammed the door and drove away.

Hatcher stalked out of the saddlery. His face was splotched with anger.

"Are you taking me to the mine entrance now, Mr. Hatcher?" Shelby asked.

He didn't answer but his expression was murderous. He started up the gravel path that cut around the shop and into the trees. Rocks ground under his booted feet. He did not look back to see if Shelby was following.

"That's the way to the mine," Emmaline said, chewing her lip. "It's hard to find if you don't know what you're looking for."

Shelby smiled and thanked the young woman. "You must be Emmaline. They told me in town you lived here with your dad. I'm sorry I've caused so much ruckus."

"Daddy doesn't like ruckus unless he's the one causing it." She sighed. "Better catch up with him if you want to find the mine. I would go with you to help but…" She shivered. "My mom used to explore all the time. She was kind of an amateur geologist, I think. I never liked it. It's so lonely up there. There are strange sounds, and at night…" She shrugged.

"I'll make sure I'm not here at night," Shelby said with a gentle smile at Emmaline. "Thank you. I'll go catch up with him." She hurried after Hatcher.

Barrett tried to think of something to say to stop her, but he came up blank.

Emmaline eyed the saddles in Barrett's truck. "Did you need those tended to, Mr. Thorn? If you bring them inside, I can write up your order."

"Thanks." Barrett hauled the saddles into the shop.

While Emmaline scrawled out the order on a notepad, he was thinking about Shelby.

It's so lonely up there.

In light of what had happened the previous night, Barrett was angry at Larraby for driving off and leaving Hatcher to lead the stubborn Shelby.

If you're so concerned, then you go with her.

He wasn't concerned, not about Shelby. The woman would do whatever she dreamed up, regardless. No, he wasn't worried about her.

Except that his stomach muscles were taut and the niggling in his nerves would not be ignored.

Barrett Thorn often thought he'd become another person since Bree died. An observer of life instead of a participator, a guy who let life roll past him like a river while he watched, rooted to the bank. But there was one thing that had not changed about him—that gut sense of right and wrong that his conscience would never let him ignore. Right now, his gut was hollering loud and clear that Shelby Arroyo should not be left in the hands of Joe Hatcher, no matter how much his father believed in Hatcher's character.

Sighing heavily, he thanked Emmaline and left the shop, grabbed a flashlight and his hat from his truck and headed up the slope the two had taken.

"Mr. Thorn," Emmaline called. "Are you going up there, too?"

"Yeah," he said, yanking his jacket zipper. "Looks like I am."

Shelby had to jog to catch up with Hatcher. She did not try to make small talk, just did her best not to slow his progress. As she trotted along, she could not help but wonder if the ground underneath her feet was laced with veins of quartz that might yield a rich gold strike, an assayer's dream. A tremor of excitement rippled through her at the thought that she might literally be standing above the answer to Uncle Ken's problems.

After several recent conversations, Uncle Ken had finally confided to her that his real estate business had been languishing. She knew the lawyers for Devon had been costly, too.

It stoked the feeling of guilt inside her. Uncle Ken had supplemented her meager earnings to pay for her college. He'd been more of a provider than her own folks, with her mother spending whatever money her father sent. She could never understand why her mother insisted that Shelby and Erin live with her instead of their father.

Why can't we just go live with Dad? she remembered shouting at her mother in one of her teenage fits. *He's got a steady job and he knows how to keep money in the bank. He misses us and you never even let us visit him.* It was bold talk since she'd only received a couple of letters and one phone call from her absent father.

Children belong with their mother, she would always reply. So when her mother frittered away yet another paycheck on new clothes for the girls or a trip to the zoo, Shelby would try to work even more hours at her part-time jobs.

It had not been enough to pay for school, so Uncle Ken stepped in. Erin had put off going to college because their mother's medical needs had been too great. When Shelby started to bring in an income that provided for her mother, she'd insisted her sister should delay her schooling no longer. Now it was Shelby's turn to funnel as much money as she could to both Erin and her mother. Shelby would help her make it through nursing school, after she got Uncle Ken's situation straightened out. Hopefully a rich vein of gold in the mine would recoup everything he'd invested in her.

Her throat thickened at the memory of his shrunken appearance when she'd arrived the week before. The toll of Devon's trial and imprisonment had cost Uncle Ken more than money. He was a shadow of the man he used to be.

Her thoughts were interrupted as she and Hatcher crested a steep hill. Down below them was a scrub-covered gorge and in front, a crumbling stone cliff. Hatcher seemed to consider a moment before he plunged through the knee-high shrubs. Grateful that she had worn her hiking boots and a windbreaker, she fell in behind him.

As they walked farther into the untamed growth, she suppressed a shiver. Was she walking into the wilderness with the man who had attacked her, thrown dynamite at her? But the police knew the situation, so surely Hatcher would not risk his own freedom by harming her. Unless the man was just plain crazy, she thought uneasily.

They stopped at a spot where the ground and the cliff intersected. All she could see was a tangle of branches and wild grasses that came up to her thighs. Hatcher pushed aside the foliage.

"Here."

She peered beyond him. At the bottom of the cliff was a dark hole about six feet across and just about her height. Across the gap was an iron fence, screwed into the rock on each side, secured by a rusty padlock. Hatcher fished out a key ring from his pocket and selected a key. She thought his look turned calculating as he removed it from the ring and shouldered past her to unlock the padlock and wrench aside the fence.

"Well, now," he said with a smile. "In you go."

She hesitated, a blast of chilled air wafting out of the entrance. It was pitch-black inside. Her nerves screamed at her not to deliver herself into that gaping maw.

"I…"

"Whatsa matter?" He came closer. "You scared?"

"No. Are you coming, too?"

"Uh-uh. Wild animals in there," he said with a cunning smile. "Some of the tunnels are flooded, too. Real slippery-like. Old guy like me can't risk falling and breaking a hip, but you're young and strong and sure of yourself, ain't you?" He laughed a wet, crackling laugh. "Won't be a problem for you at all, going into the mine all alone."

"She's not going in alone."

Shelby whirled to see Barrett Thorn standing right behind Hatcher, his expression calm and implacable as always.

"You don't have to…" Shelby started. "I mean, I can go in by myself."

"Isn't right."

Barrett's lips drew together in a determined line. Shelby understood that there was no way she was going to change this cowboy's mind. She was not sure whether she should be flattered or infuriated. Somehow, the feeling that rose to the top was relief.

"Awww, ain't that chivalrous?" Hatcher said. "If you two are both stupid enough to want to crawl around that mine, then go right ahead. I'll be in the shop. If you need me, just whistle." He moved back, the grin still wide, allowing Shelby to step inside.

The darkness engulfed her immediately, so she switched on her flashlight. Barrett crowded in behind, ducking to squeeze his head under the ceiling of stone.

Shelby beamed her flashlight above, the light sparking on the moisture seeping from the rock.

A loud clang shook the walls and made her cry out. They spun around to see Hatcher slam the gate and click the padlock closed.

Chapter Seven

Shelby was at the bars in a moment, striking her palm on the metal. Barrett crowded behind her.

"Open this gate," she yelled.

There was no answer, no sign of Hatcher.

"Hatcher," Barrett boomed, bracing his arms around her body and calling over her head. "You better unlock it right now before I kick it down." She could feel his breath warm on her neck, the anger turning his arms to steel.

Still no answer. Her heart hammered against her ribs. It was lunacy to lock them in here with the police knowing where they were. She'd left a note for Uncle Ken this time, as well. What was Hatcher trying to prove?

Barrett shouted again and to her relief, Hatcher appeared, laughing.

"No need to go all Rambo," he said, reaching for the padlock. "I was just joking around. You should have seen the look on your faces," he said. "I'll open it up."

He fiddled with the lock, bending closer until his nose was inches from the old metal. "Just one more minute... Oh." He stared at the lock and then straightened. "Would you look at that?" He held up the key, now broken in half. "Busted. Other half's stuck in the lock."

"And I'm supposed to believe that was an accident?" Shelby said.

"Don't matter what you believe, missy," he said. "Key's broken. Gonna have to go back to the workshop and get another. I think I got a spare somewhere in the back room. I'll just go get it, shall I?"

Shelby squashed the sensation of panic at being locked in. "Yes."

"And if you aren't back here in a half hour," Barrett snapped, "my brothers will come with a pair of bolt cutters if I don't have it kicked down myself."

"Sure, sure," Hatcher said, waving an airy hand. "Call 'em up on your cell, why don't you? I'll be back as quick as I can. You enjoy that mine now, Miss Arroyo." He left, whistling, his pace leisurely and relaxed.

Barrett kicked at the bars so hard Shelby almost screamed. Again and again he slammed his booted foot into the metal with such force it caused debris to rain down on them.

"Stop," she said, grabbing his arm. "It might be unstable."

He grunted in frustration.

Shelby got out her cell phone. "I have no signal here. You?"

Barrett stepped away, breathing hard, and checked his phone. "Nothing. That explains Hatcher's cat-in-the-cream look." Barrett's own look was that of a caged lion. "He knew we weren't going to be calling for help."

Shelby shook her head. "So we're really locked in here until he gets back?"

"Looks that way."

"And he's going to take his sweet time, isn't he?"

Barrett fisted his hands on his hips, flashing her a look of pure exasperation. "Well, what did you expect?"

"I didn't expect a welcome mat, but I figured with the cops here, he would comply at least."

Barrett's eyes blazed in the gloom. "You forced his hand. That wasn't smart. He threatened to kill you, and here you were ready to climb inside an abandoned mine all by yourself."

Tipping her head up so she could look him in the eye, she folded her arms across her chest. "You don't have to yell. I didn't ask you to come."

She heard his teeth grind together. "I'm not yelling. I'm talking forcefully."

"Well, you can stay here and talk forcefully to yourself. I'm going to look around."

He caught her hand. "Not a good idea."

Her pulse skittered as she felt the strength in his grip, caught the musky scent of his soap. "You don't get to give me commands. I'm not one of your horses."

"Horses would have more sense."

She pulled away. "This is what I came here to do, locked in or not. I might as well make use of the time." She turned before he could toss back an answer. He was right, of course, she had forced Hatcher into a corner, but there hadn't seemed to be another choice. His reluctance to let her in surpassed mere orneriness. The guy was desperate to hide something.

Her flashlight picked out a downward slanting tunnel that disappeared to the left. It was high enough for her to walk easily, the stone walls glimmering with moisture. The air was chilled and damp, but she sucked in a deep breath of it anyway. It was the fragrance of things long hidden and undisturbed. For some reason she found it comforting, always had.

"Owww," Barrett said, and she realized he was a few steps behind her.

"Ceiling's a little low here."

"Thanks," he said, taking off his hat and rubbing a hand across his forehead.

"I really don't need an escort," she said stiffly. *Especially not a disgruntled cowboy.*

"Oh, I think you do."

"I'm not helpless."

"More like disaster prone."

She did not dignify that with an answer. There might be a whiff of truth to it anyway, since she'd been in a perpetual mess since she came to Gold Bar.

Barrett ducked around a low-hanging cone of rock. "What are you looking for?"

"Oh, you know, big chunks of gold sticking out of the walls. Jewels, maybe, like that scene from Snow White."

"I'm not an idiot," he snapped. "I know a little about the mining process."

She could not resist a smile. "Sorry. Just trying to lighten the mood. I'm getting acclimated right now. Looking at the formations, the layering in the rock. I'll probably drill for a sample later, but right now a hand grab would work."

"All right. Grab the nearest rock and let's get back to the entrance."

"Why the rush? Scared, cowboy?" she said, raising an eyebrow, enjoying teasing him.

"Not scared, smart. The rock is sopping wet and slippery, or didn't you notice?"

"I did," she said. "I'm hoping the lower levels of the mine aren't completely flooded."

"Then let's be smart about it and come back tomorrow with battery-powered flashlights, rubber-soled shoes and someone standing guard at the fence."

"Right now I want to see what's around the corner."

He stopped as if he'd got an electric shock.

"What?" His face was stark in the glow of her flashlight. "What's wrong?"

"Nothing."

She touched him on the shoulder to keep him from turning away. "Not nothing."

He rubbed a hand over his close-cropped beard. "I, uh, my late wife, Bree. She was always saying that the best was right around the corner." The dripping water marked the seconds of silence.

"I'm sorry," Shelby said. "I didn't mean to cause you pain."

He looked away. "Not pain, so much. Less now anyway. More like…" He shook his head. "I'm not so good with words."

She wanted to touch a hand to his chest, to let him know that she understood. "It's hard to find the words when your life gets flipped upside down."

He cocked his head. "You, too?"

She didn't want to tell him about her father. How could the impact of what she'd learned about him possibly be on par with the loss of a spouse? Choosing her words with precision, she tried to explain. "I believed something that was a lie for a long time and I blamed my mother, misjudged her and now…it's too late. I can't fix it. It's just too late." She was horrified to feel tears pricking her eyelids.

"Hey," he said, taking her free hand. In spite of the cold air, his fingers were warm on hers.

"I'm a black-and-white kind of person," she babbled. "And I was sure, so sure, my mother was selfishly keeping us from our father, but now that she's impaired, well, I learned…" She swallowed hard. "Never mind. Family drama. Too messy to talk about. Let's just say I have regrets."

"I get that. After Bree died, I got mired down in that feeling. All the things I could have done, should have done." He cupped her hand in his hard, calloused palm. "If I've learned one thing it's that we can't live in regret. God doesn't want that for our lives."

She wanted to let those words loose inside and allow them to find the hurt place that throbbed bright with pain. Instead something completely different came out of her mouth. "I am sure my cousin Devon regrets what he did," she said quietly.

The distance sprang up between them, as thick and solid as the stone walls. She knew she should not have brought it up, but her comment lay between them like a ticking time bomb. He let go of her hand and stared at the slick stone under his feet.

Barrett finally spoke. "I do believe that Devon is sorry. He wrote me a couple of letters from prison. Took me a long time to be able to read them. I've really been praying that I can fully forgive him someday. I'm on my way, I think."

She wondered if she would be strong enough to forgive such a thing. Not on her own, she was certain. "Uncle Ken says the accident destroyed Devon, too. He'd give anything to undo what he did."

Barrett stared at her. "What about your uncle?"

"I don't know what you mean."

Barrett's voice grew hard as stone. "Does he regret his part in my wife's death?"

"His part?"

The whites of his eyes glinted like hard marble. "Your uncle coddled Devon. Bought him anything. Horses, cars. Never set limits. Made him think he never had to pay the price for his misbehavior."

"You don't know that."

"Yes, I do," he said bitterly. "Good old Daddy paid for Devon's speeding tickets, fixed his car when he banged it up, let him live at home with no job, no purpose but having fun."

She recoiled at the acid in his tone. "That's not true."

"It is. Your uncle didn't do his job as a parent and it cost me everything. Never once has he expressed regret for enabling his son to kill my wife."

The quiet was broken only by the sound of trickling water and the low moan of a draft wafting through the tunnels. She was chilled down deep to the bone.

"Maybe you're right about exploring today," she said softly. "We should wait by the entrance for Hatcher to come back. I'll just look around the corner. You go ahead back and I'll catch up."

She hastily moved a pace up the trail, not wanting Barrett to see the emotions she battled.

Uncle Ken had been a permissive father, she knew. His wife died of a hemorrhage giving birth to Devon and he'd tried to make it up to the boy in every way he could. Maybe it was a family trait.

That thought startled her. Was that what her own mother had tried to do? Shower her girls with nice things to fill the hole left by their father's departure?

No, not departure, abandonment, she corrected. The pain pinched her heart again.

That was a different situation, she told herself angrily. Devon was a good kid, kind and generous like his father, charming and funny to boot. Barrett was wrong about Uncle Ken. He'd tried his best like any parent. She would not bring up the topic again and she would make sure Barrett was not her escort when she returned for more samples.

Her next footstep landed on a narrow strip of rock and the one after that, on nothing at all.

Barrett heard Shelby's sharp intake of air and he was moving as she started to fall. His fingers grazed her shoulder, her sleeve, and he scrambled for a handhold, finally grasping the hem of her jacket. Too late. She catapulted into the darkness below. Because he would not allow himself to let go, he tumbled through the gap in her wake.

The fall was maybe fifteen feet, ending with a frigid splash into neck-deep water. His boot heels hit the bottom with a jarring thud. Shelby popped up next to him, heaving in a breath, coughing and choking.

He grabbed her elbow to keep her from ducking under the surface again. The water leveled off just under his chin, which meant it would be up to the crown of her head. He pulled her close. "Hold around my neck."

She did, still coughing.

"Hurt?"

"No," she gasped. "Cold."

"Yeah." The water had to be somewhere in the neighborhood of forty degrees and she was already shivering violently. His skin prickled. They did not have much time before their body temperatures would drop dangerously low. "Got your phone? I lost mine."

"Yes," she said, teeth chattering. She pulled it out from her back pocket and touched a button. "It's wet, but still working." A tiny glow punched through the gloom. "Unfortunately, we don't have coverage down here."

"At least the flashlight works," Barrett said, but the dot of light did not have much impact.

The dark was so profound that he could not see more than the vague white gleam of her face right next to his. He clamped his right arm around her waist and pulled his left up above the water line.

"Can you push the button on my watch?"

She did and the illuminated face let off a scant glow. It was enough for him to see that they were in a lower tunnel with smooth walls. About six feet past them, a ladder leading up into the darkness was bolted to the wall. "Keep pushing the button if you can."

She did, though her hands were trembling. "And here I thought watches were obsolete."

"Some people say the same about cowboys."

She managed a giggle and it made him feel better somehow.

He sloshed closer to the ladder, holding her with one arm, his elbow bumping something. She lost her grip on his watch light as he moved to snatch at it. "Flashlight," he said triumphantly. He flicked it to life, catching her surprised smile.

"It still works?" she said.

"It was my granddaddy's flashlight. Tough as he was."

"Are all the Thorn men so tough?"

"Yep, but not as tough as the women."

Another giggle, this time softer. She was weakening from the cold.

He shined the light upward. The ladder led to an upper tunnel that vanished into the darkness. The rungs looked to be sturdy enough, though they had to be rusted in the face of all this moisture. He pushed on one with his foot and it held against the pressure.

"Here's the flashlight. Climb up slowly," he told her. "One rung at a time. It may not hold all the way to the top, but at least it will get you out of the water." He helped her settle her feet onto the lower slats. Climbing gingerly, one step up at a time, she advanced almost to the top.

"It connects to another tunnel," she called down. "I can't see much, but the air feels warmer so maybe it leads out."

"Climb in if you think it's safe."

She continued on to the top. Once there, she lay on her belly, shining the light down for him. "Your turn."

He climbed up, the metal groaning under his weight. The cold made his legs feel like they were made of stone. He pushed on, boots slipping against the iron.

With a loud shriek, the rung under his right foot gave way and he tumbled back into the water with a splash. He heard Shelby scream above him. He wanted to reassure her, but the cold and the impact took the breath clean out of him.

She was halfway down the ladder before he managed to stand, coughing and spluttering. "Stop. Don't come any farther, the ladder's not in good shape."

She froze. "Are you okay?"

"I've been better, but nothing broken I think. Go back up. I'm right behind you."

She ascended again and he picked his steps carefully, skipping over the busted slat and getting to the top without any further incident. He heaved himself up to join her on the ledge. His wet clothes clung to him, his boots waterlogged and soggy. He huffed out a breath as he considered. "This is terrible."

"I know." She groaned. "I have no idea which way is out."

"Not that. I lost my hat."

To his surprise, she started to giggle.

"That funny?"

"Well, you could have been killed falling off the ladder and right now we may be closing in on hypothermia, but you're most upset about your hat."

"It's my favorite hat," he said to clarify. "I got it all broken in just right."

She laughed afresh, the sound light and airy in the dank atmosphere of the mine. He cracked a smile as he looked around, but he couldn't find too much amusement in it. Her comment about hypothermia wasn't too far off.

He recalled the time when he was just a teen and Gold Bar experienced torrential rain for days. His family had helped the woefully overworked volunteer fire department rescue a man from where he'd been trapped in a waterlogged storage room. The man had died from hypothermia.

"I don't mean to ruin your happy mood, but we need to figure out a way out of here," he said. "Any ideas?"

They both looked as far as they could see in both directions. The tunnel stretched away into the darkness but by now he hadn't got a clue as to which avenue, if either, led back to the surface.

Shelby did not look as though she had a clue either.

"I was hoping you would have a plan," she said through chattering teeth.

A disoriented assayer and a clueless cowboy. It was turning into a mighty long afternoon.

Chapter Eight

Shelby did not think she'd ever been so cold in all her life. Her hands and feet were numb and even her breath felt cool when she blew into her hands. She wanted to curl up in a ball on the ground, but Barrett would not let her. He pulled her close and chafed her shoulders, rubbing his cheek against hers. "Gotta keep moving."

"Your beard tickles."

"Don't complain. It's warming you up, isn't it?"

"I'm not sure which way is out," she said, allowing her head to drop down against his chest. "I'm… I'm sorry for getting you into another jam."

His arms were strong around her body as he cradled her close, tucking her head under his chin. "Doesn't matter much, 'cept you owe me a hat."

"If we manage to get out of here, I'll buy you a new one, I promise."

"Deal." He stepped away, unzipped his jacket and put it around her shoulders. "It's still wet, but maybe another layer will help."

"No, I can't take it," she said, eyeing the soggy flannel of his shirt. "You'll freeze."

"Too stubborn to freeze. Just ask my mom." He zipped her firmly up to the chin and slid on the hood for good measure. "There. You could be in a fashion show."

She fingered the buttons on his shirtfront. "You must really like this clothing company. It's the same style you were wearing when you pulled me out of the ravine."

He ducked his head and examined the shirt as if he'd forgotten what he was wearing. "Got ten shirts all the same 'cept the color."

"Really?" Shelby goggled. "You like it that much?"

"Can't stand to shop. When my mom drags me into a store and I find one that fits, I get a lot of them."

She started to laugh but her body was too cold to cooperate.

"We've got to get out of here somehow," she muttered. With great effort, she forced her limbs into action, running her numb fingers over the stone walls, straining to get some glimmer from either direction that would help them determine an exit. The fall had disoriented her and she simply could not get her bearings. Barrett played the light over the black stone surface. It caught on a flash of color.

"Wait," she said. "What's that?"

He trained the light again, stopping on a small red mark, a splotch the size of a dime. "That couldn't have been here from the mining days, it's too fresh."

She pointed. "And there's another one."

Barrett followed her along, playing the light over the walls.

She peered closely at the colored spots. "There's another one, ten feet away. What do you think they're for?"

"Dunno. I don't see any in the other direction."

"They're not like any official markings I've ever seen. Maybe some kids got down here? Should we follow?"

"That's your call. I'd say we don't go more than fifty yards past the ladder. Don't want to get even more lost," he said.

"There's either lost or found. No such thing as more lost or less lost."

He shook his head. "You don't spend much time in the woods, do you?"

She was about to retort when Barrett grabbed her arm. "Did you hear that?"

"What?"

"Listen."

They both strained to hear.

"Mr. Thorn." The voice floated like a wisp of fog through the tunnel. It was high-pitched, breathy. It made the skin on the back of her neck prickle.

"Who's there?" Barrett called out.

"This way," the voice called again. It was followed by a sound, a soft thud, like someone whacking a rock against another.

At first Shelby could not tell where the sound originated. She placed her palms on the rocks in different places until she was rewarded by a faint vibration.

"Over there," Shelby said, hardly able to contain her excitement. "It's coming from up the passage."

He went first, following the tunnel away from the ladder, beaming the flashlight at the rock projections so he didn't brain himself again. Shelby followed, her fingers holding on to his belt. Her legs were rubbery and weak but she tried to keep up the pace as best she could.

They stopped when they lost the tapping sound.

"I don't hear it anymore," he said. "Do you?"

"No, but the air here is warmer and I think the slope is heading up toward the surface."

Another tap, this time with a voice following. "Hurry. You've got to hurry."

They pushed as fast as they could, stumbling now and then on the dark rock, easing around occasional puddles and broken bits of wood.

When Shelby saw the first glimmer of light, she almost cheered. As they hurried along, the view changed from pitch-black to light gray. They looked above their heads and saw a half-moon-shaped cutout in the rock wall about six feet above them, a threshold between the mine and the glorious surface. It had never before occurred to her that the sunshine was utterly magnificent.

A memory shot through her brain, a little prayer her mother had taught her about thanking God for the golden sun. She'd forgotten to be thankful lately, allowing too many other things to get in the way. When they got directly underneath the opening, Barrett cupped his hands. "Come on. I'll boost you."

"But how will you get out?"

"You'll go get my brothers or call the cops."

"But you could be hypothermic by then."

"I'll try to avoid that."

"But…"

He put a finger to her lips. "Ma'am, this is the way it's gonna be. You're climbing out right now, or I'm going to have to try to shove you through that hole and that's gonna be awkward for both of us."

She closed her mouth. Her determination was nothing compared to his ruthless cowboy chivalry. He would not go until she did. Period.

Before he could protest, she unzipped his jacket and

handed it to him. "In case the rescue takes a while. You promise you're not going to die, right?"

"I will do my best, ma'am."

Acting under some impulse she did not understand, she brushed a kiss across his lips.

He didn't say anything, but she felt the echoes of a tender yearning in him, or was it in herself?

"Come on now," he said, voice low and throaty. "Quit stalling. Time for you to get out of here."

Ignoring the lingering tingle on his lips from her kiss, Barrett cupped his hands again and she stepped into them. He lifted her easily and after some wriggling, she made it out. Relief flooded through him. He could hear hollering now, and at first he was worried that Hatcher might be up there until Keegan's face appeared above him in the opening, silhouetted in brilliant sunlight.

"And I thought we were in the ranching business. Decided to try your hand at gold mining, Barrett? You want a little pickax for Christmas?"

Barrett's teeth were chattering too hard for him to rustle up much of an answer. Keegan lowered a rope and in a matter of moments he was hoisted out into the daylight, which nearly blinded him.

His father threw a blanket around him. Shelby was already swaddled in a second blanket, he was happy to see. She appeared alert and interested, all good signs. In fact, her relief at the sight of him was written across her face clear as the words on a page.

Barrett filed that thought away for later and tried to stop shivering. "How'd you f-f-find us?"

Keegan jutted his chin. "You can thank her. She called us and then led us to you."

Emmaline moved closer. "Daddy came back for the key. He wasn't, um, in a big hurry, so I sneaked away and called Mr. Thorn. Then I ran back to the main entrance but you two weren't there. I knew about this other way to get in. I used to explore when I was braver." Her smile was shaky.

"Thank you, Emmaline," he said. "I think you were pretty brave, especially since your dad might be mad at you for helping us."

"Never mind," she said, an unexpected spark of determination in her eyes. "I did what I had to do."

"And Shelby and I appreciate it," he said.

Shelby nodded over chattering teeth. "We sure do. Thank you, Emmaline."

Hatcher ambled over with Officer Larraby at his side.

Larraby eyed them. "Came to check on you. Hatcher said he lost the spare key. What happened?"

"They almost got killed is what happened," Keegan snapped. "Could have kept an eye on Hatcher to make sure this didn't happen, couldn't you?" The anger in his tone brought an answering glare from Larraby.

"Not my job to tend to your family, Keegan." Larraby put a slight stress on the word *your*.

The two were biological half brothers, though Larraby's father had never publicly acknowledged Keegan as his child. The rage that simmered between them marked them as enemies.

The last thing they needed at the moment was more antagonism. Barrett hastened to intervene. "This is Hatcher's responsibility, not Larraby's."

Hatcher rolled his eyes. "The key broke. I was looking for the spare. It was an accident, like I said. You two were fool enough to go up against the mine and the mine won. Your fault, so don't blame it on me."

"You're not an innocent party here, Hatcher," Keegan started. His father put a calming hand on his arm, but it was Shelby who spoke.

"He's right. I shouldn't have gone wandering without being prepared. Barrett said the same thing, but he came along reluctantly to make sure I was okay. This isn't Mr. Hatcher's fault, at least, not all of it."

Barrett gaped at her.

Hatcher nodded. "Now that you've seen how dangerous the mine is, I guess you're done with this fool business?"

"For now," Shelby said.

Barrett didn't buy it for a second. Those captivating green eyes shone with a determination that said Hatcher might have won the skirmish but she would never let him win the war. He had to admire her spark, as much as he did not want to admit it.

"Good," Larraby said. "I've got other things to do than come out here on a regular basis. Do either of you need medical attention?"

Both Barrett and Shelby refused to go to the clinic, so Larraby departed. Barrett insisted on driving Shelby back to her uncle's place himself.

"Just to make sure you're done wreaking havoc for today," he told her. Owen followed in Ken's pickup, though the look on his face said he wasn't happy about it.

It jolted Barrett to think how Bree's death had affected all of them, carving a line of hatred between the Thorns and the Arroyos that rippled across both families. How was it that he could begin to pray for forgiveness for Devon, but refuse to do so for Ken?

Because Ken doesn't deserve it, he told himself fiercely.

He opened the passenger door for Shelby.

"What are the pickles for?" she said as she slid in, eyeing the case in the back.

"Oh, uh, I'm bringing them to the church. They run a soup kitchen and, er, we have a lot of pickles."

"Homemade, huh? Your mom?"

"Well, actually, no. I made them." He waited for the reaction he knew was coming.

"You make pickles? I'm impressed. How did you learn to do that?"

He sighed. "After Bree died, I sort of withdrew from life. The only thing I wanted to think about was the horses. I guess I got to worrying everyone because they did this intervention type thing and demanded I either join a line dancing group or pick a hobby."

"You're not up for line dancing."

"I'd rather be boiled in oil. I found an old cookbook of my grandma's and the first ten pages were all pickles, so I figured I'd give it a try."

"That's incredible."

"Yeah. I made so many pickles it filled the entire pantry. We gave them away to everyone we could until people started hiding when they saw me coming. It's, uh, kind of a family joke now."

"Perfect. I really needed a chuckle."

He blasted the heater and Shelby pressed her fingers right up to the vent. Her eyes closed in pleasure. "I will never take warmth for granted again. Thank You, God," she breathed.

Yes, he thought, *thank You*.

Enough of the light and easy conversation. "So what are you plotting?" he said.

"What do you mean?" Her face was as innocent as a newborn lamb's.

"You know good and well what I mean. You gave up too easily with Hatcher. What scheme are you cooking up?"

"I'm scheming to take a hot bath, for one, complete with bubbles and a rubber ducky if I can find one."

"No jokes. Spill it."

"Barrett Thorn," she said, "just because you're too stubborn to freeze does not mean I owe you anything."

"Oh, yes, you do."

"What?"

"I lost my favorite hat because of you."

Her face lit with a gorgeous smile that did something to his insides.

"You got me there. Okay, so I owe you a hat, but not an explanation."

They pulled up in the gravel drive, Owen right behind. Diamond grazed along the fence, cropping grass with an elegance characteristic of her breed. Lovely, hot-blooded, strong and intelligent. Like Shelby, he thought unexpectedly. He blinked hard and fiddled with the steering wheel.

She hopped out of the truck before he could get out to open the passenger door for her. Leaning in, she gave him a rueful smile.

"Thank you, Barrett. It seems like I'm always thanking you."

"I'll try not to let it go to my head."

She laughed. "You go on with your pickle deliveries, cowboy. Don't worry about me."

"But, Shelby," he said before she got away, "joking aside, you aren't planning on going back in that mine, are you?"

Her smile vanished. Up went her chin. "I am going to keep my promise to my uncle."

"Even if it kills you?"

Shutting the door, she walked purposefully toward the house without looking back.

Chapter Nine

Shelby was grateful that Uncle Ken was closed in his office when she let herself into the house. If he knew what had transpired in the mine, he would have forbidden her to return. Tiptoeing upstairs to the guest room, she sank into the hottest bath possible and stayed there until her toes turned to prunes. Dressed in clean clothes with her hair washed and dried, she returned to find Uncle Ken in the dining room with a small duffel bag.

"Hello, Shelby," he said, sinking into an armchair. "I didn't hear you come in. I was just paying some bills." He offered a wry smile. "Could use a gold mine right about now."

"I'm going to make that happen if I can, Uncle Ken."

"I know you will."

She pointed to the bag. "Going on a trip?"

"I have to fly to England. I have property there that's up for sale and I'm signing papers. I really don't feel right about leaving you now, but I have to make this deal happen." His smile was sheepish. "I've got some creditors that won't be put off anymore. I'll be back in five days, tops."

"It's okay. I'll be perfectly fine."

"All right. Zeke will be by tomorrow morning to check on the horses. He'll come morning and evening to tend to them and get them settled for the night. Diamond is a handful so I don't want you trying to deal with her all by yourself."

"Did you buy Diamond from Joe Hatcher, Uncle Ken?"

"From his ex-wife, Cora. Her father died and left her a dozen horses, all beautiful. Couldn't believe she wanted to sell and I didn't really need any more, but Diamond was too beautiful to resist. Her daughter, Emmaline, was sure attached to that horse. Never made sense to me, but I'm not a man who can pass up a specimen like that. She's spirited, though, so be careful when you ride her."

"I've already reintroduced myself to Diamond. We get along fine."

The clock over the mantel bonged. She thought how dark and dreary the room looked without the barest hint of any holiday decorations.

"Well, I'd better go. Are you sure you'll be okay here?"

"I'll be fine. I want to do some research on the area geology anyway."

"So nothing dangerous up your sleeve, right?"

She wriggled her fingers. "Nope. Nothing dangerous."

He sighed, the late-afternoon sunlight catching the careworn creases in his face. There was no harder job than being a parent, she thought. It made her long for her mother.

"Uncle Ken," she said suddenly. "Did you know my father well?"

He arched an eyebrow. "Eric? No, not really." He drummed nervously on the table.

"My sister found—" she forced down a lump in her throat "—letters from my father. All this time I thought my mother was preventing us from living with Dad because she was selfish and didn't want to be alone."

"But the letters proved otherwise, didn't they?" Ken said softly.

"Yes. Did you know?" She caught his gaze, her own eyes wet.

"Your mother didn't out-and-out say so, but I suspected."

"He didn't want us. He said as much in the letters. He stopped sending money and left us to my mother, who made it sound like it was her decision to keep us from Dad. She lied because… To shelter us from knowing that our father didn't want us." Shelby had not said it aloud to anyone but her sister, Erin. The words stung like a scorpion.

Didn't want us.

Unwanted. The most painful word in the English language. What hurt more was knowing how she'd fought her mother tooth and nail, blaming her for being selfish when the truth was the exact opposite. But her mother shouldn't have lied, should she? Would the truth have changed anything? Would Shelby have believed it?

Her uncle was shaking his head. "I can't imagine not wanting a child. Opal and I, we tried for years to have a baby. Opal lost five to miscarriages and it devastated both of us every time. People say they aren't really babies when they aren't fully formed, but that's not true. Each heartbeat was our child's and we grieved when none of the babies survived."

She sat next to him and took his hand. He looked at her through tears. "And then there was Devon. He represented the best day of my life, and the worst. I had what I'd prayed so hard for, and I lost my wife at the same time."

"I'm sorry."

"I tried every day to show him that I loved him. I guess I didn't do some things right, but I wasn't supposed to go it alone, you see?" His tone was pleading. "Opal was supposed to be my partner in it."

She clenched his fingers.

"And now…" He waved a hand around. "Well, he's got another year in prison but what will his life be like after? He can't even hold his head up after what happened."

"He'll learn to forgive himself," she murmured. Forgiveness, there was that word again, though she did not feel she had the right to use it. "And maybe some good will come out of it somehow."

Ken stared at her, hollow eyed. "'And we know that all things work together for good to those that love God, to those who are called according to His purpose.' Romans 8:28," he recited. "Do you believe that?"

She did not know how to answer. Her past and present and all the things that had happened at the Gold Bar seemed to have jumbled up her thoughts. "I'm not sure, but I want to."

"Opal said the good comes from becoming more like Jesus." He pressed her hand to his forehead. "I don't see Devon becoming anything. He's broken, he's ruined."

"But he's asked Barrett for forgiveness. That's a first step."

Ken wrenched away. "I know Barrett will never forgive him."

"I think he will, Uncle Ken. He's already started the process."

Ken's face was clouded in disbelief. "No, he won't. And Barrett blames me, too."

She stayed silent.

"Well, I am not guilty of anything but loving my son," Ken said, getting to his feet, "and I will never seek forgiveness for that. Not from God and not from Barrett Thorn."

He grabbed his bag and stalked to the door. With his hand on the knob he turned back, eyes like slabs of granite, sparkling with rage.

"Don't let the Thorn family fool you, Shelby. They hate me, they hate Devon, and for all their religious spouting, that will never change."

The door slammed behind him.

The horses watched Barrett with their usual complacent curiosity on Saturday morning as he stacked the bales of hay in the feed room, checking for leaks in the roof. He always had a sense of peace when he worked on or near the horses, a feeling that everything was right as it should be, the universe in perfect order.

Friday had passed quietly, the routine chores of the ranch helping him forget his and Shelby's near-fatal experience in the mine. Now as the weekend before Christmas dawned in a swirl of pink and gold, he was not completely at ease. Though he'd heard nothing from Shelby since their escape from the mine on Thursday, he knew she was cooking up a plan and he also knew deep down in his gut that Joe Hatcher would do anything to get in her way.

What was driving the man? The question circled in

his brain. Pride? Paranoia? Stubbornness? Heaving the bales of hay worked his muscles, but it did not seem to clarify his thinking. Finishing the loading job, he saw his father preparing the trailer, so he joined him.

"Taxi job?"

His father nodded. "Returning Brownie. She's ready to go home."

Barrett fetched the mare and led her to the trailer. Brownie was a beloved horse on the Bar Seven Ranch, a nice piece of property owned by a married couple who ran a dental practice. Doctors Joan and Bobby Kinley traveled when they could and Brownie was a regular customer because he required daily medication and specialized care that their other horses did not. The bay had been fearful of the trailer at first, but after hours of patient work by Barrett and Jack, Brownie was a self-loader, though Barrett still kept a wary eye.

Walking next to the horse, he offered encouragement and gentle pressure on the animal's flank until Brownie walked into the trailer. "That's a girl, Brownie," he praised, giving her a scratch as he secured the lead rope and closed the tailgate.

"Can you stand some company, Dad?"

His father chuckled. "Sure, unless you're going to pressure me like Keegan does about allowing four-wheeling on the property."

"No, sir. I'll take four hooves over four wheels any day."

Barrett climbed into the passenger seat and they rumbled slowly away from the ranch.

"Can I ask you a question, Dad?"

"Fire away."

"What do you know about Joe Hatcher?"

His father shifted a little in the seat. "I don't know as it's right for me to talk about someone else's life, son. Don't know as I'd want someone to hash out mine when I wasn't there to defend myself."

"Not gossip, just facts. How's that?"

"All right. The facts." His father's calloused hands played with the steering wheel. "Joe lived on his dad's property, inherited the land and the saddlery business. Met his gal, Cora—" he squinted in thought "—Cora Felton, when her father came to the area looking for a place to stable his horses. Joe was in his late thirties when they married, I think, and Cora somewhat younger. Your mother would know the details."

"Okay. So they settled on Joe's place?"

"Yeah. Cora's dad died when Emmaline was real little and Cora inherited his horses."

"Were they, uh, happily married?"

"Not for me to say. Cora kind of kept to herself. Used to travel often, I know." He eased the truck and trailer toward the main part of town. "Joe stayed back with Emmaline and the horses when she would travel. When Emmaline graduated high school, Cora up and sold the horses, every last one of them."

"Why?"

"Dunno. Practical decision maybe. Horses aren't an inexpensive hobby, as you well know."

He knew, but that would not stop him from going without food or water before he walked away from his horses. Bree had felt the same, though she hadn't grown up with horses and she was always a little fearful around them except for Swanny.

His father continued, "After the horses were sold, she left town for good. That was almost five years ago.

Haven't seen her since. Heard they divorced, but Joe doesn't talk about it. He's a proud man."

"Can you think of a reason why he's so reluctant to allow Shelby to survey the mine?"

His father raised an eyebrow. "Would you want a stranger coming onto the Gold Bar who could potentially give the green light to a mining operation?"

He considered. "No, sir, but if the law says she has the right, I wouldn't stand in her way."

"Joe will come around. He just needs to blow off steam about it so he feels like a man. Rough having your wife divorce you." He sighed. "If your mom left me alone to raise the four of you, I'd probably go a little berserk, too."

Barrett chuckled. "Yeah, we've been more than a handful, haven't we?"

"That's an understatement." His dad ran a hand over the crown of his head. "All this white hair came directly from the Thorn sons' shenanigans." He laughed. "But you're all God-fearing, honorable men who know right from wrong, so I guess we've done okay."

"Yes, sir, you have."

His father was never effusive, but Barrett could hear the pride in his dad's voice. Tom Thorn was a tough man, quietly passionate about God, his family and major-league baseball. He would, and had, dropped boxes of food anonymously on people's doorsteps if he heard they were hungry and stepped in to raise an unwanted child when the Thorns were struggling to keep the Gold Bar afloat. Barrett's parents had always been and always would be his heroes.

They were traveling through the sleepy main street, past the ancient oak tree outlined with colored lights when Barrett saw Ella Cahill entering the Sunrise Cafe coffee shop. "Dad, would you mind letting me out here? I'll catch up with you in a bit."

"All right."

Barrett got out, noticing his father eyeing the window of the Treasure Trove Gift Store.

"Uh, Dad?"

"Yes?"

"Mama said to tell you that she doesn't want any more aprons or scented candles for Christmas."

His father's mouth quirked. "Oh, yes? And what does your mama want for Christmas then, Barrett? I'm sure she gave you explicit marching orders."

What did his mother really want? For her sons to be married, he thought. For the house to be filled with grandchildren, for a daughter-in-law she could love as much as she had adored Bree. He swallowed. "She said she'd settle for a new checkerboard since the other got water damaged up in the attic."

His father laughed and then grew thoughtful. "So she's hankering for another family game night?"

They hadn't had one since Bree was killed. For a moment, Barrett was transported back in time, hearing the click of checkers, the crackling of the fire, Frank Sinatra singing holiday carols and the laughter of a family celebrating Christmas together. His mother was ready to resurrect some of that joy, to put the pain in its proper place.

Was he ready? Part of him thought so. The grief would never go away but now it was not the core of his being. There was something else burning deep inside, though. Anger at Ken still flamed in his heart, forgiveness he could not offer. He was not ready and was not sure he ever would be.

God help me, his soul whispered.

His father looked at him as though he knew exactly what Barrett was thinking, the acid feelings about Ken. "All right," he said softly. "I guess it's time. Your mama will get her new checkerboard." He hesitated. "You okay, son?"

"Yes, sir," Barrett said, even though his heart was very far from agreeing.

Chapter Ten

Barrett caught up with Ella as she finished ordering her frappe-latte-whatever-it-was and counting out her payment in coins. Aside from water, he'd only ever understood the values of coffee, black and as strong as he could get it, and ice-cold root beer on a sizzling summer day. The barista handed her the steaming beverage.

She gazed at the drink with a look of rapture and he realized this was a treat for her. He wished he'd got there a moment earlier to purchase it for her. Money was tight for Ella and it had been ever since she'd been a kid. Nothing came easy for her or her sister, never had.

"Ella. Got a minute?"

She carefully snapped a plastic lid on her cardboard cup. "Sure, Barrett. Everything okay with the horses?"

"Yeah, this is about another thing."

"Yeah?" A mischievous smile crossed her face. "Are you wanting some help tuning up your truck?"

"No, thank you. I still have the notes you gave me from last time." When it came to engines, Ella was as good as or better than him or any of his brothers, and that was saying something.

"I, uh, I wondered what Shelby Arroyo was giving you the third degree about yesterday."

She tucked a strand of red hair behind her ear. "Maybe I shouldn't have mentioned it. She wasn't rude or anything. It just surprised me since, I mean, your family isn't exactly tight with the Arroyos."

"It's okay. I was just wondering."

"She wanted to know if we had a history museum of some kind, where old documents are kept."

"Documents?"

"Like topographical maps."

His stomach contracted. "Oh."

"So I told her to go talk to Shep. He'd be the guy to have them, wouldn't he?"

"Yeah, I suppose so. Thanks, Ella."

"As a matter of fact, I saw her driving through town heading in that direction about fifteen minutes ago."

Pulse jumping, he made his way to the door.

"Barrett?"

He turned.

"Why are you so interested in Shelby Arroyo?"

His face went hot, an unaccustomed feeling. Why was he interested? At that very moment, he could not come up with the words to explain it to himself or to her.

"No reason," he said.

"Okay. Betsy and I are looking forward to the Christmas Eve bash at the Gold Bar."

Christmas meant a lot to Ella, he knew. "We are, too. See you later." He felt her curious stare as he hastened out the door.

Shelby thought maybe she'd got the wrong directions, but the mailbox read 103 Lone Pine, which matched her Google search.

Ella Cahill told her Shep ran a tourist spot, though this didn't look particularly inviting. The small town was charming enough, every light along the main street twined with green garlands and pots of poinsettia plants clustered in front of the shops. Gold Country at Christmas time, perfect for a holiday postcard.

But Shep's place was a couple of miles out of town, set back from a road that could use some repaving. She saw no other vehicles on this lonely stretch. Peak season for folks looking for the gold mining experience was probably the summertime when they didn't mind splashing around in the cold water.

As she drew closer, she found a sign above the mailbox that read Gold Panning Adventures and Historic Gold Mining Museum. In the wide expanse of the front yard was a series of raised troughs and stacks of metal pans. There were no festive Christmas touches here.

Her temple throbbed, a sign that a migraine was still threatening. She hadn't helped things along by skipping breakfast in her haste to visit Shep. Her mother used to sneakily stow a granola bar in Shelby's bag before she left for her marathon school/work sessions.

In case you feel a headache coming on, she'd say. There would also be a couple of candy kisses there, too, in spite of Shelby's tirades about how she wanted to eat healthy. Odd. Her craving for a candy kiss at that moment was intense. She shook it off.

The office was a small wood-sided affair. At first she thought no one was home, until she noticed a glimmer of light from the side window. Hoping the proprietor would be more welcoming than Joe Hatcher had been, she approached the shop, letting herself inside to the jingle of a bell hung on the front door.

No one manned the small counter. "Hello?"

There was a cough from the back and a voice called out, "One minute."

Soon a man emerged, thin and tanned with a brown beard much fuller than Barrett's and a thermos in his hand. "Lookin' to try your hand at gold panning, miss?"

"Actually, no. I called earlier and left a message. I'm interested in your history museum."

His faint smile disappeared. "Oh, yeah."

"I was told you have some old maps and I'd love to take a look."

"Uh-huh."

She thought at first he had not understood her. "I'm Shelby." She decided not to provide her last name since that didn't seem to be earning her many fans in Gold Bar. He didn't offer his own name.

"Oh, I know who you are," he said. After a few seconds, he added, "I'm a good friend of Joe Hatcher's."

His face was as cold and hard as a rocky cliff. The hairs on the back of her neck went up. "I'm happy to pay for a ticket or something, in order to see the museum. I'm not asking for any favors."

"I won't take your money."

He said it as if her money was somehow dirty. She forced her gaze right back at him. "Shep, I'm here to see the museum. That is the point of a museum, to be seen, isn't it? I'm not going to cause any trouble. I just want to look at a few maps. Surely there's no harm in that."

He didn't answer.

A warm flutter of anger started up in her belly. "I don't have all day. Yes or no? Do I get in or not?"

Still the stony stare.

"All right. I'll leave." She went for the door. "And they say people in small towns are friendly," she grumbled. She had almost cleared the threshold when he called out to her.

"Down the path between the two pines. It's on the right. It will be dark inside, so turn on the lights yourself." Shep took his thermos and retreated to wherever it was he'd come from.

Still steeped in disbelief, she quickly headed down the path as directed before he had time to change his mind.

The museum was really just a long narrow building with a front and back door, which might have been a warehouse at one time or another. Now it was covered with aluminum siding and a sign on the front advertising Two Hundred Years of Gold Bar History.

She pulled open the door and it squealed as if it had not seen a can of oil in a few decades. The inside was ripe with the smell of dust and mildew, which did not bother Shelby in the slightest. Groping for the light switch, she found the area partitioned into smaller spaces by floor-to-ceiling screens that formed little rooms.

In the first area, she jumped when she saw what she thought was a man. It was a mannequin, dressed like a prospector, kneeling with a pan in his hands. Shep would probably have laughed himself silly at her fright. There was a display detailing the influx of would-be miners looking to strike it rich after James Marshall had made his historic discovery in the waters of the sawmill he was running with John Sutter. One man, one moment, had caused the entire country to go west.

She continued on toward the second partition, which was an overview of the various groups who gave up their domestic lives and headed in droves to the goldfields. People of all races and situations had joined the mad rush for the metal.

Shelby mused over the fake gold nugget on display for the museum goers. The geology geek in her marveled that gold was delicate enough to be hammered into the thinnest of wires and so versatile that it could be injected into the muscles of rheumatoid arthritis sufferers to ease their pain. The element was so rare that all the gold in the world could be compressed into an eighteen-yard cube and so common that every cubic mile of seawater contained twenty-five tons of gold. Plentiful and nearly impossible to extract.

The science of it never failed to awe her. In truth, it was the reason she believed in God. There could be no other explanation for the minute order of the metals, minerals and crystals she'd spent years studying. He was there in every minuscule detail, master creator, His signature in the gorgeous order of it all.

It puzzled her. Why would He so carefully create such marvels and yet allow His people, His most precious creations, to hurt each other so grievously? War, famine, abuse, neglect. If He was a loving father, why did He not intervene? And the most painful question of all? Why had he not helped Shelby see the truth instead of blaming her mother and making an enemy of the one person who loved her the most?

And the veins of gold she so eagerly sought for her uncle? They would have to be pried out of the earth at great expense and trouble. For all its beauty, the quest for gold could be an ugly business. All the blood, death, sweat and toil that went into finding a paltry flake or two.

Her own emotions surprised her. Checking her phone, she was surprised to find that she had frittered away more than thirty minutes. "What's the matter with you?" Slipping her phone into her pack, she moved on.

The next room was exactly what she'd been hoping for. Set against the back wall was a map of California, hand drawn to reflect the territory as it was during the late 1800s. Underneath was a set of long, flat drawers. With eager fingers, she pulled open the top one, finding it full of maps of the stagecoach routes. The next drawer was a hand-drawn map of the nearby towns. Encouraged, she was about to open the bottom drawer which was labeled Gold Bar, Topo.

A sound brought her upright. The scuff of a shoe on the floor.

"Shep?" There was no answer but her own thundering heartbeat. She waited, feeling silly. Had she imagined the sound? *Just look at the map and get out of here.* She crouched down and grabbed the bottom drawer, just as Joe Hatcher stepped into view. Her body went cold.

He didn't say a word, just stared at her, hands behind his back.

She stared back, unwilling to let him see her fear, while her mind churned. He was blocking her exit from the small room. She could yell, but who would hear her? Only Shep, and he'd made his alliance clear. Her phone was in the small pack on her back.

Okay. She would stand up to him and do whatever was necessary to get out of there unharmed.

"What are you doing here?" she demanded.

He shook his head. "You are one stuck-up lady. What am I doing here? This is my town. I thought I'd stop and see my friend Shep. You're the stranger. Maybe you should tell me why you're here?"

"Visiting the museum. Isn't that what strangers do?"

His eyes glittered, the thick grizzled brows pulled together in a line. "You're trying to pull the topo maps. I figured that would be your next step. Still researching my mine."

"My uncle's mine."

"Didn't you learn, lady? You and Barrett stuck down there in the water, almost drowned? It ain't safe. All you're gonna get from investigating is a coffin."

"Thank you for your concern."

"For some reason, Barrett seems to feel responsible for you. Ain't you gonna feel guilty if he gets hurt traipsing after you?"

She remembered how she'd felt leaving him behind in the tunnel. "I'm not responsible for Barrett Thorn."

He stepped closer. She caught the tang of dried sweat on his body. "Hasn't your family done enough to Barrett?"

That guilt rippled through her like an earthquake. She recalled her uncle's words. *They hate me, they hate Devon, and for all their religious spouting, that will never change.*

"The Thorns don't want anything to do with me." Straight from Barrett's mouth.

"Funny how Barrett turns up where you are."

She was tired of being in this uncomfortable standoff. "I want to go, Mr. Hatcher. Let me pass."

He moved his hand to his belt and pulled out a knife. The blade gleamed in the low light. He smiled, stepped quickly forward and pressed the knife to her throat. She went still, paralyzed with fear.

Hatred simmered in his eyes, his breath hot and sour on her face. "What's the matter?" he grunted, the blade cold against her skin. "Scared?"

Yes, her gut screamed. "No," she said, forcing out the words. "Because you're not going to kill me here in your friend's museum, are you? That would be messy."

For a moment, his gaze flickered. She'd called his bluff.

Then he leaned in closer until she could see every crease on his weatherworn face, the sheen of crazy nestled deep in his eyes. The breath froze in her lungs.

He chuckled. "Sometimes life is messy, isn't it?"

Chapter Eleven

Barrett figured since he was in town, he might as well stop by the church and see if they needed any handyman help for the soup kitchen. The kitchen was Bree's brainchild, a biweekly offering of food to any in the area who needed it. Unfortunately, there were always plenty of hungry people. If Bree had her way, they would have offered food daily, but the small town didn't have the manpower or finances to make that happen.

The church folks were busy at the moment in a meeting, planning out the Christmas festivities, so he left without disturbing them.

His father picked him up after dropping off Brownie. They drove along in silence, Ella's question ringing in his ears.

Why are you so interested in Shelby Arroyo?

It made no sense. He had plenty to do. *Mind your own business*, his head told him. *Got sixty horses and a family to take care of.* Instead, he blurted out, "Dad, you mind taking the long way back, by Shep's place?"

"Got a sudden hankering to do some gold mining?"

"No, sir. I heard from Ella Cahill that Shelby was heading there and, uh, I just got this bad feeling."

His father nodded. "All right."

He was grateful his father did not pry further into his motivation, which he did not fully understand himself. He simply could not shake the sensation that she was about to step in a hole so deep she'd never get out. Something about her combination of earnest and stubborn attracted him like a bear to a beehive. *Attracted? No, just friendly concern, right?*

But why should he care, as Ella wondered? *Because you're supposed to care about your neighbors, even the ones that you have the most reason not to.* God made that pretty clear. Barrett settled back on the seat, his mind more at ease until they reached Shep's place.

His heart lurched to a halt along with the truck. Ken Arroyo's vehicle was there all right, and so was Joe Hatcher's.

"Be right back," he called to his dad.

"I'm here if you need me."

Barrett found no one in the office, so he jogged up the trail to the museum building. Throwing open the door, he ran inside.

"Shelby?" he yelled.

"Here," she called back. His lungs started working again. Was it his imagination or was her voice tight with fear? He ran toward her, finding her jammed in the corner of a makeshift room with Hatcher next to her, a knife in his hand.

Barrett stopped short, hands loose and ready, as if he was approaching a treacherous horse, angling his body between Hatcher and Shelby. "Put down the knife."

Hatcher gripped it tighter. "You tellin' me what to do now, too?"

"Trying to save you from doing something stupid."

"Stupid?" Hatcher's eyebrows raised to his hairline. "All I'm doing is what Shep asked." He pointed up to one of the flickering lightbulbs. "Needs to be changed but it's rusted solid in the socket. He asked me to come jimmy it out on account of his bad back, and that's what I'm here for." He sneered. "What did you think I was gonna do, boy?"

Shelby's face was dead white, her lips pressed tight together. "He put the knife to my throat, Barrett. He only stepped back when he heard you coming."

"She's lying."

"No, she's not," Barrett said, rage gathering like floodwaters. "You're going to jail."

Hatcher lifted a shoulder. "Well, it's her word against mine and the cops think she's nothing but trouble already."

Shelby touched Barrett's arm. "Let's go. I'll tell the police. We'll let them sort through it."

Barrett looked at her, puzzled. The spirit seemed to have gone out of her. Had Hatcher scared her that badly?

Hatcher grinned and lowered his voice as if he was confiding a secret. "Anyway, if I was going to kill you, you wouldn't even see it coming."

Barrett shoved him in the chest. "Get out."

Hatcher stumbled back, the knife still in his hand. "Watch yourself, Barrett. We ain't enemies yet, but that can change."

"I said get out," Barrett repeated. "Now."

Hatcher fingered the knife handle, and Barrett tensed, staying between him and Shelby.

Hatcher slid the knife back into the sheath on his belt and walked away without another word.

Barrett followed far enough to be sure the front door creaked shut behind Hatcher before he returned to Shelby. She was hugging herself, her curtain of hair gleaming like wet autumn leaves in the low light.

"We'll go to the police right now," Barrett said.

"He'll just talk his way out of it. It won't do any good." She squinched her eyes shut for a moment.

"You okay?"

She nodded, but he saw a ripple of pain cross her face.

"He didn't hurt you?" Barrett pressed.

"No, I'm getting a migraine headache."

"Uh-oh. Have you eaten today?"

A flicker of surprise showed through her discomfort. "My brother Jack gets migraines when he forgets to eat or hasn't been sleeping well. It pretty much puts him down for the count if he doesn't take steps early on."

Her shoulders were sort of hunched, as if it hurt too much to stand up straight. "I'm okay."

But she didn't look okay, not by a long shot.

With a groan she bent to open the bottom drawer and let out a bitter yelp. "It's empty. Hatcher and Shep never intended to let me see the maps anyway. All this for nothing."

Hatcher had something to hide. Something big, big enough to draw Shep into the conspiracy, though Shep was probably doing his friend a favor without asking why. "They are putting a lot of thought into this."

She squeezed her eyelids together and rubbed her temples. "I'll figure out a way, but right now I can't think straight."

"Come on, we'll drive back to the Gold Bar and get you something to eat. I'll drive you in your truck back to the ranch."

"I can drive myself home."

"No offense, but no, you can't." She allowed him to take her around the shoulders. "Besides, you should come with me."

"Why?"

"You need food and I want to show you something."

He could feel the muscles of her neck, knotted like rope.

"Why are you here anyway?" she said.

"Dad and I were just passing through."

"I don't buy that, but my head is throbbing too much for me to grill you about it."

"Excellent, it will be a much nicer drive then."

He knew she must be feeling pretty bad since she did not even bother to fire off a retort as he led her to the truck and sent his father on ahead.

Shelby closed her eyes. Barrett was silent, which was a relief, since her head felt like someone had driven a spike through it, even though she'd taken a minute to swallow some of the migraine medicine she kept in her pack.

The feel of the knife pressed to her throat would not go away, leaving her muscles on high alert. She did not want to allow such a man to intimidate her, but she found her hands were shaking anyway, and not from the migraine.

Joe Hatcher may have intended to kill her right there in the museum. And he knew how to torture, too.

Hasn't your family done enough to Barrett?

She tried not to lean against Barrett's warm shoulder. *It's not like I'm asking him to take care of me.* Yet there he was again at the museum, and she'd been profoundly grateful to see him. Things might have ended differently if he had not come to her rescue.

She had no idea what it was that Barrett had to show her at the ranch, but the agony in her skull would not permit any deep thought. In a few moments, she found her head resting against his hard shoulder as the truck and trailer bumped them to Gold Bar Ranch.

Barrett took her hand and led the way into the quiet kitchen, which smelled of coffee and bacon. "Mom's run to the neighbor's, but there's always something to eat around here."

"I'm not hungry, really."

"Just a little bit in your stomach. Toast, maybe, with a slick of peanut butter."

She wanted to ask him exactly how much a "slick" was, but instead she watched through a cloud of pain as he toasted the bread, spread on a layer of peanut butter and presented it on a plate with a glass of milk.

She looked at him through bleary eyes. "Are you going to sit there and watch me while I eat?"

"Yeah."

"Can you at least eat something, too, so I don't feel like a zoo animal at feeding time?"

"Okay." He plucked an apple out of the bowl on the counter, took a big bite and sat down opposite her while she nibbled at the toast.

The bread was homemade and the peanut butter melted into a comforting ooze. She finished half before her stomach rebelled. "Thank you. That was great."

The food helped, but her meds had not yet started to dull the agony.

He tossed his half-eaten apple into the bin and stepped behind her. His long fingers massaged her shoulders, gently kneading the tension away. Her head leaned back against his torso and she accepted his tender ministering.

"Does your brother get this kind of treatment?" she joked.

"Naw, but I take care of his chores for him when he's got a migraine."

Barrett was a gentle giant of a man, she mused. The kindhearted cowboy who would try to ease the pain of a woman whose family had devastated his own. Yet he couldn't forgive… But who could? Nobody, as her uncle told her.

"I really should go home, Barrett." She pushed away and tried to stand, clutching the edge of the table as sparks danced in front of her eyes. "I'm not good company."

He stood and took her hand. "Come with me."

Unable to resist, she allowed him to lead her to a small family room furnished with a worn sofa and a pair of rocking chairs.

"Sorry, we don't have a guest room because it's filled to the rafters with stuff for the Christmas Eve party, but you can lie down and sleep here until it passes," he said.

"Oh, I don't need…"

"Yes, you do." He grabbed a quilt. She sat on the sofa, eyes closed, trying to summon up the courage to walk herself out of the Thorn house. He knelt and pulled off her boots. Before she knew it, she was lying on the sofa and he was covering her up to her chin with a quilt that smelled of fresh air, as if it had been dried on the line.

"I don't want you to take care of me," she tried to say. "I don't want to need you, any of you." Instead, the warm comfort washed over her, the darkness soothing as he pulled the curtains closed, the whinnies of the horses outside blending into a lullaby.

In the corner of the room was a small tree, covered with silver ornaments and a hand-stitched tree skirt. The faint scent of pine told her it was real, probably cut down right here on the Gold Bar property. He bent and connected a plug, and a sparkle of delicate lights shimmered.

"There now. That's about right," he said.

"Barrett," she whispered, "thank you." But he had already left the room.

Chapter Twelve

Barrett ordered his noisy brothers to hush up on account of their sleeping visitor. His mother looked particularly pleased to have a guest to fuss over and promised to give her a proper meal when she awoke.

"Jackie always likes a grilled cheese and coffee when he shakes off his headaches. I'll just see if there's more bread in the freezer. And I'm sure I've got some of that extra sharp cheddar left over."

Though Jack never corrected his mother, Barrett knew he did not enjoy her nickname for him. Still, it was good to see her smiling as he left her humming along to the ancient Christmas records she refused to part with. It reminded him how the ranch used to be a revolving door for visitors when Bree had been alive, especially during the holidays. His mother missed the bustle and the chance to exercise her gift of hospitality.

"I'm glad to see your smile, Mama," he said. He dropped a kiss on the top of her head before he headed outside to leave a message for Larraby and then muck out the stalls.

Owen caught up with him in the stables. "What's going on?"

"What do you mean, what's going on?"

"I mean, you're getting pretty tight with Shelby Arroyo."

"Not tight," he said. "Just being neighborly." He grabbed a shovel and went to work on the closest stable, scooping up mounds of soiled hay.

"Uh-huh."

Barrett stopped and faced his brother. "Uh-huh what?"

"Since Shelby blew into town, you two are together every time I turn around."

"That's an exaggeration."

"Is it? First you fish her out of the ravine, then you both are stuck in Hatcher's mine and now she's actually bunked on the sofa."

"Not bunked. She's sick with a migraine. Did you want me to leave her on the street corner?"

"No, but it all seems weird to me that she's suddenly welcome here, considering."

His jaw tightened. "Considering?"

"Come on, Barrett. Let's put it out there. Her cousin killed your wife and her uncle allowed it."

Anger flashed through him like white-hot lightning. "I know it, Owen. I'm crystal clear on the facts. It was my wife, remember? I have more reason to know that than you. If memory serves, you weren't even here when it happened."

He shouldn't have said that. It pained his brother that he had not been in the United States for the worst time in their family's history. And then the injury had left him a virtual invalid. Owen was born a protector. Barrett felt shame that he'd struck at his brother's vulnerability. He should apologize, but Owen was enraged.

His shoulders stiffened and he stood up to his full height, about an inch shorter than Barrett. "Yeah, I was somewhere else, wasn't I? Well, you know what I learned in Afghanistan? Two things, brother." He stabbed two fingers into the air. "One, never go anywhere without your body armor, and two—" his eyes blazed at Barrett "—know the enemies from the friendlies."

"Shelby loves her uncle, but she's not the enemy." When had he decided on that, he wondered?

"Yeah? Somehow I think her loyalties lie with another family, Barrett."

"Why is this your business?"

Owen folded his arms across his chest and looked down at his boots. "Maybe because I wasn't here, and now that I am, I want to do my part for the family... and you."

Barrett felt his ire drain away. His brother had fought his own battle and it followed him right back home to Gold Bar. "I get that."

"I don't want to see you hurt again," Owen said quietly.

Barrett blew out a breath and nodded. "Thanks. I know what I'm doing."

Owen looked at him long and hard before he nodded. "Okay. I'll trust your instincts unless I have reason not to." He turned and limped away.

Barrett put all his energy into mucking the stables, working until he was hot and sweaty in spite of the December temperatures. When the stalls were filled with sweet-smelling bedding, he checked on Swanny and tended to his other chores. By that time, it was well into the afternoon. He found Shelby and his mother on the porch, the Thorn family's old hound, Grits, sprawled on the bench between them with his head in Shelby's lap.

He laughed at the sight of Grits's eyes rolling in pleasure while Shelby rubbed his ears. "I see you've made friends with Grits."

"I miss having a dog." Shelby paused. "We took in a stray after my dad left. My sister and I named him Filbert and we doted on that dog until we had to give it away. We moved around a lot and most rental places aren't so dog friendly." Her fingers were slender and delicate as she soothed the fur. Grits let out a sigh that billowed his fleshy lips.

"How are you feeling?" Barrett said.

Her cheeks flushed a rosy pink. "Much better, thank you. I'm sorry to have been such a bother."

His mother waved a hand. "No, none of that. Happy to have you." She looked her son over. "You missed lunch, honey. Want a grilled cheese?"

Shelby giggled, a small dimple he had not noticed before showing alongside her mouth. "Your mother is a champion grilled cheese maker."

"You should see what she can do with a lasagna." He shook his head. "Don't need a sandwich, Mama, but thanks. I want to show Shelby some of Granddad's old things. Is that okay?"

"Of course it is." Her eyes danced. "You take your time and then she can stay for dinner."

"No, Mrs. Thorn. Absolutely not. I've taken advantage of your hospitality long enough. Besides, my uncle…" She paused. "Well, anyway, he's out of town and I need to keep an eye on things. Larraby is going to call and I want to have my thoughts together."

His mother looked slightly downcast. "Oh, well, if you change your mind, there's always plenty. I'm going to make chili and corn bread. The boys love it."

Barrett shooed Grits off Shelby's lap. "Let her up, boy."

Shelby stood and Barrett led the way along a shaded trail behind the ranch house. The air was cold, but she was zipped to the chin in her jacket, hair loose and dancing on the breeze. The sun glazed her fair skin and he was struck by the beauty of her face. Not so much the features as the passion that illuminated her from the inside, a kind of wonder at the path under their feet and the oak trees that towered above them.

"This place is gorgeous," she murmured, stumbling on a tree root because she had been eyeing a scrub jay. He reached out a steadying arm but she did not take it.

Message delivered. Jamming his hands into his pockets, he tried to clear his mind. The small cabin sported a coat of fresh ivory paint and deep burgundy trim. "Cheerful," his mother had declared when she'd chosen the color. "Just like Granddad."

He opened the door to the two-bedroom home where Granddad had lived for a decade after his wife had passed. They'd had talks about what it was like to lose your soul mate.

"Like when I lost my leg to the diabetes," Granddad had said. "It's gone but it still hurts like crazy."

"Does the pain ever stop?" Barrett had asked.

Granddad had gone quiet then for a while. "No, son. It dulls down to a softer hurt, but it never goes away."

Barrett's loss had dulled down to a softer pain, too,

but now it was twirled together with a strand of guilt. Guilt that he could not forgive Ken Arroyo, as he knew Bree would have wanted him to. Guilt that he was more than a little attracted and preoccupied by a new woman? He gritted his teeth and quickened his pace.

Shelby gazed at the photos on the top of a scarred upright piano. She laid one fingertip on the family shot of all four boys, each clutching a fish they had caught. Barrett was the tallest even then, gangly, in his midtwenties, she guessed. Next to that photo was a picture of Owen in his military uniform, tall and proud, without the hostility she'd recently detected in his eyes.

"It must be something to have a family like this," she murmured. "All the old memories and history you share."

"Got plenty of stories, that's for sure. What about you? You close with your sister?"

She nodded. "I love her like crazy. I've almost sent her enough money to start on her training. She wants to be a nurse," Shelby said, pride creeping into her tone. "She's going to be a fantastic nurse because she's smart, determined, super detail oriented and so compassionate." She let loose a breath. "She got a lot of practice with our mom before we had to hire full-time care for her."

"Not doing too well?"

"She has dementia triggered by her stroke. There's a great care facility in Phoenix near where my sister will be going to nursing school."

"You ever see your mom?"

"Not as much as I should. I wish… I wish I had

found out sooner that she was keeping the truth from me about my father."

She could see Barrett wanted to ask, but he probably didn't wish to come across as nosy. He stayed silent and she answered his unspoken question.

"He left us," she said simply, "and I thought my mother was the one that kept us from seeing him, that she was selfish and didn't want to share us with him." Moisture collected under her lashes. "I discovered last year when we had to pack up my mother's things that it was my father's choice, actually. He didn't want us. Part of why he left was that he never wanted kids."

Barrett shook his head. "I'm sorry, Shelby. That's a terrible thing to find out about your dad."

He could hardly conceive of it, she was sure. The Thorn family was as tight as any she'd known. "It hurts, but I can take it. The point is—" the confession dribbled out before she could stop it "—I was horrible to my mother about it and I never asked her to forgive me and now she doesn't even know who I am." Pain almost cut off her words. "It's too late."

"Maybe not," he said.

"What good would it do to apologize now?"

His eyes shifted in thought. "Well, Granddad said the hard stuff comes along to make us more like Jesus."

More like Jesus. It was an echo of her conversation with her uncle.

Barrett fixed her with a gaze bluer than the California sky. "Are you a believer, Shelby?"

The question startled her. "Yes," she said after a pause.

She could tell he was spooling the words out carefully. "Then maybe you should talk to your mother, not for what it will do for her, but for what it will do for you, for your soul, you know?"

"Maybe." Looking at his handsome face, chiseled and strong, she felt emboldened to ask a question of her own. "But if you believe that, Barrett, if you really believe forgiveness is for your own soul, then why don't you do the same with my uncle? Not for him, but for you?"

Emotions unrolled quickly across his face, anger, hurt, fear and last of all shame. "I... I can't."

"Then that doesn't speak well for your faith, does it?"

"No," he said, the word sounding strangled. "So I guess I should keep my advice to myself."

It got so quiet in the cabin she could hear the scuttle of a squirrel on the roof. She made a show of looking around the tiny spot. "Well, anyway, this is a nice place and I appreciate you showing it to me. I think I'd better go."

He yanked open a handmade wooden cabinet. "What I wanted you to see was Granddad's collection."

"His collection of what?"

Barrett unfurled a long cylinder of yellowing paper. "Maps," he said, finding a spot and pointing. "Look at that."

She hurried to see, her body brushing his arm. Her mouth fell open. "That's a rendering of the mine entrance on Joe Hatcher's property."

"It was Hatcher's father's at the time this was drawn, or more likely his grandfather's."

She peered closer, soaking in the faded details. "Wait," she said, peering closer. "This, this here. What is this?"

Barrett frowned. "I'm having second thoughts about telling you."

"Tell me, Barrett."

"It's a cave that Granddad said used to connect to the mine."

"Here? Right here on your land?"

"Not ours. The neighbor's. Oscar Livingston owns the adjacent property. He runs the Nugget Country Inn in town."

"Do you think he knows something about those red marks? Would he give me permission to access the mine via his property?"

"Maybe."

"Well, why didn't you tell me that earlier?"

"I forgot. The map didn't occur to me until I heard you were looking at Shep's museum. Granddad forbade us from ever sneaking over there and exploring because he said it was unstable and we'd be buried alive."

She caught his gaze. "Four boys and a forbidden tunnel? You tried anyway, didn't you?"

He looked sheepish. "Yeah, but he got wind of it before we even made it out of the house and asked Oscar to bar up the entrance."

She felt like kissing him. Instead she grabbed him around the shoulders in a hug. He embraced her, and she marveled at the sheer muscle of his torso.

Elated, she moved to kiss his cheek but he shifted at just the same moment, so her lips grazed his. Electric sparks rolled through her.

A shadow flickered across the window and she jumped away from him.

"Uh, problem?" Barrett asked.

"I thought I saw movement, like someone was looking in the window."

He stepped away, clearing his throat. "I'll check. Stay here."

He went outside, returning in a few moments. "I don't see anyone."

She sighed. "I think I'm getting paranoid. I'm sorry."

"No harm done, but I'm showing you this map on one condition."

She hoped she didn't sound as breathless as she felt after the accidental kiss. Further, she hoped her cheeks weren't flushed red. *Business at hand, Shelby.* "What condition?"

"That you will promise me not to go down into that mine shaft alone."

"But…"

He raised a finger and glared at her. "No buts."

"But…"

"What did I just say?"

She glared right back. "Your mama wouldn't like you bossing me around."

"Well, I'm bossing anyway, and don't drag my mama into this."

She expelled a long, slow breath. "Okay. I promise I won't go down there alone."

"Good. So when do we go?"

She grimaced. "Hey. Just because I have to take someone, doesn't mean it has to be you."

His look was purely sarcastic. "And who else would be insane enough to head into an unstable tunnel with a half-crazy assayer besides me?"

The seconds ticked by. She could not think of a single person.

"Oh, all right. How about now?"

"How about no? I've got horses to feed and Mama

said something about chili and corn bread. She would be mortally offended if I wasn't here to eat it."

"Fine, tomorrow then, and no fair dragging your mama into this if I'm not allowed to. Did you get your cell working after it got doused in the mine?"

"No. It was ruined. Using my old one. You?"

"Borrowing one from Uncle Ken. Give me your number so we can connect about a time."

She punched her number into his cell and he did the same with hers. He offered a smug smile that she found irresistible. "But it's still not fair."

He lifted a careless shoulder. "My mama, my ranch, my rules."

"You're one stubborn cowboy."

"So sue me," he said, returning his granddad's map with a chuckle.

Chapter Thirteen

Shelby was practically giddy as she drove home and fixed herself a peanut butter sandwich. Another entrance to the mine meant she would not have to fight Joe Hatcher anymore. She could take her samples without his consent or cooperation. The weight she'd been carrying around dissipated in a cloud of relief.

Curiosity kindled afresh. Those red marks she'd seen in the mine tumbled through her thoughts. With unfettered access to the mine, she could find them again and decipher the message they were obviously intended to deliver.

The sandwich was a far cry from Mrs. Thorn's chili and corn bread, but she did not want to risk spending any more time than necessary with Barrett.

The man befuddled her, plain and simple. He awakened trifold feelings: attraction, though she hated to admit it; anger, that he was so free with spiritual advice and so reluctant to take his own; and pleasure when she was sharing time with him. How could all of those feelings coexist? Black-and-white, that's how she liked things, and Barrett represented all the millions of shades in between.

The easy solution was to cut him out of her life, yet she found herself depending on him at every turn. It was simply maddening.

She liked him, or was it more than simple fondness?

No, it's not, you ninny. Focus on the anger, she told herself. *You're here for a job and that's it.* Barrett was bossy, a hypocrite who did not have the right to tell her what her soul needed when his own was far from spotless. She wanted to dismiss him outright, but his words continued to turn in her mind, twirling like a single leaf clinging to a winter-blasted tree. *Then maybe you should talk to your mother, not for what it will do for her, but for what it will do for you, for your soul, you know?*

It hadn't occurred to her that the act of asking for forgiveness was as important as the forgiveness itself. Maybe Barrett was right, because the change in her Uncle Ken from the man she'd known in her younger years was dramatic. He used to be loving, softhearted, but now his eyes burned hollow and hate filled, poisoned from within.

I am not guilty of anything but loving my son, and I will never seek forgiveness for that. Not from God and not from Barrett Thorn.

Her uncle's rage, Barrett's hypocrisy, her own inability to face the mother she had wronged. All three of them were caught in deep tunnels of despair, like veins of gold imprisoned in stone.

"God," she started, "help me to fix things with Mom."

Far from eloquent, it was the first prayer she'd uttered about her relationship with her mother in a very long time. The words were rough, as if they had lingered too long in some abandoned mine shaft.

"God, help me," she repeated, louder, insistent. There was no answering feeling of comfort, no dawning certainty about what to do.

Her thoughts were interrupted by Larraby's phone call. It was clear from his tone that he thought she was making up or exaggerating her encounter with Hatcher. It was a relief to end the call.

Darkness filled every corner of the house, so she turned on a few lights and played some Christmas music on her phone: Bing Crosby, Tony Bennett, Burl Ives, all her mother's favorites. She opened the newest issue of *Geology Today*, which would normally enthrall her, but she found she could not concentrate on the articles.

It was as if her heart longed to be somewhere else. The smell of the cozy quilt and the twinkle of the lights in the Thorn family room felt so very far away as she lay down on the couch and pulled on a blanket until her senses were finally overcome with sleep.

Shelby sat up with a start, disoriented, heart thumping. Her cell phone told her it was after midnight. The house temperature had dropped because she'd forgotten to set the thermostat.

She blew on her fingers as she tried to figure out what had awakened her. Tiptoeing to the window and pulling the curtains aside, she looked out onto the front lawn, but there was no sign of any visitors. Across the drive, the land dipped away and the roof of the barn and stable was barely visible.

Uncle Ken had downsized considerably, but he still kept Diamond, an older mare named Pattycake and her beloved companion, Buddy. The three were stabled for the night since Diamond was finicky about being in the rain and Pattycake and Buddy had grown used to night-time stabling with their previous owners.

A flicker of movement caught her eye. Diamond's coat gleamed in the moonlight as she trotted away from the stable. How had she got free? Had Zeke been careless about securing the animal?

Shelby considered. The pasture was fenced and Diamond could stand a night out in the cold since the temperature would not drop below freezing. Even if Shelby chased after her and offered an apple, Diamond's favorite treat, there was no guaranteeing the headstrong horse would come when summoned.

High-spirited indeed, as Barrett had said.

"You're on your own then until morning, you stubborn horse." A moment later her worry shifted to the other two. How would Pattycake and Buddy do, wandering at night with another storm threatening? What if Zeke had simply not stabled any of them for some reason?

With a sigh, she pulled on a pair of boots and a jacket, grabbed a flashlight from the kitchen drawer and shoved her phone in her back pocket.

As the weatherman had promised, rain had begun to fall and she eased her hood over her head. At least her migraine hadn't made a return appearance. She flashed on the sensation of Barrett's strong hands kneading comfort into her tense shoulders.

"Can't you keep him out of your mind for five minutes, Shelby Elizabeth Arroyo?" Yanking up the zipper so hard it caught her chin, she strode toward the stables.

Back in the more profitable years, Uncle Ken had

built a lovely wood-sided barn with adjacent stables that could accommodate ten horses, securing them comfortably in roomy stalls that opened up onto the main pasture. Most of the stalls were empty now, except the three on the end for Diamond, Pattycake and Buddy, who needed to be within hearing distance of each other. Normally two powerful lights mounted on the exterior of the stables would be switched on, but at the moment they were not.

Zeke had not done his job, apparently. She hastened into the barn, nearly tripping over a small can of red paint and a broom, shining her light on the control panel. The switch that controlled the exterior lamps was already in the on position. Figuring a circuit must have popped, she moved it to the off position and then on again. Nothing happened.

She turned on the interior barn lights, and the lamps set high into the ceiling flickered to life. Uncle Ken had not replaced the ones that had burned out so it was scant help, but it provided her enough of a glow that she felt more confident. "Must be some kind of a problem with the exteriors only."

Flashlight ready, she headed to the stalls. Her shoes crunched on the wet ground as she drew nearer. Beaming her light at her feet, she realized she was stepping on broken glass from the exterior lamps. Several feet away was another pile of shattered fragments, the remains of the other lamp. One broken lamp might be a bizarre accident, but two wasn't. A chill snaked up her spine.

She switched off the flashlight and melted as quietly as she could into the shadows. Sweat beaded her brow when she detected the low squeal of someone opening the door of the farthest stall. She heard Pattycake's soft nicker of surprise.

The person wore a black coat, and Shelby caught no gleam of hair, which indicated that whoever it was wore a ski cap.

Whoever? She knew exactly who it had to be. Joe Hatcher.

What he was doing in the stables she had no clue, but it was meant to hurt, of that she was positive. Creeping backward, Shelby inched around the side of the stable, yanking out her phone and shielding it with her shaking palm in case the light could be seen.

Someone's here in the stables, she texted Barrett. But it was almost 1:00 a.m. He would not be awake. There would be no help from Barrett and the Thorns. She could not call the police from her hiding spot because the stranger would overhear. Gripping the phone, she tried to keep her breathing steady and silent.

She needed a weapon. Uncle Ken kept a shotgun in the house and he'd taught both her and Devon how to use it. Would she remember? Could she actually pull the trigger? *Get somewhere safe*, her mind screamed. The house was her best option. From there she could call the police and defend herself.

Fear gripped her so tight she was paralyzed. "Move, move, move," she silently commanded her body. After a slow count to three, she sprinted toward the house, not daring to look back. She would not be able to hear the sound of pursuing feet over her own frantic breathing. *Go.*

Stumbling over clumps of soaked grass, she fell, rocks biting into the knees of her jeans. Scrambling to her feet again, she ran faster than she'd thought possible, not bothering to undo the pasture gate, instead clambering up and hurtling over the top rail. Splinters jabbed into her palms but she did not slow her pace until she exploded through her uncle's front door.

Slamming the door closed, she turned the bolt and sucked in precious lungfuls of oxygen. The police call took only a moment to place, but she knew it would be twenty minutes or more before they arrived at her uncle's place. Until then, she would be her own defender.

She pounded down the hallway and retrieved the shotgun from the closet and the shells from the shelf. She slid a round in the chamber and slid the action forward. Then she loaded the remaining rounds into the magazine.

Returning to the front window, she drew aside a corner of the curtain. The view was quiet, undisturbed. Shrouded moonlight glistened on the wet grass with pockets of deep shadow in between. She could not make out the barn. Needing a higher vantage point, she jogged upstairs to look through her uncle's bedroom window.

At first, she saw nothing, just darkness and rain. Then an orange spot flared into her field of vision. Her brain did not make sense of it for several moments. The orange spot danced and grew, shooting up in ragged tongues, obscene in the blackness.

Fire.

The stables were on fire.

She could not breathe, could not move. She imagined Joe Hatcher holding a lit match to the clean hay, watching while it caught, observing the mounting terror of the trapped horses, listening to them die. He would be smiling, enjoying the pain and misery.

Rage unlike any she'd ever known enveloped her in

a white-hot grip. A rush of adrenaline lit her from the inside out.

"I will not let you murder those animals," she hissed in a voice she did not even recognize.

Shotgun over her shoulder, she yanked open the front door. Sprinting, she raced back to the stables. The smoke was pouring from the end stall where Pattycake and Buddy stabled together. She yanked open the door, shotgun ready, but there was no sign of an intruder, only the terrified horses.

"Don't worry," she murmured to the panicked animals. "I'll get you out." She eased around them to gently prod them toward the door when a shadow of movement made her tense. She had only enough time to hold her arm up, but the blow caught her on the shoulders, knocking her to the floor beneath the horses.

Covering her face, she tried to avoid being trampled and shield herself from further attack.

There was the sound of the stable door swinging shut and the scrape of a wedge being kicked under it.

She crawled toward the door, head down to avoid the thickening smoke. Pressing her palm against the wood, she confirmed what her instincts already told her.

She was locked in.

Chapter Fourteen

Barrett didn't bother saddling a horse. He gunned the engine on his truck, tires churning up grit as he took the road to the Arroyos' property. Owen was in the passenger seat, tight jawed and silent, a rifle across his lap. He'd been awake in the kitchen, the perpetual victim of pain and insomnia, when Barrett had staggered in.

"I'm coming," he'd said. "You need backup."

Barrett had not argued.

Leaves torn loose by the incoming storm slapped against his windshield, the wipers keeping time to the panicked beating of his heart. Someone in the stables?

"Police are en route," Owen said. "She reply to your text?"

He shook his head. Would Shelby play it smart and stay locked inside as he'd advised, no, ordered, in his text? Would he, if the situation was reversed? If he thought someone was threatening his horses, he'd grab his gun and charge out like an angry bear. Any of his brothers would do the same.

The rain sheeted on the glass, his headlights picking out pockets of water collected on the road. He had to slow a few times when his tires caught in several pot-holes, jarring them both. The house came into view, some lights showing on the bottom floor.

They cut to a hard stop behind Ken Arroyo's truck. The smell of smoke hit them immediately, the crackle of flames jerking their attention toward the barn. "The stables are on fire."

"I'll get the horses out," Owen said. "You see if Shel-by's hiding in the house like you told her to."

Owen disappeared into the night. He was a crack shot, a trained soldier, and he had way more experience with this kind of situation than Barrett. Barrett made it to the front door in moments, stomach plummeting when he found it ajar. He pushed it open with his boot.

"Shelby?" he called softly. Then louder. No answer. The eerie stillness of the house telegraphed the truth. She'd done what he would have. Gone to save her horses. He texted his brother. Shelby's at the stables. Coming now.

Then he ran, flat out pounded down the sloped drive and onto the graveled trail that led to the stables. Drifts of smoke filled his nostrils. He found Owen trying to unjam the door at the end, but the wedge was driven too deep.

"Let me," he said, grabbing an ax and striking at the hinges. It took Barrett a half dozen chops to knock away the metal. He hauled open the door. Owen went for the horses when a shot exploded through the air, sending him to his knees.

"Don't touch my horses," came a faint voice from the corner.

"Shelby?" Barrett yelled, smoke stinging his eyes.

"Don't shoot. It's Barrett and Owen. We're here to get you out."

Crouched in the corner, she looked at him, peering through the smoke. After a moment, she struggled to rise but crumpled back into the hay. He gathered her up and carried her to the barn, laying her down while Owen tended to the horses.

She lay on her side, sucking in air, coughing. He brushed the hair from her face. "Easy does it. Just focus on breathing."

She sucked several more lungfuls before she struggled to sit up.

"The horses are out," he soothed. "Just stay put until we get an ambulance here."

She sat up anyway. He felt a thrill of relief. "What happened?" he asked, figuring he could keep her still for a while if she was talking.

She coughed violently. "I saw someone setting a fire in the stables. Whoever it was knocked me down and locked me in."

"Hatcher?"

"It had to be."

Barrett frowned. "Did you actually lay eyes on him?"

"No," she admitted. Her face was smeared with black streaks. "But I know it was him."

"So you came to stop him? With a shotgun?" Barrett was incredulous.

"It stopped your brother, didn't it?"

He almost laughed out loud.

Shelby was not smiling. "The horses would have died. Diamond was loose before I got here. I was trying to let Pattycake and Buddy free when he locked me in." Her expression darkened into a mask of rage. "He was going to let the horses burn alive. What kind of monster would do that?" Her lip trembled, just a little, and he could stand it no longer. He wrapped her in his arms and pulled her close. She pressed her face into his shirtfront and he knew she was trying desperately not to cry.

"It's okay now," he whispered. "It's okay."

She gulped and sniffled and he breathed in the comfort of her presence, the knowledge that she was safe, and pressed his lips to her hair. She raised her head, tears staining her cheeks.

He carefully wiped them away with his thumbs. Her skin was satin soft, warm, and he cradled her head between his palms, easing away the shivers, the fear.

"How could anyone do that?" she said so softly he could barely hear her. The eyes that met his were tortured, cut through with a pain he desperately wanted to ease.

"I don't know, honey." He let his palms cup her cheeks. "But the important thing is you're okay and the horses are all right."

She raised her head to his, and without thinking he pressed a kiss to her warm mouth. For a moment, her lips melted into his and his soul felt an ease that he had not experienced since his wife's death. The feeling was so intense it startled him and he drew back, staring.

"I, uh…"

She pulled away and stood. "I have to go find the horses. They're scared."

He regrouped, trying to shove away the reality of what had just happened. "You should wait to be checked out by the paramedics."

"No. I'm okay." She headed toward the pasture.

"I'll help."

Owen met them outside. "Stables are clear of any

intruders and the horses are uninjured as far as I can tell, but we'd better have Doc Potter check them over. I got the fire mostly contained, but I'll keep working on it." The sound of sirens pierced the night. "Cops are finally showing up."

"We're gonna take a look at the horses." Barrett hoped his voice didn't sound strange, but Owen just nodded.

"I'll stay here to keep more water on the fire and brief Larraby when he comes."

Shelby grabbed a few apples from the barn and several lead ropes.

Barrett was struggling over what to say when she stopped short. "There they are. All three of them."

The horses were gathered under a dripping oak. Diamond gleamed as if she had been carved out of marble. She tossed her mane when she saw Barrett and Shelby.

"I think Pattycake and Buddy will cooperate, but Diamond might be tough." Shelby handed him two apples. "Can you get them while I try to coax her?"

Barrett agreed. Shelby was right. The frightened horses were only too happy to nibble their apples and allow themselves to be fastened to lead lines. They followed him back to the stables eagerly enough. There was still the stink of smoke in the air but it was quickly dispersing in the wind.

The two did not want to be parted, the smaller gelding whinnying pitifully when he tried to stable them separately. Barrett put them together in an undamaged stall, stroking their trembling sides. He dried them down and gave them water and oats, talking softly until they settled.

Larraby had finished with Owen by the time Shelby had returned, wet to the boots, with Diamond.

"Miss Arroyo," Larraby started.

She shook her head. "I'm taking care of this horse first. Then I'll answer your questions."

Barrett hid a smile at the look of annoyance that crept over Larraby's face. Owen's expression said he was enjoying it, too.

"Quite a woman, isn't she?" Larraby said in an uncomplimentary tone.

Yes, Barrett thought with a growing sense of awe that scared him. *Yes, she is.*

Shelby was only half paying attention to the police officer's questions.

Barrett's kiss had enflamed her already amped emotions. Why would he do such a thing at such a time? And more significantly, why did his kiss make her feel like the tight bands holding her heart together had sprung wide open? Out of control. That situation must not be allowed to continue. There was no future with Barrett, a man who despised her kin and distracted her from her duty to save her uncle. She squeezed her hands into fists and brought her thoughts into focus.

"So are you going to go arrest Hatcher?" she demanded.

"I will question him and if he can't provide an alibi, then we'll go from there." Larraby shoved his pen in the pocket of his rain slicker.

"He's guilty," she said.

"Yeah, but we got this little thing called 'innocent until proven guilty' here in this country and you didn't witness him committing a crime." Larraby looked at Barrett and Owen. "Can either of you make a positive ID?"

The brothers shook their heads. "No," Barrett said, "but that doesn't mean she's wrong."

"Doesn't mean she's right either," Larraby said. "I'll take some pictures and look for prints." He walked off.

The horses, Shelby thought with a start. Would Hatcher return to try again? How would she protect them?

Barrett seemed to read her thoughts. "The horses should come to the Gold Bar until your uncle returns." He paused. "And so should you."

"I…" She took a breath. "I would appreciate it very much if you could take them for a few nights in case that monster returns, but I'll be fine here." The thought of staying in the empty house all alone made her skin crawl, but she could not, would not, impose on the sympathy of a family who hated her uncle. Besides, the less time with Barrett, the better.

Barrett glowered. "Not safe."

She held up the shotgun. "I'm a pretty good shot. Ask Owen. He can confirm."

"Well, my head is still attached to my shoulders, so I guess that's something," Owen said, clicking off his phone. "Jack and Keegan are on their way with the trailer. We'll get the horses settled in at the Gold Bar."

She nodded. "Thank you. I am grateful and my uncle would be, too."

"I doubt that," Barrett muttered.

She straightened. "I'm going back to the house to call him. Thanks again for your help." She hurried away a few paces.

"I'll walk with you," Barrett said.

"I don't need an escort," she tossed over her shoulder.

"Yes, you do."

She turned to face him. "Look, Barrett. It's…it's just not a good idea for us to be in close proximity."

"Probably not."

"Then why are you still following me?"

"Dunno." He wiped the rain from the brim of his hat.

"Yes, you do. Tell me." Her face went hot, remembering the kiss. He seemed to read her thoughts.

"Yeah," he sighed. "I don't understand why I…" He looked up at the watery moonlight. "I mean, considering my feelings about your uncle and all…" He stopped again. "But I can't stop thinking about you, and you make me feel, I dunno…" He shoved his hands in his pockets. "Awww, never mind. Forget I said that. I'm comin' at least until you get inside and lock your door, so that's that."

She didn't know what to do but force her legs into motion while her mind reeled. *Can't stop thinking about you…?* How could he possibly have put into words the same emotions flailing around her insides?

It was ludicrous, dangerous, ridiculous.

Keep walking, Shelby. Just keep walking.

Mercifully, Barrett did not speak at all on the way back to the house. By the time they got there, Shelby had herself firmly under control.

"Thank you, Barrett. I'll come for the horses as soon as my uncle gets back. We'll pay you to board them, of course."

"Naw, you won't."

"Yes, we will. You don't want to do a favor for my uncle."

He grimaced. "Could be God's giving me the opportunity to change myself." A soft sigh escaped him. "I hate it when He does that."

She could not help giggling at the plaintive look that showed through the weariness. There was just something about the guy, the way he struggled with his faith, yearned to do the right thing in spite of the flaws that got in his way, that made her want to kiss him again.

"Anyway," he said. "I'll see you tomorrow."

"Tomorrow?" She blinked hard. "Oh, right. Our mine expedition."

"Yup," he said. "And don't even think about going without me. I…" He cleared his throat. "I know I upset you tonight with that kiss and all my crazy chattering, and I apologize. It won't happen again."

His gaze was firmly fixed on his boots.

"It's okay," she said softly. "It was just a kiss and some words. No harm done."

He looked at her then, something wild and wounded and yearning in his expression. "Yeah," he said. "No harm done." He turned away.

"Barrett," she called.

He stopped.

"You aren't by chance planning on sleeping in your truck and keeping an eye on me tonight, are you?"

His eyebrows shot clear up to his hairline. "Me?" His tone dripped with innocence. "Why would you accuse me of such a thing? I'm not a stalker, you know."

She knew, and she also knew that was exactly what he intended to do. She opened her mouth to complain when he waved her off.

"Go on now. Starting to rain again and I'm getting cold."

"I thought you were too stubborn to get cold."

"Must be turning weak or something."

She smiled, taking in his proud form, tall and strong, as if he defied the rain to fall on him. Not weak, not anything close to it.

The door was ajar, as she'd left it in her haste to protect the horses. The smell hit her first. As she flipped on the lights, it took a moment for her eyes to adjust to the darkness.

She screamed.

Chapter Fifteen

Barrett bolted through the open door, almost plowing into Shelby from behind. Blood oozed down the walls, dripping in scarlet rivulets to the wood floor. No, not blood, his brain corrected. The chemical scent of paint permeated the space.

Shelby was staring at the wall. Written in the paint was a message: You'll Die. By the time he had the presence of mind to take out his cell phone and photograph the horrible phrase, the letters had smeared and dripped, drying in ugly trails, yet still shouting out their message of hate.

You'll Die.

He put a hand on her shoulder. She was trembling under his touch.

"I saw the can of paint at the barn," she whispered. "While you and I were securing the horses, he came up here and did this."

Barrett did not know what to say. Ken Arroyo's living room was desecrated. The man did not deserve that, no matter how Barrett felt about him. Nor did his niece.

"I'll get Larraby," he said, anger humming through

his veins. "And when we're done here, you're staying at the Gold Bar. Period." His tone brooked no argument and she did not offer one. That worried him almost as much as the fact that whoever had gone after the horses had been at large here, too.

Would Hatcher actually do such a thing? Barrett couldn't fathom it.

His phone call summoned Larraby and another officer who began printing and photographing. At the end of the process, they allowed Shelby to try to clean up the spilled paint before it dried on the floors. Barrett helped, but they succeeded only in smearing the color over the walls and in bright arcs across the wood planks.

"I'll leave an officer posted out front to keep watch tonight," Larraby said, his tone more conciliatory than it had been earlier. "You can call him if you feel uncomfortable."

"No need," Barrett said. "She's coming to stay at the ranch."

Larraby mulled it over. "Okay. We'll schedule some drive-bys to check on the property anyway."

Shelby called her uncle. Barrett stepped outside to allow them some privacy while she packed an overnight bag and he phoned his mother.

"Can we accommodate a houseguest, Mama?" he asked after he filled her in.

"You have to ask?" she scolded. "I'll put some clean sheets on the bed in Granddad's cabin. She'll be snug and safe as anything there."

Perfect, since Barrett's bedroom window looked directly out on the cabin.

"And when Ken gets home," she said firmly, "we will help him clean up the mess properly."

Help Ken. The idea would have disgusted him a week before, but now it did not feel quite so distasteful. "Yes."

"You know," she said softly. "God's going to work good out of this. I can see it happening in you."

In him? God had to be pretty amazing to work good out of the present mess with Shelby. Was it possible he could rid himself of his long-simmering rage and forgive, not for Ken's sake but for his own? It would be a tall order, very tall.

"Be home soon, Mama."

Shelby locked up the shotgun, pulled the front door closed behind her and secured it. "Uncle Ken is going to try to catch an earlier flight, but he still won't make it home before Monday afternoon. He's really upset, of course, but he's appreciative that your family is looking out for me."

Appreciative. Little did Ken know that Barrett was intrigued by his niece to the point where he could think of nothing else. Odd.

Maybe he should be feeling guilty about having such strong feelings for another woman, but he knew Bree would want him to find another partner. She'd told him as much on one of those long summer nights when they'd sat on the porch, talking and watching the fireflies paint the skies over the ranch. She was unselfish like that. But to love someone whose uncle enabled his son to kill Bree? How could God mean for that to happen?

God's working good out of all this. I can see it happening in you.

With an effort, Barrett pulled himself back to the reality of the situation. Problem solving, the soothing list of things to be done, details to work out. That's what he craved.

He mentally worked through the logistics of housing three extra horses, who to ask about how to clean paint off Ken's hardwood floor and how to structure his chores so he could be sure Shelby did not go sneaking off into the mine without taking him along. He did not like the angry glint to her eye and the set to her chin. If Hatcher intended to scare her off from her explorations, he'd missed the mark by a mile.

Something odd and primal pulsed in Barrett's stomach as he pulled into the Gold Bar property. He had the feeling that he was bringing Shelby to the place she belonged, his home, his world, as if she was his woman, his soul mate. It was the way he had felt about Bree, that she was his and he would do anything in the world for her, anything at all.

Struck motionless by the thought, he stared out the window, the truck idling in the front drive. She reached out her hand and cupped his fingers in hers.

"I feel like I'm trespassing."

"No," he said softly. *I wouldn't want you anyplace else*, he wanted to add, but he'd already made a fool of himself one too many times that day. "You're welcome here. Don't think anything different."

She gathered up her purse while he hopped out and opened the passenger door for her. His father had the front door ajar before Barrett made it there.

"Shelby, I am so very sorry that this is the kind of treatment you've got from Gold Bar. It's beyond comprehension."

To Barrett's great surprise, Shelby started to cry. Tom Thorn, who was strong enough to fight for his family and love a complete stranger, folded her in an embrace.

"It's going to be all right," he said, patting her back. "When you're staying here, you're an honorary Thorn and nothing is going to happen to you. I guarantee it."

Barrett saw Owen, Jack and Keegan standing behind their father. Their faces showed varying degrees of emotion: Jack complacent, Keegan enjoying the whole spectacle and Owen reserved and still suspicious. He knew all three of them would honor their father's words and protect Shelby Arroyo, no matter their own feelings.

Pride mingled with his confusion. God made something special when he put the Thorn family together. He watched his mother draw Shelby inside, no doubt to try to tempt her into eating something. He busied himself with fussing over the horses, who didn't need it, and checking the supply of hay, which was more than adequate.

When his mother was finished, he walked Shelby to Granddad's cabin. His mother had left the lights on and turned down the bed. She'd even placed a plastic-wrapped plate of Christmas cookies on the table.

Shelby sighed. "Oh, I wish she hadn't gone to the trouble."

"Trouble? You made her whole holiday season, and this way Keegan won't eat the entire batch all by himself."

Barrett went to the corner and plugged in a string of lights, illuminating the small tree that had been in the family room. Shelby gasped, the lights reflecting in the pools of her eyes.

"There was no need to move it here for me," she whispered.

"Like Dad said, you're an honorary Thorn, and that means you get the full holiday treatment."

He made sure the windows and back door were locked, just for extra good measure.

"Good night, Shelby."

"Good night." Her voice was soft and tender.

Though he wanted to look back and see her silhouetted in the lamplight, he forced himself to keep walking, distancing himself from feelings that his heart could make no sense of.

Shelby was up with the sun, alerted to morning by the soft sounds of ranch life. Peeking out the window, she caught her breath at the sight of Barrett forking flakes of hay down into his truck to deliver to the waiting horses. His breath steamed in the cold air. He worked alongside his brother Jack.

The lights were on in the ranch house where she imagined Evie was busily preparing breakfast. Shelby dressed quickly, tying back her hair and swiping on a quick brush of mascara and lip gloss, chastising herself as she did so.

Who is this vanity for? Barrett? You're not going to be a couple, get that through your head. Her head was not the problem, unfortunately. It was her heart that did not want to listen to the list of reasons why Barrett was an unsuitable match. The list was compelling enough.

First, there was the problem of her uncle and their mutual familial hatred. If that wasn't enough, Barrett had obviously been desperately in love with his wife and he was simply confusing a mild attraction with something deeper. Furthermore, she had no intention of staying around after the mine was properly assayed. Aside from visits to her Uncle Ken, she had plans to open her own assayer's office in Arizona where her sister was attending school, close to their mother.

Her stomach clamped tight at that thought. There were so many things she should say to her mother, things which would not be received by the woman who no longer even remembered who Shelby was.

She realized she was standing as frozen as a statue, while her mind ran rampant. "Get it together," she hissed at herself, pulling on her jacket and yanking open the door.

Barrett and Jack looked up as she strode purposefully toward the stables.

"Good morning. I thought I'd check on Diamond and her partners in crime."

"We've got them in the western pasture by themselves for now. They were skittish after their eventful night." Barrett peered at her as if wondering if she felt the same.

"I'm going into town," she announced, "to talk to Oscar Livingston about access to the mine."

"I'll go with you," Barrett said.

"No need."

"I've got to get some brackets to put the tables together for the Christmas Eve dinner and your truck is still at your uncle's place, so why don't you hitch a ride with me?"

Why? She'd just given herself three good reasons why. "But…"

Barrett was talking to his brother.

Evie called from the house, "Time for breakfast."

Shelby wanted to flee, but how could she face that smiling woman and turn down her gracious hospitality? Feebly, she followed Jack and Barrett into the kitchen.

The scent of sausages and scrambled eggs made her mouth water. Tom greeted her with a cheerful smile. Evie gestured her to a chair and poured coffee into mugs at the wide table. The wood bore the scars and nicks from generations of people who had gathered around it over the years.

Shelby imagined the little grandchildren that would come along one day, sitting at that same table, hunched over coloring books or learning to roll out piecrusts like Grandma Evie. Her own childhood had been punctuated by moments like these, until their father left. Then it was as if a darkness had settled over the family, in spite of their mother's desperate attempts to lighten it.

The anger had gradually taken over Shelby's soul, and with it a need to punish the person she felt was responsible, the wrong person. Her father did not want the children he had made. She should be brimming with rage at him, shouldn't she? But she found she was only filled with sadness at what she had lost, the years she could never get back.

Did the Thorns understand what a precious thing they housed between the old ranch house walls?

She looked at Barrett, Evie, Tom, and she knew the answer was yes. They had all endured great sorrow at the death of Bree and they knew how fragile a blessing could be.

Owen and Keegan joined the group, cheeks ruddy from the cold morning. Before she knew what was coming, Barrett had taken one of her hands and Evie the other. The brothers completed the circle and Tom said a simple grace. The company broke into a lively conversation about ranch duties.

Evie dished up a plateful for Shelby. "We're going

to the evening church service tonight, honey. You're invited, of course. They added that service for those ranching types, who have plenty of early chores."

"Or just can't get up in the morning," Owen said, laughing at Keegan who was in midyawn.

"Thank you," Shelby said, trying to figure out a way to politely decline. She feared it would be awkward, downright painful, to attend church with everyone's eyes on her, the whispers about the newcomer whose life had been threatened on a regular basis.

"Meg at the church said she could use more pickles for the soup kitchen's Christmas Day luncheon," Evie said to Barrett.

Keegan laughed. "Better start rationing. We're down to the last fifteen cases."

"Funny," Barrett said. "You're just jealous because you don't know how to cook anything but toast."

Jack startled Shelby by speaking. "He doesn't know how to make toast either."

She joined in the laughter, marveling at how the levity buoyed her spirits and pushed away the fear from the night before.

She was halfway through her eggs when there was a knock at the door. Jack admitted Officer Larraby, who declined the offer of coffee and breakfast. He looked ill at ease in the Thorn house. Shelby's nerves went taut as she waited for him to report his findings.

"I came to let you know that Hatcher has an alibi for last night."

Shelby dropped her fork. "I don't believe it."

"His daughter, Emmaline, says he was home all night."

"She's lying because she's scared of him," Shelby said. "He's a tyrant."

Larraby shrugged. "Possibly, but his truck engine was cold, hadn't been driven."

"He could easily have come on foot," Barrett put in. "It's not more than a mile to Ken's place."

"He wasn't the least bit wet when I spoke to him. Hair dry, coat dry on the rack, boots dry, too."

"So he changed, dried his hair," she said. "You can't possibly think he's innocent."

"It doesn't matter what I think," he snapped. "My job is to enforce the law and there's no evidence to arrest him. No prints at your uncle's place, no tire tracks, no eyewitnesses and nothing to refute his alibi."

Barrett threw down his napkin. "How about all the threats he's made to Shelby? The knife he pulled on her at the museum? Guy's clearly out to get her."

"Like I said, not enough," Larraby said, moving toward the door.

"When will it be enough?" Shelby said. "When I'm dead?" The words dropped like bombs in the quiet kitchen.

"We'll keep digging," Larraby said. "I'll let you know if we come up with anything. Sorry to interrupt your breakfast."

"Where's his ex-wife?" Shelby blurted.

Larraby blinked. "What?"

"I heard in town from a waitress at the coffee shop that his wife, Cora, left him almost five years ago."

"Yeah, I'm sure the gossips loved that whole drama. What does it have to do with the present situation?"

"Emmaline said Cora was an amateur geologist, that she'd spent time in the mine. When Barrett and I were down there, it was clear that someone had done some exploring, left some marks behind."

"That mine is more than a hundred years old."

"The marks were recent."

"I still don't see where you're going with all this."

"I wondered if Cora would be willing to talk to me about what she saw down there. It might explain why Hatcher is so reluctant to let me in. Maybe he knows there's a rich vein of gold and he wants to keep it for himself."

Larraby shook his head. "Sounds like you're cooking up some wild theories."

Shelby stared at him. "What happened at the stable last night was not my imagination. I'm going to find out who is responsible, with or without your help."

Larraby folded his arms across his chest. "We're investigating and I'm doing my job."

"And I'm going to do mine, also."

"You do that, Miss Arroyo, but whacking on the hornet's nest by prying into Cora's life is asking for trouble."

"They're divorced. He doesn't get to decide who Cora talks to anymore."

"She chose to leave Gold Bar and as far as I know, she never looked back."

"Yeah," Shelby said, thinking of her own father. "Well, maybe it's time she did, whether she wants to or not."

"Like I said, if you mess with the nest, you're likely to get stung, but I can see my advice is falling on deaf ears so I'll go about my business." Larraby departed, the door slamming shut behind him.

Shelby realized everyone in the kitchen was now staring at her.

"I'm sorry. I think I've ruined your breakfast."

"No," Owen said, his blue eyes so like Barrett's.

"But Larraby does have a point. Hatcher's divorce is his business."

"My horses almost burned to death and there's a threat painted on my uncle's living room wall, so I'm not so concerned about Hatcher's feelings at the moment."

Owen's face was contemplative rather than hostile as she got up from the table. The men stood to be polite, a gesture which made her blush. Still courteous in spite of the trouble she had brought right into their midst.

Barrett caught up with her outside.

"Ready to head to town?"

She arched an eyebrow. "I didn't think you'd still want to be involved with a woman who's whacking a hornet's nest." She'd thought he'd smile, instead his face was dead serious.

"Like Dad said, you're an honorary Thorn. Thorns stick together, even when we disagree."

She swallowed. "Your brother Owen might not accept that."

"Owen has his own battles to wage. This family is all he has left and he'll fight to the death to protect it."

"Seems to me like that would describe all four of you."

He nodded. "Yes, ma'am. Now, are you ready to go?"

"Yes."

"All right. I just gotta load a case of pickles into the truck."

She smiled as she watched him go. For some reason, she'd been provided the comforting shield of the Thorn family.

You'll Die. It was a threat she could not allow to spread to Barrett and his kin. She would risk her own life for her uncle and the truth, but she'd make sure no danger would fall on the Thorns.

Chapter Sixteen

Barrett delivered the pickles before he picked up the boxes of brackets and a dozen folding chairs that the hardware store owner loaned out on a regular basis. Shelby helped him load the chairs into the bed of the truck, though he didn't want her to.

"Chivalry is nice and all that," she said, as they slid the wood in the back, "but four hands are better than two and my hands are pretty strong."

He had no doubt of that. Across the street from the hardware store was a thrift store with colorful dresses and handbags displayed in the window. Shelby's attention was caught and he followed her gaze.

Emmaline was exiting with a shopping bag. Shelby hastened over, Barrett following.

"Hi, Emmaline," Shelby said.

The woman shied like a startled colt. "Oh, hi."

"Doing some Christmas shopping?" Shelby asked.

Emmaline shrugged. "Not really. I just needed a plain apron so I can add some holiday trim. There was a skirt, too, I've been admiring with this really pretty beading along the hem. I love fancy clothes even though I have no occasion to wear them."

The sadness of that statement tugged at Barrett's heart. "You're coming to Christmas Eve at the Gold Bar, right?" Barrett suggested. "That's an occasion if I ever heard one. I even wear my best jeans, the ones without the hole in the knee."

She offered a tentative smile. "Imagine that." She twisted the handle of the bag. "Um, I know you probably want to talk to me about the thing that happened at your uncle's place. The police did, too. I told them everything. My dad was at home with me and I'm not going to talk about it anymore no matter how much you pressure me." She clamped her mouth closed.

"I understand," Shelby said. "I'm not going to ask you to speak out against him."

Barrett was surprised. He admired Shelby for not trying to force the girl to possibly betray her father.

"I have something else to ask you. I wondered if it might be okay for me to contact your mother."

Emmaline's mouth dropped open. "My mother?"

"Yes. You said she liked to explore the mine. I wanted to ask her about her observations and if she knows anything about the marks down there."

Emmaline's gaze dropped to the ground. "My mother's gone. She left us when I was in high school. Mom and Dad are divorced."

Shelby touched her very gently on the shoulder. "That's hard. I understand."

Emmaline's eyes glittered with anger. "Oh, really? You understand how it feels when your mother leaves you? When you're not a big enough reason for her to stay?"

"Not my mother, my father."

Surprise flickered through Emmaline's anger. "Oh," she said. "Well, anyway, I don't know where my mother is. I wouldn't know how to find her."

"Can you tell me her last known address? Any family members she might have contact with?"

Emmaline shook her head. "No. As far as I'm concerned, I don't have a mother anymore."

Barrett wondered if Shelby felt the same way about her father. How unutterably sad to lose someone who was still walking the planet. What a waste.

"I didn't mean to upset you," Shelby said. "I'm sorry."

Emmaline gathered her bag close and blinked hard at the tears that had formed under her lashes. "It's okay, but please don't talk to my father about it, all right?" Her tone was pleading. "He can't think straight about her. He goes a little crazy when her name is brought up, so I've learned not to mention it."

What kind of life did this girl have with a mother who abandoned her and an unbalanced father?

"I won't," Shelby said, and Emmaline looked relieved.

"We'll be sure to save a seat for you on Christmas Eve." Barrett hesitated.

Emmaline laughed. "Don't worry. I know what you're worried about, but my father never goes to any gathering. You don't have to be concerned about him showing up." She held up the bag and smiled brightly. "But I'll be there with a fancy new skirt on. Well, new to me anyway."

"Emmaline," Shelby said. "I heard that you were really attached to Diamond before she was sold to my uncle."

Emmaline bit her lip. "Yes. She is the most beautiful horse I've ever seen. If she were mine, I would never have sold her. Ever. I can't understand how my mother could do it. Even my dad didn't want to sell Diamond because he knew how much I loved her, but they were my mother's property." A look of disgust curled her lip. "That's how she saw Diamond, as property. We both begged her to keep the horse but she wanted out, out of ranching and out of our lives."

Christmas carols played softly in the store behind them, at odds with the tragic story unwinding on the sidewalk. Barrett wasn't sure what to say but he wished he could think of something. Words eluded him, as they often did, but Shelby broke the silence.

"Why don't you come by and ride Diamond sometime? She needs more exercise and my uncle wouldn't mind."

Her brows shot up. "Really?"

"Sure. It would be good for Diamond."

And good for Emmaline.

"Um, okay. Maybe when my dad is away. He wouldn't like it. He doesn't like me to do anything that reminds him of my mother."

"Whenever you'd like. Right now, Diamond is at the Gold Bar, but in a few days she'll be back home." Shelby gave Emmaline her cell number. "Text me when you want to come and I'll be sure there's somebody there to help you."

Emmaline nodded. "Okay. Thank you."

Shelby stood watching Emmaline walk away, coat collar pulled up to her chin.

"That was a nice thing you did there," Barrett said.

Shelby continued to gaze in the direction Emmaline had taken until she disappeared among the throng of people stringing lights along the eaves of the Grange Hall. "I understand how she feels."

"Maybe you can help her process what happened with her mother."

"I've got to figure out how to process my own situation first." Her smile was rueful, but he saw a touch of hope there, and it lifted his spirits. "Anyway, I'm itching to talk to Oscar Livingston. If your granddad's maps are accurate, there's a way in from his property."

"All right," he said with a sigh. "Let's go."

The Nugget Country Inn was a picture-perfect Victorian house set on the edge of town, backed by a rugged stretch of foothills that gradually gave way to the Sierras. The meticulously painted two-story building boasted quaint gingerbread trim twined with lighting for the holidays. The small lobby was warmed by a crackling wood fire and guests sat on plush settees and chairs, enjoying mulled cider and gingerbread cookies.

Shelby breathed in the scent of the spices and the decked-out fir tree crammed in the corner of the room.

Oscar Livingston was behind the counter, an enormous man as tall as Barrett and three times as wide. His full white beard was at odds with his perfectly bald head.

"Welcome," he boomed. "Morning, Barrett."

"Good to see you, sir," Barrett said, returning the man's vigorous handshake.

"Brought a pretty guest, I see. Can I get you a mug of cider, miss?"

"I'm Shelby Arroyo," she said. While she craved the offered cider, she decided it was best to keep things businesslike. "No, thank you for the cider, even though it smells delicious."

"Arroyo?" He mused. "Ah. Ken's niece."

She held her breath but did not see any ill will creep across his broad face at the mention of her surname. "Ken is proud as peas about you. Tells everyone who will listen about his niece, the assayer."

Her cheeks warmed. Uncle Ken was her father and her uncle all rolled into one and how good it felt to know she'd made him proud. *And I'm not done yet*, she silently reminded herself. "That's nice to hear. Actually, I've come on assaying business. I'm surveying the mine for my uncle."

"I heard you were taking a look on Hatcher's property." He cocked his head. "Didn't take it well, did he?"

"No."

"He's making things more difficult than they have to be," Barrett put in. "So we're looking for another way."

Oscar nodded, a frown wrinkling his forehead. "Oh, I get it. You want to access the mine via my property."

"Yes," Shelby said. "That's exactly what I want."

The phone rang on his desk, an ancient rotary model in a shade of avocado green. "Excuse me just a minute." He listened and then called to the back. "Hazel, can you come here a minute, sis?"

A large woman with the same full cheeks and warm smile stepped out of the back room. "Well, hello," she said. Bypassing the counter, she planted a kiss on Barrett's cheek and extended a plump hand to Shelby. "I'm Hazel Livingston and I see you've met my big brother."

Oscar chuckled. "She's always happy to remind folks that she's two years younger."

"Girl's gotta hold on to her youth," Hazel said.

"How's Shannon?" Barrett asked. "Coming home for Christmas?"

Hazel beamed. "Shannon's my daughter," she explained to Shelby. "She's studying in New York. Premed. Can you imagine that? Premed, and her mama never even went to a day of college."

"Her uncle neither," Oscar put in. "Too bad she's probably not coming back for Christmas." He gave Barrett a sideways glance. "But since she's not, uh, maybe we'll come to the Christmas Eve dinner, if we can get free. We'll bring pie."

Barrett laughed. "Pie would be great. I'll tell Mama." He paused. "You know, if Shannon does make it home, it would be okay for her to come, too."

Hazel twisted up her mouth. "Oh, no. We wouldn't want to make Jack uncomfortable."

Shelby read between the lines. Shannon and Jack had a tumultuous past. Life in a small town might be harder than she thought with everyone knowing everyone else's business.

"Folks in the Hickory Room need more towels," Oscar said. "I'll just go bring them up while you watch the front, okay? Be right back."

Hazel nodded as Oscar slipped away. "He's good to me." She pointed to her leg, which Shelby now noticed was a prosthetic. "Lost it to diabetes last year. Don't know what I would do without Oscar." A guest approached the desk and Shelby and Barrett stepped aside to allow Hazel to take care of her customer.

Shelby felt restless at the delay. To pass the time, she perused the enormous collection of photos mounted on the side of the enclosed spiral staircase. They ranged from black-and-white snapshots to modern colored ones, showing the parade of guests that had spent time at the inn over the last fifty years, she estimated.

"There's a lot of history here," she mumbled.

"For sure," Barrett agreed.

As she scanned the collection, her attention was caught by one in particular. "Look," she said, grabbing Barrett's arm and pulling him closer. He bent to look.

"It's Joe Hatcher, and that must be his wife, Cora, next to him."

Hazel had come over to join them, leaning on a cane for support. "Yes, they spent their honeymoon here right after they got married."

"Do you remember Cora?" Shelby asked. "What was she like?"

"Yes, I remember her. She was an elegant woman with lovely clothes and jewelry. I remarked to Oscar what an unusual couple they made since Joe is such a homespun kind of fellow."

Shelby took another look at the tall slender woman in the photo. Cora Hatcher was indeed elegant, her hair done in a soft chignon, handbag matching her pumps. "Do you know where Cora went after the divorce?"

"I don't really know."

Oscar returned. "Hazel, it seems these youngsters want to go exploring the mine using the entrance on my property."

Hazel's face blanched. "Oh, no. You can't do that."

"Why not?" Shelby said.

Hazel shook her head, fingers pressed to her mouth. "It's dangerous. People have disappeared, young people, doing just what you're proposing." She looked as though she might cry.

Oscar stroked his beard and patted her soothingly.

"One of our guests about three years ago was a prospector at heart. Young kid, college boy, name of Charlie. Had the gold fever pretty bad. We warned him not to go down into those mines, and of course I forbade him from going on my property. He went missing. Some boards were loose that I had nailed over my entrance so the cops searched the tunnels, but they never found him. We figured he went exploring, found a way into the mine, fell down one of those shafts and broke his neck or something."

Hazel gripped her brother's arm. "Don't say it. I can hardly bear to hear the words."

Oscar stroked her hand comfortingly. "We searched every spare minute. His family came out, too, clear from Nebraska. They were broken up and there was never any resolution for them. Terrible, never to know what happened to your son."

"Yes," Shelby agreed, suppressing a shiver. "That is terrible."

"So you see," Oscar continued, "that's why I can't allow you into that mine, not today or ever. I'm real sorry."

Chapter Seventeen

Not even Shelby's persistent arguing would sway Oscar from his decision. He shook his head firmly, chins wobbling. Finally, Barrett led Shelby outside, Oscar following.

"Please reconsider," she tried one more time. "I promise I will be careful and I won't go down in the mine alone. Barrett's agreed to come with me."

He shook his head. "I'm sorry. Risking two lives is worse than risking one. I can't allow it."

She took his big hands in hers. "Mr. Livingston, this mine may be the only thing standing between my uncle and bankruptcy. If I can't get in through your entrance, I will have to have the police force Hatcher to comply, and I believe he's already tried to kill me to prevent that from happening."

Oscar gaped. "What? That's…that's hard to believe. Why would he do such a thing?"

"I don't know, but someone wants to keep me from doing my job." She told him about the death threat written in paint and the fire in the stable. Her voice wobbled once, and Barrett wished he could embrace her.

"Please," she said. "Your entrance is the safest way."

Oscar stroked his beard. "Let me think about it." He took down Shelby's cell number. "I'll call you tonight with my decision, okay?"

Shelby thanked him profusely and they returned to the truck.

"Well, all I can do now is wait," she said.

Waiting was not her strong suit, Barrett knew. Judging by her fingers twisting together and the frantic tapping of her foot on the floor, evening was going to be a long time coming.

Having tried unsuccessfully to get Shelby to attend church with the family, Barrett had to settle for insisting she lock herself in the cabin with old Grits for company.

As added insurance, he made sure the two younger dogs, Ida and Pockets, were on patrol. Ida was a border collie who would do nothing more than try to herd any strangers into manageable groups, but Pockets, the German shepherd, was protective of the property. Both of them would raise a ruckus if anyone approached who was not a member of the Thorn family or a long-time ranch hand. He double-checked that her cell phone was charged and his number programmed in.

"Phone is working. Go already," she said. "I'll be perfectly fine."

Of course she would, and it was not like she was his kin or even his sweetheart. But why did his concern for her safety gallop first and foremost in his thoughts?

"'Cause you're losing your mind," he muttered to himself, earning a look from his mother.

"What, honey?"

"Nothing, Mama," he said, helping her on with her coat as they got into the truck.

Still, he worried through the service as he sat and tried to listen to the pastor's message. The tiny church was decorated with pine boughs he'd personally cut at the Gold Bar. The creative ladies in the congregation had twined little white lights around the branches and added scarlet ribbons. He wished Shelby was there to see it.

It was astonishing to him that this woman whom he had fished out of a ravine not even a week ago had changed his life, like it or not, and made him face head-on his most uncomfortable feelings. *What's happened to me?*

When the service was over, he left his brothers to shuttle their parents home after the coffee-and-cookie hour was done, while he drove back to the ranch faster than was legal. It was almost eight thirty when he rolled up the drive, and the skies were clear, spangled with a brilliant carpet of stars.

The lights were on in Granddad's cabin and Ida and Pockets greeted him with wagging tails. A good sign that all was well, Shelby was safe. He breathed out an enormous gust of air. Then Pockets stiffened, tail erect and ears swiveling. Both dogs let out an earsplitting round of barking before they tore around to the back of the cabin.

He sprinted after them. The dogs continued their crazed barking, circling through the dense coyote bush that served as a backyard to the cabin. Their intensity told him something was hiding under those bushes. Or someone? Twigs crackled as he pushed forward.

A light shone behind him. "What's going on?"

Shelby stood with a flashlight, shivering in the cold. The dogs ran to her, barking, before they about-faced and dived once more into the bushes.

"Go back in the cabin," he said. "There's something out here." He didn't wait to see if she complied, but grabbed an ax from the woodpile and charged into the bushes himself. Wet leaves slapped at him, snagging his shirt. He pressed on, shoving through the foliage, lifting the lower branches with his ax to look underneath. A heavy bough snapped as he lifted it, and whatever was underneath rocketed out.

Claws scrabbled against the bark of a knotty pine tree.

The dogs went wild, lunging and scratching. A raccoon peered angrily down from a branch, eyes showing red in the night.

"All right," he said, exhaling. "That's enough, dogs."

Reluctantly, the dogs broke off their frantic search, trotting back over to Barrett, their mission ended. He shouldered the ax. He was about to say something when he noticed an impression in the mud underneath the side cabin window. The outline was blurred. Might it be a partial footprint? Before he could examine closer, the dogs barreled across the wet ground, obliterating the print.

"Was it an animal?" Shelby said.

Were the raccoons solely to blame for upsetting the dogs? Or was it possible that someone had been spying through the window? His mind was beginning to see danger everywhere. No need to spread his paranoia to her. "Raccoon." His eyes met hers. "You're cold. Let's get you inside."

She allowed him to usher her back into the cabin, and

she sat shivering on the sofa. He closed the curtains and fetched a quilt from the closet, draping it around her, then started a log burning in the fireplace. Grits lumbered over and eased his way onto the cushion next to her. She stroked his droopy face.

"It's unlikely anyone would be able to get onto your property undetected, right?" Shelby said. He wasn't sure if she was comforting herself or him. "Just coyotes and raccoons and things."

"Sure." His gut was not nearly as convinced, but he had no proof. When daylight came, he intended to make a more thorough search, in case the raccoon wasn't the only thing prowling the night around Granddad's cabin. He sat and faced her. "What if Oscar says no?"

She cocked her head and drew her slender legs up underneath her, tucked her hands into the long sleeves of her sweater. "He'll change his mind. I'm sure of it."

"But if he doesn't and there's no other easy way in? After hearing what Oscar said about that college kid, are you willing to possibly risk your life over this thing?"

"It's not just a thing, Barrett," she said, hugging her knees. "I wasn't exaggerating about my uncle's financial position. He needs this mine to work out."

Barrett felt the old familiar anger at the mention of Ken. "He'll land on his feet," Barrett couldn't stop himself from saying. "He'll sell some property and bail himself out."

"He's already spent most of what he had trying to help Devon."

Anger flashed through him. "Helping him avoid prison was expensive, huh? Maybe if he'd have stopped enabling his kid to escape responsibility, they'd both be better off." The words flew out like poison-tipped arrows. He breathed deep, trying to get some control.

She stared at him and he could see his own ire reflected in her eyes. "He lost his wife," she said.

"Me, too," Barrett growled, wishing immediately that he hadn't, but the floodgates were open. "Did you know that I fished Devon out of a ditch two months before the accident? He was drunk, wrecked his motorcycle. I took him home, talked to your uncle. Told him he ought to make sure the boy was straightened out before there was real trouble."

"I didn't know that."

He scrubbed a hand over his face. "Know what your uncle did to punish him? Bought him a car to replace the motorcycle."

He heard her expel a breath. "Aunt Opal, his wife, died in childbirth after losing five babies to miscarriages. I know it's not an excuse, but Uncle Ken tried to be everything to Devon that he'd lost, to fill up the holes. He made mistakes. He knows that." Her voice broke.

"We all make mistakes," he said, "but a real man takes responsibility for them. Devon has tried to do that and he's still practically a kid, but Ken can't face the fact that he failed as a father."

She took his hand, her fingers silk soft on his roughened ones. He wanted to pull away, but he couldn't.

She gazed into his eyes. "I thought a real man was one who could forgive." She hesitated. "Like Christ did."

He sighed heavily, his inability to beat his own anger defeating him. "I'm nothing like Christ."

"Both your mother and my Aunt Opal would probably have said that's the point, that we're supposed to become more like Him, through all the troubles and tragedies."

He squeezed his eyes shut. "I can't." He felt her hand caressing his cheek and he kept his eyes closed in hopes she would not stop.

"I'm not sure I can either," she said. He opened his eyes to find her kneeling in front of where he sat on the couch, expression so earnest it took his breath away. "But I... I'm going to go see my mother and say the things I should have said earlier, even if it doesn't change anything."

"What made you decide to do that?"

"Being here, with your family. Seeing what my mistakes have cost me."

He looked into her jade eyes, so rich and deep, and he wanted more than anything to say that he could forgive Ken Arroyo. But the hard stone in his heart would not be broken, and it had taken the place of the soft flesh that used to beat there.

"I am glad for you," he said.

She wanted more, and so did he, but he could not give it. Her hand fell away and he realized the truth. His anger was a mountain between them that could never be crossed. He'd followed God all his life, he knew that he should do what God demanded of him, but he was too wounded, too weak.

He got up, shame weighing him down like a rockfall. "I should go." She walked him to the door, standing on the porch. He was torn with the intense desire to leave, yet his feet would not let him.

Her phone buzzed and she answered. Barrett was grateful for the distraction. He gazed up at the stars, hands jammed in his pockets, trying to accept the gulf that lay between them, that always would.

When she disconnected, her smile was jubilant.

"Oscar said yes. He'll meet us at the entrance at 6:00 a.m. tomorrow morning."

He nodded. At least he could help her find the answers in the mine that would put her life in order, and maybe Ken's, too. If that was all he could offer, so be it.

"Dogs will keep watch tonight and I can look over your cabin from my window. I probably won't sleep much, so text me if you hear anything. I'll see you in the morning," he said. He let himself out of Granddad's cabin and trudged back to the house.

Shelby kept her focus on the task as she packed supplies into her backpack and double-checked that she had extra flashlight batteries and some food and water just in case. The memory of her conversation with Barrett intruded anyway.

Ken lost his wife.

Me, too.

In those two words, there was such a flow of hurt that had hardened over the years like igneous rock. In his voice, she'd heard the underlying message. He was unchangeable, immovable, frozen in his pain and unforgiveness, just as Uncle Ken was frozen.

"Lord," she said, squeezing her eyes shut. "I don't deserve to ask, but please help them both out of this darkness."

The prayer did not dull the edge of her unhappiness, but for some reason it felt right to say it, just as it had the moment she'd told herself it was time to go and see her mother. Would unburdening herself before her mother change anything between them? No, but perhaps it would change something inside Shelby's soul.

More like Jesus.

Her breath came out in a rush. Like Barrett, she had a long way to go.

The sky was dark, the horses munching their morning meal, when she let herself and Grits out of the cabin. Grits lamented their early departure with a low moan and a full body shake that sent his long ears whirling around his snout.

"I know, sweetie," she said, giving him a pat. "But the early dog gets the bacon, right?"

Grits did not look convinced as he trotted off toward the main house.

Barrett showed up wearing a Giants baseball cap.

"No cowboy hat today?"

"Don't want to lose a second one," he said. The words were light, but his eyes did not have their usual sparkle. He wore hiking boots and a jacket, a small pack over his shoulder. He sported his usual style of shirt in a different color and she hid a smile. She'd seen him exploring the ground around the perimeter of the cabin, and his scowl told her he was unsatisfied with whatever he had or had not found.

"Did you get breakfast?" she said. "There's time if you want to grab something."

"No, I'm okay. Let's get this over with."

Over with. The phrase stuck in her ears as they headed up the road. A wall was up between them now, and it was clearly Barrett's desire to keep it that way. Grief cut at her heart. He was right. The only thing left to do was get the job done so they could each go their own ways. She tightened the straps on her pack and quickened her pace.

It was much faster to hike to Oscar Livingston's property than to drive the truck, so they took a narrow path cut through a grassy hillside.

Barrett finally broke the silence. "I told my brothers and Dad what we're up to. If for some reason they don't hear from us by noon, they'll come running."

"Good to know."

"Keegan really wanted to come, but he's working with a new horse today. He's kind of unpredictable."

"Keegan or the horse?"

"Come to think of it, both of them."

They walked the rest of the way in silence until they let themselves through the gate onto Oscar's property. Since Oscar lived at the inn, the small house was empty, showing signs of wear and weathering. The land itself was overgrown with tall grasses on the low, flat plain, which eased down into a gorge peppered with old, gnarled trees poking out at odd angles.

Oscar waved a meaty hand, the other clutching two hard hats, which he presented to them.

"Got lights on them, too, so you don't brain yourself hopefully."

"Thank you so much, Mr. Livingston."

"Call me Oscar."

They put on the hard hats and Barrett shoved his cap into his back pocket.

Oscar led the way to a wood-framed entrance, wedged into a scrubby hillside on the near side of the gorge. It was boarded over, but the plywood was beginning to rot, the rusty nails popping free from the wood. Oscar handed Barrett a crowbar.

"Here you go, son. Better your strapping young back attacking this thing than mine."

"Yes, sir," Barrett said. It did not take him more than five minutes to pry loose the boards. The black maw of the mine opened before them. A ripple of excitement raced up Shelby's spine.

Oscar put a hand on each of their shoulders, his face troubled. "I have a bad feeling about this, and so does Hazel. Is there any way I can talk you out of it?"

"No, Oscar, but we'll be fine, I promise."

"You both need to be careful, extra careful."

"We will," Barrett said, and Shelby nodded her agreement, pressing a kiss to Oscar's round cheek.

He shook his head. "I'll just never forgive myself for what happened to that young fella, Charlie. I wonder sometimes if I had just been stronger with him, told him louder, forbidden him from going prowling around this place." He shuddered as if the frigid air from the mine had chilled him. "That hunger for gold," he said, "can get a person dead."

You'll Die. The memory dripped like blood through her thoughts.

You won't scare me off, Hatcher. No one will.

She squeezed Oscar's hand. "Nothing will happen to us, I promise." She turned toward the entrance and Oscar gripped Barrett's arm.

"I'm old-school, son," he said. "In my day, a man looked out for a woman's safety."

"In my day, too," Barrett said.

"Okay, then. You bring her back safe and sound."

"I will, sir."

"All right. I have to go help Hazel with the break-fast service. We still haven't got cleaned up from yesterday's Christmas tea, even though she hired on extra help. Hazel works too hard unless I'm there to share the load, but I will come back when I can."

Barrett nodded, shaking hands with Oscar as if they were concluding a business meeting.

Shelby was grateful that Barrett still intended to keep her company, in spite of the distance between them. With Barrett right behind her, Shelby switched on her headlamp and eased into the crypt-cold darkness.

Chapter Eighteen

The hard hat was not comfortable, but Barrett figured it was better than getting bashed on the skull again. He tried to edge up in front of Shelby, but true to form, she led the way.

The mine had obviously been worked at one point. Busted-up tracks indicated there had been a system to move carts back and forth.

"The rails were for the ore cars," Shelby said, as if she read his thoughts. "They must have found a workable vein here. The miners would dig out the ore and haul it outside where it was put through a crusher to extract the gold."

He breathed in a damp lungful. "Air seems okay."

"They dug a shaft for ventilation and to release any dangerous gases."

"How do you know that?"

She grinned. "I spent the wee hours poring over your granddad's maps. There's one that shows the entrance and the shaft. That's about it."

"Sketchy."

"Yep, but that's the fun of it, right?"

He shook his head. "If you say so."

"Actually, reading the topography, I'm guessing this shaft connects to Hatcher's somewhere north of here. If we follow these tracks, I'm sure we'll get there."

"Does your uncle own the mineral rights to this whole area?"

"No, mostly just what lies under Hatcher's property, unfortunately."

Barrett was secretly relieved. If Arroyo wound up in the gold mining business, at least he wouldn't disrupt Oscar's land, too.

Shelby was busily taking pictures and writing notes on a spiral pad. He stayed quiet, allowing his vision to adjust to the gloom. The entrance was no more than ten feet high and maybe twice that wide. A rusted, over-turned ore car lay on its side and something, he suspected rats, rustled in the recesses of the space.

At least the floor was dry and for that he was grateful. It was his mission to get them both in and out with no more plunges into icy underground lakes. He noted the timbers wedged into the rock to support the over-head portions of the tunnel. "So what's the shelf life of a support beam?"

She joined him in examining the wood. "I don't see much in the way of rot. Fortunately, it's dry and you don't get termites down here."

Awesome. At least they didn't have to worry about bugs.

His light caught on a metal box covered with dust. He could read enough that his heart skipped a beat. "TNT," he said.

She stared. "Reminds me that someone tossed a stick at me shortly after I arrived in this town."

He nodded, stomach muscles tight. "I remember."

"Barrett?"

"Yeah?"

"Those boards came away pretty easily from the entrance, didn't they?"

"Yeah."

"As if they could have been removed and then nailed up again, wouldn't you say?"

"I might."

"As much as I hate to admit it, someone could have grabbed themselves some TNT from this mine, instead of Hatcher's."

"Or a million other places. This is Gold Country. The place is riddled in every nook and cranny with leftovers from the mining industry."

"The dynamite, those red marks in the tunnel and the mysterious disappearance of Charlie, Oscar's guest at the inn. What's going on in Gold Bar, Barrett?"

"I wish I knew." Then again, maybe he didn't. Just keeping her safe was all he could think about.

She grew quiet as she stepped past the dynamite and followed the tracks. "Okay. It's six thirty already. We'd better start moving if we're going to get in and out before the Thorn cavalry arrives."

They crept into the narrow tunnel, and he had to hunch to keep his hard hat from scraping the rock. No need to generate any sparks, he thought uneasily. Debris covered the floor along the rails so they had to step carefully to avoid twisting their ankles.

She stopped, beaming her lamp at a patch of rock that looking like nothing special to Barrett.

"What? Something sparkle at you?"

His comment caused her to chuckle. "I'm looking at the quartz veining here in this fracture."

Her index finger traced something that must be significant, though it looked like more rock to his ignorant eye.

"Not gold?"

"No, but it can be a good indicator." She pulled a hammer from her pack and began to whack off some rock chips, which she slid into a heavyweight bag. The sound echoed and boomed down the tunnel. "Certain elements are telling, too. Arsenic, antimony, mercury, selenium, thallium. It's like being a detective, in a way. The lab will give us the final verdict."

He whistled. "Well, you certainly got the smarts for this job, I'll say."

He thought she might be pleased by his compliment, and that made him feel good.

"Thank you. I studied hard every moment and worked two jobs, but I still couldn't have done it if my uncle hadn't paid most of my tuition."

Her uncle. Somehow they always came back to him. It had not occurred to Barrett that Ken Arroyo had been supporting anyone but his spoiled son. He tucked the information away to examine at a better time.

Right now, Shelby was making her way to a spot where the tunnel forked into two shafts. One was considerably larger than the other, which was no more than four feet high, the air chilled as a tomb.

"If I'm right," Shelby said, "one of these tunnels will connect with the main shaft on Hatcher's property. That's the one I need to sample to get the best reading."

He looked hard at both. "I don't imagine we're headed into the roomy one, huh?"

She slung her pack on her back and got onto her knees. "In for a penny, in for a pound," she said.

"I never liked that expression," he grumbled.

"Come on, cowboy." She unwrapped a light stick and snapped it to life. The green glow cast an eerie color on the black walls. She set it just outside the entrance. "So your brothers can find us. See? Safety first."

Barrett didn't bother to mention that if the whole place caved in, her little green light was as good as useless.

He hadn't realized until he peered after her into that narrow opening that he might be a touch claustrophobic. Claustrophobia or not, there was no way he was going to stay back and leave Shelby unprotected. On hands and knees, he squeezed his shoulders through the opening.

This had to be the craziest thing he'd done since he was a teenager, all because Shelby Arroyo had got under his skin and into his heart. If he could just get through this wackadoodle adventure and bring her out safely, she would have everything she needed.

He began to squirm his way past the rock that seemed to be trying to smother him. "In for a penny." He sighed.

Shelby wanted to charge ahead but the rocks biting into her palms and kneecaps kept her at a slow pace. That, and the muttered comments from Barrett, who was hard-pressed to stuff his big frame into the narrow tunnel.

Every twenty minutes or so, she activated another light stick to mark the way. The time crept past seven thirty and on to eight o'clock. Though her stomach growled, she ignored it, inching along until a sound brought her up short.

"Barrett? Did you say something?"

"Naw. It's taking all my powers of concentration to crawl along. What did you hear?"

"I thought…" What had it been? A faint gasp of pain? The sound she caught, or imagined, had come from behind them.

Barrett was staring at her, head scrunched under the rock ceiling. "What?"

She shook her head. "Never mind. Just the rock settling or something." She continued on for what seemed like hours until her mouth was parched and her stomach could not be ignored.

"Break time," she announced, her muscles relieved to settle into a sitting position.

Barrett folded himself into an awkward arrangement next to her, accepting the granola bar she provided and guzzling some water from his bottle. "Plan?"

She pulled out her digital thermometer. "The air is getting cooler. It's dropped five degrees in the last five minutes."

"And since Hatcher's tunnel is lower than Oscar's, you figure we're heading in the right direction."

"You're getting good at this," she said, grinning at him. "You could be an assayer."

"Think I'll stick to horses."

A loud thud startled her. "What was that?"

Barrett grabbed his flashlight and scrambled down the tunnel they'd just traversed. Pulse thumping, she scooted behind him. They crawled fifteen feet or so, training their lights into every crevice.

"Nothing," he said. "Some loose rock falling, maybe."

Maybe, she thought. Wasn't that the likeliest explanation? But for a woman who had been shoved in a truck, nearly blown up and almost burned to death, it was easy to jump to other explanations. She didn't want Barrett to see her sinking into paranoia.

"That must have been it," she agreed, and they returned to their spot. Still, the hair on the back of her neck prickled as if stirred by an icy wind. *Don't let Hatcher get inside your thoughts.*

Finishing their snack, they crept onward until the tunnel pinched off completely. She shined her light, sucking in a shocked breath.

"It's blocked."

Barrett stuck his head over her shoulder, his beard giving her shivers.

"Can you switch places with me a minute?"

She flattened herself against the cold rock and he edged forward.

"This is recent," he said grimly. "Someone has rolled a rock across the entrance and filled in around the bottom with debris."

Shelby's nerves twanged. "To what purpose? Was it Hatcher trying to prevent explorers like Charlie?"

"And us?" he offered, not without irony.

She didn't answer. He put a shoulder to the rock and felt it shift. "It's not as heavy as it looks. I can move it."

In a few moments, he'd levered the rock aside and turned to stare at her.

"Shelby, this is getting weird. Someone's been down here. I think we should go back."

"Oh, no," she said. "I may not get another chance. I'm going to get as far as I can in the next few hours before we need to turn around and meet your brothers."

He sighed. "I thought you'd say that. At least let me go first."

"Okay, I…" She stopped.

"Shelby?"

Her whole body was gripped by an icy blast of fear. "Barrett," she said slowly, shining her light to the rock over his head.

He followed the beam. The light caught a clump of hair clinging to a sharp bit of stone.

"Whose hair?" she whispered. The gloom made it impossible to tell the color. Blond? Black? Brown? Red?

The confusion on his face told her he had no clue either. Whoever it was who had passed this way recently had unintentionally left a calling card. Joe Hatcher, her mind screamed.

The only problem was, Hatcher's hair was snow-white.

The prowler wasn't Hatcher then, Barrett concluded, but that left a million other explanations. Random trespassers who'd done their exploring before Oscar had closed up the mine. Others who enjoyed the fun, breaking in and then boarding up the entrance behind them. Charlie?

The whole thing was giving Barrett a case of the creeps. He didn't suggest turning back, though. The only end to this adventure was through it.

Shelby had pressed on, leaving him to crawl along after her. The tunnel sloped downward and mercifully enlarged, so he could resume a cautious standing position.

The walls, he noticed, were growing damper, trickles of moisture oozing down and muddying the dirt caked on his hiking boots as the passage branched off yet again. He trusted Shelby knew what she was doing, but he could not tell one passage from another except for the glow of the light sticks she was dropping along the way.

She cried out, and he rushed to her. "Look," she said. "Those marks again."

There was indeed another series of red marks, about shoulder high on the wall, speckled with moisture. "They're marking the way to something," she breathed, "I know it."

What kind of weird scavenger hunt was this? Ahead, a scatter of rockfall piled up to the side of the tunnel.

"Odd," Shelby said, shining her light on the ceiling. "Look at the marks. They're scraped and gouged, like someone was using a shovel to bang the rock."

To free the rock detritus that now littered the floor?

She knelt and began pushing away the bigger rocks, rolling them aside. He joined her, a sense of urgency that he did not understand fueling his actions. They'd cleared enough that they were both sweating and had nothing to show for it but sore fingers.

Shelby sat back, shaking her head. "I just don't…"

Barrett held a finger to his lips. "Wait."

They sat in silence for some thirty seconds, listening. "What do you hear?"

"Air, like a rush of wind from somewhere below us."

Barrett turned on his granddad's flashlight and stuck his face almost to the rock floor where the debris pile had been. One more cluster of rocks remained in the way and he heaved them aside. There in the gap between the tunnel floor and wall was an opening wider than a manhole cover. He eased back to let her see.

"It's too dark. Can I borrow your flashlight?"

He handed it to her, putting a palm on her back to

hold her steady as she wriggled her torso into the opening. Her scream cut through his senses.

He grabbed her shoulders and yanked her up. Her eyes were wide with panic, her breath coming in shudders.

"What's wrong?"

She was breathing so rapidly she could not answer.

He took her face in his hands. "Shelby, it's okay. Breathe in and out, real slow."

She tried to comply, but her chest heaved with the effort. He spoke softly to her, soothingly, concentrating on the simple act of breathing. He did not ask again what she'd seen, his only desire to still her panic.

When she calmed down enough that he did not think she would pass out, he took the flashlight from her clutched fingers. The panicked breathing started up again.

"I'm just going to look, that's all. Okay?"

She clamped her lips together and gave him the barest of nods.

He crept to the edge and shone his light down. At first he saw nothing but darkness, the bottom of a subpassage some fifteen feet below. Then the light picked up the gleam of something terrible, unnatural.

Something very, very still.

Chapter Nineteen

Barrett returned to Shelby and sat quietly next to her, his arm around her shoulders, wiping her tears as they fell. Her limbs shuddered with horror, knees drawn up under her chin.

Barrett had seen no more than a twisted body with a shock of hair, the gleam of skin somewhat well preserved due to the cold, no doubt, but subject to decay nonetheless. The dead man lying sprawled against the rocks wore a nylon jacket and sneakers.

"It has to be Charlie," he said. "The hair, it's dark, it must have got caught on the rock back there. He fell in the hole while he was exploring." Even while his mouth constructed impossible scenarios to explain what he'd seen, his brain insisted on coughing up the facts which he knew Shelby was considering, too.

The rock rolled across the entrance. The tunnel debris loosened by some sort of tool to conceal the hole.

"Charlie may have died of natural causes," Shelby finally managed, "but someone tried to hide his body."

"Which makes me think it probably wasn't natural causes after all."

Shelby shivered and he gripped her closer. He could hear her struggling to breathe deeply, to drive away the shock of what she'd seen.

She cleared her throat. "The police sent in searchers looking for Charlie but they didn't come this far in, or if they did, they didn't notice the hole in the tunnel floor," she finished.

"We need to get out of here and contact Larraby."

After one more deep breath, she nodded and they got to their feet.

Reluctantly, he settled on his belly, leaning over the hole to take photos of the body with Shelby grimly holding the flashlight and avoiding looking at the grisly mass. Two more light sticks marked the gruesome find to prevent any search-and-recovery personnel from falling into the exposed hole.

They'd done all they could for poor Charlie. Now at least his parents would have closure, the chance to properly mourn their lost son. He pitied them the years they had agonized, not knowing the truth, and the painful years that would stretch on after they did.

Quietly, he said a prayer, feeling the warmth of Shelby's hand joining his. She squeezed his palm and that tiny gesture in the vast darkness lit up a small corner of his heart.

When they were done, he picked up his pack. "We'd better go."

This time she did not argue. When she took a step, she stumbled and grabbed his forearms for support. He folded her close, knowing he shouldn't, understanding there could not be anything between them but feeling an overwhelming urge to comfort her that would not be denied.

"I'm sorry," she whispered, her face pressed to his chest. "My legs aren't working right."

"It's okay. Take your time. We'll go slow and easy on the way back, when you're ready. Not until then."

He wouldn't have minded if she took hours there, leaning on him. It felt so right to be needed by this woman, this flawed, determined, contrary lady from a family he despised. His senses reeled from the shock he'd just experienced and the profound joy of holding her close.

Yep, he was definitely losing what was left of his mind.

She pulled away, wiped her eyes and took in a steadying breath.

"I'm ready. Let's get out of here."

They traversed the way back much slower, the green glow of the light sticks a welcome sight around each corner. When it was time for them to crawl, the distance seemed insurmountable, the cold burrowing into his skin, rocks jabbing his knees and shins.

He decided that he wouldn't care how many tons of gold lay buried deep in the earth, he'd never go into another mine without a very compelling reason. They got to the place where the tunnel pinched in and the clump of hair clung like some horrible fungus.

Barrett went through the gap first, scraping his shoulders as he did. He was turning around to help Shelby when the sound of a shot fractured the stillness.

Barrett dived instinctively, even though the shot was nowhere near them. He succeeded in bringing Shelby to the floor.

"Gunshots?" she panted.

"Yes," he said. "Near the entrance."

They locked eyes. The entrance where the box of

TNT sat innocently in the corner. He did not have time to mouth the words as, a second later, an explosion rang through the caverns, shaking the walls and sending a cascade of debris down upon them.

Shelby screamed and he hauled her close, sheltering them as best he could under a shallow rock projection. All around them the rock seemed to writhe and undulate as if it was a living thing. The tunnel shook so violently he was sure the whole place was going to collapse.

He tucked her head under his torso as the patter of rocks slapped against his back. Thoughts flashed through his mind in a crazy kaleidoscope. He was not afraid to die, he knew a better place awaited, a place where Granddad and Bree were free of pain and suffering. But it occurred to him that he would be leaving behind anger, hatred even, a part of his soul that had not been properly formed into what God intended it to be.

I thought a real man was one who could forgive... like Christ did.

It grieved him that things might end this way. Shelby cried out as a rock bounced off her hip and he tried to pull her closer. She deserved the chance to find her own forgiveness and make peace with her mother. He wanted to holler and shout at the hard stone all around them.

Suddenly, the noise died away and the ground settled itself again. Shelby uncovered her face, breathing hard.

"The shot exploded the dynamite," she panted.

"That would be my theory, too."

"The whole mine might have collapsed. We could have been killed."

There was nothing to be said to that. He watched her expression change from shocked to angry.

"Someone is trying to kill me and it's really starting to get on my nerves." Her voice rose to a shout that bounced off the stone walls, as she swiped the debris from her hair.

He repressed a smile.

"Do you think this is Hatcher's handiwork again?" she demanded.

He didn't want to take the time to dwell on the who-dunit. Instead he shook the mess from his hair and beard like a bear emerging from hibernation, and took several cautious steps into the darkness. Turning the corner, he stopped short.

The space was completely filled with shifting rubble that reached fully up to the ceiling. He shoved a hand into it, pushing at the mass, but the rocks pushed right back, pressing him into retreat.

"Guess you got your wish," he said dully, as he returned to her.

She stood with her arms folded, dust coating her hair and clothing. "I'm afraid to ask what that means."

"You wanted to explore the mine and now you're going to have the chance because we're not getting out that way." He jabbed his thumb in the direction of the entrance.

"Completely collapsed?"

"I'm not sure, but in any case it's too filled with debris to pass."

"So we're trapped in here."

"Until we find another exit, yes, or until my brothers and Oscar can shovel us out."

"But...that could take days."

"Months."

She gaped. "Then why do you look so calm about it?"

Because he'd already decided how to play it. It was

like working with horses; the calmer you were, the better. "You've mapped this, right? You know it connects to Hatcher's property and we can get out that way."

"That is a theory, mind you, but even if I'm right and we can make our way to Hatcher's entrance safely, his gate is padlocked, remember? And he's supposedly lost the key."

He patted his pack. "I'm prepared this time, but we could also use the escape Emmaline showed us if we can locate it again."

Her eyes narrowed. "Are you being Mr. Cool and Confident because you don't want me to panic?"

He'd told her it might take months to free them, but with the explosion possibly destabilizing the whole mine, there was the chance that it was impossible to clear no matter how much time they had. Considering their limited food and water supplies, the clock was already ticking. Better for her to be searching for a solution than coming to that sobering conclusion.

He pasted on a self-assured smile. "Plenty of people know we're down here. Might as well get out on our own while they're considering what to do." He kept his tone light. "Agreed?"

She searched his face as the seconds ticked by. She was a very smart woman, and he realized he couldn't fool her, not for a minute. She was well aware of the difficulties of moving tons of rock under unstable conditions, but the look on her face said she'd chosen to take a page from his book. Cool and confident beat trembling and terrified any day.

"Yes," she said, tone steady. "But I wasn't going to panic, just for your information."

He admired her for this decision, and for not allowing him to coddle her. Dirty, disheveled as she was, he'd never seen a more beautiful woman. His pulse revved up a notch. *Knock it off, Barrett. Big problems here, or haven't you noticed?* "I didn't figure you would."

"Maybe we can find out more about those red marks while we're poking around down here."

He nodded. "Why not?" he said, squeezing back through the narrow gap. Inwardly, he sighed. God had given them a chance at survival and he would give it everything he had, but it had to be nuts to venture deeper into the mine that had almost killed them.

No, not the mine, he corrected himself. The person who'd shot at the dynamite, who was ready to commit multiple murders to keep them from doing precisely what they were now going to do.

"This is all kinds of crazy," he muttered to himself, thinking she would not hear.

"For sure," came her reply from behind him.

Shelby put on the second jacket she'd packed and checked her supplies. She had twenty or so light sticks left, two bottles of water and several protein bars. How long before they reached Hatcher's end of the mine? If they could find the way.

The light in her headlamp chose that moment to flicker, reminding her that when the batteries ran out and she'd gone through her refills, they would be in total darkness.

The thought sent a jolt of fear through her. *Plenty of time before that happens*, she silently told herself. *You're not gonna panic, remember?*

More than panic, she felt an overwhelming sense of guilt. Many people had warned her and now, once again, she'd fallen into a disaster, but the worst thing was she'd dragged Barrett right along with her.

His choice, she reminded herself, but the thought rang hollow. Barrett was the sort that would give the shirt off his back for a person in need. Plus, he had that cowboy chivalry thing going that both drove her crazy and made her feel warm and fuzzy.

You're just going to have to get him out of here alive, she told herself sternly.

They reached the spot where the glow sticks marked Charlie's makeshift grave. The path of red marks continued on. She wondered again who'd made the marks. Charlie? Joe Hatcher's wife? Emmaline?

They trudged on for what felt like hours, but her cell phone told her it was only noon. The Thorn brothers would be mounting a rescue effort if they hadn't already been alerted by the explosion.

She had no idea if the entrance collapse had been loud enough to attract attention, or if she and Barrett would be able to receive text messages. Barrett had already tried to send one to his family just in case, and received no reply. The tunnel continued on endlessly until it again branched off.

"Which way?" Barrett said.

The million-dollar question. "I… I don't know." She tested the air temperature of both. "Almost identical."

Barrett played his flashlight over the rock. "Hey, there's one of those red marks."

She joined him. "At least we know someone has been this way before. That's a good sign, right?"

"Yeah." She heard the hesitation in his voice. "Unless it's a trail to lead someone back to Charlie's body."

"For what reason?"

"To make sure they disposed of it properly at some future date, so no one would ever find it."

Like no one would ever find their bodies if they didn't get out of the mine.

"Let's follow it for a while. We can retrace our steps if we need to." She activated a light stick and prepared to move out.

"Lunch break first," Barrett said.

"I don't need a lunch break. I'm not hungry."

"You need water or you'll get dehydrated. Besides, I've got a great snack here." He spread his spare jacket on the ground and patted the spot next to him. She took a seat.

Her mouth fell open as he pulled out a jar of pickles. "You brought pickles with you to go explore a mine?"

"Naw. I brought them to give to Oscar, but I forgot." He popped the lid. "These are the best pickles in California. Believe me, it took me almost a year to master Nanna's recipe."

She accepted a pickle spear and took a bite. Savory with a hint of spice. "You're right," she said with a giggle. "They are good."

He grinned. "I know."

"I never imagined I'd be trapped in a mine with a cowboy, eating homemade pickles."

"Life is a funny thing, isn't it?" They took several swallows of water and capped the bottles, making an unspoken decision to ration their supplies.

Barrett sat up and checked the phone.

She pressed close to see, a flame of hope rising in her.

"Nothing," he said. "Too much interference down here, but it was worth a try."

She finished munching her pickle and checked her own phone. No messages but she noticed the charge was down to 56 percent. "How long will your phone stay charged, Barrett, in case we can somehow send a text when we get closer to the surface?"

"Got the screen turned down and it's running on low power mode. We'll probably be out of here before it dies."

His tone was again Mr. Cool and Confident, but she saw in the twitch of his mouth that he was worried, too.

"I'll power mine off to save the battery." She suppressed the shiver that threatened to march up her spine. How much longer before the phones died?

And how long before their own time ran out?

The muscles in Barrett's shoulders were screaming from being hunched over, but he did not complain. After their lunch break, they'd headed into the tunnel with the marks, but another two hours later, they had encountered no signs that they were headed toward the surface or Hatcher's property.

Making her stop for more water, he pretended to drink deeply, but only took a shallow swig. Still no texts and the charge on his phone continued to drop.

Shelby had fallen silent, trudging along, avoiding the fragments that littered the floor. "So who knew we'd be down here?" she mused aloud.

He understood exactly what she meant because he'd been puzzling over it himself. Who had known they were accessing the mine that morning? "My family, Oscar Livingston and anyone at the inn who might have overheard his conversation with you." He recalled the rustling in the bushes. "If anyone was snooping around Granddad's cabin and heard us talking on the porch."

She shook her head. "It has to be Hatcher. He killed Charlie and doesn't want anyone to discover the body."

"Still doesn't make sense as to why. What reason would he have for killing Charlie in the first place?"

"I don't know."

He sighed. "I'm hungry, time for another pickle break."

He opened the jar and handed her one.

"Thanks."

He took another and fastened the lid back on.

"You're—" His sentence was ripped away, buried in an avalanche of sound as the floor gave way beneath them. He felt himself falling, the jar sailing out of his grasp, and he grabbed at nothing as they plummeted. Shelby tumbled next to him, hair flying, fingers splayed in search of a handhold.

He tried to grab for her but gravity continued to suck him down.

The breath whooshed out of him as he struck the ground. His senses spun, a whirl of pain, confusion and dizziness.

"Shelby," he tried to yell, but his vision narrowed to a tiny pinpoint before darkness overtook him.

Chapter Twenty

The dripping woke him, a ceaseless monotonous tapping that brought him to consciousness. He realized he was on his back on a pile of rubble, both arms thrown wide as if he was making some ridiculous snow angel on the cavern floor. His body screamed with pain and cold. At first he could not tell if his eyes were open or closed in the profound darkness. He tried to sit up, succeeding only in flapping his arms a bit.

"Shelby," he croaked.

There was no answer but the incessant dripping.

Fear, reminiscent of the terror he'd felt at pulling Bree from the wrecked car, invaded every pore in his body. "Shelby," he shouted again, thrashing his legs around to free them from the blanket of rock. His voice echoed back at him, mocking his fear.

He heard a cough and froze. "Shelby?" he said softer. "Are you hurt?" *Please let her answer. Please.*

A flashlight sprang to life and he squinted against the glare. Rocks crunched against each other and the light swam closer. Still, he tried without success to free himself until he felt a hand on his chest and light blinded him, making him blink.

"Stay still," she said, voice barely louder than a whisper.

"Are you hurt?" he said, unable to see her clearly.

"No, but you are."

"Naw," he started, but she was already moving away. He heard her blow out a breath as she struggled to pull rocks away from his legs. He tried to help, but his limbs behaved as if they were made of rubber.

When she returned, she shined her flashlight around his body, running her hands along his arms and legs, smoothing them over his face, gentler than a spring breeze. He closed his eyes and allowed her touch to push away the pain.

"I don't feel anything broken or out of place, but I only know basic first aid. Did you hit your head on the way down?"

"I hit everything on the way down." He could just make out her faint smile. Score one for the busted-up cowboy. "But I'm okay," he insisted, trying again to sit up with no success. The pain shooting through his side would have made him cry out if he hadn't gritted his teeth.

She gripped his hand. "I think you may have some bruised or broken ribs."

"Yeah," he grunted. "That feels like the right diagnosis." He'd cracked a few ribs getting thrown from horses a time or two. Ribs mended eventually, but he knew full well the injury hurt like gangbusters. He fought back the pain. "Where are we?"

"An underground cavern. It's got a lake and everything."

"Swell. I've been sad that we haven't come across another lake to this point."

"There is some good news."

"By all means, share."

"We're not the first people to hang out down here. Look."

He forced his eyes to focus. In the far side of the cavern sat a couple of wooden barrels, a metal ladder and some old wheels for the ore cars.

"And there's more good news. This was used as some sort of storage area, so that means we have to be getting close to a way out. Miners wouldn't have kept their materials in a place that was completely inaccessible, right?"

"Right," he grated out past the dust in his throat.

She stroked his cheek, her voice soft and comforting. Holding a bottle to his lips, she encouraged him to drink. The liquid was bliss on his tongue.

"In a few minutes, I'll explore our options, but right now, I need to get your other jacket out of your pack. This one is ripped and you have to stay warm to make sure you don't go into shock."

His ears were still ringing but he nodded. "Okay. Where's my pack?"

"You're laying on it. I think it broke your fall. Otherwise you might be dead."

"I'm not totally convinced that I'm actually alive."

She pressed her forehead to his, and spoke nose to nose, her warm breath stirring life back into him. "You're alive, cowboy, because you're groaning. Dead people don't groan."

"Ah. I'll make a note of that." Her lips were so close and he wanted to kiss her. His lips seemed to be the only part of him still working. Certainly his brain had taken a vacation. She pressed a kiss to his cheek and eased away.

After some scrabbling, she managed to pull the pack from underneath him.

"Okay so far?"

"No sweat," he said. At least he had not cried out.

"Can you move your arms and legs at all?"

"'Course." He did an awkward marionette maneuver.

"Nice. If you feel like you can, let me help you sit up on the count of three."

She counted, and with her assistance and a very loud groan, he sat up. The pain flashed bright and hot for a minute before subsiding. Easing on one sleeve at a time, she pulled his jacket over the one he was wearing.

"Are you sure you aren't hurt?" he said. "That was a nasty fall for both of us."

"I was able to hang on for a second before I dropped, but I lost my hard hat. Plus, I fell onto a pile of sand, so that helped. They must have stored sandbags down here at one time." She zipped the jacket to his chin. "Stay put while I check around."

"I can help," he said peevishly. "All my parts work, more or less."

She forced the flashlight into his hand. "You sit here and shine the light around. That's helping."

Grumbling, he complied. His head was still spinning, though he wouldn't admit it to her, but he didn't like being treated like a child. He yanked his phone from his pocket with one hand, biting back an oath. The thing was completely smashed to bits.

"My phone's busted," he griped.

"Mine survived the fall, but still no texting, I just

checked. Hey," she cried out, "you won't believe what I just found."

"A walkie-talkie?" he suggested hopefully. "Or a couple of jet packs?"

"No," she said, grin wide as she returned to him. "Better. Your pickles landed in the sand, too. They're not broken!"

He bit off a hearty guffaw when it hurt his ribs too much. "Aside from pickles, what did you find?"

"More good news."

The words were a little too cheerful. "Uh-huh. Let's hear it."

"This cavern is really spectacular actually. Lots of interesting rock formations."

"How about an exit?"

"Oh, there's an exit, all right. It connects to another tunnel and I can see tracks from the ore cars."

"And?"

"And it's the way out onto Hatcher's property, I'm sure of it."

"And?"

"Well, there's a glitch."

He opened the jar and ate a pickle, waiting for the other shoe to drop.

She sighed. "There has been some ground failure so there's about a ten-foot gap between the cavern where we are and the tunnel."

"Ten feet between us and the way out?"

"It appears that way."

He swallowed the pickle and struggled to his feet.

"You should be sitting down," she blurted. "You could pass out."

"Then I guess you should be helping me instead of scolding."

She hooked an arm under his shoulder and he stood, woozy at first, but relieved to find that he did not notice any new areas of pain. Together they staggered over to the cavern's edge.

"Careful," she said as he peered below. The view was obscured by darkness. Only when she shined the flashlight across could he see the tunnel ahead, the edge of the rails twisting off where the ground had collapsed underneath them. She was right, the distance was a good ten feet.

He stared down into the abyss. "How far down does it go?"

"I'm not sure."

Painfully, he bent to pick up a rock and tossed it over the edge. Time stretched out endlessly until finally he heard a splash, seemingly fathoms away, as the rock connected with some hidden lake.

His gaze fastened on hers.

"So all we need to do is figure out a way across," she said.

"Yep, that's all there is to it." He let out a deep sigh. "Right."

Shelby wished she could light a fire to keep them warm, but there was not enough flammable material to fuel it, and it was a risky idea anyway with all the trapped gases she might ignite with a mere spark. Instead she sat side by side with Barrett, shivering, sharing a protein bar to quiet their aching stomachs.

She was deeply grateful that he had not suffered any worse damage, but she worried that he might slip into shock, or that he could have internal injuries. Their options were narrowing with every passing moment, along with their supplies. They were down to less than two bottles of water since Barrett's had both been smashed on impact. Her mouth was already parched. She allowed herself a swallow of water and insisted Barrett drink one, too, in spite of his protests.

His phone was crushed and hers low on charge, so she powered it down after she checked the time. It was almost four o'clock in the afternoon. Had the Thorn brothers started trying to dig them out via Oscar's entrance? Or might they have decided the best way was to go through Hatcher's property? It grieved her to think how Barrett's brothers and parents must be frantic with worry, Oscar, too.

But you had to go through with it, didn't you? she chided herself. No matter that it put Barrett's life at risk or flew in the face of good sense. She deserved the consequences of her bullheaded determination, but Barrett and his family did not.

Anger at her helplessness bubbled up. *But people don't always get what they deserve, now do they?* she thought.

Bree hadn't. Her own mother hadn't. Right then in the crippling darkness, she remembered her mother's soft touch, always smelling of scented lotion. She missed it desperately, craving the chance to hold her mother's hand again.

The memory doused the anger and lit her with a new determination. She and Barrett would get out of this and she would go to see her mother. Period.

Enough with the sentimentality. Figure out an escape plan, she commanded herself.

She played through the scenarios in her mind. There was only one way out and that was to get across to the tunnel. Could she leap across the chasm? Even running at full speed, she doubted she could make the jump, especially in her weakened and hungry state. Barrett most certainly could not. So how were they going to cross the gap?

The only workable idea she could think of was the long metal ladder left to rust for who knew how long in the forgotten cavern. She got up and examined it. It had to be at least fifteen feet, made of heavy iron, built to last. Pressing a foot to the rungs, she figured the metal was as sound as it needed to be. It only had to support her weight long enough for her to get across. Then she would summon help somehow. She'd just have to pray that she could get a text out or scream loud enough that someone would cut through the lock on Hatcher's gate, if that was indeed where she wound up.

If…if…if.

Barrett joined her. "No way," he said, as if reading her thoughts.

"I'm just testing out an idea."

"Well, quit it 'cause it's a very bad idea."

"I didn't ask for your opinion."

"I'm providing it free of charge."

She ignored him, dragging the ladder over to the edge of the crevasse. He followed, issuing a steady stream of discouragement, which she disregarded. "Can you put weight on this end and keep it from angling downward? I'm going to slide it out and see if it will reach the other side."

"This is a…"

"Bad idea, I know," she said, straining all her muscles to slide the ladder out into the darkness. Inch by inch she pushed it forward, Barrett weighing the other end down to keep it horizontal. He grunted with pain but he did not slow his efforts. Sweat dripped down her face as the metal grated against the rock on the other side.

"It worked," she said, wiping her hands on her jeans. One end of the ladder rested on the lip of the tunnel, the other on the sandy floor of the cavern. Hope flickered to life.

Barrett watched her, arms folded. "So you think that ladder is stable enough to support a human body?"

"Yes," she said with certainty.

"And you figure the tunnel edge isn't going to give way as soon as we put any more weight on it?"

"Pretty sure, yes." Was she? There was no way to be certain that the lip of rock would hold. A lump formed in her throat and she longed for a deep drink of ice-cold water. Seconds ticked by accompanied by an incessant dripping from somewhere in the cavern, mocking her thirst.

He finally shook his head. "Shelby Arroyo, there is no way on this planet I am letting you crawl across that ladder."

Her chin went up. "You can't stop me."

"Yes, I can."

He stepped forward, towering over her. She feared he was going to put her over his shoulder, injured ribs or no injured ribs. Instead, he stepped around her, blocking her from the ladder.

"What are you doing?"

He rolled up the sleeves of his jacket. "I'm going to cross and then I'll get help."

She tried to edge in front of him, but he moved her aside. "You're in no condition to do this, Barrett."

"The only condition a person needs to be in to do this is to be out of his mind, and I reckon I fit the bill."

"Barrett, no." She grabbed his arm. "You're heavier than I am, you're injured. I got you into this mess. I should go."

"I walked into the mess of my own accord. Eyes wide open."

"No. This is my fault and I am going to get us out of this."

He took hold of her hands and held them to his chest. Though the darkness dulled the hue, she imagined the intense blue of his gaze riveted on her face.

"Shelby, I cannot watch you risk your life. I am going to cross first because it's the right thing to do."

Tears gathered in her eyes and she whacked a palm against his chest, making him wince. "That makes no sense, it's just dumb cowboy chivalry."

"Maybe, but it doesn't change my decision."

"I can't let you do this." Her voice shook. "You've been in trouble since the moment we met."

"That is true," he said, something wistful in his voice.

"And I don't want you to sacrifice yourself for me, do you hear me, Barrett Thorn?" The tears trickled down and he put his mouth to her forehead. She held him close, fiercely, ignoring the pain it might cause him, trying to squeeze some sense into him.

"My dumb cowboy chivalry says a man needs to do what he can in this world," he murmured in her ear. "I've disappointed you and myself. I can't be the kind of man you deserve, but I can do this and I'm gonna."

"I won't let you."

"It's not your decision to make." He pulled away, kissed her on the temple and then on the cheek. She found her head tipping up to meet his mouth and for a split second it felt as if her heart reached out and joined with his.

Sparks tripped across her senses, and she grasped the nape of his neck, holding him close, kissing him. He released her and trailed a hand through her hair. Desperately, she tried to think of something that would change his mind.

Bending, he picked up his hard hat and put it on her head. "It's going to be okay."

But what if it wasn't? What if he fell? What if…?

Before she could rally another argument, he got on his knees and crept out onto the first few rungs of the ladder. The metal creaked, twanging her nerves. Time ground to a halt and even her shallow breaths seemed loud to her frazzled senses. Two more rungs out and he was well away from the side, perched on the rickety ladder, hovering over a drop that would certainly kill him.

She could make out the white gleam of his hands, a flicker of his cheek, ashen in the darkness. Twisting her hands together, she realized they had not prayed together before he put his life on the line.

"Lord God," she breathed. Another creak of the ladder made her stop, pulse slamming in her throat.

Light. He needed more light than the glow from her headlamp and the flashlight. With clumsy fingers, she pulled out a glow stick from her backpack. "Barrett, I'm going to throw a light stick over to the far side to help you see, okay?"

"Fire away," he said.

She activated the chemicals and launched the stick

across the chasm. It arced through the black, a whirling pinwheel of green, landing on the lip of the rock.

"Good shot," he called. "I can see where I'm going now."

Inch by painful inch, he crept forward. Each movement had to be tugging on his ribs, but he made no complaint. She kept the flashlight trained as best she could to make out his progress and help light his way. Only three feet to go as he inched closer to the luminescent green marker. She blew out a breath to relieve the excruciating tension.

With a smack of flesh on iron, his right hand slipped off the rung and he fell heavily against the ladder, grunting as his torso impacted the metal. She screamed, body stiff with terror. He clung there for a minute. It hurt to breathe, her every muscle taut as steel wire as the seconds ticked by.

Barrett, please don't fall. Please...

With excruciating slowness, he got into a crawling position again.

Finally able to draw breath, she felt like laughing and crying all at the same time.

You're going to make it, Barrett.

He had only a few feet to go now. The insane plan was actually working. Barrett was gradually creeping across to safety. She realized her hands were balled into fists and she forced her fingers to relax.

Wishing she'd thought to urge him to carry his pack with some food and water, she considered his next steps. The tracks would take him to the surface. They had to, or at least close enough that he could yell for help. Her lungs began to return to a seminormal rhythm as he eased along the rusted iron rungs.

She could practically hear him now saying, "That was all kinds of crazy."

It would be a story to tell his family, for sure.

The smile died on her face as the ladder snapped in two with a shriek of metal.

Chapter Twenty-One

Barrett felt the ladder give way underneath him. He clung to the metal with all the strength he could muster, his knees and elbows scraping against the rock wall as the ladder ricocheted off the rocks, plummeting downward. The spiraling movement and the rain of debris dizzied his senses.

He managed to hook an arm over the end of the twisted rail that jutted out over the chasm. The sudden stop in momentum jarred every nerve into an avalanche of pain. Hanging there by one arm, the pieces of the ladder fell away beneath him until they made a distant splash as they plunged into the water far below. Shelby's screams ricocheted off the cavern walls.

He knew he could not hold on for long. His ribs sent ribbons of fire through his body as he wriggled to get his other arm around the rail. The metal was cold and damp, like something long dead, but at the moment it was his best friend. Hanging there cost him every bit of effort but it was not enough. His only hope was to hook a leg up over the rail, which would give him enough leverage to shimmy his way out of the chasm. Muscles tensed to the breaking point, he tried to heave his leg over, but he could not manage it. Panting, he allowed himself to rest a moment.

"Barrett," Shelby screamed again into the darkness. She appeared to be lying on her stomach staring down. Her voice was brittle as glass, edged with hysteria.

"I'm okay," he shouted up, but he was not sure it was enough to carry back to her. Knowing she was up there, frantic, perhaps thinking him dead, fueled him to try again and he swung his leg up a second time, managing to curl just the heel of his boot over the edge of the beam. He'd done it, but he was too depleted to do anything more. His muscles were hard-pressed even to hold him there, growing weaker by the moment.

"Move, move," he ordered his aching limbs, but he did not have the strength.

The weight of his failure pressed in on him. If he did not succeed, who knew how long it would be before help arrived for Shelby.

Arms trembling, he focused on breathing, despair permeating his bones like the relentless cold. *Shelby*, he wanted to call out, *this isn't your fault*. His sweaty palms began to lose their grip on the clammy metal.

"Lord, save her," he breathed. "Don't let her die here alone."

Seconds ticked into minutes. He became aware of shouting from somewhere above him, low voices, deep and masculine. His mind wanted to consider that strange fact but he could not bring his mental powers into focus.

Something thudded against his shoulder and still he clung, sweat rolling down his face.

"Barrett."

Then Jack was somehow next to him, tethered to a rope.

"How…?"

"Not important. Hold on." Jack wrapped a rope around his middle and grabbed him up in an enormous bear hug. "Ready," he shouted.

From somewhere above, the rope was hauled up, cinching around his middle and squeezing until he thought he would pass out from the pain.

"Shelby," he murmured. "You've got to get her out."

"One rescue at a time," Jack said. Moments later, they were lifted out into the tunnel by Owen and his father. Oscar was right behind him, standing ready with a sturdy twenty-foot aluminum ladder.

His father gripped Barrett's arm after Jack lowered him onto the floor. "That was not a sight I ever want to see again."

"Me neither, sir. How are we going to get her out?"

"Keegan is setting that up right now," Jack said.

Keegan. Good. If there was anyone skilled at cheating death, it was his youngest brother. Once Barrett quieted his breathing, he could hear Keegan, along with Owen, shouting directions across the gorge to Shelby. He watched as Owen and Keegan used the same procedure he and Shelby had with their sturdy ladder, easing it out across the chasm, a rope looped through one of the rungs.

"Tie the rope around your waist," Keegan shouted to Shelby.

"Her hands are numb with cold. The ground is unstable," Barrett said. "The rope might not be enough. I need to cross over to her."

They ignored him.

"Hey," he said, earning a look from Keegan, "this isn't safe."

Keegan cocked his head. "Considering Oscar's entrance is covered under three tons of rock, this is the only option. Besides," he said with a grin, "I've done stuff like this plenty of times. It'll be fun and she'll have a great story to tell afterward."

Barrett opened his mouth to retort, but his father stopped him. "There is a rescue crew on its way, but I think we are her best chance just now."

Barrett tried to breathe his way to some sense of calm. "How did you find us?"

"Heard the explosion. Couldn't get through the rock-fall so we let ourselves onto Hatcher's property."

"He allowed you into the mine?"

His father shook his head. "He wasn't home so we let ourselves in."

"You trespassed?"

He shrugged, a mischievous twist to his mouth. "Not going to let my boy and his girl die, am I?"

She's not my girl, he wanted to say, but right then the group grew silent as Keegan and Owen steadied the ladder. Barrett struggled to his feet.

"Stay put," Jack said.

"I need to be there," he hissed through gritted teeth. His brothers had brought lanterns that illuminated the chasm much better than their meager flashlights. Vast, silent and unforgiving, the tomb of stone had been left undisturbed for years. He paid attention only to the small figure on hands and knees, making her way across the sturdy aluminum slats.

"That's it," Keegan said. Owen, Jack and his father

had all taken hold of the other end of Shelby's safety rope, legs braced in case she fell. Barrett's stomach was a tight knot.

Her face, ashen and scrunched in concentration, swam closer and closer. He could hardly hold himself back from scrambling across that ladder to retrieve her. Metal creaking, an icy wind blowing through the pitch-black, he gritted his teeth and waited.

"You got this," Keegan said. "Piece of cake."

Another five seconds of agony and she was across.

When she was safely past the rock lip, Barrett could not wait any longer, grabbing her up in a hug that sent pain through his side.

She was shivering, breathing shallow. Jack wrapped a blanket around her back. Owen pressed a water bottle into her hand but she was shaking so badly she could not open it.

Barrett uncapped the bottle for her and held it to her lips while she drank. With a sudden roar, the ground trembled under them as the lip of rock gave way and the ladder spiraled into the depths.

Keegan let out a low whistle. "Gonna have to get ourselves a new ladder."

Barrett laughed and held Shelby close.

Shelby did her best to keep up with the Thorn family and Barrett as they crept through the tunnel. If she showed the slightest signs of faltering, they would pick her up, and she could not allow that.

They'd moved a safe distance away from the collapsing rock and given her time to get her body working again, but her limbs still shook as they walked back to

Hatcher's property. It was a small comfort to know that she had been right; the passages did connect.

She stopped, fished a bag out of her back pocket and collected a sample of rock, stowing it in her backpack along with the other.

Jack and Owen looked on in astonishment.

"Still on the job?" Owen asked. Even in the dim light, she could read the distrust on his face. She couldn't exactly blame him. Her bullheaded dedication to her job had almost cost their brother's life. Instead of answering, she pushed ahead, filled with a burning desire to get out of the rocky tomb.

When they finally exited the mine into the moonlit night, she thought she'd never experienced air so pure and precious. Barrett must have felt the same, too. He stood with his face tipped toward the sky, pulling in deep breaths, one hand pressed to his side. Evie Thorn greeted them, squeezing them both into a joyous embrace, her face stark with emotion.

Hatcher was there, too, arms crossed, glowering, Emmaline peeping over his shoulder. "Cut through my lock," he grumbled. "Destroyed my property."

"And as I told you, we will reimburse you in full for the replacement of that lock," Evie said. "And you won't raise a fuss, because if it was your daughter in the same predicament, you would have trespassed on our property without a second thought, wouldn't you?"

He looked at his boots.

"Wouldn't you?" she repeated.

His mouth twisted. "Yeah, I'd do most anything for Emmaline."

Shelby was astonished with Evie Thorn's powers of

persuasion as the woman turned her attention to Barrett. "You're going to the clinic," she told her son.

"Yes, ma'am." Shelby thought he must be in significant discomfort to have agreed without a word of argument.

"You, too," she said to Shelby.

"I'm not hurt."

"Your jacket sleeve is torn and I can see blood through the tear. You're both dehydrated at the very least. We'll let the doctors clean you up." With that, she marched to the truck and opened the passenger door, waiting while Shelby meekly shouldered her pack. She passed Barrett on the way.

"Don't worry," he whispered. "Even Keegan does what Mama says when she takes that tone."

"I heard that, Barrett," Evie said. "It's a twenty-minute drive to the clinic and you're both shivering, so quit talking and get into your brother's truck."

"Yes, ma'am," he said.

Shelby slid into the front seat of the other vehicle between Tom and Evie. When the heater fired up to high, she felt the delicious warmth bringing her limbs back to life and every scrape and bruise made itself known with a throb. Evie made sure Shelby's lap was draped with another blanket. Then she sat, hands clasped in her lap while Shelby told her about the body they'd found. Tom's forehead creased as he listened. Evie gasped.

"Was it that poor boy who stayed at Oscar's inn?"

"I think so. He might have died accidentally, but someone tried to hide his body."

Evie stared at her. "Shelby," she said quietly, "this has got to stop. Whatever is going on with this mine has created too many close shaves. You were both almost killed today. Please tell me you're not going back into that mine. Not again."

"I don't have any plans to." She wanted to stop there, but she owed these good people the truth. "Unless I need another sample."

"No," Evie repeated firmly. "That's not good enough. I want to hear you say you won't go back down there, not with my son."

"Evie…" Tom started.

"I can't stay quiet." Her eyes searched Shelby's. "Barrett is obviously fond of you and so are we. He feels a duty to protect you, a commitment that I haven't seen in him since Bree was alive, but he's already lost one woman he loved and I don't want that to happen to him again."

"I don't want him to risk himself for me. I didn't ask him to."

Her eyes flashed. "Don't you see that you didn't have to? I think he's falling in love with you, and that means nothing would ever prevent him from standing by your side."

Falling in love with her? "You're wrong," she wanted to reply, but Evie had taken Shelby's hand.

"Say you'll walk away from the mine and never go back."

A pang of regret stabbed her heart. Evie was right. Any mother would insist on the same thing, but she could not make a promise to Evie Thorn that would mean she had to break the one to her uncle. "I still haven't completed my work for Uncle Ken. I can't make a promise like that."

Evie chewed her lip. When she finally spoke, her voice was a ragged whisper. "Then promise me you'll stay away from my son."

Tom cleared his throat. "We don't have the right to interfere, Evie."

"Yes, we do," she said, tears sparkling on her lashes. "After what he's endured, I can't stand by and watch another disaster in the making. He's finally begun to heal."

Tom sighed. "Let's talk about this later when we've got our nerves under control."

Evie nodded, mouth tight, and stared out the window.

Shelby kept her own gaze front and center, willing herself not to cry. *Stay away from my son...* How could they not understand her desire to protect her uncle? Did it really come down to betraying him in order to follow her burgeoning feelings for Barrett? She recalled the absolute terror she'd felt when the ladder had collapsed, throwing him into the abyss. Did she care for him enough to walk away from her uncle?

Is that what love meant? Turning your back on your family?

No, she told herself. She'd turned her back on her mother, busied herself with school and her career, allowing anger and resentment to cement the wall between them. Whatever she felt for Barrett was not strong enough to drive her to abandon Uncle Ken.

Besides, Barrett had said he could not give her what she deserved, so deep were his own feelings of resentment. Thoughts whirled through her mind along with a cascade of hurts and hopes. She could not be with Barrett unless she gave up on Uncle Ken, and Barrett was not able to give his heart to her because of his endless rage at that same man.

Oh, Lord, she pleaded silently, *what should I do?*

There was no answer in her soul, no comfort as the miles unrolled before them.

Chapter Twenty-Two

After Barrett was thoroughly poked, prodded, hydrated and had his ribs taped, he found Officer Larraby waiting. He'd refused any pain medicine other than a couple of aspirin and fatigue was not helping him concentrate on the questions. Nor was the detached look on Shelby's face. Was she experiencing delayed shock? He didn't blame her. As the hours after their escape ticked by, the magnitude of the whole trauma was starting to sink in.

They sat in an empty waiting room with Larraby and another officer while his parents and brothers clustered nearby.

Barrett explained again about the body and did his best to describe the location. "I took pictures..." His voice trailed off. "But we used my phone," he said, "and it was smashed in the fall."

"We might still be able to lift something from it." Larraby held out a palm.

Barrett felt his cheeks warm. "I left it in the cavern."

"I don't suppose you picked it up?" Larraby cast a peeved glance at Shelby.

She shook her head. "No, but I can confirm everything he said. You should be able to find the spot where the body is buried and maybe the place where we found the hair."

"Oh, you think so, do you? Not until we get some engineers to shore up the place and a backhoe to remove a ton of rubble. Oscar's given us carte blanche to do whatever we need to, but we'll still have to bring in people from outside the county to make this happen and that costs time and money."

"Do it, then," Barrett said irritably. "The family needs their son's remains. It's only right."

"Your family is fortunate we aren't digging out *your* remains," he said, glaring at Barrett, before he cast a glance at Shelby. "Or yours. We contacted your uncle on his cell phone and he's half-frantic. He's on his way home right now."

Shelby looked at the floor. "I didn't mean for any of this to happen."

"Well, that makes it all better now, doesn't it?" Larraby said.

"Hey," Barrett snapped, "no harm done and we discovered a possible murder. You should be thanking us."

"That'll be the day."

"The red marks," Shelby said suddenly. "Someone left them as a set of directions. Maybe it was the murderer, who intended to come back and remove the body at some point."

Larraby held up a palm. "First off, we don't know this was murder. Second, red marks could have been left by anyone. We'll investigate, but for now, stay out of the mine."

"I concur," Barrett's mother said. He saw an odd

look on her face as she gazed at Shelby and he wondered what the two of them had talked about on the way to the clinic.

All he could think about was how petrified he'd been watching Shelby crawl across that ladder. He wanted to touch her, to hold her, to reassure himself that she really was there and not lying broken at the bottom of the chasm. He itched for the others to move away and give him a moment alone with Shelby.

She straightened and checked her phone. "It's a text from my uncle. He's on his way home from the airport."

Barrett's heart sank. He'd not realized until that moment how much he liked having her on the ranch.

"I have to go," she said.

"We'll drive you," Barrett said, giving his brothers a look.

Jack nodded. "Sure. We can stop at the ranch first and get your things if you'd like."

"No, thank you," she said. "I will find my own way home."

Barrett started to object but she simply walked out of the waiting room. His mother tried to put a restraining arm on his shoulder but he got painfully to his feet and followed. "Shelby, wait."

When she did not slow, he tried to hurry but his legs felt battered and scraped. "Shelby." She did not pause until he touched her arm. Finally, she turned.

"What is it, Barrett?" Her eyes looked pained and he wondered if she'd been hurt more seriously than she let on.

He felt suddenly tongue-tied. "Well, I mean, I don't think you should be leaving alone."

"Why not?"

"Um, I… I'm worried about you."

She caught her lip between her teeth and he could see moisture glittering in her eyes. "Barrett, I am sorry I got you into more trouble, but it won't happen again. I appreciate all you've done for me, I really do, but it's best if we go our separate ways."

"Separate ways?" he repeated dumbly.

"Yes. I'm going back home to my uncle and you're going with your family. That's the way it should be."

Of course she was right. His life had been simpler, easier without her, but the words stung like wasps. "Did I…did I say something wrong back there in the mine?"

She tilted her head and he wanted to reach out and push the strands of hair from her forehead, but he stood frozen.

"No, not at all. You've been so good to me and gone way out on a limb to help me, and so has your family, but my first loyalty has to be to my uncle and your family expects your loyalty to be to them."

"My loyalty is not in question."

"It will be, and so will your safety if you hang around with me. Please take good care of yourself, okay?"

"Shelby," he started.

She moved quickly, pressing a kiss on his cheek, and left through the sliding exit doors.

He felt a presence behind him and turned to find his mother. "I begged her not to go into that mine anymore, and she could not promise that she wouldn't, so…"

"So?"

"So I asked her not to be involved with you."

For a second, anger licked hot inside his gut. "Mama…"

"I know it wasn't my place, but I was scared. She said her first duty was to her uncle."

He let out a gush of air. Ken Arroyo…the root of all the heartbreaks in Barrett's life. If things had been different, he mused, if Shelby wasn't the man's niece… but she was, and all that Shelby and Barrett had gone through was for the purpose of helping him out, the man who'd raised a feckless son, the boy who killed Barrett's wife.

He looked at his mother, pain that began when Bree died etched deeply in the crow's-feet around her eyes. He realized how he must have reawakened that pain by his dangerous interactions with Shelby. He could not be mad at her.

"If you…if you want her to be a part of your life," she said, "I will apologize to her, Barrett. I'll drive over there right now."

My first loyalty has to be to my uncle.

His mother was right. He folded her in his arms and kissed the top of her head. "I love you, Mama."

She sighed softly against his chest. "Can we go home now, honey?"

"Yes, ma'am," he said. "Let's do that."

Shelby could hardly keep her eyes open when she arrived by taxi back at the Arroyo Ranch late that night. Her uncle met her with both anger and rejoicing.

"You never should have gone. What were you thinking?" Then he clutched her in a bear hug that nearly squeezed the air out of her.

She endured his relentless questions. "The bottom line is that I got the samples."

That stopped him short. "You did?"

She nodded. "I've arranged with an assayer in Copperopolis to analyze them tomorrow at his lab."

His eyes widened. "I would never have wanted you to risk your life, but I am glad to know something good came out of it."

"Maybe. We'll know after I complete the analysis."

"Well, I'm going with you, of course."

"It's a date," she said, smiling. "Ten o'clock."

"And I'm contacting the Thorns to have my horses returned ASAP."

She frowned. "They were very gracious to take them."

He lifted a shoulder. "Yes," he admitted. "I suppose they were. I'll be sure to thank them."

After the hottest, longest shower she could manage, she pulled on some blissfully clean clothing. Her body felt less achy in spite of the gouge on her arm, but the throb in her chest had not dissipated since she left the clinic. The look on Barrett's face had almost broken her will to leave.

But he'd made it clear, hadn't he, before the cave-in? There could be no future for them anyway. His mother had only confirmed that. The Thorns were good people and Shelby would not threaten their future simply to chase after her own fleeting happiness with a man who did not want her enough.

Fatigue overwhelmed her and she lay down on the bed, pulling the covers up to her chin. As she drifted off to sleep, she thought of the Thorn family room, the smell of Evie's cooking, the good-natured ribbing of the brothers and the sad blue eyes of one particular brother.

Shelby decided that a dose of sunshine might help lift the gloom the next morning. The December frost had long since melted away, leaving the ground damp. She'd just crested the slope moving toward the stables when she caught sight of the Thorns' horse trailer parked near the pasture.

She froze. "Oh, quit it, you ninny. After the horses are delivered, you won't see any more of Barrett." Besides, she thought, it was likely Barrett wasn't even participating in the process with his banged-up ribs and the way they'd ended things at the clinic.

Standing tall and pushing her hair behind her ears, she marched toward the pasture, face flushing when she realized Barrett was indeed there, coaxing Diamond from the trailer. Pattycake and Buddy were already freed, close together and happy in the pasture.

Emmaline was also there, to Shelby's surprise, elbows propped on the pasture fence watching Barrett. Shelby joined her.

"Are you okay?" Emmaline asked.

"Yes, a little worse for wear, but not bad."

Emmaline cocked her head. "It's like you are invincible or something."

Shelby laughed. "Not anywhere close."

Emmaline quirked a grin. "I hope it's okay that I came. You said…" She shoved her hands in the pockets of her jeans. "You said I could come and see Diamond anytime."

"And I meant it."

They watched Barrett ease the nervous horse from the trailer before he led Diamond to the pasture and let her loose, shutting the gate behind. After a moment's hesitation, he joined them.

Emmaline moved away a few paces, pulling an apple from her pocket, face shining.

"Here, Diamond. Remember me? Come here, girl."

Barrett kept his gaze on the horse.

"Thank you for taking care of them," Shelby said.

"Your uncle already thanked us and offered to pay."

"Which you didn't accept."

"Correct." Now he glanced at her. "They weren't any trouble. Are you…okay?"

She nodded. "Scraped is all. You?"

He shrugged in typical fashion. "No lasting damage. Did you, uh, get your samples safely home?"

She nodded. "Taking them to a lab in Copperopolis at ten to analyze."

Emmaline stretched her arm farther over the fence. "Diamond," she crooned softly. "You used to be mine, remember? Red apples were your favorite and I brought you one every day."

The horse sniffed the air, nostrils flared.

"That's it," Emmaline said. "You remember now."

The horse suddenly wheeled around and raced away, legs flying swiftly over the green grass. Emmaline sagged, the apple falling from her fingers. "She doesn't know me anymore."

"It may take some time," Shelby said, "but she will learn to trust you again."

"That's what my father used to say about my mother. 'It will take some time, but she will grow to love it here in Gold Bar.'" Emmaline's features hardened. "Do you see any sign of her coming back?"

Shelby pitied the girl. Abandoned by her mother, with an angry man like Joe Hatcher for a father. Where was the tenderness in this girl's life? "I'm sorry, but please don't give up on Diamond."

"Too late," Emmaline said. "She's got you now."

"Emmaline..." Shelby started, but the girl had already trudged away.

"She's had a hard life," Barrett said.

"I'll find her later and encourage her to try again with Diamond."

He nodded. "So, uh, I guess I'd better be going."

She tried for levity. "Horses waiting for your attention?"

He huffed out a breath, rubbing a hand across his close-cut beard. "I've been banned from most duties until my ribs heal. I had to throw a fit to get to bring the horses over here. Now I'm relegated to building tables for the Christmas Eve dinner."

"I hope it's a great event," she said.

"I wish..." he started. "Nothing. I've gotta go. I picked up a new phone, same number, you know, if you need anything. Hope your samples turn out the way you want."

Nothing has turned out the way I want, she thought, watching him climb back in the trailer and drive away.

Chapter Twenty-Three

Shelby carried the samples to the truck and her uncle climbed behind the wheel. "Ready to find out once and for all?"

"Yes," she said. "More than ready."

As they clattered over the drive, she gripped the samples tight. She and Barrett had almost died for this small bag of rocks. Her mind wandered, thinking of his laughter in the cavern, the taste of pickles trickling across her memory.

"That went better than I expected," her uncle was saying.

"Oh, I'm sorry. What did you say?"

He smiled at her as he took the turn onto a quiet stretch of highway that curved away through the wooded foothills. "My business trip. I have someone who offered full price for my property. I hate to let go of the land, but it will ease the pressure for a while anyway, maybe until Devon is released."

"Next year?"

"Or sooner, maybe." He shifted in his seat and

cleared his throat. "Devon told me that Barrett Thorn sent him a letter."

She started. "Really?"

"Said Barrett made it clear he forgave Devon, that he was praying for him."

Shelby swallowed a lump in her throat. "That's wonderful."

Uncle Ken's lips twisted in thought. "Yeah. I don't know how I feel about it. Devon's life is ruined and it's not like Barrett's forgiveness is going to make one bit of difference."

It will make all the difference, she thought.

"And who is Barrett to be offering prayers for my son, like he's some kind of perfect man himself?"

Who was Barrett? A man learning to forgive. Something warm and soft washed over her heart. She hoped his actions would give him and his family peace.

Uncle Ken opened his mouth to talk when his glance went to the rearview mirror.

"What in the world…?"

Shelby jerked around to see a battered pickup bearing down on them. The glare made it impossible to see the driver, but clearly the driver saw them, pushing the truck forward, closing the gap between them.

"He's going to hit us," Shelby screamed.

Uncle Ken jammed his foot to the gas pedal. "Hold on," he shouted. Their truck was bigger, which made it more ungainly, so their pursuer had the advantage. At first it looked as though they would be able to outpace the smaller truck.

"Look out," Shelby cried. "Sharp turn."

Ken cranked the wheel hard and tried to slow enough to safely navigate the tight bend in the road.

With a crash of metal, the truck behind them plowed into their fender.

Shelby was jerked hard, hitting her shoulder on the door frame. Uncle Ken fought the wheel but the impact slammed their vehicle and it skidded sideways off the road.

Time slowed as the truck began to tip over, twisting and turning as it plunged down the hillside. Dark tree trunks flickered in a dizzying parade by the windshield. There was a crack, and the windshield shattered. Bits of metal and glass flew around her face. Finally, with a massive bang, the truck crashed headfirst into the twisted trunk of an oak tree. The impact jarred them both violently.

For several moments, Shelby was unable to do anything but breathe. The truck had righted itself, but the front end was mashed against the tree trunk. She forced herself to look sideways. Uncle Ken was slumped against the driver's door, eyes closed.

"Uncle Ken," she said, trying to reach him, but her seat belt was jammed. She heard the distant sound of a car door slamming up on the road. Was it help? Or the person who had just tried to kill them? With frantic fingers, she yanked at the seat belt but it would not give.

Phone.

She wriggled and thrashed until she could free the pocket of her jacket from under the belt. She texted Barrett.

Help. Accident.

She added the last route marker they'd passed.

Now there were footsteps approaching their truck,

warily, stealthily. Not a passerby, come to rescue them. A killer, come to finish the job. Her skin crawled.

She again pressed the seat belt button and this time it gave way. She grabbed her bag of samples. If someone was ready to kill for the rocks, they might be her only bargaining chip to keep her and her uncle alive.

The door was stuck, so she kicked aside the broken glass and climbed out, fighting dizziness. Listening hard, she heard the footsteps off to her right, behind a screen of prickly shrubs. Head down, she raced over the grass, looping around to circle back to the road where she had a better hope of flagging down help.

Fear for Uncle Ken made it hard to move. Was he dead? Bleeding out? Was she leaving him behind to die? *Just run, get help.* Fighting dizziness, she scurried behind a pile of rocks and stopped to get her bearings. Shadows loomed all around her but she poked her head above the rocks, identifying a relatively clear route leading up to the road. Unfortunately, it was exposed.

Stay put and hide?

Run for help?

The agony of indecision nearly overcame her. One thought pounded repeatedly through her mind.

Run.

She counted to three, hugged her sample bag tight and sprinted.

Adrenaline fired her muscles. She covered several yards before she heard the footsteps pursuing her. Stumbling over fallen branches, panting, she pushed on until a hand grabbed her hair, yanking her back and sending her sprawling. She tried to scramble away, but the arms that turned her over were strong, one forearm pressed hard on her throat.

She looked up into the hard face of Joe Hatcher. He ripped the samples out of her grasp.

"Listen," he said, "I didn't want it to be this way. None of this would have happened if you could have kept your nose out of my mine."

"What is down there?" she breathed. "What are you so scared for me to find? Did you kill Charlie? Is that it?"

He pulled her hair until she stopped talking. "Just give up, you wretched troublemaker. Why won't you get out of Gold Bar and never come back? When I pushed you in the trunk I was sure that would scare you off for good."

She blinked back tears of pain. "Give me back my samples."

"I told you," he said, breath hot on her face, "you have to get out of town or…"

"Or you'll kill me like you've been trying to do since I got here?"

"I didn't want to hurt you," he hissed. "You just wouldn't let it go." He pulled a knife from his pocket, the blade glittering.

Shelby writhed and tried to scream but he clapped a hand over her mouth.

"Remember that I didn't want to," he said, lifting the knife.

She closed her eyes, breath still, waiting for the bite of the knife into her throat.

There was a dull thud. Her eyes flew open as the knife fell from Hatcher's grip. Before she could get to her feet, Hatcher toppled over sideways, unconscious. Uncle Ken stood, ashen faced, blood running down his cheeks, a rock still gripped in his hand.

"It's over," he said, before he fell to his knees.

* * *

Barrett arrived at the Copper Creek Hospital within a half hour. As soon as he'd received Shelby's text, he'd called the cops and raced to the scene to find that both Shelby and her uncle had already been discovered by a passing officer, who had summoned an ambulance and got them to the hospital.

Barret's mind still spun with the information he'd heard from Larraby, that Joe Hatcher had been arrested at the scene and was on another floor of the hospital being treated for a head injury inflicted by Ken Arroyo as he defended his niece's life. Barrett forced himself not to run along the tiled hallways as he made his way to Shelby.

He found her pacing, arms hugged around herself. She looked over and saw him, stopping her endless laps around the waiting room. She didn't move, but tears streaked from her eyes. He didn't say a word, just pulled her close and let her cry onto his chest. When her tears were spent, he guided her to a chair.

"How is he?"

She sucked in a breath. "He was bleeding internally and he's in hypovolemic shock. They've given him a transfusion and medicines to help his heart beat more efficiently. They said they would have a better prognosis in the next twelve hours. He might be strong enough to recover, or his organs might shut down." Her voice wobbled.

"Okay," he said, squeezing her hand. "And how about you?"

"I'm okay." She laughed bitterly. "It's like Emmaline said, I must be invincible. Only the people around me get hurt."

The misery in her voice made him pull her closer. "It's over now."

Larraby approached, sinking into a chair next to them. "I'm glad you are okay. We'll keep your samples as evidence until we've cleared the scene, then you can have them back," he said. "May I ask how your uncle is?"

Shelby repeated the diagnosis, her voice shaky.

Larraby nodded. "We're all hoping he pulls through."

"But why did this happen?" she said. "Why did Hatcher risk everything to steal the samples? They could be worth nothing at all."

"I think I have an answer to that," he said. "He can't take the chance that the samples pave the way for excavation of the mine."

"Because he killed Charlie?"

"That might be part of it."

They both stared at Larraby.

He continued. "We found another way into the mine on Oscar's property and sent in a team with a dog. They found Charlie's body, just like you said—" he paused "—and another one down there."

Barrett gaped. "What? Whose?"

"The remains appear to be female. She was wearing a necklace with C.H. engraved on the back."

Shelby gasped. "Cora Hatcher? Joe's wife?"

"Looks like she's been dead about five years, right about the time he told everyone she left town." They fell into stunned silence for a few moments.

"Why Charlie, though?" Barrett said. "What did he have to do with Hatcher?"

"Nothing, except he was probably at the wrong place at the wrong time. He was getting close to discovering

Cora's body with his exploring, so Hatcher killed him and covered up the body." Larraby tapped a finger on his notebook. "Hatcher might have figured he would go back and dispose of the remains more permanently at some point."

"Which would explain the red marks he left to point the way to the bodies," Shelby said. She shivered and Barrett rubbed her shoulders. "It's over now," he said again.

Shelby shook her head, exhaustion shadowing her face. "No, it's not. Emmaline's father is going to stay in prison for his whole life now because he murdered her mother. It's never going to be over for her." Her eyes flooded again. "And my uncle. What if he doesn't survive?"

Barrett took her hand and they stood. "Come on."

She allowed him to help her to her feet. "Where are we going?"

"To the chapel. We'll see you later, Larraby."

The officer gave a short nod before speaking into his radio.

They made their way to the empty chapel and linked hands to pray. Shelby clung to Barrett, hands shaking, while he prayed for Ken Arroyo. At first the words were forced, until something loosened inside him and he felt his hatred slipping away like a blanket of fog, dissipating in the warmth of the sunlight. When the prayer ended, he hung on to the feeling, marveling, grateful, awed.

They sat in silence, each lost in their own thoughts, as the time passed away. When Shelby began to droop, he led her back to the deserted waiting room where she lay down on an upholstered couch. He covered her with his jacket. She fought to stay awake.

"But what if the doctors come? If Uncle Ken wakes up?"

"I'll stay right here. I'll wake you if there's any change."

Her lovely green eyes fixed on his and her voice was very small. "I'm scared to be alone."

He knew what it cost her to admit it. "I'm here," he said, while he watched her slip into sleep.

Barrett felt caged by the confines of the waiting room. He wandered to the threshold of Ken Arroyo's room and then found himself standing at the man's bed. Ken's face was scratched and battered, lined with wrinkles too pronounced for a man of his age. Though he was a big guy, almost Barrett's height, the hospital bed and the crowded machinery dwarfed him.

There were no words to explain why Barrett laid his hand on Ken's forearm, just the urging of his soul. He closed his eyes. "I know…" he began, then his breath failed and he needed to take another one. "I know that you love your son as much as I loved my wife."

"Yes," came a croak of a reply.

Barrett's eyes flew open to see Ken Arroyo watching him, irises bright with some unnamed emotion.

"And…and I know that you tried to be a good father."

Ken didn't answer, but his chin quivered and a single tear ran down his cheek.

"I've been wrong to hang on to hatred," Barrett said. "I guess I need to ask for forgiveness as much as I need to offer it."

Slowly, Ken reached out until his shaking hand was inches from Barrett. Barrett grasped the cold fingers and he felt the hard stone of hatred dissolve in his heart.

In Ken's eyes, Barrett saw that he, too, had moved toward a place of peace.

Barrett heard someone behind him and turned to find Shelby moving next to him, her own eyes streaming with tears, mouth trembling. She joined her hand to theirs, her crying twined with the soft sounds of the machinery.

Shelby awoke on the hard hospital couch, Barrett sitting quietly next to her. It took her a moment to realize that the previous day and long restless night had not been a dream. The most incredible part had really happened, her uncle had awakened, and he and Barrett had shared a divine moment of forgiveness.

Through the fatigue and worry, the thought circled light and airy in her heart. So what did it mean for her and Barrett, she wondered? But it was not the time to think about it.

Barrett's family had arrived in shifts throughout the previous day and all through the night, making sure she was never alone. Now, when it was Evie's turn, she sent Jack and Barrett off to fetch the Styrofoam container of soup that she had left in the truck.

"Piping hot. It's much better than the hospital cafeteria food, and I thought you might like some since you did not have dinner last night," she said. Then she cleared her throat. "Shelby, I am so sorry about all that's happened. I wish... I mean, I shouldn't have..."

Shelby gripped her hand. "You love your son. There's no need to apologize for anything."

Evie bit her lip and took a breath. "I want you to come to Christmas Eve dinner at the ranch. Your uncle, too, if he is released."

"That's a very kind offer but…"

Evie held up a palm. "It's not an offer, it's an invitation. I want you to be there, and so does our family."

Shelby blinked against the tears. "Thank you."

The doctor found them in the waiting room.

"He's improving steadily," she said. "I would venture to say he is going to make a complete recovery in the next week or so."

Shelby could not help but hug her around the shoulders.

The doctor laughed. "I wish I could deliver this kind of news all the time. Now, why don't you go home for a bit?"

"No, I want to stay here."

"Your uncle is sleeping peacefully and there's no reason you can't pop home for a nap and a change of clothes."

Shelby looked down, realizing she was wearing the same ripped and stained jeans, though Evie had insisted she put on one of Barrett's flannel shirts.

"Go on, honey," Evie said as Barrett and Jack arrived with a paper sack and the container of soup. "Take the soup home and eat it. Jack and I will stay right here while Barrett drives you home. He'll pick you up whenever you're ready to return, since you seem to have trouble with vehicles."

Shelby laughed. "All right. Just for a little while. I want to be sure the horses are taken care of." She shot a look at Barrett. "Are you sure you don't mind?"

"Naw, I'm pretty sure Mama packed some Christmas cookies in this bag so I will take that in lieu of a taxicab fee."

She followed him to his truck, happy to sink down on the seat and watch the scenery go by. The soup container in the cup holder let off a cloud of savory scent. Her senses felt dull and slow with the shock of all that had happened, mostly that Joe Hatcher had killed his wife and Charlie, and almost added her, Barrett and Uncle Ken to the list.

Barrett scurried to open the door for her when they arrived and she let him. "I want to make sure Zeke has been seeing to the horses before I allow myself that shower," she said.

They walked up the slope and down toward the stables. A figure stepped from the shadowed barn. At first she thought it was Zeke until they got closer.

"Emmaline," Shelby said, her heart breaking. "I am so sorry for everything that's happened."

"I'm not," Emmaline said, pulling a gun from behind her skirt and firing.

Chapter Twenty-Four

The bullet creased a hot trail along Barrett's temple, hurling him to his back on the ground. He heard Shelby scream and drop to her knees beside him.

"Why did you do that?" Shelby panted. "Barrett," she whispered, fingers skimming his face as she tried to ascertain his injury.

"Diamond doesn't even know me anymore," Emmaline said. "My mother gave me that horse and now…"

Though his vision was blurred, Barrett could see Emmaline's face twisted into a mask of hatred. He would not have recognized her.

"You can have the horse," Shelby said. "Take her, just leave us alone."

Emmaline did not appear to hear. "My mother sold her, just like that, wanted to move away from here. She didn't care that I loved Diamond, loved Gold Bar. She never cared what I wanted. I hated her."

Barrett felt a sick sensation creep through the pain in his head. "You…" he wanted to say, but the words wouldn't come.

"So…" Shelby started, then stopped. She sucked in

a breath as she must have come to the same realization. "Oh, Emmaline. You killed your mother, didn't you?"

The girl didn't answer.

"And your father, he did all these things to keep us out of the mine…in order to protect you."

"I did some of it," she said proudly. "I'm handy with TNT and paint, and I've been snooping around the Thorns' property, keeping tabs on your activities. I am a good snooper. I knew Dad's idea to lock you in the trunk wouldn't be enough, so I had to take the reins, so to speak."

"Charlie," Barrett croaked in a desperate bid to keep her talking. "Why?"

"I didn't want to kill him," Emmaline said. "He was handsome and funny. I got to know him when I helped out at the inn sometimes. I didn't want to hurt him, but he kept on pushing deeper into the mine. I really did like him, but I couldn't let him find Mother so I got him to take me along, and one shot, that was all. It was peaceful."

Shelby gasped. "I can't believe this."

"Maybe you'll believe it when I shoot you," Emmaline said with a cunning smile. "Bullets are very convincing. I didn't want to hurt you at first either. I mean, I helped you escape the mine and all, just to keep you safe and Daddy out of trouble for his dumb practical joke, but see where that kindness got me."

"But you can't hide the truth anymore, Emmaline," Shelby said. "The bodies have been discovered now, Charlie and your mother."

"And Daddy has already confessed. He will stick to the story because he loves me. I am all he has, you know, since Mother is dead, but if you persist in analyzing the samples, eventually the mine will be fully excavated and there will be evidence found to incriminate me."

"What evidence?" Barrett said.

"I was angry. I painted messages on the tunnel walls sometimes, like I did at your uncle's house." She frowned. "It was stupid. I should have covered over them or moved the bodies, but I never got around to it."

"The police are investigating. They'll find your messages soon," Shelby said.

"No one will find them," she snapped, "unless your assaying causes mining to start up again, but I think when you disappear and are found dead eventually, your uncle will lose interest in his mining adventure."

Shelby's voice was high and taut. "How are you going to explain our murders?"

"I don't have to, but really, you're nosy, and nosy people get into trouble, don't they? Poor Barrett, getting mixed up with the likes of you. His wife was much better. She brought us Christmas cookies every year. It was a shame your cousin killed her. She didn't deserve to die, not like you."

Don't talk about my wife, Barrett wanted to say. *And Shelby doesn't deserve any of this.* He eased a little onto one side, grabbing a handful of gravel. Shelby squeezed his arm to show she'd noticed. She knew what they had to do.

"You don't have to do this," Shelby said, slowly standing. "We can explain it to the police. I am sure you didn't mean to kill her. It could have been an accident."

"No," Emmaline said, eyes blazing. "It was not an accident. My mother was a selfish shrew. My father fawned all over her like a puppy and she didn't care about him, or me. She sold the horses and told Daddy she was leaving us. It wasn't an accident," Emmaline snapped. "I shot her with this gun in the back of the head, just like I did to Charlie. Daddy has spent his whole life trying to cover it up, and now he's even gone to jail for it, so it's all up to me. You two are the only ones who know the truth."

She's insane, Barrett thought. His fingers tightened around the gravel. Without warning, Emmaline stomped down hard on his wrist. He grunted in pain, losing his grip on the bits of rock.

"If you think you're going to try something heroic, Mr. Thorn, you are making a mistake. Now, get up. We're going to walk to your truck and drive."

Shelby hooked an arm under his elbow and he got unsteadily to his feet, blood dripping from his face onto his shirtfront. "Where?" he said.

"Somewhere remote, where you won't be found for a while. It will be fun watching them search for you."

They made their way toward the truck, Emmaline behind them, gun aimed. Once they were out of town, there would be a much smaller chance they would survive. The window of opportunity was narrowing.

Barrett squeezed Shelby's hand. Her fingers trembled in his. In that touch, he wanted to tell her so many things about how he'd changed since he met her, about what he'd learned deep down in his soul. Above all, he hoped she knew he would not give up fighting for her until his very last breath, and he had no intention of breathing his last to clear the way for Emmaline to cover up two murders.

"You drive," Emmaline said, prodding him in the back when they reached the vehicle.

"Can't," he said. "Double vision, thanks to your shot."

Shelby flicked him a worried look from the corner of her eye. Head turned away from Emmaline, he winked.

"You, then," she said to Shelby. Barrett handed her the keys. She dropped them and Emmaline cursed at her. While she bent to retrieve them, he yanked open the passenger door and started to climb in. There was only one thing he could use to save them. Praying, he grabbed the container. He had it in his hands, the soup still hot enough that the container was warm against his fingers. Whirling, he flung the soup into Emmaline's face.

She recoiled, raising her arms reflexively to her eyes, gun pointed at the sky. Shelby swept an ankle out and hooked Emmaline's legs. The gun went flying and Barrett pinned Emmaline down, turning her onto her stomach and holding her hands behind her back.

"Don't touch me," she hissed into the dirt. "Let me go."

"Happy to oblige as soon as the police arrive," he said, panting.

Shelby grabbed a coil of rope from the back of the truck and tied Emmaline's hands. Together, they knelt over Emmaline's prostrate form, breathing hard. Barrett still could not quite believe that the young girl they held had killed her own mother and an innocent college student.

And nearly killed them both as well, he reminded himself. Shelby shivered next to him and he figured she was running through those chilling thoughts, as well.

"All kinds of crazy?" she said, a sliver of a smile on her face.

"That's exactly what I was about to say."

Christmas Eve morning, Shelby was at her uncle's side, prodding him to eat from a dish of applesauce while she explained what had happened at the ranch. He was still pale, weak, but improving at a steady rate, according to the doctors. She had stopped in the chapel on her way to his room to thank God for her uncle's deliverance and theirs. The world had spun out of control for so long, she hardly knew what to do with herself now that He'd put it back in order.

Barrett had not wanted her to spend the night alone at her uncle's and she suspected he might have even slept in his truck outside, but she did not feel frightened anymore. Emmaline, poor twisted girl, was in custody and there would be no more threats to Shelby or her uncle. Shelby had wrapped up in her blankets, cried, prayed, thought about her mother, about Barrett and her future and prayed some more, sleeping intermittently until morning dawned.

With effort, she brought her mind back to the present. "When the police release my samples, I'll get them analyzed as quickly as I can."

Uncle Ken pushed the applesauce aside. "No need."

"What?"

"I'm okay, for a while, like I said, and it doesn't feel right to pry open that mine anytime soon. Too much grief contained in those tunnels for my taste."

She felt her eyes well up again. "Charlie's parents will arrive soon to take home his remains."

Uncle Ken sighed. "That's good. Some closure." He patted her hand. "So what are your Christmas Eve plans?"

"I'm going to stay here with you. I'll see if I can smuggle in some cookies or something."

"Not necessary. Evie Thorn called just before you arrived to say she and Tom will be here precisely at noon to deliver me a Christmas luncheon that will fill me to the rafters."

Shelby gaped. "And you're...well, you're okay with that?"

He was quiet a moment. "Let's just say I've learned a few things recently. It will take time," he said, eyes damp, "but I want things to be different."

She blinked back her own tears and kissed him on the cheek. "I'm so glad, Uncle Ken."

"So," he said, after clearing his throat, "you are to attend the Christmas Eve gathering at the Gold Bar Ranch tonight, Shelby, no arguments."

"I'm not going to leave you here alone."

"Trust me, after Evie's lunch I think I will be napping the day away. Nothing sounds better to me than a night of uninterrupted sleep. Please," he said, catching her hand, "I want you to go."

It doesn't seem right, she wanted to say, but she found to her surprise that it did. Spending Christmas Eve with Barrett was the only thing her heart craved. She did not know where things stood between them, but she knew she had to see him again.

"If you're sure," she said.

He pulled her hand to his mouth and kissed her knuckles. "I'm sure. Go."

On the way down in the elevator, she made plans. First, a call to her mother to tell her caregivers she'd be coming for a visit soon. Then a proper shower and an attempt to make herself presentable. And one very important stop in town...

The Christmas Eve service at the church was packed as usual. Everyone greeted Barrett with extra hearty hugs that made his ribs throb and he heard "I just can't believe it" more times than he could count. He was still having trouble believing it himself.

And further, he could not stop wondering about Shelby, where she was and if he had done the right thing on his afternoon errand after his mother confirmed that Shelby would likely be coming to Christmas Eve at the ranch. Barrett was not prone to indecision, but now his stomach felt tight.

As the choir sang the last Christmas carol, his eye caught a glimpse of brown glossy hair pulled into a soft pile. Shelby? He strained to see, but he was caught up in the throng of churchgoers filing down the aisle. Most of them would be heading to the ranch directly. His mother tugged on his arm.

"Come on, Barrett. We've got mouths to feed."

"Right behind you, Mama." He strained to look for Shelby but there was no sign of her.

At the ranch, he was immediately engulfed by his duties. The long wooden tables he'd constructed were covered and set with pine garlands and flickering lanterns. He activated the tall heat lamps and his father threw more wood into the crackling fire pit. Jack stood at the fence, armed with carrots that he dispensed for the children to offer the horses that stood expectantly on the other side. Owen poured endless cups of cider and hot coffee. It was good to see him smiling.

It seemed like this year the eight-foot tree standing near the front porch sparkled with more lights than in recent memory, and the buffet table was jammed with an unbelievable assortment of offerings, everything from roast turkey to mashed potatoes, cranberry relish and plates of his mother's famous stuffing.

Keegan was posted at the dessert table, ostensibly to keep the kids from raiding it before supper, but Barrett saw his youngest brother sneaking cookies to the kids and nibbling on them himself. Barrett chuckled. Tonight would be a night of rejoicing, finishing up with a rousing family game time and a midnight prayer.

Thorn family Christmases. He'd taken them for granted. The last four years he'd been so steeped in grief, in hatred, that Christmases had come and gone in a meaningless parade. Bree would have tugged on his earlobe and told him not to waste a minute being regretful on Christmas Eve. Bree had always relished the life God had given her, and Barrett was going to try to do the same.

"I'll always love you, Bree," he whispered, looking up at the spangle of stars. A feeling of peace filled his soul.

But he had not yet seen Shelby. What if she did not come?

"Is it okay to start with dessert and work my way backward?"

He spun on his heel and found Shelby standing there, clutching a box. Her hair was piled up like he'd noticed in church and she wore a red sweater and a white scarf.

"Pretty as a Christmas present," he murmured.

She smiled, looking away. "Speaking of presents..." She handed him the wrapped box.

"You didn't have to get me a gift," he said.

"Yes, I did. Open it."

He tore off the paper and pulled off the lid. Inside was a cowboy hat, sturdy and unadorned.

"I know it's not as good as your favorite hat that you lost in the mine," she said.

He clapped it on his head. "It'll be perfect, once I beat it up a little. Thank you."

She laughed. "Glad I didn't get the one with rhinestones on the side."

He chuckled. "Good call. I, uh… I got something for you, too."

He took her hand and led her over to the glistening Christmas tree. From underneath it, he took a tissue-wrapped package. "Hope you like it."

With nerves zinging, he watched her open it. Her laughter drifted through the air like snowflakes. "A jar of homemade pickles," she cried. "I'm going to keep them forever, unopened, to remind me of you."

He pointed to the ribbon around the edge. "Maybe, um, you could keep that instead."

Eyes wide, she untied the ribbon and slid off the gold ring. "Barrett?"

"It's an engagement ring." He could hardly swallow. "I mean, if you want it to be."

She stared at him, the ring clutched between her fingers.

"I love you, Shelby," he said. "You brought my heart back to beating and you helped me see that I was wasting my life on hatred."

She cocked her head, her expression…puzzled? Confused? *Upset?* he thought with a trickle of fear.

"I thought I didn't have any more right to experience joy after Bree, but being with you has changed all that. I want you to be in my life."

"But you almost died because of me."

"No," he said quietly. "It's the opposite. You taught me how to live again."

Tears glimmered on the edges of her thick lashes.

Tears of joy, he told himself stubbornly as he eased down to one knee, slid off his hat and took the ring from her hands.

"Will you marry me, Shelby?"

Her mouth opened in a circle of surprise, but she did not speak one reassuring syllable.

He cleared his throat. "If it feels rushed, we can have a long engagement, as long as you want. I know you want to set up your own assayer's office, and there's your mother to think about. I don't want you to give up anything, so if you need time, I understand, but tell me that you want a future with me." He sucked in a breath. "I'm just a simple cowboy, and I know that's not much to offer, but I promise I will love you forever, Shelby. Tell me that you love me, too."

The wind carried the sounds of Christmas music and laughter. Maybe he'd been wrong, misread her heart and mistakenly equated her feelings with his. Suddenly he felt cold, foolish. He got to his feet.

"I, uh…"

She leaped into his arms. Astonished, he lifted her off her feet as she pressed her face to his.

"You know what, Barrett Thorn?" she said, cheeks rosy and eyes glittering.

"What?" he breathed, experiencing an upwelling of hope.

"I would be honored to be the wife of a simple, pickle-making cowboy. I love you."

Jubilation filled his soul and he knew Bree would be happy, too, that he had found another remarkable woman to love. He kissed Shelby long and slow.

She giggled. "Are you sure you're going to be able

to handle it when I beat you at checkers during family game night, cowboy?"

"I'll never surrender," he said, laughing. Then he swept her closer and kissed her properly.

Cowboy-style.

* * * * *

HOLIDAY SECRETS

Susan Sleeman

For all the families waiting for their prodigal son
or daughter to return home.

Acknowledgments

A special thank-you to Amanda Williams
for naming Kendall's horse Beauty.
To Leslie McKee for naming Gavin's horse Lightning.
And to Lizzi Rizzi for naming Lexie's horse Misty.
Your help was greatly appreciated!

Then you will know that I am the Lord;
those who hope in Me will not be disappointed.
—*Isaiah* 49:23

Chapter One

Lexie Grant's father had to pick today, of all days, to come back from the dead.

"Not a word from you in over a month." She glanced at his prop plane rumbling in the distance on the abandoned airstrip, the winds from a blue norther howling across the field. "I thought you had to be dead."

"Why in the world would you think that?" Her father raised his chin in his usual haughty manner.

"Your house and office. They were ransacked. Then you go missing. The sheriff couldn't find you, and he suspected foul play. What else was I supposed to think?" She sighed and wished her father cared enough about her and her fourteen-year-old brother, Adam, to have told them he was leaving town. "Where have you been?"

He stepped closer to the crumbling maintenance building shielding them from the harsh wind racing through the Texas Hill Country. "There's no time to explain. I have another appointment and have to leave."

Right. Leave. He'd left her and Adam to be raised by their mother's sister, Ruth, when their mother died giving birth to Adam. Why should Lexie expect him to stay and give her an explanation?

"So why are you here, then?"

"To give you this." He held out a large manila envelope, his hand trembling.

She watched him for a moment, trying to determine if he was shaking from the twenty-five-degree temperature drop in the last hour or if it was more. He stood strong as usual, but something was off. Maybe something to do with his disappearance.

Thankfully, her fears for his safety had been unfounded, and he was alive. Tears of gratitude sprang to her eyes, surprising her, what with their troubled relationship.

He shook the envelope. "Take it."

She might be glad he was alive, but she wanted nothing from him. Nothing at all. She shoved her hands into her pockets.

"The envelope." He glanced over his shoulder to make a furtive sweep of the area.

"If you're worried that someone is watching us, I should tell you Gavin is coming out here to meet me. He needed to talk to me tonight, too."

"You're meeting your old boyfriend? Here? Tonight?" His voice rose as he cut his gaze over the towering copse of bald cypress trees shadowing the abandoned property.

"Yes," she replied, trying not to think about seeing the man she'd once thought she'd spend the rest of her life with, before he'd bailed on her three years ago.

"He's FBI now... I can't... I have to go." He waved the envelope. "C'mon, take it. Everything you need to know is inside. It's insurance to make sure you're safe."

"Safe? Why wouldn't I be safe?"

He opened his mouth to respond but a rumbling noise sounded from the far side of the field, taking his attention.

A dirt bike burst from the shadows and raced straight for them.

"Gavin?" her father asked.

"No. He's riding over on his horse."

"Take this. Now!" Panic wove through his tone. He shoved the envelope toward her.

She'd never seen the all-knowing doctor this rattled. Should she be afraid, too?

"Now!"

She reached for the envelope. He let go, but she didn't have it in hand. The wind whipped it into the air.

"No!" He charged after the envelope dancing toward his plane.

As a pilot, he could jump in the cockpit and take off anytime he wanted, but he seemed more concerned about getting the envelope.

"Are you coming back or leaving?" she called after him.

He didn't respond. She stepped away from the building to get a better look. He charged ahead, then froze in place, staring at the bike rumbling closer. He suddenly bent to grab the envelope. A gunshot rang out, cutting through the night.

Was it the biker? Was he the one shooting at them?

Her father took off, running toward the plane. The bike veered right, bearing down on him. He'd barely made it a few feet when another shot split the air. Then another. Her father went down.

Dad! No! She opened her mouth to scream.

No. Stop. The shooter will hear you. Maybe come after you.

She clamped a hand over her mouth as panic raced along her nerves. What should she do?

Hide. Yes, hide. Now!

She slipped behind the building. Held her breath. Fought the panic. Her horse Misty, tethered a few feet behind her, nervously shifted. Lexie raced to the mare.

"Shh, girl. Don't give me away." She scrubbed her hand down the mare's velvety nose until she calmed. "What do I do, girl? I can't just leave Dad out there."

But could she do otherwise and not be shot?

She had to try. She couldn't lose him when she'd just gotten him back. She was an ER nurse, after all, and she was sure she could help.

Hoping the shooter hadn't seen her, Lexie left the horse behind and peeked around the corner. The biker roared close and came to a stop ten feet from her father. The biker sat there, his gun outstretched, his bike idling. Her father didn't move.

"Stupid old man," the biker yelled as he dismounted.

Gun waving, he strode toward her father.

Was he going to shoot her dad again? Should she intervene or would he shoot her, too?

She had to do something, but if she died, she'd be of no help to anyone. So she had to be careful. Smart. Assess the situation before acting.

She crept around the back of the building. *Good.* Dark shadows clung to the crumbling siding. She eased through the inky blackness. Not only did she have an improved view of the action now, but she would also have a better chance to offer aid if the opportunity presented itself.

The bike's engine cut out and died, but the dying motor only stopped the biker for a second as he paused to look back. He shrugged and continued walking, holding out his gun in a gloved hand. He poked her father's side with a pointy boot. Her father's tortured moan rose into the stark night.

Yes! He's alive!

"Stupid, stupid man," the gunman said. "Running when bullets were flying."

The shooter was tall. Over six feet. Thin. Lexie searched the darkness for his face, but his tinted helmet hid his features. She'd never heard his voice before, but he had a deep Southern accent, so he could be from around their rural Texas county.

He kicked her father again. "You didn't actually think I'd let you meet with the head of the syndicate today, did you?"

The syndicate? Her dad mumbled something, but she couldn't make out his response. She desperately wanted to know what type of trouble her father had gotten into. Even more, she wanted this man to take off so she could tend to her father's injuries.

"You should have known I'd never let you bring me down," the shooter continued. "Not when I'm facing three strikes. I'm not going to prison again and never coming out. You're a smart man. How come you don't know by now that I'm smarter than you? That I'd hunt you down?"

A sick laugh rolled from his mouth and he moved closer.

Lexie held her breath. Waited for a fatal shot to sound.

Instead, the gunman jerked the envelope from her

dad's hand and peered around. "So, who's meeting you here tonight?"

Lexie strained to hear the answer.

"No one," her father said, his tone weak and wavering. If she didn't get to him soon, he might not make it. "Was just hiding the envelope. That's all. I swear."

The shooter bent down and pressed the gun against her father's forehead.

Lexie almost gasped but caught herself in time.

The shooter waved the envelope in her father's face. "Thanks for this. I also have the copy you left with your attorney in Mexico. You should never have given him the information. Now he's dead."

"No."

"Yes." His voice was calm, like committing murder was an everyday occurrence for him. "You obviously planned to hand this over to someone tonight. Who?"

"No one," her father insisted.

"Not even your precious Lexie?"

Wait—the shooter knew her name? Knew who she was? Did he know her father was meeting her here? Would he come after her next?

Her heart stammered and panic ricocheted through her.

"Well, old man?" he demanded. "Lexie. Is she meeting you here?"

"No. I was hiding it. In the building. Would've called her later. Told her where to find it." Her father's voice was growing weaker, blood loss likely taking his strength. She hated seeing him in this situation, suffering at the gunman's hand, but she appreciated his effort to distract the shooter from learning she was there.

A noise sounded from across the field. She listened.

Heard a horse trotting. *Gavin?* Or was it just wishful thinking?

The gunman spun. "So, you were meeting someone, after all. No worries. I'll be long gone by the time the horse reaches us."

He shoved his hand into his pocket and came out holding a cell phone. He pressed his thumb to it, the phone coming alive and illuminating his face shield. She squinted to get a better look at his face, but the light reflected against the shield.

"I'm assuming you have another copy of these documents on the plane. Well, buh-bye, plane." He tapped his phone.

The plane erupted in a ball of fire. The ground beneath her feet rumbled in concussive waves. Fragments of the plane flew through the air and hit the dusty ground. A rush of heat washed over her face even at this distance.

She stared in stunned disbelief. Just who was this guy and how was he involved with her father?

"See how much you underestimated me," he shouted. "And don't think I believe you when you say you didn't give this information to your daughter. I won't rest until I'm sure she doesn't have it. Even if that means she has to die, too." He laughed, the sound high and maniacal, his craziness sending her fear skyrocketing.

He was willing to kill her father, so what would he do if he spotted her?

Horse hooves thundered on the open field.

Please let it be Gavin. As a former local deputy and now an FBI agent in Houston, he'd be armed and know what to do—how to save them.

Are You there, God? Listening? Please don't let this psycho fire on him, too.

The shooter mounted the bike. Kicked the engine awake then screeched to a start and roared forward, stopping to take a final shot at her father. The gun report sounded like thunder.

No. Oh, please, no. Had he done the unthinkable and killed her father?

Her head swam. Her leg muscles turned to mush. She grabbed the wall to keep from dropping to the ground.

Breathe deep. Keep it together.

The biker laughed again then shifted his bike into high speed, passing right in front of her. She held her breath so even the tiniest movement didn't give her away. The whoosh of wind from the cycle blasted her face and heavy fumes irritated her nose. He glanced her way. The gun lifting.

Had he seen her? She couldn't be sure and remained frozen in place.

When he moved out of sight, she ran for her dad. Knelt beside him. Spotted gaping chest and stomach wounds.

For a moment, all of her medical training and experience as a trauma nurse fled and panic won out. Her pulse skyrocketed. She felt woozy. Like she might collapse. She wanted to give in. To forget her father lay in front of her with wounds only a skilled surgeon could treat.

"Dad... I..." She didn't know how to continue as blood oozed from his body. If she'd listened to the many times he'd nagged her about becoming a doctor, she could help, but with his extensive injuries, only a doctor could save him now.

He moaned.

She let her gaze flick over the area. Searching for what, she didn't know. Maybe she was just avoiding the obvious.

Cut it out. He needs you to be strong. To think. Get it together.

She ripped off her favorite Christmas scarf, wadded it into a ball and pressed it against the most critical wound. Blood saturated the cashmere in moments and she suspected an equal amount of blood spurted from his back, too.

Please, she begged. *Don't let him die.*

"Lexie," he muttered, his voice not more than a whisper.

"Shh." She bent forward. "Don't try to talk."

He struggled to breathe, his chest barely moving. "Be careful…dangerous. He took it. Your insurance. I should have…couldn't…my reputation. Legacy. He'll come after you, Lexie. He'll kill you…"

Gunshots. Lexie.

Gavin McKade cleared the tree line to see a fireball rising into the sky over an airplane torn in pieces and a dirt bike racing away from the maintenance shed.

Had Lexie given up on him because he was late and boarded the plane to go somewhere? Or were the gunshots directed at her and she'd been shot?

Dear God, don't let me be too late. Don't let Lexie be on that plane.

He jerked his unruly stallion's reins to keep him from bolting and searched for any sign of Lexie. He would call out, but with shots fired, he wasn't about to draw more attention to himself than Lightning's pummeling hooves might have already done.

Was she by the shed or in the plane?

He'd check the plane first. He kicked Lightning into motion. They tore across the open field, the biting wind hitting him full-on and carrying heavy black smoke in his direction. The heat soon forced him to pull up.

Dancing flames illuminated fragments of the plane lying scattered around. No one could have survived the fiery explosion. If she was in there— No, he wouldn't go there. Not until he checked by the shed.

He whipped Lightning around and took off. Nearing the shed, he spotted someone on the ground. Someone moving. Small. Slight. A woman. Leaning over another person. Performing CPR.

He threw caution to the wind and shouted, "Lexie!"

"Gavin!" she screamed. "Hurry."

Thank You, God, he prayed, though he had no idea if God heard him. After shooting Emily, Gavin had been hard-pressed to trust in his faith.

Gavin pushed Lightning into a gallop, the stallion's breath coming in hard puffs as he quickly closed the distance between them. To be safe, he drew his weapon as he dismounted.

"Lexie," he said, afraid he was wrong, that she'd turn, it wouldn't be her, and he'd learn she'd perished in the explosion.

She looked up from doing CPR on a man.

It *was* Lexie. His Lexie. No…not his. Not anymore. He let out a slow breath of relief. "Are you okay?"

She stopped her compressions, held up blood-covered hands and peered down at the man lying in front of her.

"It's Dad. He…he's gone." A sob tore from her throat. "Gunshot wounds. I saw it all. He tried to give me an envelope and the guy shot him twice. Then took off. I tried to help Dad and failed."

"Oh, sugar, I'm so sorry." Gavin didn't think of the years that had passed...of the turmoil when they'd broken up. Instead, acting on pure instinct, he dropped down beside her and drew her into his arms. She snuggled tight against him, and he cradled her head against his chest as her body heaved with pain-filled sobs.

She needed his comfort, and he was only too happy to hold her, but with the shooting, he had to keep his gaze roving the area, just in case the killer hadn't really taken off.

He gently pushed back and gazed at her. "You said the shooter was gone."

"He took off on a dirt bike."

That explained the bike he'd seen.

"This can't be happening. Not really. Can it?" She suddenly grabbed Gavin's arm. "The killer can't get away with this. We have to go after him."

"He's long gone by now and we won't catch him on horseback." Gavin dug out his phone. "But I'll call Dad to get an alert out on the bike. Can you describe it?"

"Black, I think, but I'm not positive. Dark colored, anyway."

"Did it have a license plate?"

"I don't know. I was too afraid. I'm sorry." She wiped away her tears. "But the rider wore a leather jacket and pants. He was over six feet. Thin."

Without a better description of the bike, the odds were bad that they'd find the guy. Especially when a dirt bike could travel off-road.

"And the plane exploding?" Gavin asked. "Did the shooter have something to do with that, too?"

She nodded. "He used his phone to detonate it. Thank goodness Dad was flying his own plane and was alone."

"I'll want more details, but first I'll get that alert issued." Gavin dialed his father, Lake County sheriff Walt McKade, but stepped away from Lexie so he could speak freely about her father. He also didn't want her to learn that conversations with his dad were still tension-filled. No sense in adding to her stress.

As his phone rang, he kept her in view while also watching for any signs the shooter might have returned.

"Sheriff McKade," Gavin's dad answered with his usual confidence.

Just hearing his father's voice made him cringe, but he swallowed down his unease. "It's Gavin. There's been an explosion and shooting at the old airstrip on Engles ranch."

"I know about the explosion. Just got a 9-1-1 call from neighbors…but how do you know about it?"

"I'm in town for a few days."

"First I'm hearing about it," he grumbled. "And you just happened to be out at the airstrip when all of this goes down?"

"I'll explain that later," Gavin said. "For now, you need to know Dr. Grant's been fatally shot."

"Well, I'll be." His words were slow and drawn out in his thick drawl. "Here we all thought he was dead and now he turns up only to be murdered."

"Lexie's here, and she saw the whole thing. The shooter took off. Heading east on a dirt bike. She thinks it's black but she's not positive. He's been gone about five minutes or so. I thought you'd like to issue an alert ASAP."

"You got that right. I'll take care of it and head out there to get started on the investigation."

Great. The moment his dad arrived, he would demand to know Gavin's reasons for being in town.

He didn't have the authority to divulge that, yesterday, Dr. Grant had become a person of interest in a major health-care fraud investigation, and that Gavin had arrived to try to track him down.

"And before you try to claim jurisdiction on the murder…" his dad continued. "You know the ball's in my court, not you Feds."

Gavin stifled a groan. As far as he knew, his dad's only experience with the FBI was watching TV shows and movies that often got things wrong. Murder investigations didn't top the Bureau's priorities, and the Feds rarely involved themselves in a case without being invited.

"No worries there," Gavin said.

"I'll be there in less than ten." His dad disconnected the call.

Gavin returned to Lexie, who hadn't moved, her gaze fixed on her father. Gavin squatted next to her and told her softly, "Dad's on his way."

She sighed. "I suppose now would be a good time for you to tell me why you wanted to see me."

Though it was no longer necessary to locate her father, Gavin would still need to interview her and serve the warrant to search her father's office and home. Obviously, there was no point in the FBI filing charges against a deceased person, but his records could contain information about other doctors involved in the fraud. Still, nothing needed to be done tonight, and he'd hold off on upsetting her until after she'd gotten some rest.

"That can wait," he said.

She shook her head in wide sorrowful arcs. "You

sound like my father. You both had these big things you needed to talk to me about. Turns out, he only wanted to give me that envelope. He tried, but it was so weird."

"Weird in what way?"

"He was acting totally out of character. All jittery and afraid. Clearly, he had a right to be. The shooter was creepy and not at all concerned about committing murder." She blew out an unsteady breath. "He said this would be his third strike, and he wasn't going back to prison. He also took the envelope and said he'd killed Dad's attorney in Mexico because Dad gave him the same information."

So Dr. Grant had been hiding out in Mexico this last month. But why? "Did the shooter mention what the envelope contained?"

She shook her head. "He did say he was part of some syndicate. Said Dad was meeting with the head honcho today, and the killer wasn't going to let that happen."

Gavin nodded but didn't speak. Dr. Grant wasn't the only doctor in the fraud investigation. Gavin hadn't yet found a connection between the doctors, but he supposed it was possible they could have formed a syndicate and this murder was related.

"And there's more," she said. "The killer knew my name. Called me Dad's *precious Lexie*. Which means he didn't know Dad very well as I wasn't precious to him. Maybe once. When Mom was alive."

Gavin had hoped she'd reconciled with her father in the past few years, but clearly she'd still had issues with him. And now, thanks to her father, a killer knew her name.

Gavin didn't like it. Not one bit. He didn't want the

killer to know anything about her. "In what context did he mention you?"

"He asked if Dad gave me the information, too. Dad said no, but the killer didn't believe him. Dad warned me before he died that this guy is dangerous, and he'll come after me. Kill me, too."

"Kill you?" Gavin's voice shot up, spooking Lexie and Lightning. He lowered his voice. "Do you have the information he's worried about?"

"I don't know what was in that envelope and Dad didn't give me anything else. But now that we know someone is looking for information, it makes sense that his office and house were ransacked." She turned her big-eyed gaze to him. "What if the killer spotted me as he was leaving? If he did, he knows I saw him commit murder." She shuddered. "Do you think he'll come after me? Try to kill me, too?"

"I won't let that happen, sugar. I promise." Gavin wrapped an arm around her shoulders to help allay her fear, but his emotions were a different story.

If this man had killed once, he wouldn't hesitate to do so again, and now he had Lexie in his sights.

Chapter Two

Lexie didn't know what to think. To feel. After Gavin's father arrived, he'd escorted her to the main road where she now sat sideways in the front of Sheriff McKade's patrol car, her feet planted on the asphalt as she waited to give her statement. She caught a glimpse in the distance of tall lights, their halos standing like beacons in the night over the plane wreckage, another set near her father's body, warning all who came close of the horrific sight.

And it had been horrific. There was no question. Even for a trauma nurse. Seeing the once-solid plane in tiny bits scattered around the area. Seeing her father gunned down. Worse than horrific.

She shuddered and stared at her blood-caked hands. Her father's blood. He'd lain in front of her, his life floating away, his eyes going blank and glazed. She'd seen death before. Of course she had. Many times in the ER. Always feeling sad for a life lost coupled with a bit of second-guessing as she ran the trauma through her brain to make sure they'd handled it right.

But tonight? What did she feel now?

Something, that was for sure, but it was hard to put a finger on her emotions. She definitely didn't feel the deep, split-your-insides-open anguish she'd experienced when her mother had died. So was it guilt for not being able to save her dad? Maybe. Actually, now that she took the time to think about it, she felt numb. Cold inside and out. Alone. So alone.

Where are You again, God? Why take someone else from my life? From Adam's life? Am I this undeserving of love?

Why was she even asking at this point in life? Nothing changed.

She wrapped her arms around her body and ran her hands up and down her arms to ward off the howling wind. Earlier, she'd tried closing the car door, but claustrophobia had set in and she'd had to open it again.

The sound of boots stomping across the road brought her head up in time to catch Sheriff McKade marching over to Gavin.

Gavin. What did she do about him? She'd been relieved to see him when he'd arrived. Practically thrown herself into his arms. But now what? Was *he* the reason for her numbness?

She shifted to get a better look at the pair. They stood strong, staring across the road, backs to her with hands on their waists in identical stances. They were both over six feet. Both had a head of thick, black hair, though she knew gray strands that had grown in numbers over the years intricately laced the sheriff's.

Gavin suddenly crossed his arms and spun. His dark gaze landed on her and that familiar, angry frustration with his dad lingered in his eyes. Walt turned, as well.

They spit a few more sentences at each other and Gavin suddenly stormed in her direction.

Lexie sighed. Nothing had changed. The same old Gavin, and the same reason he'd left town. Left *her*.

Gavin was the firstborn in a family of four siblings, and his father held his son to lofty standards that no one could live up to. Still, Gavin had wanted a career in law enforcement and the only option without leaving Lost Creek was to work as a deputy for his dad. He'd tried to make a go as a deputy for years. Really tried. Even if it meant he wasn't always happy.

Then one day he'd disagreed with direct orders from his father on how to handle a domestic disturbance. Walt had wanted to sit back and wait for things to play out. Not Gavin. He was more of a "take action and sort things out later" kind of guy. Fearing for the wife's safety, he'd stepped in. Tensions escalated and he'd ended up in a shoot-out with the husband, catching his wife in the cross fire. Emily had survived, and Gavin wasn't hurt, but from that day on, his father no longer trusted him.

No matter how hard Gavin worked to right things between them, he failed and couldn't continue to work with his father. His only choice was to leave town. At least, that was what he'd thought. Lexie still didn't agree.

Didn't matter now, though. She'd had enough of her pity party and it was time to shake it off. To go on. For Adam. Her brother needed her.

Gavin continued toward her, his strides long and powerful, his gaze focused.

Why was he in town, anyway? If it was solely to talk to her, why wouldn't he just tell her what he wanted to discuss? Why the big mystery?

Gavin stopped before her and squatted down.

How many times had she gazed into Gavin's rich brown eyes and known he was the man she'd wanted to marry? He'd dashed that dream when he'd moved away and left her behind without a second thought.

"Dad will take your statement," he finally said. "I was hoping to put it off till tomorrow, but he refused. So I wanted to see if you needed anything, and I'll take care of it while he's talking to you."

For a moment, he worked the muscles in his jaw then forced a smile. The left side tipped up just a fraction higher, a quirk that never failed to make Lexie's heart skip a beat.

"I could get some water for you," he offered. "A blanket. Or maybe I could call your aunt Ruth."

"Ruth? No. She's on a much-needed vacation, and I don't want to burden her with this until she gets back in a few days. But I do need to tell Adam about Dad." Lexie saw Walt approaching. "I'll give my statement to your dad and get going."

Gavin crossed his arms and gave her a steely look. "You're not going anywhere alone until this killer is caught."

"So you really *do* think he'll be coming after me," she said, letting her fear usurp her unease over his sudden bossiness.

"Yes," he said, but his narrowed gaze told her that he didn't like admitting it. "I'll drive you home, and make sure you have a protective detail. I can help you tell Adam, too."

No way she wanted Gavin to talk to Adam. The two of them had formed a strong bond and Gavin had destroyed the kid when he'd moved away. She'd have to tell Adam he'd lost his father. Why add the unease of talking to Gavin?

"I'm glad for the protection," she said. "But I'll deal with Adam on my own."

Walt arrived before them and slapped his hat on his head as he peered at Gavin. "Our first priority is to keep little Lexie safe. Since Ruth is in Florida, I planned to bring Lexie back to the ranch when I finish up here. I'll send a deputy to get Adam, too."

Lexie disliked it when he called her "little Lexie" and when he talked about her as if she was a child. It came across as demeaning, even though she knew he didn't mean it that way. He was just referring to her barely over five-foot height compared to his children, most of them six feet or more.

"I'm not letting Lexie out of my sight until I'm sure she has a strong detail assigned to her care," Gavin said. "Not with the threat the shooter made—and we have no way of knowing if he saw her. If he did, well…"

His worried tone sent her heart beating faster. "Do you think Adam could be in danger, too?"

"I suppose it's possible," Gavin said. "But I wouldn't expect your father to confide obviously valuable information to a kid. There'd be no point. If I was the killer, I'd focus on you, and then if I struck out, I'd move on to Adam."

"I concur," Walt added. "Especially since your dad has never even lived with Adam and isn't much involved in his life."

They both made valid points. Her father had blamed Adam for the loss of the love of his life. Not a legitimate blame, but her dad had associated Adam with the pain and never bonded with him. He'd also claimed

Lexie resembled her mother and had hardly been able to look at her. He'd promptly moved her and Adam into Aunt Ruth's house, where they'd both lived for the last fourteen years. So when Lexie's heart was shattered by the loss of her mother, she'd lost her father, too. Now she'd lost him for good. Tears threatened again, but she firmed her resolve to keep it together until she was alone.

"Still, we'll take no chances, and we'll watch over Adam, too." Gavin lifted his chin as if daring his father to disagree.

"That we will." The sheriff kept his gaze leveled on Lexie. "So what'll it be, sweetheart? Gavin drives you home or you come to the ranch?"

Even with the simmering tension between her and Gavin, being at Trails End Ranch with this strong law-enforcement family was a safe place while she thought through the implications of all that had happened tonight. Besides, she missed his mother, Winnie, and his grandparents, Jed and Betty. Jed would offer to protect her and both of the women would fuss over her, and right now, she could use a little comfort along with the added protection.

"I rode Misty over here, and I need to get her home and brushed down."

"You can do that at the ranch. 'Sides, Tessa and Kendall would let me have an earful if I didn't bring you home. I won't even put voice to what Winnie would do to me." At the mention of his daughters and wife, a slow smile slid across Walt's lips.

"Tessa and Kendall are both at the ranch?" Gavin asked.

"Not just yet. But seein's how you're in town for

once, I figured we should get the whole family together, so I called them."

"I don't think Lexie wants to get into the middle of all of that." Gavin puffed out his chest, his white dress shirt straining at the buttons.

Irritation shot through her. He'd not only gotten bossy, but he also seemed to think he could make her decisions for her when he had no right.

"I'll be glad to come to the ranch," she said, ignoring Gavin's disappointed look. "But I want to be sure no one tells Adam about Dad. I want to do it."

"Matt's on duty," Walt said, mentioning Gavin's younger brother. "I'll assign him to pick Adam up. Matt'll keep it on the down low if I tell him to."

Gavin took a sharp intake of air through his nose, his nostrils flaring. He couldn't have missed his dad's less-than-subtle message that at least one son listened to him.

Gavin turned to Lexie. "I'll round up our horses and we can ride over together."

"Little late to be riding, isn't it?" Walt asked.

"We both got here just fine on horseback. We can get home the same way." Gavin eyed his father for a moment as if challenging him to argue.

Instead, Walt faced Lexie.

Gavin strode off into the dark.

"Stubborn boy," Walt muttered.

"Gavin's thirty-five. Not much of a boy anymore."

Walt scowled at her and pulled a small notebook from his uniform pocket. "I'm guessing you have a horse trailer nearby as you sure as shootin' didn't ride cross-county on your horse."

"My truck and trailer are down by the cutoff at Wheeler's old gas station."

"Then I'll make sure someone escorts you back there at the end of the night and helps you load your horse."

One of the things she liked about Walt McKade was that, behind all his bluster and bravado, he had a compassionate side. Despite being ornery at times and tough on his kids, he was a gentleman through and through, and he'd raised his sons to be fine, responsible men.

"I'm sorry about your father, Lexie," he said, his words filled with earnest compassion.

The soft tone coming from such a tough lawman made it even harder to keep tears in check, but Lexie managed it.

"Thank you," she said.

He stroked his salt-and-pepper mustache for a moment as if trying to decide how to move forward. "S'posin you give me the details of what happened tonight."

She replayed the night, making sure to include every point she could remember, and he recorded them in his notebook.

"Did you know before today that your daddy was back in town?" His pen hovered over the page.

"No. He called after dinner, and that's the soonest I heard about it."

"And he came back just to give you the envelope that was stolen?"

She shrugged. "The plane was on the ground when I got here, so I don't know how long he'd been here. He did say he had another appointment, so who knows how many people he talked to before me, or would have after, if he'd lived." A lump rose to her throat but she swallowed hard. "The shooter mentioned that Dad was going to meet the head of a syndicate."

"Syndicate, huh?" Walt made a production of closing his notebook and stowing it with his pen, then tipping his hat back even farther and leaning on the car door. "A syndicate doesn't on the surface suggest illegal activities, and I'm not at all saying your daddy was involved in something illegal, but being killed in relationship to it is a whole other ball game."

She'd been thinking the same thing—that was, when she could forget the horror of seeing him gunned down and think clearly at all. "All I know is it's not normal for a man to disappear for a month, and when he does resurface, he's killed."

"Agreed. Matt's already working on tracking down the biker." He pursed his lips. "We've secured the area and I've called in the ATF to investigate the explosion."

"ATF?" Lexie asked.

"Bureau of Alcohol, Tobacco, Firearms and Explosives. They investigate bombs and have resources we don't begin to possess and can pinpoint the type of explosion."

"How will that help find Dad's killer?"

"Forensic evidence from the bomb could lead us to where the suspect purchased or stole his supplies. Finding that could then lead us to the suspect."

"And what will your role be?"

"My team will work the murder angle and try to locate this syndicate you mentioned. Since we've already tried to find a lead as to your father's disappearance this past month and failed, I'm not sure how successful we'll be, but I aim to try." He shifted his duty belt. "I'll also come up with a plan to make sure you stay safe, sweetheart."

"I'd appreciate that." Her gaze drifted to Gavin, who

was standing by the horses, his phone to his ear. She couldn't help but wish he would stay in town and hunt down this killer. Despite their differences, with his FBI experience, she'd feel safest if he was the one to protect her.

How crazy was that? He'd walked out on her—left her heart shattered—and here she was, wanting him to protect her. Or was she simply fooling herself? Trying to believe she needed him to keep her safe when in reality she was simply happy to see him again?

Gavin kept Lexie in view as he waited for his supervisor to call back. She still sat in the squad car, but his dad had stepped away. The dome light caught the golden strands of her hair, wavy to her shoulders. Her icy-blue eyes, dark with angst, stared across the field, her arms wrapped around a slender waist. She'd always been a beautiful woman, but it was all he could do not to stare at her and let her know how much simply looking at her impacted him.

Was she thinking about her father or about their past? He suspected both. Man, he wanted to help her through this, but that was the last thing she would want. He'd hurt her in the worst possible way. He'd acted just like her father and put her second in his life.

He hadn't meant for things to end between them, least of all to end so badly. Just like he hadn't meant to shoot Emily, but he had, and she now had a permanent limp thanks to him.

His phone rang. Assistant Special Agent in Charge Zachary Harrison's name flashed on the screen. Gavin quickly answered the call, but took a breath to make sure he displayed the confidence needed for lead agent on the investigation. His first lead. Exactly what he'd planned when he'd taken a series of online business classes so he could be assigned to the white-collar crimes unit, a division with great potential for advancement. Sure, Harrison had made Gavin lead agent on this investigation because of his connection to Lost Creek, but he still felt the need to prove himself.

He quickly and succinctly explained the latest developments with Dr. Grant. "A syndicate could mean the doctors on our list are connected."

"I concur," Harrison replied.

"I want to remain in Lost Creek and work with County on the murder investigation. I have the feeling it ties in with the other doctors involved in the Medicaid scam."

"You could be right," Harrison said. "Your connections could very well pay off for us. Making you lead might just be the smartest move I've made all week."

"If you remember, my dad and I don't see eye to eye on investigative protocols, so my working with him isn't as certain as you think."

"Still, he's your father and, from what you've told me, he's a good sheriff. He'd be a fool to reject our help."

"Did I mention he's stubborn?"

"Then the apple doesn't fall far from the tree." Harrison chuckled.

Gavin wouldn't discuss the point further. One way or another he'd find a way to get his dad on his side. Since the job was all he had in his life right now, it was imperative that he advance, and that wouldn't happen if he failed on this investigation. "I'll need to fill in my dad and his investigator on the Medicaid case."

"Go ahead. Who knows? Maybe working a joint investigation with your father is just the thing you need to learn how to let go of controlling every little thing around you. It could even improve your teamwork."

In Gavin's last evaluation, his skills and abilities received high marks. But being a team player? Not so much. His fault totally. He compensated for shooting Emily by controlling everything and didn't trust others. If he ever hoped to advance, he needed to change. He'd known it for some time, but hadn't found a way to do so.

"Anything else?" Harrison asked.

"With Dr. Graves's death, I think his daughter would be more apt to cooperate if I share her father's suspected Medicaid fraud."

"Keep the information superficial, and I'm okay with that."

Gavin agreed and ended the call by promising to keep Harrison apprised of the situation.

He stowed his phone then grabbed Misty and Lightning's reins and led the pair across the field.

Lexie flipped up her faux-fur-trimmed hood and started toward him. She wore the same worn red cowboy boots she'd owned for years. Man, he'd loved to tease her about those boots. Her feet were tiny, and she'd had to buy them in the children's department. Despite the circumstances, he smiled.

She took Misty's reins. "Looks like you think something's funny."

"Your boots."

She shot him a look, but frustration quickly melted into an impish smile that never failed to tug at his heart. "I know you like to make fun of them, but you wouldn't laugh so hard if you knew how much less I pay for my boots than the rest of you do. Besides, I look far less comical in my boots than you do getting ready to mount a horse in your city-slicker pants and shiny shoes."

Gavin grimaced. Right…his shoes. He'd planned to talk to her, take Lightning back to the ranch for a quick brush-down then head for his motel for the night before he ran into his father. Now here he was, looking out of place with all his old wounds raw and on display for Lexie. She'd seen enough of his ongoing issues with his father over the years. Something he wasn't proud of. He was a grown man. Old enough to be a father himself, for crying out loud. He sure should be old enough not to let his father continue to push his buttons. Not something he could change standing here.

"We should get going," he said. "Let me give you a leg up."

Her eyes narrowed for a moment but then she nodded. Misty was getting on in years, so he suspected her agreement was for the mare's well-being, as a shorter person mounting a horse from the ground was hard on the horse.

Gavin hoisted her into the saddle then climbed on Lightning. His shoe slipped in the stirrup and he regretted being so hasty in not changing his attire. He'd regretted it even more when his father eyed his shoes and chuckled.

Lexie set Misty in motion and he directed Lightning to move into position beside her. He kept his head on a swivel, carefully watching the trees dipping in the wind.

Maybe his behavior was overkill, but he'd learned the hard way that things could go sideways in a hurry. He wasn't about to make the same mistake again. Not with Lexie's life in the balance.

Chapter Three

Gavin led Lexie under the wood sign stretching over Trails End's driveway. His ancestors had burned the ranch name and MK brand into the wood that had been erected in 1895 when the ranch was first established. About the time the first McKade had become county sheriff. With minor repairs, it had stood the test of time and always gave Gavin a sense of pride in his family's long history.

They trotted down the familiar drive until the two-story home with a long porch holding strings of garland and colorful Christmas lights came into view. Lights glowed from the lower windows, which meant his family was gathered in the living and dining rooms that faced the front of the house. A patrol car sat at the end of a circular drive—Matt's car, Gavin presumed.

He veered off shy of the house and dismounted at the corral abutting a large barn and stable. "We'll leave the horses here. I'll make sure someone takes care of them."

Gavin thought to help Lexie dismount, but he knew she'd balk, so he secured the reins and they made their way up an incline to the house. They'd barely stepped onto the porch when the door flew open and his mother barreled out like a bronc in a rodeo shoot. She was thin and tall, with leathery skin from time spent outdoors, and had a solid look about her as if she'd sunk her roots into the ground like the mighty cypress trees in the area. She'd always worked the ranch with the hands and kids, and never taken a day off.

"Welcome home, son." Her arms outstretched, she jerked him to her as if he was a rag doll, and he went willingly.

After getting her fill, she set him away and stepped to Lexie. "You poor dear. Come here."

His mother's strong arms swallowed Lexie and she started to cry.

Gavin's heart ached, and he felt like a dolt standing there when he knew if he hadn't moved to Houston, she would be crying on his shoulder, not his mom's. But he didn't have long to dwell on it as his grandmother burst through the door and made a beeline toward him. She wore a gingham top over a T-shirt, and when she pulled him close, she was soft and squishy and smelled of baking spices. She did all the cooking, and he'd never found a better meal than the hearty ones she served up.

"Nana." He hugged her back.

A clap on his shoulder had him pulling back to look into the sharp blue eyes of his granddad's lined face. "About time you got here. S'posin your daddy kept you sitting around all this time."

"Crime scenes take time to process." Gavin was surprised he was defending his father.

His granddad hooked his thumbs in his red suspenders. "In my day, we wouldn't make a little bit of a thing like Lexie wait around. We'd drive her home and have a civil conversation over a cup of coffee."

"Coffee sounds like a good idea." Gavin's mother took Lexie's arm. "We'll settle you and Adam in the dining room by yourselves, and the two of you can take as long as you want."

"Dad will likely have additional questions for Lexie when he gets here," Gavin said.

"Then he'll just have to wait." His mother's jaw firmed, meaning his dad would indeed be kept waiting, as Winnie McKade was the only person with the power to make that happen.

"I'll see to the horses," Granddad said.

"I appreciate that."

"Don't worry so much, Grandson," Nana murmured. "God is faithful and He will work all of this for Lexie's good."

If only Gavin could be certain about that, but he hadn't been certain about anything since Emily had been shot other than needing to leave town. He followed his family into the wide foyer holding a towering Christmas tree filled with handmade ornaments dating back as far as his granddad's childhood.

Lexie glanced back at Gavin and, if he didn't know better, he'd think she was begging him to join her to help break the news to Adam. But Gavin *did* know better. She didn't want his help. She'd made that perfectly clear. Besides, he'd given up the right to sit by her side in good times and bad, and no matter how much he hated seeing her pain, he wasn't a comfort to her now.

He closed the door behind them and headed across the house's original wide-plank floors. Through a wide archway, he saw the other family members settle in front of a roaring fire, the woodsy campfire aroma he loved mingling with the scent of pine.

Matt stepped out to meet Gavin in the foyer. Though an investigator, Matt still worked patrol when needed and was dressed in the department's basic navy patrol uniform. He looked tired and concerned, but had a ready smile.

He gave a light punch to Gavin's arm. "You sure do know how to make an entrance in town, bro."

"I'm surprised to see you here. I'd have thought you'd be out investigating the murder."

"You know Dad. He has to make sure the department is fairly represented. So he'll be in the thick of this one to make sure we don't garner any bad press." Matt frowned, disturbing his pretty-boy face that assured he always had his share of women to date. "And if you must know, I *am* involved. I've been tracking the suspect's dirt bike."

"Any luck with that?" Gavin asked.

"You know Dad wouldn't want me to share investigative details outside the department." A single eyebrow arched, looking so like their dad's mannerism.

Gavin had to work hard not to comment. "And I also know you're going to tell me everything, so why hassle me in the process?"

"I am, am I?"

Truth be told, Gavin wasn't as confident as he'd once been that Matt would spill the beans. His brother had grown up a lot in the last few years. He'd be making a run for sheriff when their dad retired, and Gavin honestly believed Matt, who'd just turned thirty-one, could handle the position.

"Okay, fine," his brother said without further prodding. "There's no harm in telling you that ATF investigators arrived on scene and have taken over. They shooed Tessa away and I hear tell she's hopping mad."

"She had to know it was coming." Gavin imagined their youngest sibling, who was a sworn deputy along with being a top forensic crime scene investigator for the county, facing off with an ATF agent. She was a nurturer at heart, but let anyone threaten her work domain, and she turned into a tiger.

"Knowing is one thing. Having a Fed toss you off the scene in your own county is another."

"Hey, now. It's awfully soon in my homecoming to be bashing the Feds, isn't it?"

Matt frowned. "Dad said you wouldn't tell him why you were in town."

"I'm here on an investigation that involves Dr. Grant."

"For real?"

Gavin nodded. "I cleared it with my supervisor to fill you and Dad in, but you'll have to wait until I get Lexie settled and make sure we've made a protection plan for her and Adam."

"Then in the spirit of cooperation, I can tell you that I located the dirt bike abandoned a few miles from the airfield."

He narrowed his eyes. "How can you be so sure it's the right bike?"

"The envelope with Lexie's name on it was in a saddlebag. Empty, of course."

"She told me the shooter has been incarcerated before. So any prints Tessa lifts should return an ID in the database."

"Don't hold your breath, bro. Lexie also told Dad that the suspect wore gloves. I doubt we'll get prints."

"What about the bike's registration?"

"Bike's not street legal, so no plates, but Kendall's looking up the VIN number as we speak." Their other sister, Kendall, had worked part-time as a deputy for nine years while she'd worked on her degree in information technology and was now a full-time deputy.

"Okay, so say this *is* the bike ridden by our suspect," Gavin said. "No way if he owns the bike that he would abandon it and let us run the title to discover his identity."

"So it's likely stolen, but we haven't had any dirt bikes reported stolen." Matt frowned. "We'll just have to wait on Kendall."

Gavin didn't want to wait. He'd rather log in to the database and get an instant answer. But taking over someone's work was the kind of thing that drove others crazy. He would hold off for a bit, but if they didn't hear from his sister soon, he would take charge and deal with the consequences later. "People around here don't always register new bikes. It could also be secondhand and not registered to begin with."

"Then if the VIN leads nowhere, we'll need another way to find the owner." Matt hooked his thumbs in the corner of his pants' pockets.

His brother might be taking the wait-and-see approach, but Gavin wasn't about to take the laid-back approach. "We need to figure it out ASAP so we're ready to act if needed."

"Whoa. When did you become such an all-fire control freak?" Matt shook his head. "City living, I suppose, but you're back home now. You'll need to learn to relax again or you'll tick people off."

Gavin wouldn't admit the incident with his dad had

changed him. Better to let Matt blame it on the city and move on. "You're running the envelope for DNA, too, right?"

Matt crossed his arms. "We may not be a big, fancy department, but we do know how to investigate a crime."

"I didn't mean it that way, and you know it."

Matt continued to eye him.

"I'm gonna grab a cup of coffee. You want one?" Gavin asked before saying something else to make his brother mad.

"Yeah, sure."

Gavin led the way to the kitchen. He glanced through the dining room's French doors to see Lexie with her arm wrapped around Adam's shoulders. Dark pain lingered in her eyes and cut Gavin to the quick. Adam, the teenager Gavin had come to care for, darted his gaze around the room, as if looking for a way to flee or for help in dealing with his grief.

Lexie met Gavin's gaze and frowned before looking away. He sighed. He hadn't meant to hurt her. He'd asked her to move to Houston with him, but her dad had forbidden her to move Adam out of town. Made no sense. Not when her father had little to do with either of them, but still, he'd had legal custody of Adam. Which meant she'd be stuck in Lost Creek for years. Gavin had suggested a long-distance relationship, but she'd shut him down fast.

Although a part of him wished he could go back and change things, he'd been right to move to Houston. Confirmed it, too, the minute he'd talked to his father tonight. But, no matter what, Gavin wasn't going to flake on her now. He wasn't going anywhere. At least not until he was confident she was safe.

Chapter Four

Lexie tightened her hold on Adam's hand, but he was trying so hard to be a grown-up that he shrugged free and jumped to his feet. He marched across the room and lifted a stuffed Santa Claus from an antique sideboard to stare at it.

"I know Dad has been a loser father," Adam said, "but I can't believe he'd get involved in something illegal."

"We don't know that he broke the law," she said, wishing the same comfort she'd once offered for skinned knees would work for Adam tonight. "Just that he was involved with a syndicate of some sort."

He spun around. "Sounds bad, though, right?"

She got up to join him but shoved her hands in her pockets to keep from reaching out to him. "That's because in our world the word 'syndicate' often refers to a group involved in illegal activities."

Adam's eyes, blue and large like their father's, narrowed. "Yeah. Dad getting shot makes it almost a certainty."

"Perhaps."

He set down the Santa and it toppled to the floor. He stared at it. "What do you think he was mixed up in?"

"I don't know."

"Had to be drugs." He grabbed the Santa Claus and settled it on the shelf with great force.

Due to his grief, she ignored the way he manhandled the keepsake item the McKades had owned for generations. "Why would you say drugs?"

"Dunno. Just sounds likely is all." He chewed on his lower lip. "Do you think I'm in danger, too?"

"I hope not." She played it down so she didn't terrify him more. "Either way, we both need to be extra careful. As of this minute, there'll be no going anywhere without me at your side."

An impish grin lit his face. "Cool. That means no school."

"You wish." She knuckled his head. "I can't have you fall behind."

"But I'll be alone."

"I'll see if Gavin or the sheriff can arrange to have someone go to school with you."

"Gavin. *Pfft.* Why's he even here?" Adam dropped onto the nearest chair, sliding down so far, she thought he'd slip off.

"I don't know, but he can help us, so we have to give him a chance." She couldn't believe she'd not only downplayed their father's actions, but now she was standing up for Gavin. What was next? Welcoming Gavin back into their lives?

No. No way.

"Like you're happy to see him," Adam muttered.

"I was when he came to my aid at the airstrip," she admitted and left it at that. The last thing either of them needed was to get into a heated discussion about Gavin. "Let me see if the sheriff arrived and we're cleared to go home."

"Home?" His voice squeaked. "Is it safe?"

Gone was his bravado. Sitting before her was the little boy she'd held during crazy Texas thunderstorms. Comforted after their beloved pets had died. When he'd gotten his immunizations...and on and on. Her anger flared. How could their father put them in this position? Easy. He thought only of himself.

She squeezed Adam's shoulder. "If Sheriff McKade or Gavin say it's not safe, we won't go there. Okay?"

"But where will we stay?"

"Let me talk to them and we'll figure something out."

She stepped out of the room, closing the door behind her. Walt had returned from the crime scene and he sat with Kendall on the old plaid sofa. Gavin and Matt both leaned against a wall as if they planned to spring into action. His mother and grandparents sat in side chairs, both ladies crocheting.

"Can I speak to you a minute, Sheriff?" Lexie called out as soon as there was a break in the conversation.

She felt Gavin's gaze on her, but she wouldn't make eye contact. His father got up and strode toward her, no questions asked. Gavin pushed off the wall and tagged along. Walt frowned at Gavin, but he held his ground as if he'd been standing up to his father all his life, when in fact all of the McKade siblings tried not to buck Walt's decisions unless it was of utmost importance.

"I told Adam about Dad," she said to them both. "But I didn't want to terrify him, so I didn't share details like Dad's warning. I'd appreciate it if you all kept it to yourselves, too."

"Makes sense," Gavin said. "But he needs to know the suspect is looking for something and will likely come back. And that he might have seen you, too."

"I made sure Adam understands enough to know he needs to be careful. For the most part, he's trying to act tough, but I can tell he's afraid."

Walt offered a kind smile. "Nothing to worry about. Gavin here has insisted on personally seeing you home tonight."

Gavin nodded and met her gaze. "I just want to be sure you're safely settled in, is all."

"Thank you," she said instead of trying to argue when she was so wiped out.

"We've got a deputy stationed outside your house for the night," Walt continued. "Kendall will drive Adam to school in the morning and spend the day with him. After we have a clearer picture of what happened at the scene and have processed any recovered evidence, we'll make a long-term plan."

Her heart dropped. "Do you really think this will go long-term?"

Walt rubbed his forehead lined from hours of working the ranch beneath the hot Texas sun. "Can't rightly say. Not when I don't have enough information."

"Regardless, it's best to be prepared," Gavin said.

She firmed her jaw, something she often felt like her slight stature forced her to do to be taken seriously. "I'd like to be in on all discussions about our protection."

Walt nodded. "Let's plan to meet over lunch here tomorrow. If you have to go anywhere before then, our deputy will follow you. That work for you, sweetheart?"

At his tender tone, she almost lost it. Walt was a hard taskmaster with Gavin, but once she'd started dating

Gavin, Walt had in many ways become the father she'd always wanted. Until Gavin had left. Then she'd made a point of trying not to run into any of the McKades if she could help it.

"Can we meet at one? Adam only has a half day tomorrow, so I'll need to pick him up from school early."

"Kendall can bring him home."

"I know, but I want to try to keep as much of our routine as possible to reduce his turmoil over losing Dad."

"I completely understand," Walt said. "Adam can have lunch in the kitchen with my parents while we talk. Mom will fill him up with her famous Christmas cookies."

Lexie smiled her thanks.

"Are you ready to go?" Gavin asked.

She nodded. "Let me get Adam."

She went to the dining room door and motioned for her brother to join her in the foyer. He started off at a good clip, his untied sneakers slapping on the floor, but then he spotted Gavin and slowed.

Gavin smiled. "Good to see you, bud."

"We're not buds." Adam jerked open the front door and bounded down the stairs.

"Hey, wait up!" Gavin went charging after Adam to grab his arm.

The teen shook it off.

"Look, I get that you're mad at me," Gavin said. "You have every right to be, but I need you to stick close by me or any deputies escorting you. For safety reasons. Can you do that?"

Adam nodded, but his sullen expression remained. "Let's just get going."

"My car is over there." Gavin gestured at his black SUV backed into a small parking area next to the house.

When they were on the road, Lexie glanced over the seat to where Adam glared at the back of Gavin's head.

How had their lives come to this? To the point that she and her little brother were in serious danger? Bad enough that she had to deal with it, but Adam was just a kid.

Adam slammed a fist on his knee and jerked his head toward the window. She caught a glimpse of pain mingling with anger in his eyes. He'd taken the news of their father's death harder than she'd expected, but part of the pain, and she suspected all of the anger, was her fault. Her breakup with Gavin had devastated Adam. He'd lost the male role model that he'd bonded with most. And now he had to deal with the emotions of losing a father who should have been that positive role model in the first place.

Lexie sighed. She would just have to limit Adam's exposure to Gavin to make things easier for him. Just like she needed to limit her own exposure.

Right. Easier said than done when her gaze kept drifting to him. Settling on his broad shoulders and strong jaw. His long, masculine fingers as he rested his hand on the gearshift. And then there was the scent of his woodsy cologne, now mixed with the smell of hay and horses. At their lunch meeting tomorrow, she'd make sure he understood that he didn't owe her anything and that if he wanted to go back to Houston, that was fine with her. But even as the thought popped into her head, she doubted it *was* okay.

"Grrr," she said without thinking.

Gavin glanced at her. "Everything okay?"

"It's nothing." A big, fat nothing that was everything to her at the moment. She followed Adam's lead and peered out the window, too.

The SUV rounded a narrow curve to where she'd parked her truck and trailer. Gavin pulled into the boarded-up gas station. The station had gone out of business when Mr. Engles had closed down his airstrip and barricaded access for vehicles beyond this point in an effort to keep out trespassers.

Gavin angled his vehicle to shine headlights on her truck before shifting into Park.

Exhausted, it took all her strength to push open the door and climb down, but she wouldn't let Adam or Gavin witness her fatigue. It was a good thing Gavin had such a considerate grandfather who'd bedded Misty down at the ranch for the night. Lexie loved her horse, but was glad not to have to take care of her on top of everything else.

Gavin headed straight for her truck. Why, she didn't know, but she didn't have the energy to question him. She opened the SUV's back door for Adam. He slid out, his shoulders sagging, his face downcast.

"I know this is hard." She forced out a smile. "But we'll get through it just like we get through everything else life throws at us. With our faith."

Right. Faith. She felt like a hypocrite. Hers had pretty much been put on the back burner since their mom died, but she didn't want to impact Adam's faith journey by letting him know she had doubts on God's faithfulness, so she put on a good front.

He gave her another sullen look and leaned against the SUV.

She stifled a sigh, something she'd been doing since

he'd become a teenager and spread wings she'd had to clip at times. Aunt Ruth was a great mother figure, but Lexie felt pressure to fulfill her mother's dying wishes. She'd known their father could get wrapped up in his practice and forget everything else, so she'd asked Lexie to make sure Adam was happy and well looked after.

She'd kept that promise and wasn't about to let a killer or even Gavin's attention make her shirk her responsibilities. She dug out her keys and started for the truck. She heard Adam's shoes thumping on the concrete behind her.

Gavin approached the passenger door. He spun around, his gaze intense. "Back to the car. Both of you."

Lexie looked past him to see her truck window shattered and the door standing open.

Her heart racing, she grabbed Adam's arm and dragged him back to the SUV.

Gavin eased forward, his feet crunching over glass. She noted her truck's dome light was out, so the person who'd broken the window had either turned it off or shattered it, as well. Lexie still had her hand on Adam's arm, which shook under her grasp. Stepping closer to him, she slid her arm around his waist. He was nearly six feet tall now and she couldn't place an arm around his shoulders or she'd do so. He started to shrug her off, maybe thinking he needed to be that tough young man again, but then stopped and moved a bit closer.

Gavin drew out his phone and turned on the flashlight app while still balancing his gun. He crept quietly around the truck, shining the beam in the surrounding shrubs and dense foliage. Then he moved to the horse trailer hitched to the back of her truck and peered inside.

He faced them. "Looks like they're gone."

Adam let out a long sigh and pushed free of Lexie's hold.

Gavin holstered his weapon. "I'll take you home, then come back to handle the scene with Dad and Tessa."

"That's fine." Lexie shouldn't let him take over for her, but she didn't want Adam to stand around looking at the destruction. "I picked up a prescription at the pharmacy and need to grab it from the glove box."

"Is that really necessary tonight?"

She nodded, thinking he didn't need to know that the doctor had put Adam on ADD medication.

"Then I need to warn you. The inside of the truck is trashed, and the medication could have been stolen." Adam got in the SUV, and Gavin walked her to the truck. He shone his light inside.

Lexie gasped and forgot all about the prescription. In the bright beam, glass sparkled from the slashed-open seats. The mats had been jerked out and the carpet torn up. The glove box hung open and items she'd stored in the jump seat were scattered across the floor and ground.

Gavin leaned in behind her, focusing his light in the cab. She felt the heat of his body, but forgot even that when the light landed on a piece of paper lying next to a cell phone on the seat.

"That's not my phone." She reached for it.

"Don't touch it," Gavin warned. He focused the light on the paper with its big bold letters and read the message.

"'I want the information. Give it to me before I have to take more drastic actions. Keep this phone with you at all times. I'll call with further instructions.'"

"The killer?" She spun to look at Gavin, finding him

even closer than she thought. She could easily imagine his strong arms going around her right now, offering the comfort he'd so often provided in the past. For that very reason, she pushed him back. "The killer must have seen me and didn't trust that Dad was telling the truth."

"So he thinks your dad gave you the information."

"But what could it be?"

Gavin met her gaze and held it. The dark worry she saw in his eyes told her bad news was coming. "It likely has to do with what I wanted to talk to you about. I came back to town to investigate your father."

"You *what*?"

"I'd hoped to do a better job of telling you, but my team has been investigating health-care fraud and your dad just came on our radar."

"No, I don't believe it." She shook her head hard. "Not Dad. He may not have been a great father, but he would never sink that low."

"I hoped the same thing, Lex, but we have to face facts now. Someone killed him. Someone who's part of a syndicate."

Gavin took her hand, but she couldn't think clearly with him touching her, so she jerked it free.

"It's looking more and more like he was involved with some unsavory people," Gavin continued, his tone deadly serious. "We need to figure out who they are and what they're looking for before they try to kill you, too."

Chapter Five

Gavin stood at the front door to Ruth Paulson's house, staring at its fragrant pine wreath and big red bow while Lexie worked the lock. As soon as she opened the door, Adam bolted inside and up the stairs.

"Thank you for driving us home." Lexie started to close the door.

He reached over her head to plant a hand on the door. "Before I go, I'd like to take a look around to make sure the place is secure."

"I'll agree on one condition." Her gaze locked on his.

"Name it."

"You steer clear of Adam," she said firmly. "He's had enough drama for tonight without having to deal with issues over your abandonment."

Another fist to his heart. He deserved this one, too. He sucked in a breath. Let it out. He had to find a way to forget their past and concentrate on the lives that could be lost if he let emotions make his decisions for him. "I'll have to check the locks on his window."

"Then I'll come with you and run interference. We'll

start there so he can get some sleep." She hooked her jacket on the newel post and marched up the stairs.

At the landing, she tucked her plaid blouse into her jeans and tugged on the thick belt boasting a silver buckle. She was a Texan to the core like most everyone who lived in rural Lake County. Something he'd forgotten since living in the city.

He followed her down the hallway and stepped into Adam's messy room to get to the window. The teen glared at Gavin, who cringed at the walls reverberating with the loud, blaring music coming from Adam's speakers. Gavin wasn't one to judge. He'd been the same as a teen. Man, that seemed like an eternity ago. Still, he wouldn't mind going back to those days when he and his dad were inseparable—his family everything to him.

Stop it. Focus.

Lexie chatted with Adam while Gavin checked the lock. Once finished, he wasted no time leaving the teen alone and then followed Lexie through all five bedrooms on the second floor and the first-floor rooms, tugging at windows and double-checking locks in the rooms with exterior doors. She didn't say a word through the tour, but the moment he finished, she marched to the front door and pulled it open. Clearly, she wanted him gone.

He had no excuse to stay, even more reason to go, but his feet were made of lead and he couldn't step through that door.

She turned to look at him, her gaze pointed.

"I know Ruth always has coffee on hand," he said, grasping for any reason not to leave. "How about I make a fresh pot and we talk?"

"About what?"

He winced at her suspicious tone, but wouldn't back down. "Your father."

She nipped on her lower lip and didn't move an inch. "I do want to know about your investigation, but you have to promise not to bring up anything personal. I'm too exhausted for that."

"I promise."

She led him into the kitchen and opened the back door. Two large German shepherds charged into the house and pawed her legs.

"Well, hello to you, too." She laughed and gave them both big kisses on their heads.

Feeling a bit jealous of the dogs, Gavin sat at the round oak table worn from years of family use. "Nice to see Salt and Pepper are still doing well."

Lexie dumped kibble into two large bowls. "They have the best vet around."

Ruth was a highly respected veterinarian, and she filled the ranch with a menagerie of animals needing homes. She brought many of them home while waiting for someone to adopt them, but they never ended up leaving.

Lexie washed her hands and prepared the coffee in a single-serve machine. He watched her every move. She wasn't what people would call an overly graceful woman. She could be, he supposed, if she didn't often rush head-on into things and stumble in her eagerness. Her father's extreme demands when she was young had taught her to hurry to please him. That was a subject the two of them had often commiserated about in the time they'd been a couple.

The nutty aroma of coffee drifted through the homey kitchen. When the first cup finished, he reached out to take it from her, but she made a point of setting it on the table as if making sure she avoided his touch. She then placed a milk jug and sugar bowl next to it.

"Thank you." The fact that she remembered how he took his coffee only added to his sadness over the end of their relationship. And the way she avoided touching him? Man, that hurt, too.

She went to retrieve the other cup and then sat across the table from him. He opened his mouth to ask how she was doing but then snapped it shut.

She met his gaze. "Go ahead and say it."

"Say what?"

"You forget... I know you like the back of my hand. You were going to say something then stopped."

"It's personal."

"Oh, okay. In that case, never mind." She crossed her arms as if defending herself against him.

He felt like such a jerk for adding to her pain. He wished things could be different, but he'd had to leave town or die a slow death working for his father.

She met his gaze. "So tell me about the investigation into my dad."

"First, you should know that I can only share the barest of details because you don't have clearance to be read in."

"Read in? Fancy talk for a guy from Lost Creek." She frowned. "What with your new way of dressing, I should have expected that, I guess."

"Now who's getting personal?"

"Sorry," she said and sounded like she meant it. "I'll be quiet and listen."

He almost chuckled, as she loved to gab, and he often hadn't been able to get a word in during their conversations. "I'm sure you know that doctors bill charges for Medicaid clients to the government. Your dad had a large number of clients who were legitimate Medicaid patients and billed accordingly. But he also billed for clients we've been tracking for suspicious charges."

She set down her cup and sat forward. "But why would he do that? He didn't need the money. Or, at least, he didn't ever let on that he did."

"He led a pretty lavish lifestyle for a country doc."

"He had a huge inheritance from his family."

"Still, a plane, fancy cars, multiple properties. That all takes money. He could have run through his inheritance long ago."

"If you think that, why didn't you get a warrant to look at his banking records?"

"We tried, but the judge wanted additional information before granting our request. He did approve a warrant for your father's patient files, and I planned to serve his office manager with it tomorrow. But first I wanted to talk to you, as I'd hoped you would know where he was."

"You thought I was covering for him?" She recoiled. "With my relationship with him, how could you even think that?"

"I've been gone for a few years, Lex. I had no idea of your current status."

"He was still the same guy. Never available for Adam. Always slamming my profession whenever I ran into him. Being a nurse still wasn't worthy of the reputation he tried to cultivate. Only a doctor would do." Her voice hitched with emotion. "Even in his last words to me he mentioned his reputation."

"What? You didn't tell us that."

"Honestly, I forgot about it until now. Guess learning someone wants to kill you messes with your thoughts."

"In what context did he bring up his reputation?" he prodded.

"He said the envelope was my insurance and he should have done something, but then his voice fell off and he said, 'My reputation. Legacy.' Like these things stopped him from acting on whatever he was trying to tell me about."

"Legacy's an interesting choice of words."

"Is it?"

"He could have been talking about his inheritance. Or maybe he knew he wasn't going to make it and meant the money he was leaving behind."

"I don't know. I mean…" Tears flooded her eyes, and she looked up at the ceiling.

"I'm sorry, sugar."

"Don't call me that." She leveled her gaze on him. "You have no right."

The vehemence in her tone felt like a physical blow.

"I apologize," he said stiffly. "It's a habit, and I'll do my best not to do it again."

She ran a hand through her hair. "I overreacted. I guess I'm at the end of my rope."

"Maybe we should call it quits for the night," he said, though he really wanted to probe deeper.

"Sounds like a good idea." She raced away as if running from a dangerous foe and faced him at the exit. "Will you be attending the meeting tomorrow?"

"Yes."

She pulled open the door. The wind howled through the opening, but wasn't as frosty as her look. "Then I'll see you there."

He nodded. "Tessa should soon be done processing the phone left in your truck, so someone will stop by with it tonight."

"What? Why?"

"Because you'll need to keep that phone on you at all times in case the person who left it calls."

She clamped a hand over her mouth and her eyes opened wide. "I hadn't really thought about him calling me. Not sure why. I mean, he said he'd call with further instructions."

"You're still in shock from everything that's happened. Just promise me if the phone rings during the night that you'll call me right away and won't go anywhere. Not even with the deputy out front."

"Trust me. If I hear from this creep, I'll call."

With her vehement tone, he had no doubt she'd comply, though he still didn't like leaving her. But what choice did he have?

He exited, each step away from her raising his concern. He almost turned back until he saw his cousin Dylan climb out of the patrol car. Dylan was a top-notch deputy and Gavin could count on him to keep Lexie safe.

Gavin met his cousin at the curb. "I'm glad to see you on duty."

"This's crazy, isn't it?" Dylan settled his hands on his duty belt. "I hate that crimes like these are creeping into the county. Mostly big-city folks moving out here." He held up a hand. "No offense meant at that, bro. You're still one of us."

At least someone still thought of him that way. "You know I have a special interest in keeping Lexie safe, right?"

"Honestly, I wondered. What with your breakup and all, but then I saw you bring her home…" He shrugged.

"Water under the bridge." After seeing Lexie again tonight, Gavin knew their feelings most definitely *weren't* water under the bridge. They couldn't be or they wouldn't react so strongly to every little thing. But Dylan didn't need to know about any of that, so Gavin would keep up the pretense for as long as this investigation lasted.

"You have my cell number, right?" he asked.

Dylan nodded.

"Then call me if anything odd happens. Anything. I mean a cat jaywalks and you call me. Got it?"

Dylan eyed him. "We've been friends from birth, man, but when it comes to my job, my loyalty is to your dad."

"Fine, call him first and then me. 'Sides, you won't report a jaywalking cat to Dad unless you want to be razzed for life." Gavin punched his cousin's arm and stepped toward his vehicle.

He heard Dylan laughing and felt certain if a problem cropped up, he'd get a call.

Back at the ranch, Gavin wasn't surprised to see the family room light burning bright. His mother never went to bed until everyone under her roof was safe and sound in bed, and that meant him if he stayed with them while he was in town. He didn't need to wait to be asked. He knew she would insist, so he grabbed his suitcase and headed up the steps.

As he closed the front door, the wind jostled a tree ornament he'd made in first grade. He stared at the yarn-wrapped frame holding the picture with his gap-toothed smile. He still remembered presenting the package to his mom and dad. Remembered the love glowing in their eyes.

He sighed heavily. How had his life strayed so far from that? Living in a threadbare apartment in the city. Working every waking hour. Filled with emptiness much of the time, which was why he worked until he dropped from exhaustion. He'd wanted to be with his family. Had wanted to be with Lexie and see Adam grow up.

As it turned out, maybe it was a good thing he'd left. With the way shooting an innocent person had caused him to start controlling every little thing in life, he'd hate to think of how he'd treat any woman he was involved with. He'd be a real bear to live with, that was for sure. Lexie didn't deserve that. No woman did.

"Good gravy," his father shouted. "Can't those blasted reporters get anything right?"

Gavin set down his suitcase and joined his parents in time to see his dad turn off the TV then fling the remote at the end of the sofa.

His father tried to make sure the public received accurate facts about his department, but accurate often wasn't sensational, so reporters embellished the facts. Part of his concern was due to his being an elected official, but also because he, like every McKade before him, had great pride in law-enforcement work. Gavin respected that. Respected him as a sheriff. Gavin just couldn't work for him.

His father eyed him. "Lexie get home okay?"

Gavin nodded.

"And you checked the locks?"

He nodded again.

"They were secure?"

The warm nostalgia brought on by the ornament evaporated. "It's all been covered, Dad, so give it a rest."

His mother stood. "Why don't I get the two of you a nice cup of hot cocoa?"

Gavin really wanted to head up to his room, but his lack of visits was hard on his mother, so he smiled and nodded.

"Don't stand there like a guest," his dad said. "Take a seat."

Gavin dropped onto a leather club chair with worn patina. His dad had hit it on the head… He felt like a guest in his own home.

"S'posin while your mom is out of the room, you fill me in on why you're in town."

Gavin had hoped to wait until tomorrow when he wasn't as tired, but he might as well get it over with. He launched into the fraud story. "I read the news reports online about Dr. Grant's disappearance."

His dad planted his hands on his knees. "So you came here thinking your FBI training gave you skills to find the doctor where I failed."

"No. I'm mostly here to serve a warrant for his files, but I also planned to interview people. Not because I didn't think you did a thorough job, but because I'm lead on the investigation and *I* have to do a thorough job."

His dad watched him for a long moment. "Guess I taught you well, then."

"Yes." Gavin meant what he said. His dad was a fine sheriff.

"That why you were at the airstrip?"

"When I called Lexie, she said she would rather not be seen with me in town. She didn't want to deal with gossip about our breakup again."

"Makes sense, I suppose. What with the way gossip travels faster than that feisty stallion of yours. So what are your plans now?"

"I'll still serve the warrant tomorrow, and I was hoping to work with you on the murder investigation." Gavin held up his hand before his father could say a word. "Your investigation. Not mine. But we share information and keep each other in the loop about what we learn."

"Sounds reasonable."

Gavin had to work hard to keep his mouth from falling open. "Do you want to talk now about how we'll handle disagreements about procedure?"

"No need to talk about it. It's my county. My case. My way."

Right. He hadn't changed.

His mother joined them with a tray of steaming hot mugs and decorated sugar cookies. Gavin had meant to chug his cocoa once it was cool and head upstairs, but he never could resist Nana's Christmas cookies. He grabbed a bright yellow star and devoured it, then polished off a few more.

"Don't you eat in Houston?" his dad asked.

"No one makes cookies like Nana." Gavin resisted taking another one and blew on his mug to cool it.

"I saw your suitcase in the foyer," his mom said. "Glad I didn't have to convince you to stay."

"Why in the world would you have to convince the boy?" his dad asked.

She shook her head and launched into questions about Gavin's life in Houston. He talked with her on a regular basis, but not with his dad. Gavin figured she updated him, but he still seemed to be staring at Gavin. Not that he turned to check.

Once the cocoa was cool enough, he made quick work of drinking it and then started for the foyer. "I'm beat. See you all in the morning."

His mother came after him and drew him into a tight hug. "I'm so happy to have my firstborn under my roof again."

He peered at her, the guilt eating at his gut. "And I'm happy to see you, Mom. Real happy."

"Since you'll be staying for the unforeseen future, you know I'll make sure there's time for us to talk about everything before you leave, right?"

"I expected as much."

"Then spend some time figuring out how you're going to find your way back home."

Gavin glanced at his dad, who jerked his gaze away as if not wanting to be caught watching. "I'll try, Mom, but you know it takes two. So far I haven't seen a change."

"Don't worry about him. I'm working on him, too. Just worry about yourself."

"Sound advice." He kissed her cheek. "Now, you should get some sleep."

He grabbed his suitcase and ran into his brother, Matt, on the upstairs landing.

"Saw your car out front," Gavin said. "Didn't know you were staying here, too."

"I'm pulling a second shift to help out and needed a fresh uniform to go out on patrol. Would be a waste of time to go home and change. So I took a quick shower to wake up, and Dad lent me one of his."

"Anything new since I left?" Gavin asked, thinking his brother would be more forthcoming than their father.

"Motor bike registration didn't pan out, but we'll get

the word out via local channels and someone's bound to recognize it."

Gavin wished he wasn't so concerned with how laid-back his brother seemed. "Local channels?"

"Dad asked me to talk to the press and give them a picture of the bike." Matt shifted his duty belt higher. "He hates reporters, but if Dad finally does retire like he keeps claiming, I don't have his track record, so developing a relationship with the press is important."

"You're going to make a fine politician, little brother."

Matt's smile evaporated.

"I say something wrong?"

He looked around then lowered his voice. "Not sure I want all the politics. I like being in on the action, but I'm not a pencil pusher."

"But Dad—"

"Doesn't always know what's best for us." Matt crossed his arms over a powerful chest built from hours of pumping iron. "You ought to know that."

"If that's how you feel, then you have to tell him."

"Right," Matt scoffed. "Like he and Mom could handle both their sons not toeing the line."

Great, now Gavin felt bad about this, too. Thanks to his leaving town, his brother couldn't say no to running for sheriff. Should have been Gavin's role, but even if he moved back to town, he felt the same way as Matt. He wasn't a pencil pusher, either. And thank goodness for that, because the world needed men and women to step up now more than ever to hunt down criminals before they hurt good people like Lexie.

Chapter Six

Lexie sat in the school parking lot as she waited for Kendall and Adam to join her. She picked at a sliver of plastic peeling from the steering wheel on the old ranch pickup. Such an old beater. Lexie couldn't rely on the relic of a truck, so she had to get her own truck repaired ASAP. Turned out, she had plenty of time to do that since she wasn't going to work anytime soon. She didn't want this current predicament to follow her to the hospital, so she'd stopped by the ER to talk to her supervisor, who suggested Lexie take leave until everything was all sorted out.

She patted her jeans' pocket for about the zillionth time since leaving home to ensure the burner phone remained there. Having something bulky in her pocket constantly caught her attention when she'd just as soon forget that a criminal, likely a killer, would call. Her. Lexie Grant. A simple nurse in a simple town. Waiting to talk to a killer. Unbelievable.

Kendall stepped out the front door and held up her hand to keep Adam inside. A few moments later, she gestured again and the teen joined her, his gaze fixed on her and not his surroundings. He likely had a crush on Kendall. Tall and slender, the beautiful brunette took after her mother in her mannerisms, her hips swaying as she walked and looking nothing like the tough deputy Lexie knew her to be.

As the duo approached, Lexie pushed open the passenger door, the rusty hinges groaning with age. Adam climbed in, and Kendall poked her head inside.

"How did the morning go?" Lexie asked.

"Uneventful."

"Says you," Adam muttered. "You didn't have to take the math test."

A wide smile found Kendall's lips and she lifted her hand as if planning to pat Adam on the head, but then thought better of it and gestured behind the truck. "Officer Ellison's got you for the drive to the ranch. I have an errand to run, but I'll drop by Trails End this afternoon, and we can catch up."

"Sounds good," Lexie said.

Kendall closed the door and stepped back.

Adam shot Lexie a look. "You said we'd go home right after lunch."

"We were going to, but having deputies with us 24/7 is putting pressure on the sheriff department's schedule. So Walt called this morning to ask if we minded hanging at the ranch where we'll be safe."

"But I have a ton of homework, and my books are at home."

"Then we'll stop home to pick up your books first. Just let me tell Deputy Ellison so he doesn't wonder where we're going."

She quickly informed him of the change and then got the truck on the road with the deputy following.

Adam plugged in his earbuds, his music loud enough for her to hear across the seat. Normally she'd tell him to turn it down, but he'd had enough going on that she let it slide. After all, he wouldn't lose his hearing in the time it took for them to get home.

On the drive, the upcoming lunch invaded her thoughts. She had to admit she was glad for the extra time it would take to get Adam's homework, as it reduced the time she'd spend in Gavin's company. But she also had to admit that she was glad he'd cared enough to check the locks last night. Not that he cared enough to make her a priority and stay together, though. If he had, they'd likely be married now. Have a child on the way or already be parents.

She let herself imagine their life. Their home together. Their children. A happy family that included Adam flourishing with Gavin in the picture.

A loud blare of a train whistle jerked her from the daydream. She saw railroad crossing lights flashing ahead and the arm coming down. It was too late to stop, so she sped up and slipped safely under the arm.

She glanced back to find the deputy's car on the other side of the arm. A moment of fear took purchase, but she tamped it down and slowed to give him time to catch up after the train had passed. She rounded a curve and spotted a car parked on the shoulder. The trunk was open and an infant car seat sat on the ground near a woman resting her head against the rear fender.

Lexie could still hear the train rumbling down the tracks, so she pulled over. When the woman didn't move, Lexie's concern mounted. Was she hurt? Not conscious?

Adam looked up and took out an earbud. "What's going on?"

"A woman with a baby is having car trouble." Lexie shifted into Park. "She's not moving. I'm going to check on them."

"But won't Deputy Ellison do that?" Adam asked.

She told him about the train.

He bit his lip, last night still clearly affecting him. "Maybe we should wait for him."

Lexie unbuckled her belt. "This woman and child could need medical attention, Adam. Don't worry... I'll be fine."

She got out and approached the car, her gaze locked on the unmoving woman.

"Ma'am," Lexie said, but she didn't respond or acknowledge Lexie. "Ma'am?"

No response again, leaving Lexie unsettled. She eased closer when a gust of wind howled down the road, blowing the woman over.

A dummy. She's a dummy. This is a trap.

A rustling sound came from the woods. Lexie spun to see a man wearing a ski mask and black clothing dart out and race toward her. She bolted for her truck, but he launched himself into the air and tackled her. She hit the ground hard, gravel slicing into her cheek. She bucked and fought. Kicking. Twisting.

She heard footsteps racing toward them.

"Leave her alone!" Adam shouted.

"No!" Lexie yelled. "Go back to the car, Adam."

Her abductor faltered for a moment. Just long enough for her to shove him off, and he rolled into the ditch. She scrambled to her feet.

"Run!" she screamed at Adam.

They raced for the truck. She fumbled to get the door open. Saw her abductor lurch to his feet and start for them.

"C'mon, c'mon," she muttered as she finally pulled the latch and jumped inside. Adam hit the seat and jerked the door closed behind him.

"Lock your door," she shouted as she punched her button down in the old truck.

Sirens screamed behind them, coming closer. Had to be Deputy Ellison, but she wouldn't relax. Nor would she take her eyes off her attacker. She shifted the truck into gear, ready to take off if needed.

The masked man fled into the woods. She sighed with relief and slumped against the wheel.

If there were any doubts that the killer was coming back for her, they were long gone.

Her life really was on the line.

Gavin careened his SUV to a stop behind the road-block and jumped out. Multiple patrol cars lined the highway, their lights flashing. Ruth's ratty blue pickup sat behind a sedan parked on the shoulder, but Gavin couldn't see Lexie or Adam.

"Lexie," he shouted as he charged toward the barricade. "Where are you? Lexie, answer me!"

No response. Gavin vaulted the barricade and took off running. Matt stepped in front of him and planted his hands on Gavin's chest to stop him.

"Lexie. Is she—?"

"She's shaken up but fine. So is Adam. They're sitting in my patrol car."

Gavin tried to sidestep Matt to go to her, but his

brother jumped in front of him. "She doesn't need to see you this upset. Take a minute to calm down."

Gavin had to see Lexie to be sure she was okay, but Matt was right. His distress would only serve to raise her anxiety. He took a breath. Then another. Tension flowed out on every exhalation and his heart started beating again. Okay, fine, maybe that was an exaggeration, but when he'd heard about her attack on the ranch scanner, it had *felt* like his heart had stopped dead in his chest.

"Tell me what happened," he demanded.

Matt arched a brow, likely at Gavin's tone, but he quickly filled him in on what had just transpired.

Gavin's fists tightened more with each detail of the chain of events leading up to the man with the ski mask charging after Lexie and then escaping into the woods when reinforcements arrived.

"Any hope of catching this jerk?"

"We have deputies scouring the area, but Ellison heard a car take off from behind the woods."

"You think he had a different getaway car parked on the old logging trail?"

Matt nodded. "No witnesses, of course, as the area isn't inhabited. Makes this a perfect location for an abduction."

"You run the plates on the abandoned car?" Gavin asked.

"It was stolen in Prineville," Matt replied. "I'll look into the vehicle's owners for any possible connection. Also check for any video of the area where it was stolen and talk to any witnesses."

Gavin clapped his brother on the shoulder. "Wouldn't expect any less of you."

Matt gave a firm nod of thanks. "Tessa's on her way, too. Not that there's much here to process."

"The attacker had to know Lexie's schedule if he was lying in wait near her house."

"You think he's been watching her?"

Though Gavin hated the thought of the creep keeping eyes on her, he nodded.

Matt grimaced. "We need to increase our protection detail."

"I got that covered. As soon as I heard the news on the scanner, I decided I'm going to insist on her staying at the ranch with us."

"C'mon, bro. You know Lexie. After her dad's heavy-handed behavior, she's not about to agree to that." Matt eyed him. "You never would have thought to make such a demand before you left town. Houston has changed you."

"Then I'll ask her. Is she free to leave?"

Matt nodded and Gavin pushed past him, not bothering to wait for his brother's permission to step onto his crime scene. Gavin needed proof that Lexie and Adam weren't injured. They both still had a huge part of his heart. If his reaction to hearing about her near abduction told him anything, Lexie claimed a far bigger part than he'd thought when he'd arrived in town yesterday. So how in the world did he handle that while keeping her safe and finding her father's killer?

First step was to remain calm. Let her see that he was capable of taking care of her. That she and her brother wouldn't come to any harm under his watch. The rest he'd have to play by ear.

At the patrol car, he squatted down by the open door. "Are you okay?"

She nodded, but it was wooden and controlled, her hands clasped together in a death grip. Her jeans were torn, revealing bloody scraped knees, and the side of her face was red and raw. The thought of some jerk putting his hands on her sent his anger soaring, but he tamped it down. Seeing how upset she was, he decided he couldn't add to her turmoil right now by suggesting she stay at the ranch with them. He would take her back there for lunch, and then, when she was more relaxed, he'd bring it up.

"If you're ready," he said. "I'll drive you to Trails End."

She kept looking at him, her eyes dark and worried, but a note of defiance also lingered. "I can't leave Ruth's truck sitting alongside the road."

"We can give Matt a key and he'll make sure it's taken to Ruth's place."

"Then how will I get home?"

"I took your truck in for repair and cleaning this morning. It's at Trails End, waiting for you."

She faced Adam. "I need a private word with Gavin. I'll be right back."

Gavin moved out of the way, and she climbed out to step to the rear of the car. "I'm still a little freaked out, so I'm glad for the ride and for Matt taking care of Ruth's truck. Even for you having my truck repaired as long as you give me the bill. But I want to be sure your offer is only for lunch, and you're not going to suggest we stay at the ranch with you all, because that's not happening."

"Not even if it means Adam is safe?" He regretted his words the minute they came out as she closed her eyes and fisted her hands.

He hadn't meant to play into her fear, but she needed to recognize their extreme danger.

Matt stepped up to them. "What about staying in one of the rental cabins?"

"Good idea," Gavin said. "You wouldn't have to be under the same roof as me, but you'd be on a secure property with all of us available to help. With our past relationship, no one would think you'd want to stay anywhere near me."

"The cabin sounds good," she said, but didn't sound convinced.

"Since we're close to Ruth's ranch we can pick up your things right now," he offered, as he wasn't taking any chances that during lunch she'd realize the plan would keep them in close proximity and she'd change her mind.

"It's okay with me." Matt peered at Lexie. "But we'll need your clothes bagged so Tessa can swab them for DNA. I can send the bag with Gavin."

"Is that really necessary?" she asked.

"Whether you like it or not, Lex." Gavin pulled his shoulders back. "You have a killer tracking you. If we can find his DNA on your clothes, we'll be one step closer to putting him behind bars."

Lexie sat next to Adam in the back of Gavin's SUV. Gavin had opened the front door for her, and while she'd been tempted to slide in next to him, she'd needed to be close to her brother. To take his hand and assure him that they would be okay. Not an easy thing to do when she no longer believed it.

What was to stop the killer from tracking her? Was he watching them right now?

She looked out the back window, searching for any vehicle tailing them. Then she remembered with Matt closing the road it would be impossible. But still, the feeling of someone watching didn't go away. She was likely overreacting, but fear did that to a person.

True, she found comfort in Gavin's strong, steady presence and she could choose to focus on that, but then she'd have to think about him more often, and she didn't need another reason to do so.

A patrol car came roaring toward them, lights and siren blaring. She caught sight of Sheriff McKade behind the wheel. If he recognized Gavin's vehicle, he didn't show it by waving or slowing to talk to them.

Adam shivered, and she tightened her grip on his hand. He may be fourteen and want to act all grown up, but he recognized the stakes here just as she did.

"Nothing to be worried about, bud. We're safe."

"Now, sure." His chin quivered. "But then what?"

"Then we'll stay with the McKades, and they'll take care of us."

"At the ranch with him?" He pointed at Gavin's head. "No way."

"We'll have our own cabin."

"But *he'll* still be around."

"You know we all care about you and will do our very best for you," Gavin said.

"Right." Adam rolled his eyes. "Like you actually care about us."

"That was rude, Adam," Lexie said, even though deep down she felt the same way. "It's our safest option right now, and I need you to make the best of it. For me, okay?"

He gave a sullen nod.

"Now, apologize."

"Sorry," he said, but she was sure he didn't mean it.

"I should have asked before we left the pickup behind," Gavin said, obviously ignoring the whole thing. "But do you still have the phone on you?"

She glanced at Adam but he seemed oblivious to their conversation. Still, she was thankful that Gavin was sensitive enough not to call it a burner phone to remind Adam of last night. She patted her pocket to assure him.

"And no calls?"

She shook her head and sat back for the last quarter mile to the ranch she'd called home since her teen years. Staring out the window, she watched the wide-open fields pass by, the many oil pump jacks dipping in rhythm and groaning with the exertion. Her father had inherited a small oil company, Grant Oil, and he'd once traded on his relationship as Ruth's brother-in-law to ask her for the rights to search for oil under her property. Thankfully, Ruth hadn't needed the money to keep the ranch going, unlike so many of their neighbors.

Their corral at the road soon came into view. Four horses grazed in the space where Misty would normally be located this time of day, but her horse was still at the McKade ranch. Lexie couldn't continue to trade on the McKade generosity in caring for and feeding Misty. Ruth's ranch hand would arrive later in the day to tend to the horses, and she'd call him to pick up Misty and schedule overtime with him to do the morning chores, too.

Gavin turned the car onto the winding gravel driveway lined with tall trees, and Lexie sighed out a breath when the familiar ranch house surrounded by Ruth's large flower beds came into view. This home had become a sanctuary after she'd lost her mother and her father had turned his back on them. She wished she could stay here tonight with Adam, but just like she'd asked her brother to do, she'd make the best of things.

They all climbed out and headed up the walkway lined with candy-cane lights. A large nativity set that had been in the family for generations sat by an even bigger manger, adding to Lexie's feeling of security but also reminding her that she hadn't prayed for God's help in many years.

Her pastor had taught her as a child to think of God like a father. A heavenly one, but a father nonetheless. She'd once found that comforting. Until her father's abandonment. Then she'd chalked up her belief in God loving people unconditionally as foolish childhood musings.

So why bother asking Him for something when for all she knew He'd abandoned her, too?

She unlocked the door, and as she pushed it open, she glanced back at Adam. "Though I hope we won't need it, I want you to pack for a few days at least. And grab all of your books so…"

His face blanched and he took a step back.

"What is it?" she asked.

He pointed at the door.

She turned, peered into the family room and gasped.

"No, oh, no…" She backed away, bumping into Adam. "Not here, too."

Chapter Seven

Gavin pushed past the pair to look into the house. Furniture, books and papers were scattered across the floor.

"Back to the car." Gavin drew his gun and hurried them to his SUV while keeping his head on a swivel.

Once settled inside, he dialed his father, who he knew was just down the road. Gavin kept checking out the windows even when his father answered.

Gavin explained their discovery. "I don't know if they're still here, but I won't leave Lexie and Adam in the car alone to clear the house."

"On my way," his dad responded.

Gavin stowed his phone and peered at Lexie. "We'll wait here for Dad to check the house."

"And then what?" Lexie's voice rose sky-high. "Dig through the mess to find things to pack? To find Adam's books?"

Gavin gave Lexie a pointed look then cut his gaze toward the boy sitting wide-eyed beside her, his focus fixed straight ahead.

She clamped a hand over her mouth then dropped it and took Adam's hand. "We're okay. Help is on the way."

He gave her an as-if look and slumped in the seat. Gavin didn't miss the shaking of the boy's knees or the trembling of his chin. When Gavin and Lexie had started dating, Adam had already thought of himself as the man of the family, protecting Ruth and Lexie. Gavin had thought it was cute back then, but now Adam was likely blaming himself for not being up to the task and for being afraid, too.

And on top of it, Gavin had put this kid through so much. He wished he could fix things between them, but he had no idea how.

"The dogs," Adam suddenly cried out. "They didn't meet us at the door."

"I'm sure they're fine," Lexie said, but Gavin heard the underlying doubt in her tone.

Sirens cut through the air and Adam shot forward. He was wound as tight as a penned-up bull.

"That'll be Dad," Gavin said, though it was obvious.

The patrol car pulled up alongside them and his father jumped out, his hand clamped on his holster. Gavin admired his dad for staying in great shape and, for once, had to admit he was happy to see him.

He drew his weapon and signaled for Gavin to stay put as he started for the door. Gavin hated sitting back and waiting, but he had to think of Lexie and Adam. If the intruder was still inside, he could come barreling out of the house. Gavin needed to remain alert.

He released the strap on his holster and rested his hand on the butt of his gun. Time ticked by slowly. Gavin's pulse throbbed in his neck, and not until his father stepped out did he start to breathe normally.

"You two stay here." He crossed over to his father.

He holstered his weapon but, just like Gavin, he

didn't let down his guard. "Found the dogs drugged in the kitchen. They're breathing, but we need to get a vet out here. And the whole place has been ransacked."

Gavin glanced back at the car and found Adam's face plastered to the window. "Lexie and Adam are going to lose it when they see the place, but they'll really freak when they hear about Salt and Pepper."

His dad gave a solemn nod. "Looks like the intruder was looking for information."

"You know," Gavin said, "if the information the killer wants is worth killing over, then I have to think it's valuable and someone else is looking for it, too."

"Possible. At least, we can't rule it out. Once Tessa is done down the road, I'll get her over here to process the scene." He dug out his phone. "Gonna be a long afternoon here."

"We can't leave Lexie and Adam sitting in the car that long, but I don't want to bring them back here later to get their things and risk exposing them to danger."

"Agreed," his father said. "I have booties in the car. We can escort them through the house to minimize contamination, and they can pack a bag."

Gavin nodded. "You take Adam. He's royally mad at me for leaving, so it would be better for you to help him."

"And Lexie isn't?"

"She's mad, all right, but she's older and can handle it better." At least, Gavin hoped that was the case.

Gavin escorted the pair to the house, where his dad waited with a box of booties. After they'd all covered their shoes, his father headed into the house with Adam.

"Ready?" Gavin asked Lexie.

She stepped inside and gasped. Gavin stepped up to

her and took her hand, not caring how she might react to his touch. Her gaze searched his for a long moment, but then she eased closer to him.

"I hate that you have to go through this." He continued to hold tightly to her hand. "If I could take it away, I would in a heartbeat. You know that, right?"

"I know that's who you are. The brave defender who wants to help others in need."

It's more than that—it's you, he thought to say, but kept his mouth shut, as he had no right to tell her that. No right to even be thinking that. Not unless he was going to commit to staying in Lost Creek and hold her hand for a lifetime. Something he just couldn't do.

On the drive to Trails End, Lexie patted the burner phone to confirm she'd moved it to her clean jeans when she'd bagged her other ones for Matt. She rested her head on the seat and closed her eyes. The attack by the roadside weighed heavily on her mind, but even more, she couldn't let go of the pictures of her home, her sanctuary, torn apart.

How was she going to tell Ruth about the dogs and the mess? Thankfully, Dr. Wilson believed Salt and Pepper had been given a mild sedative and would be fine. Just to be sure, he'd taken them to his practice so his staff could keep an eye on them. Lexie had thought to call Ruth, but she wasn't about to ruin her aunt's vacation. There was nothing she could do here, anyway, and hopefully this would be over before she was due back two days from now.

The car came to a stop and Lexie was surprised to see they'd reached the ranch. Once Tessa had arrived at Ruth's place, Walt had departed, and his car, along with a patrol car, was now parked outside the ranch house. The front door opened and Winnie and Betty stepped out.

Lexie was glad to see them both, but after the recent incidents, she had to force a smile for them. She waited for Adam to join her and tried to put her arm around his back, but he shrugged it off. Something had changed while he'd packed. He'd gone from being afraid to being mad. Once they were alone at the cabin, she planned to have a long talk with him.

"Cabin's ready, Gavin," Winnie called out. "Why don't you take Lexie's and Adam's things over there?"

Gavin peered at Lexie and looked like he didn't want to leave her, but she needed him to go. She'd already let him hold her hand, and she could only imagine what more she might allow if he stayed nearby. Maybe hold her. Even kiss her.

A far-too-dangerous temptation for her peace of mind.

"Do you mind?" she asked.

"Not at all." He smiled. "You and Adam go inside, and I'll be back in a jiffy."

Lexie and Adam climbed the stairs.

"C'mon, Adam." Betty opened the front door. "Let's you and I head into the kitchen and have lunch together."

"What are we having?" he asked.

"Beef stew and some lovely rolls I baked this morning. And if after that you still have room, I've set aside a plate of Christmas cookies with your name on them."

He stepped inside and Lexie hoped he could actually eat after everything that had just happened. And she was grateful that Walt had arranged for Adam to eat in the kitchen so he wouldn't have to hear the up-coming discussion.

"Now, what about you?" Winnie asked. "Hungry?"

Lexie shook her head and felt tears pricking her eyes.

Winnie gathered Lexie in a hug and didn't say a word. She had open arms for anyone in need, reminding Lexie of her own mother. A trauma nurse, just like Lexie, her mom's heart had been the size of Texas, and her nurturing spirit had drawn everyone to her. She'd also been a spitfire in the ER. Lexie tried to emulate her mother and hoped she succeeded.

"I'm sorry for everything that's happening, sweet-heart." Winnie pulled back and studied Lexie's face. "I think we'll all rest easier with you staying in a cabin. I heard Gavin pacing at all hours of the night, and I sus-pect he was worrying about you and Adam."

Lexie had to admit it felt good to think he was look-ing out for her again even if she didn't believe he'd stay by her side for the long run, but she wouldn't share that with Winnie. "He was probably up thinking about his investigation."

"Hogwash." She stepped back. "It's plain to see he still cares for you."

"Good gravy, Winnie," Walt called out from inside. "Let little Lexie get in here and close the door before we pay to heat the entire state of Texas."

Winnie shook her head. "You can still join us for lunch in case your appetite returns. And don't forget what I said about Gavin. He does care for you."

Before Lexie could argue more, Winnie led the way to the dining room, where Matt and Walt sat at the table Lexie had dined at nearly every Sunday after she and Gavin had gotten serious.

"Let me get lunch on the table," Winnie said.

"Can I help?" Lexie offered.

"I wouldn't hear of it. Have a seat and I'll be right back." Winnie went through the swinging door to the kitchen.

By the time Lexie sat, Gavin joined them. He went straight for a carafe of coffee.

"Want some?" he asked Lexie.

She nodded.

After he filled a mug to the brim, she cupped her hands around it for warmth and shifted her gaze to Matt. "Anything new in the investigation?"

He nodded. "We located the dirt bike owner. An Odon Walmet. He claims the bike was stolen, but he has a sketchy past that involved extortion."

"And he doesn't have a solid alibi for last night." Walt slid a photo across the table to her. "Could he be your guy?"

She studied the pockmarked face with its scraggly beard and skin toughened from the Texas sun. "I didn't get a look at the killer's face, so I can't say. He looks thin, though, and the shooter was thin. Do you have a full body shot?"

Matt shook his head. "No, but I talked to him and he fits the build you described last night."

"Does he have any connection to my dad?"

"He's a patient, but hasn't seen your father for years." Matt slipped the picture back into the folder. "Since we can't rule him out yet, I'll continue looking into him. If it turns out he's a viable suspect, I'll arrange a voice lineup for you to determine if his voice matches the killer's."

Lexie was about to comment on the lineup, when

Winnie came in and placed a big pot of stew on the table. The savory scent of garlic and onions filled the air and got Lexie's taste buds working again.

"If one of you will ladle out the stew, I'll be right back with rolls Betty just took out of the oven." Winnie didn't wait for a response, but bustled to the kitchen.

Needing to keep busy, Lexie stood and filled Walt's bowl with meat and vegetables covered in rich brown gravy.

"Thank you," he said. "I believe we should focus on figuring out what your daddy was involved in and what was in that envelope to warrant murder."

"I'm hoping the answer can be found in his patient files," Gavin said.

"Since that's the only real motive we have right now for murdering Dr. Grant, I have to concur," Walt said.

Lexie ladled an overflowing scoop of stew into Gavin's bowl. "I was planning to go to Dad's house and office today to look at his records."

"You can still go, but I'll be escorting you." Gavin's tone was unyielding.

She paused, ladle midair, to study him. Had Gavin always been bossy and controlling like her daddy—like his father—but love had blinded her to it?

No. He'd never pushed her around, and now that it seemed to be a big part of his personality, she didn't like it. Not one bit. But she wasn't a fool. She wanted to be safe and wouldn't argue about being accompanied.

She could and would argue about who did the accompanying, though. "I'm sure you have things you need to do for your investigation. Perhaps Matt or your dad could escort me."

He folded his arms across the broad chest she'd

rested her head against so many times and issued her a nonverbal challenge. "It has to be me."

She wanted to cross her arms, too, but she still held the ladle. "Why?"

"Remember I mentioned the warrant last night? Well, I can't have you going through files that I have legal authority to seize."

Right. The investigation, not her safety, was his priority. Even more reason not to go with him. "But I—"

"Should just agree. We can review the files together. He was your father, and you may notice something I miss."

Her broken heart told her to continue arguing, but logic said it was time to give in. "I didn't really know him any better than you, but I want to see the files, so I guess we'll go together." She grabbed Matt's bowl. "So let's agree on a protection plan for Adam and me, and then we can head over to Dad's house."

Spoon in hand, Walt paused in lifting it to his mouth. "As I mentioned this morning, my resources are tapped out, but with you staying here, that will help."

"I'm thankful you agreed." Gavin's words came out choked and reminded Lexie of Winnie's recent comment.

After their breakup, Lexie had often imagined, maybe even wished, Gavin's suffering equaled or exceeded hers. Now that she could hear his pain, she was sorry for thinking that way. She shouldn't wish him or anyone else emotional distress, and she was ashamed she'd done so.

Winnie stepped into the room with a basket of golden rolls, the smell of warm yeast overpowering the stew. She handed them to Walt, but her gaze roamed between

Gavin and Lexie. She was such an intuitive woman that even if she hadn't been in the room, she noticed the emotions zinging between the two of them.

Oblivious to the undercurrent of tension, Walt helped himself to a roll and passed the basket to Gavin. "I don't want you to think by staying at the ranch that I'm leaving you high and dry. I'll keep a deputy in reserve if needed, and I'll continue to have off-duty deputies who volunteer their time escort Adam to school and spend the day with him." He cleared his throat. "And Matt and I can fill in for short time frames, but each hour we do will take us away from the investigation, so I'd rather curtail that as much as possible."

Lexie spooned her own stew then gave Walt an earnest smile. "I really appreciate all you're doing for us."

"You're practically family, Lexie. I can do no less." He pressed a warm hand over hers.

Practically. The word stuck in her throat and she couldn't respond. She'd been so close to being a McKade. To having this amazing family adopt her through marriage. It would have been so wonderful. Not only for her, but also for Adam. Having such strong men to serve as role models on a daily basis at this vulnerable stage in his development would have been so incredible. Gavin could have been such an important part of Adam's life. If only…

Stop.

It wasn't going to happen. Not now. Not in the future.

"Time to get some of this hearty stew in your stomach." Winnie took Lexie by the shoulder and settled her in the chair. She squeezed her hand before releasing her. "I'll leave you to your discussion, but don't get so caught up that you forget to enjoy your food while it's still warm."

Lexie smiled up at the woman who would have been a wonderful mother-in-law, then quickly turned her attention to the stew to keep her wayward emotions from spiraling out of control. There was no point in thinking about what could have been, as God had made it clear that such a traditional family was out of the question for her right now. Maybe for forever. She just didn't know.

They ate in silence and Lexie suspected they were all thinking about how to proceed after the near abduction and break-in at Ruth's house.

After a few minutes, Matt's spoon clanked on his bowl as he raised his napkin to wipe his mouth. "We can't all look at records, so we should come up with a suspect list to spread the work around. I'd start with guys in the area who have the skills needed to blow up a plane."

"The ATF report said dynamite was used for the charge, which is far too common round these parts to track down," Walt said. "And the device had a simple timer with an action circuit controlled by his phone."

"Can't buy a circuit like that around here, but it can be purchased online and won't narrow down a suspect list," Gavin said. "So we're better off looking at people with explosives experience and a basic knowledge of electrical wiring."

"Good thinking, son," Walt said. "There's Earl Clark over at Clem's Garage. Clark knows about wiring from working on cars. Plus he used to handle demo for an oil company. He also fits the killer's build."

"Know him, Lex?" Matt asked.

She shook her head. "Jose fixes all of our vehicles."

Gavin pulled a small notepad from his pocket and jotted down the name. "We should also consider Norbert and his son Freddie Nash, who live up near the county line. I remember from hauling them in a few times for drug possession that they both have electrical skills. Plus Norbert handled explosives."

"If they're involved, their drug use could indicate a syndicate," Matt said. "Though there's never been any suggestion that these guys are more than low-level users."

"It's common for drug users to escalate and often move into peddling drugs to pay for their habit," Gavin stated, noting the names on his pad.

Matt's gaze turned pensive. "That's true, but is it true in this situation?"

Lexie couldn't believe the direction the discussion had gone. "Surely you don't think my dad was a drug dealer."

"At this point we have to entertain all possible leads," Gavin said. "And illegal drugs can easily mean a syndicate. Plus drugs are always a strong motive for murder."

"Let's not forget Silas Ross," Matt chimed in, changing the focus. "He has a record, too, and last I heard he was still working in explosives with one of the oil companies. I haven't seen him around lately, so maybe he's moved."

Walt nodded. "You know Silas or the Nash men, Lexie?"

She shook her head. "It's great to have names, but why would any of these men want to kill Dad other than a drug connection, which, honestly, I find hard to believe?"

"Well, I'm still thinking the syndicate is related to

the Medicaid fraud," Gavin said. "And the killer somehow learned your dad was using their social security numbers to defraud the government. Maybe more."

"Best way to figure that out is bring them into the office for a little one-on-one." Walt pushed to his feet. "I'll get interviews set up, and if they don't have an alibi for the near abduction and the time of the murder, then I'll press for their connection with Dr. Grant."

"And I'll arrange the voice lineup for Walmet," Matt added and stood, too. "We can do the same thing for the others if their alibis don't pan out."

Walt nodded and turned his attention to Lexie. "If all goes well this afternoon, you could soon be hearing the voice of your father's killer."

Goes well? Lexie shuddered. How could hearing the voice of the man who'd killed her dad be considered a good thing?

Chapter Eight

Gavin dropped the folder on Dr. Grant's desk. He'd been sitting next to Lexie for an hour, reading her father's financial records. He was in his element here. Doing what he'd trained to do. So why was he having to work so hard to focus? Was it the sweet scent of Lexie's vanilla shampoo bringing back so many memories? Or the warmth of her body reminding him of how wonderful it had once felt to hold her? Especially after he'd argued with his father or had a miserable day.

He missed her big-time. He sighed, drawing her attention.

"Mind scooting a little further away?" she asked pointedly.

"Sorry—can't," he replied, though he really wasn't sorry, as he loved being close to her. He'd felt that way since they started dating. "I have to see the records, too."

Her chin went up in her usual attempt to make herself appear taller and more formidable. She obviously felt a need to defend herself like she'd done with her father. Gavin didn't want to be compared to her father. Not ever. But he'd acted like her dad. Moving to Houston.

Susan Sleeman   341

Not talking to her since. Then coming back here and telling her what to do without any regard to her feelings.

But she's in danger.

Not an excuse and he knew it. It was all about his need to take charge and keep his finger on every action in his life to stop bad things from happening.

Look how well that's been working.

She suddenly cleared her throat and pushed back from the desk. "It's clear that Dad wasn't destitute, so maybe this has nothing to do with money at all."

Right, business. They were there to work, nothing personal between them anymore, and he needed to remember that. "Don't be so quick to jump to that conclusion, Lex. These statements are from the last six months, so we have no way of knowing where the money came from without accessing older records."

"But there isn't anything else in his file."

"His bank will have more." Gavin closed the drawer.

"You can't get a warrant for them, though, right?"

"Not at this point, but hopefully I'll find enough information at his office to satisfy the judge."

Lexie's phone rang from her coat pocket and she fished it out. She got a puzzled look on her face, but answered.

"Hello?" A frown soon drew down her very kissable lips.

Don't go there, man.

She picked at a sliver of leather curling up on her father's desk blotter, her frown deepening as she listened. "Thank you, Mike."

Mike? Maybe Mike Alexander, her father's attorney.

"His will," she said, confirming Gavin's suspicion. "Does it contain his burial wishes?"

She pressed the leather back down as if trying to repair it and her life.

"Then I appreciate the call, but honestly, I have no interest in hearing about what Dad wanted to have done with his worldly possessions." She hung up and stowed her phone.

"Mike Alexander?" Gavin asked.

She nodded. "He wanted me to stop by for a reading of the will. He said it was kind of complicated, and I should hear about it sooner rather than later." She turned to peer out the window overlooking a lush lawn. "I haven't even made funeral arrangements yet. I'm not at all ready to hear what Dad wanted done with his stuff."

Gavin thought the will could give them insight into her father's thoughts and maybe his finances, but she was in no frame of mind to be pushed into a reading. He could also request a warrant for the will, but at this juncture, they didn't have enough probable cause for the judge to approve the document.

Hoping the office visit would turn something up, he got up and stacked several boxes filled with records that he planned to take into evidence. "Let me get these boxes out to the car, and then we'll head over to his practice."

Lexie nodded but continued to stare into space, so he carried the first load outside. The crisp northerly wind swept over the area, reminding him that Christmas was just weeks away and he hadn't even considered where he'd be for the holiday. He'd spent the last two years working. His life had taken such a sharp turn away from family and friends. How pitiful was that, and how in the world had he let it happen so easily?

He settled the boxes in his vehicle with a pensive

Susan Sleeman 343

sigh. Had he been wrong in leaving town? Could he have survived under his dad's thumb? No. No way. He shook his head and went back inside.

Lexie jumped, but didn't look up at him.

He desperately wanted to console her, but there was no point in trying to offer comfort when his touch would only make things worse. But, man, what he wouldn't give to have her in his arms one more time.

Shaking off those foolhardy notions, he picked up the final box. "This is the last one, and we should get going, as Helen is waiting for us."

"Helen Byrum," Lexie said as if reminding herself of the name of her father's office manager. "I haven't been to the practice in years, and I can only imagine what Dad told her about why he didn't live with Adam and me."

Not something Gavin thought was a good idea to dwell on. "Let me get this last box in the car and then I'll come back for you."

He quickly departed before she asked about his reasoning and he'd have to tell her that he needed his hands free to go for his gun if necessary. Before returning to the house, he made a quick sweep of the area, checking shadows and blind spots. Convinced there was no immediate danger, he escorted her to the car and got them on the road.

He didn't speak for the entire drive, as after the attempted abduction yesterday, he had to keep his gaze moving over the area and checking the mirrors. Even when they hit Lost Creek, a town he'd always considered safe despite it being the largest city in Lake County, he searched storefronts and vehicles.

Satisfied by what he was seeing, he parked in front

of the office. "I'll come around to open your door. Stay close to me."

She nodded, but looked like she'd swallowed some bitter medicine. Still, she'd listened and remained by his side until they stepped inside the office. Lexie greeted Helen as Gavin turned the door lock behind them and went straight to the blinds to close them.

Though he knew Helen, he displayed his credentials for her. "Are you alone?"

"Yes," she replied.

"You don't mind if I take a look, do you?"

"What's going on?" she asked.

"Let me look around and then I'll explain." Gavin stepped through the open door leading to a hallway with three exam rooms and several offices.

How many times had he as a kid come down this hall to have something stitched up or to get an X-ray for an injured limb from horseback riding or sports? Twice needing a cast, one time suffering a concussion. Now here he was, checking each room and the bathrooms for a killer. Surreal for sure.

On his way back down the hallway, he heard Helen talking about him.

"Seems like he's forgotten all about being one of your dad's patients," she grumbled. "Got to be a big shot in Houston, I guess."

Why was everyone thinking that? He was just doing his job. Sure, maybe he was more formal, more in control, but his job required it.

He stepped into the small waiting area and Helen eyed him through thick glasses. She sat behind the reception desk, her lips puckered. Was this the same woman who'd given him lollipops after his appointments? Maybe she was right. Maybe he was acting too tight-laced for the small-town atmosphere.

"I'm sorry to be so terse, Helen." He smiled amicably. "Is there a place we can all sit down to talk and I can explain?"

"My office." She stood. "Follow me."

She clipped down the hall and they trailed her to the smaller of the two offices. She dropped behind her desk that was neat and organized. Lexie settled in a chair facing the desk.

Gavin remained standing and pulled the warrant from his pocket. "As you can tell, I'm not here on a social visit but official business. I have a warrant authorizing me to seize Dr. Grant's records."

Her thick eyebrows rose above her glasses as she held out her hand for the document. She took her time reviewing it before looking up.

"Do you understand the request?" he asked.

She crossed her arms. "We may be a small office in rural Texas, but this isn't the first court order we've ever received to produce records. What are you looking for?"

"I'm afraid I can't divulge that."

"But you must think Doc did something illegal or you wouldn't have a warrant."

He nodded but said nothing.

"You're not going to tell me because you think I'm in on whatever it is you hope to find."

Again, Gavin couldn't deny it, so he didn't speak.

She looked at Lexie. "You knew about this?"

Lexie nodded.

"Your father's not even in the ground and you can come here demanding such a thing?"

Lexie recoiled. "We hope the files will help us find who killed him."

"But you don't think either of us did anything illegal, do you?"

Lexie shrugged.

"Tell me this isn't happening." Helen clamped a hand over her mouth.

Gavin would like to ease her mind, but if Dr. Grant was defrauding the government, she could very well know about it. "As the warrant says, I'll be taking all patient files and billing records."

She crossed her arms. "I'll help you with the files, but billing records aren't kept here. Doc had a local gal do all the billing electronically, and she gave the files to him every month."

"I hope you'll understand that my job requires me to search the office anyway."

"I understand."

"So you never saw the bills?" Lexie sounded surprised, but she didn't have much to do with her father, so it made sense that she didn't know how he ran his practice.

Helen sniffed. "Only ever saw one if a patient put it in front of my face to ask a question, and I referred him to the biller. I was always glad I didn't have to deal with any of that. I'd hate to know which of my neighbors didn't pay Doc on time."

"Did you not handle the office finances at all?" Gavin asked.

"Doc took care of all of that. I gave him expense reports at the end of the month and he paid the bills."

"Sounds like my dad," Lexie said. "Keeping the money all under his purview."

Helen peered up at Gavin. "Before we go any further, suppose you answer a question for me. Do I need an attorney?"

"Did you do anything wrong?"

"No, of course not."

"Then you shouldn't need an attorney."

Lexie peered up at him, a deep scowl on her face. She thought he was being too harsh with Helen, but he was simply doing his job. Sure, if the same situation occurred when he'd been a deputy, he might have softened the blow, but he wasn't a rural county deputy any longer. He was an FBI agent with strict standards to uphold.

Okay, fine, he could relax a bit, but he wouldn't. That led to thinking about this town. The people. His family and Lexie, when he needed to think only about putting the killer behind bars and bringing this Medicaid investigation to a swift and thorough closure.

"Can you think of anyone who might want to kill Dad?" Lexie asked, maybe because she felt a need to step in before Helen got mad.

"You know your dad," Helen replied. "He could be hard to get along with at times. But his patients loved him." She frowned. "Well, maybe not all of them, I suppose."

"Are you thinking of someone in particular?" Gavin asked, trying not to sound too eager.

"Three people actually. The month before Doc went missing. He refused to fill their prescriptions and they stormed out of here. Next thing I knew, they canceled future appointments, and we got requests from the Lowell Clinic for the patient files."

Gavin's interest perked up at the clinic name, as Dr. Lowell was another potential suspect in the Medicaid fraud. "The same doctor for all three patients?"

She nodded.

"And you didn't think that was odd?" Gavin asked, as he sure did.

"This isn't like the big city, where you can choose from a long list of doctors. We only have two GPs in the county and Lowell is the closest."

He took out his notebook. "I'd like the patient names."

"Look, your warrant doesn't force me to give out their names, so I can't do that." Helen bit her lip. "But it does give you access to the schedule, where you might notice a few canceled appointments."

She pushed an appointment book toward Gavin and he picked it up to flip through the pages. He ran a finger down each day until he hit on the first crossed-off names: Rex Sanderson and Billy Howard. He jotted the names in his notebook and continued down the list until he found the third name and had to work hard to stifle his enthusiasm.

He tapped the calendar and peered at Helen. "Billy Howard, Rex Sanderson and Silas Ross. These are the patients you were referring to?"

Helen nodded. "But remember, I didn't say anything."

"Silas," Lexie said. "Didn't you mention—?"

"I assume I'll find the patient files in your records," Gavin interrupted before Lexie mentioned they'd already put Silas on the suspect list at lunch. Gavin added a pointed look to tell her to keep it to herself.

"Don't worry," Helen replied. "The files are right where I put them."

Perfect. Now all Gavin had to do was pack up the records, cross-reference the names and addresses with his list of suspicious Medicaid clients, and they could very well have a suspect angry enough to commit murder.

Chapter Nine

Thankfully, the doc only kept patient files for the current year at the office and the remaining files were already boxed and in a secure storage facility, limiting the number of files that Gavin had to pack up. He was able to load them into his SUV, put a seal on the office door and the storage unit, and then get Lexie back to the ranch within a few hours.

He still had to go back into town and serve the warrant on the woman with the billing records. He wouldn't expose Lexie to more danger for that, and he also wouldn't leave her alone. Which meant he'd have to wait for his dad or Matt to stop by for dinner before taking care of business.

He pulled up to the house and spotted Ruth's ranch hand stepping down from his truck, the horse trailer hitched behind.

Gavin shifted into Park. "What's Jose doing here?"

"Taking Misty home." Lexie unbuckled her seat belt.

"With you staying on the property, there's no point in moving her, is there?"

She firmed her jaw. "I can't impose on your family to care for her or pay for her feed."

"As Dad said, you're practically—"

"I'm not family, and I never will be," Lexie snapped.

Her bitter tone cut him to the quick, but he wouldn't ignore her barb again.

"My family loves you, Lex," he said, careful not to say he loved her, too, though he did and always would, he supposed. He just wasn't sure if he was still *in* love with her. "They're happy to help you out."

"And I appreciate it, I really do, but..." She drew in a long breath. "But being with them when we're no longer a couple is awkward."

He swiveled to get a better read on her emotions. "You seemed right at home with them, so I never considered that."

"I am at home here, and I like being with them. All of them. But..." She shook her head.

"But what, sug—" Her fiery gaze at his almost slip had him physically pulling back, but he wouldn't let this drop. "But what?"

"But spending time with them only to have you leave again will make it harder for me."

"Another thing I didn't think of." He resisted sighing, as this wasn't about him. "I'm such a dolt."

She peered at him and her lips started turning up in a grin. "For an FBI agent, you do miss the obvious sometimes."

He should smile with her but he couldn't. "I don't miss a thing on the job, but I have to admit, I haven't been as in tune with you as I should be."

"Why do you think that is?" she asked softly.

"Honestly?" He paused for a second. "Because I

don't know how I feel about you and I've been trying to avoid thinking about it."

"Me, too," she admitted. "And I think it's a good idea that we keep on avoiding it." She grabbed her door handle. "I'll just help Jose get Misty loaded up."

"I wish you'd reconsider."

"I'm already imposing. I won't be a financial burden, too." She opened her door. "Once Misty is on the road, I'll help you carry in boxes."

She jumped down and crossed the driveway. For a moment, Gavin watched her go. Her thick head of hair, gathered into a high ponytail, swished as she walked. She wore her little red boots and dressier jeans, along with the same parka from last night. The big hood seemed to dwarf her, adding to her look of vulnerability.

Tessa stepped outside and waved when she spotted them. She'd gotten in late last night and was out of the house by the time he'd come down for breakfast, so he hadn't seen his sister yet. Eager to talk to her, he headed for the stables.

She opened the gate and stood back. A fiery redhead, she took after their nana and was the only sibling without dark hair. They'd often teased her growing up that she was adopted among other things and still did. She'd balked as a kid, but took it all in stride now and gave as good as she got.

"I'm sorry for your loss, Lexie," she said, her eyes, more russet than the McKade deep brown, filled with sadness.

"Thank you." Lexie smiled a soft, sweet number that Gavin wished she'd offer him. "It's good to see you."

"You, too. We should have kept in touch better."

Tessa closed the gate behind them, then launched

herself at Gavin and gave him a fierce hug. Regret tugged at him. He hated what he was doing to his family by staying away. Man, if only he could change it.

"Wish you'd get it in your stubborn head to leave those Feds and come home where you belong," she whispered.

She smelled of her familiar scent of lab chemicals mixed with horse. A huge tomboy, growing up, she competed in rodeo barrel racing and could rarely be found with her boots on the ground instead of in stirrups. Somewhere around high school, she discovered boys and found her feminine side. Still, she wasn't afraid to get dirty on a crime scene and was more at home in boots and jeans than heels and a skirt.

He pulled back. "Anything new on any of the crime scenes?"

"Still waiting on the ATF to give us something of value, and the other scenes are a bust." She sighed. "So you're going to be working with Dad on this, huh?"

He nodded.

"Does that mean maybe you can see your way to work with him again on a full-time basis?"

"It's way too early in my visit to go there, squirt." He ruffled her hair. "I'll just see if Jose needs help getting Misty ready to leave."

"Watch where you step," she said. "Wouldn't want you to mess up those fancy shoes."

"Careful, squirt." Gavin planted his arm around her shoulders and rubbed his knuckles over her hair. "You're still the smallest one in the family, and I can easily still wrestle you to the ground. You wouldn't want to get your pretty red hair dirty."

"You two never change." Lexie chuckled before a wistful look settled on her face.

"Let's get Misty on the trailer," he said to move them forward and away from dwelling on all that she'd lost out on.

In the stable, he breathed deep of the hay, feeling like he'd come home again. Tessa squirmed out from under his arm. She was a handful to hold on to, all muscle and little padding. Lexie, on the other hand, was soft and sweet and oh, so wonderful to hold.

He dragged his gaze away from her and from the corner of his eye caught Tessa watching him. She pushed boundaries in much the same way he did, but she didn't have the added burden of being the oldest sibling. Before this trip was over, he suspected he'd get an earful from her on why he shouldn't have left Lexie behind.

Manners had him wanting to take over Lexie's work, but he knew she loved caring for Misty, so he stood back and said nothing until Jose was heading down the drive with the trailer.

Gavin tipped his head at his vehicle. "After I unload the boxes, I have some paperwork to catch up on. You can either stay at the main house with me, or I'll grab my things and come to the cabin."

"Main house is fine," she quickly said when she looked like she really wanted to say neither.

At his vehicle, Gavin grabbed the first few boxes, stacking them in his father's office. He made another trip and Lexie helped carry in the boxes. Once upon a time, they would be laughing and cutting up, but now tension lingered between them, making the job seem like it took longer to complete.

Finally, she dropped the last box in place. "I'll go see if your mom or nana need help making lunch."

"Thank you, Lex," he said. "I know they both like having you here."

He caught her frown before she left the room. No matter what he said, it was the wrong thing, and he needed to get used to that. He shook it off and removed the disgruntled patients' files. To spread out on the desk, he moved the glass appreciation plaque given to his dad after twenty-five years of service to the county. Gavin remembered the award ceremony and how he'd thought at the time that he would receive such a plaque someday, too. Wishful thinking and no point indulging in it.

He laid out his files then opened his laptop, where he called up a database of patients for nearby clinics suspected of Medicaid fraud. He entered Silas Ross's name and clicked Search.

The Lowell Clinic in Cumberland had recently added Ross's name, just as Helen had mentioned. His search of Billy Howard and Rex Sanderson produced the same results. For kicks, he entered Earl Clark and both of the Nash men's names, but they didn't return any records. He didn't know what to make of his findings at this point other than those three patients had moved on to the nearest clinic.

He plugged each name into law-enforcement databases and learned that Sanderson had prior arrests for drug possession and confirmed Ross's record, too. Howard was clean.

Given a choice, Gavin would go with the men with priors, and of the two of them, Gavin knew Ross possessed the skills to detonate the plane. He flipped to Ross's patient file and tried to read Dr. Grant's notes, but he couldn't decipher the handwriting. Same was true of Sanderson and Howard.

Maybe Lexie could read the chicken scratching. He grabbed the files and found Lexie with his mom and nana in the kitchen. Lexie wore his nana's apron, her hands covered in flour as she cut out biscuits. She was humming until he stepped into the room and her frown returned.

Was she ever going to forgive him? Probably not until he got her to see things from his point of view, which she'd never done. But then, had he really taken the time to try to understand what she was feeling or had he needed to escape so badly that he'd focused only on himself?

"Did you need something?" She wiped the flour-covered back of her hand across her forehead, leaving behind a white trail that he wanted to brush away.

Instead, he held out the top folder. "I'm hoping you can decipher your dad's handwriting and help me figure out why these patients were seeing him."

She went to the sink to wash her hands then sat at the small table and scanned the folders. "Looks like they were all pain management clients, and Dad prescribed narcotics." She stabbed a finger at a few of the notes. "See? Here and here?"

He peered at the files. "And does their reason for moving on to a new doctor match with Helen's statement?"

She nodded. "He refused to prescribe additional meds and they left. She didn't mention narcotics, though. Do you think my dad was writing too many narcotic prescriptions and his death is somehow related to that?"

Gavin shook his head. "We checked that out already. He's not on the DEA's radar for writing excessive scripts. So, no, I don't think it has to do with prescriptions he generated."

"But you mentioned drugs as a good motive earlier."

"I did, and I'm not ruling out his death being related to drugs. Just not the prescriptions he wrote."

She furrowed her brow. "But what else could there be?"

"I don't know at this point," he admitted. "But locating these men so I can talk to them could very well help us figure that out. I have a last known address for all three of them and that's a good place to start."

She stood and turned to his grandmother. "Mind if I bail on the biscuits so I can help Gavin?"

His nana waved her hand. "Go on now. I like seeing you two together and not at odds with each other."

"Mom." His mother's tone warned his nana not to go there, but Gavin could see his mother shared the sentiment.

Honestly, he liked not being at odds with Lexie, as well. Liked it too much for his own good, so as he headed for the office where they'd be alone together, he warned himself to keep things professional.

He took a seat behind his father's big desk and Lexie came to stand behind him. Her sweet scent caught his attention and it was all he could do to remember his thoughts of a moment ago to remain professional. He forced his attention to the computer and entered the patients' names into the DMV database. The search returned the same addresses.

"They all live in apartments in various cities in the county. Silas resides here in Lost Creek, but Matt mentioned he may have moved. I'll give the apartment managers a call to see if they're all still at the same addresses."

As he picked up his phone, Lexie went to stare out the window. He had to admit to being thankful that she'd chosen to put some distance between them, making it easier to concentrate on his calls. It was all he could do not to stare at her framed in the sunlight and make his calls.

When he'd finished talking to the managers, he swiveled to look at her. "They've all moved on. No forwarding address."

She turned. "Don't you find that odd?"

"I do for Silas, as he's older and he was holding down a steady job. But people who live in apartments are more mobile, and if they have any issues with the law, they often take off without forwarding addresses."

"So now what?" she asked.

"Now we move on to Facebook."

She snorted. "What? Like they'll brag about being involved in drugs on Facebook?"

"You'd be surprised. Criminals aren't often the brightest, so it may sound far-fetched, but many cases are solved when they brag on social media. But even if they don't, you can often locate people just by reading through their posts."

Since Silas was the only one of the three on both lists, he entered Silas's name and his profile came up. In his picture, he had a crooked smirk and his hair hung in eyes that were glassy, leading Gavin to think Silas used drugs.

Gavin clicked on his picture to enlarge it. "Is he of the right build to be the biker?"

She leaned closer. "Could be."

Gavin pointed out for Lexie that Silas's About page had listed him living in Cumberland.

"Let's look at his feed to see if there are any pictures of the complex where he lives." Gavin read down the posts, mostly about beer brewing, but one item caught his attention.

"Look at this." He pointed to the screen update and read, "'Lowell Clinic rocks. 'Bout time I found a decent doctor. If he shows up on time tomorrow afternoon.'"

"He has an appointment tomorrow." Lexie's voice rose with excitement and her eyes gleamed.

"See? Social media helps in many ways." Gavin smiled up at her and got caught up in her beauty.

"You can catch him when he goes to the appointment. And thanks to Facebook, you'll have no trouble recognizing him." She suddenly threw her arms around his neck and hugged him.

Her touch caught him off guard but it felt so right that he came to his feet and pulled her closer. Surprisingly, she didn't push him away but settled her head on his chest. Holding her was just like he remembered, and he wanted more. So much more. Starting with a kiss.

He pulled back, and as he lowered his head, she shoved him away.

"I'm sorry," she said, looking shocked by her actions. "I should never have done that. I don't know what got into me. It doesn't mean anything, though. I was just so happy to have a lead, and you were…well…convenient, so I… Anyway, it's good news about the lead."

Right, the lead. He had an investigation to solve. A career to advance, a killer to find, and he should be equally happy. Then why was his heart aching and his stomach tied up in knots?

Chapter Ten

Walt had just finished the lemon chicken and red potatoes Winnie had kept warm for him after a big accident caused by an unexpected snowfall had kept him from getting home on time for dinner.

Due to their higher elevation, they often got a light snowfall each winter and Adam was outside playing in the fluffy powder. Lexie wanted to join him, but she didn't want to miss the update from today's investigation, which Walt declared he'd reveal from his recliner in the family room.

Matt, Jed and Gavin were already seated in the cozy room when she stepped under the large archway. A fresh scent wafted from the cinnamon-infused pinecones on the fireplace mantel above a roaring fire, and her gaze landed on the Christmas stockings quilted by Betty. Lexie couldn't resist running her fingers over Gavin's embroidered name. She looked up to find him watching her as he'd been doing a lot today. She dropped her hand and focused on Walt before he came over to join her.

"I talked to Norbert and Freddie Nash today." Walt lifted the recliner handle on his chair. "They both have alibis. Course, I'm not taking their word for it, and I've got Kendall running down the alibis right now."

"Anything in any of the interviews to suggest our suspects partnered with the doc or have a grudge against him?" Gavin asked.

"Not so far. Earl Clark wasn't at home or answering his phone. Checked a couple of times. Then I called the garage and Clem told me Earl works tomorrow. So I plan to pop in on him unannounced in the morning."

"I'll go with you," Gavin said.

Walt raised his brow, and Lexie wasn't surprised to see father and son duke it out without saying a word.

"Wouldn't two investigators be better than one?" she said before Walt said no. "You might pick up on something the other one misses."

"Good point," Walt conceded. "But I'm taking lead."

"No problem," Gavin replied. "Someone will need to stay with Lexie while we go."

"I can spare Dylan for the morning, but need him on patrol by noon."

Gavin gave a quick nod and explained what they learned from Facebook about Silas Ross. "He's Dr. Grant's former patient."

"Facebook," Walt scoffed. "You can't believe what you read on there. His DMV records still have him listed in Lost Creek."

Lexie waited for Gavin to dispute his father's claim about Facebook, but he simply blew out a breath. "I called the manager for Silas's last known address. He's moved on."

"No wonder we haven't seen him in town," Matt said. "But even if it takes an hour to get to Cumberland from here, it seems kind of drastic to move just because he changed doctors."

"His company is up that way, too, right?" Jed said. "So that would make more sense."

Gavin nodded. "Whatever the reason for his move, he posted on Facebook that he has a doctor's appointment in the afternoon, so I'll stake the place out."

"Sounds like a good plan," Matt said.

Walt frowned but didn't say anything else.

"So if that's it…" Matt stretched. "I haven't slept in over twenty-four hours and I need some shut-eye."

"Lightweight," Gavin joked. "Going to bed and it's not even seven."

"Give it a rest," Walt said. "He works hard and needs to sleep."

"I get it, Dad. I was just razzing him."

Lexie cringed at Gavin's sharp tone and waited for Walt to respond.

"That's okay, Dad." Matt winked and punched Gavin in the arm on the way past. "We all know the Feds are slackers."

The brothers laughed.

At one time Lexie would have joined in, but felt like laughing now would send the message that she'd forgiven Gavin when she wasn't anywhere near doing so.

She heard the door open. Assuming it was Adam, she went to the foyer. He closed the door and stomped the snow from his boots. His cheeks were apple red and he wore a cute grin she hadn't seen in years.

"Looks like you had fun," she said.

He shed his boots and jacket in a pile on the rug then started to step away.

"Um, hello," Lexie said and pointed at his clothing on the rug.

He turned, the smile gone, and an exaggerated sigh slipped from his mouth as he hung up his jacket and set his boots off to the side. Then his phone came out and he headed under another archway into the dining room, where his schoolbooks awaited him.

Though the house had separate rooms, the wide openings made it feel like one big space and Lexie could hear Gavin and Walt arguing.

She was too hyped up to join them, and they didn't need a witness to their discord, so she stayed in the entry and prowled around the space, pacing past the big arches a few times. She finally stepped up to the tree and fingered a few ornaments as she heard the argument end.

"I hate to see you this way," Gavin said from behind her.

Startled, she spun. "What way?"

"Unsettled. Nervous. I understand it, but you have to know you're safe with us."

With the way he'd been trying to ignore her, she kept forgetting how well he knew her and could read her nonverbal signals if he wanted to. "I know but..."

"Why don't we go on a trail ride? That always relaxes you and it'll be beautiful with the fresh snow."

Yeah, he knew her, all right. Whenever life got her down, she'd turned to Misty. Too bad she'd insisted Misty be taken home.

"You can ride Beauty," he said, preempting her first line of defense.

"You don't think Kendall would mind?"

"She won't. But if you'd like, I can text her to ask."

"That would be great. But only if you think it's safe."

"The killer would be a fool to come here with all the law-enforcement officers in place." Gavin smiled, one of those crooked boyish ones that always got to her. "And if it'll make you feel better, we'll only ride up to the pond."

The thought of the pond with snow covering the ground, the skies clear now and the moon shining off the crystals, cinched her agreement. "Text Kendall."

He took out his phone and tapped the screen. "I'll change clothes while we wait for her to respond."

Lexie nodded, but her mind had already gone to the upcoming ride. They'd be together. Just the two of them. Heading for the spot where she'd once expected he'd propose under a starlit night. Maybe the ride wasn't such a good idea. She'd invite Adam, but he didn't need to be around Gavin. Plus her brother wasn't much of a horseman. Despite how often she or Ruth had tried to coax him onto a horse, he'd rather sit in the house with a computer or his phone in front of him.

Winnie entered the foyer.

"Gavin and I are going for a ride up to the pond," Lexie said, as she thought someone should know they'd gone out riding.

"Perfect night for it with the fresh snow." Winnie's eyes twinkled.

Her attempt at matchmaking was far from subtle.

Walt joined them, his empty coffee cup in hand. "See that Gavin's mind stays on checking the surroundings and not on how pretty you look under the stars."

Adam's head shot up at that one.

"Do you want to come with us?" she asked her brother. He shook his head and bent over his phone again.

Grrr. She needed to help him find an interest other than what he could do with electronics. She appreciated her phone for being able to check email and social media. Catch up on the news. Check the weather. But having it in front of her face nearly every waking moment was beyond her understanding.

She looked at Walt and Winnie. "Do either of you want to ride with us?"

She received a shake of heads. "You don't know what you'll be missing."

"A sore rear end and frostbite, you mean?" Winnie laughed and traded her full mug for Walt's. "Sit, and I'll fill yours for you."

They departed, and Lexie went to Adam. She put a hand on his shoulder so he would look at her.

"I have my phone. Call or text me if you need anything. We should be back in an hour or so."

"I got it. I'm not a baby." He was good at pushing boundaries, but he was rarely rude like this.

"When you're under my roof, Adam—" Walt's voice came from the other room "—you'll respect your elders. Now apologize to your sister."

"I'm sorry," he said, real contrition in his tone.

She squatted next to his chair. "We're all under a lot of stress. I get it and understand that it can make us short-tempered."

"Yeah, well…yeah. Right."

She squeezed his hand. "We can head over to the cabin when I get back, okay?"

He nodded eagerly.

"See you in a bit." She stepped back into the foyer to wait for Gavin and turned her attention to the tree.

She spotted a varnished dough ornament of a pair of

snowmen wearing Santa hats. Her name and Gavin's were painted below the snowmen, along with a date four Christmases ago. Winnie had snowmen ornaments with each child's birth date. When Lexie and Gavin had gotten serious, she'd added this one so Lexie had a place on their family tree. Lexie searched and found the one Winnie had gotten for Adam, too. She rested the delicate ornament in her hand, her eyes filling with tears. For the McKade kindness. For the loss of her mother. The loss of her father. Of Gavin.

Father, why? Why put us through all of this? Are You really not there or do You just not care about Adam and me?

"Ready to go?" Gavin asked.

Lexie jerked. The ornament went flying.

He lurched forward and caught it a foot from the floor.

"You scared me," she said. "I almost... It would have been horrible to break Adam's ornament."

Gavin studied her face. "Everything will be okay."

Not wanting to respond to what she felt was a platitude, she grabbed her jacket from a hook and stepped onto the porch lit by the moon's bright glow. She took a few deep breaths of the sharp air and sighed out her tension. She heard Gavin say goodbye to his parents as she descended the stairs. Snow covered her boots and she stared at it as she waited at the bottom.

She looked up to see him step onto the porch, and her thoughts shifted. He was dressed in worn jeans that fit as if custom made for him. He wore scuffed boots and a denim jacket and had settled his favorite cowboy hat on his head. The sight of him standing before her, looking so ruggedly handsome, pulled at her heartstrings.

And her mind wandered to a place it had no business going.

His formal agent attire had helped her keep her feelings in check, but seeing him like this? Seeing the old Gavin. The Gavin she used to know, and love, was almost more than she could bear.

She whipped around and started for the corral. A moment later, she heard him jogging to keep up.

"I need you to stay closer to me." He shifted the rifle in his arms.

"But you said it was safe."

"Nothing is one hundred percent safe, Lexie. We can never let our guard down."

At the urgency in his tone, she shot him a look. "You've changed."

"What do you mean?" he asked.

"You're always on edge."

"It's the situation."

"No, it's more," she insisted. "Even at Dad's office, you were tightly wound. Like you're expecting something bad to happen at any moment and you have to be on guard for it."

He shrugged. "That's the life of a law-enforcement officer."

"True, but you weren't like this when you were a deputy. Sure, you were cautious and carried all the time… but this? This over-the-top need to control. That's new."

He peered at her as if he wanted to say something but thought better of it and then suddenly grabbed the gate and opened it.

Fine. Be that way. It would be far better on the ride if they kept this wall up between them anyway.

They saddled the horses and Gavin dropped a pair

of binoculars in his saddlebag and his rifle into the holder. She knew he was just taking precautions, but still, her nerves were fried, and she really needed to gallop across the field with Beauty. She mounted the horse and urged her into a slow walk. Gavin rode up beside her, and they galloped toward the lake, the crisp air whipping at Lexie's face. Each strike of Beauty's hooves kicked up snow, and Lexie felt like she was in a winter wonderland painting.

She let go of the stress. Let go of the worry. The fear. A killer may be stalking her, but right now, there was nothing but her and Beauty, the wind and the man she was trying so hard to ignore.

By the pond, Gavin watched as Lexie slipped off Beauty and literally pranced through the snow, throwing her arms out in excitement. She spun in a circle then dropped to the ground and swished her arms and legs over the fluffy powder to create a symmetrical angel. "Isn't it breathtaking?"

"Gorgeous," he said and meant it, but he only had eyes for her.

Lexie lay for a moment, her smile wide and warming his heart. She suddenly jumped up like a little child and brushed the snow from her clothes then rushed over to a rock at the edge of the pond. Plopping down, she raised her face to the stars, her contented look making Gavin suck in a breath.

Her smile broadened. "This was such a good idea."

Gavin dismounted and moved closer to her, but there was no way he was sitting down. Not with a killer out there. He kept his gaze roving the area. "It must feel good to catch your breath after dealing with the hordes of McKades."

"You exaggerate. It's not a horde until they all show up." She grinned. "Besides, I love your family. Sunday dinners with them are some of my fondest memories of when we were together."

"Ouch." He faked pulling a knife from his chest.

She tsked. "I'm serious. You've always taken them for granted. I mean, sure, you don't get along with your dad, but for the most part, he's a good father. Not like my fa—" She pressed a hand over her mouth. "I guess it really hasn't hit me that he's gone."

"I'm so sorry, Lexie."

She shook her head as if shaking away her pain. "Besides passing each other on the street, I only saw him a couple of times a year, but you know… I'm… It's…" She pulled her feet up on the rock and rested her chin on her knees. "I think it's the thought that we'll never have a chance to reconcile that's hitting me the hardest. Despite years of being ignored and belittled by him, I always hoped a day would come where we could bury the hatchet and go back to the way we were before Mom died."

She suddenly jumped to her feet and grabbed Gavin's hand, her fingers insistent. "You have to let this serve as a lesson to you. Find a way to get along with your dad. Now. Before it's too late."

"I…" he began, but couldn't even put words to a thought he didn't believe. Sure, she was right. He didn't have forever to patch things up with his dad, but a peace accord had to be a two-way street, and the ornery old guy wasn't likely going to meet him in the middle.

"Just promise me you'll try, okay?" She sought his

gaze and held it with a tearful one of her own, resurrecting memories of their time together after run-ins with her dad. Times when Gavin would have done most anything to erase those tears and he was helpless to deny her anything.

"I promise," he said, wondering how in the world he was going to hold to his promise.

They were locked in each other's gazes, tension crackling between them. He didn't even try to come up with a subject, as he figured anything they might discuss would end awkwardly. They'd been in love. Deeply. And yet he'd had to walk away, leaving her hurt and confused.

Maybe he'd been confused, too, as he'd chosen to leave town, and yet, as she stood before him, looking so beautiful and achingly vulnerable, he realized how very much he missed her. He hadn't met another woman who compared to her. Not that he'd been looking. Not with his heart still raw years after their breakup.

But despite the pain, he couldn't move back here. He just couldn't. Being a lawman was in his blood. From generation to generation, and he couldn't bear the thought of doing anything else. Working for his father was the only law-enforcement gig in the area, and that he couldn't abide. So he had to stay away. Even if it meant never being with Lexie.

Gavin scrubbed a hand across his jaw and released a long, frustrated breath. He couldn't stand there in limbo—wanting her and yet knowing he couldn't have her. "Do you want to ride again?"

Looking forlorn now, she nodded, and he boosted her onto Beauty's back. She didn't argue or frown at his assistance, which was a huge improvement over yesterday, as far as he was concerned. He wouldn't put any stock in it, though, as he was sure her sudden compliance stemmed from being distraught over her father.

He got Lightning moving and they meandered along the trail toward the ranch. Taking it slower on the return trip gave him time to look around at the ground covered in a pristine white blanket. Why couldn't he find a way to cover his life this way? To forget his issues with his father and make a fresh start?

Because life didn't work that way, that was why. You couldn't simply lay a blanket over it and—presto—have all your problems solved. It simply hid them for another day, and when that blanket of snow melted, they were still there.

He heard a branch snap in the distance and would have thought he'd imagined the sound except Lightning's head picked up at the noise. Could be related to the snow clinging to the branches, but Gavin wouldn't take any chances.

Grabbing his binoculars and rising up in his stirrups, he scanned the area. At a scenic overlook on a nearby road, he saw movement and stilled Lightning so he could zoom in. He scanned again.

His heart rate kicked up and he dropped into his saddle. "We need to go, now!"

Lexie's eyes widened. "What's wrong?"

"There's a man at the scenic overlook watching us."

Chapter Eleven

Lexie kicked Beauty faster, the wind biting into her face. Why had she sent Misty home? She knew how to handle and communicate with her. Sure, Beauty was usually a gentle ride, but the sudden change in movement left her unsettled and her hooves pummeled over the ground in wild abandon. The last thing Lexie needed was to fall from the horse. Actually, the last thing she needed was for the man watching them to come after them.

She glanced over her shoulder. No one was chasing them. Had they gone far enough so if this guy fired a gun that a bullet wouldn't reach them? She wasn't familiar with weapons, so she had no idea. Which meant keeping Beauty racing fast.

At the house, Gavin dropped from Lightning before fully stopping. He looped the horse's reins on a rough wooden fence and then jerked Lexie from Beauty's back. Her feet had barely hit the ground when he grabbed her hand and flew toward the steps, pulling her behind him. She tripped on the bottom stair, so he scooped her into his arms and kept moving in one seamless motion.

Terrified or not, the awareness of being in his arms cut through her feelings. He pushed open the door and she wished he'd set her free as much as she wished he'd keep holding her. She longed to be held by him again and the reality was even better than her memories.

He looked deeply into her eyes. "Are you okay?"

"Fine," she replied, though her heart beat as fast as Beauty's hooves had struck the ground.

Gavin scooped her closer. Held her tighter. She circled her arms around his neck. Wanting to kiss him, she lifted her face.

"What's wrong, Lex?" Adam called out from the dining room. He was a teenager, but they were so close that he had the ability to sense her distress.

"Don't worry, bud. I'm fine." She dropped her arms and tried to squirm free.

Gavin held fast and carried her into the family room, where his parents and grandparents were watching television. He gently set her on her feet. She heard Adam follow them into the room.

"There was a man watching us from the overlook," Gavin said. "I'm leaving Lexie here and going after him."

Walt jumped up from his chair. Winnie's eyes narrowed and Betty sat forward.

"Then let's get after him," Walt said.

"Not so fast." Gavin held out a hand. "I've got this. You stay here with Lexie."

His father eyed him. "It's my county, and if anyone does the staying, it'll be you."

Gavin seemed to weigh his decision and finally looked at his grandfather. "You good to watch over Lexie, Granddad?"

"Course I am." Jed came to his feet. "But don't be in such an all-fire hurry that you forget defensive tactics."

"Be careful," Winnie called out, but they were out the door in a flash and Lexie didn't know if they'd even heard her.

Lexie's fear started to abate and her legs felt like rubber. She nearly collapsed but Jed grabbed her elbow. "Whoa, there, little filly."

Winnie rushed over to her. "C'mon, sweetheart. You need to sit down."

The siren on Walt's car sprang to life outside while Winnie helped Lexie to the sofa, where she gratefully sank into the worn plaid cushions.

"I'll get you some water," Betty offered. On her way, she stopped next to Jed, who was staring out the door, his hand planted on his waist. "I know how much you want to go with them, but there's no holster at your side anymore, dear."

"I know that. How I know that." Yearning lingered in his tone as he closed the door and locked it tight. "I'll go up and get my rifle just in case this weasel comes calling."

Lexie heard his quick footfalls on the stairs and was surprised he could still move that fast. These McKade men would remain protecting others as long as they were physically able, and she, for one, was extremely grateful to have them on her side.

"Are you sure you're okay?" Adam's eyebrow rose, looking so much like their father that Lexie felt tears coming on.

She blinked them away. "I'm fine. How's your homework coming?"

"Need to finish math."

"Go ahead and finish up so when Walt and Gavin get back we can head to the cabin."

Usually he'd argue about the homework, but he gave a clipped nod and, after a long look, left the room. Her mama-bear instincts told her to go after him and talk about the incident, but they also told her not to do so when her emotions were so raw.

Winnie clicked off the television. "I'm sure the last thing you want to listen to is an old episode of *Bonanza*."

"Actually, it's comforting to see the four of you still like to watch it. At least there's something that hasn't changed."

Winnie leaned closer. "I have to admit, the show is more Walt and Jed's joy. Betty and I put up with it and let the men pretend they're in the Old West working the Cartwrights' ranch and protecting their community. But please don't tell them."

Lexie laughed. Oh, how she loved this woman. Lexie wanted to fall into her arms and cry. For herself, sure, but mostly for Adam and the danger he could be in. For the loss of Gavin in their lives. For the pain of seeing him again. For losing this family. This beautiful, wonderful family that she'd hoped to become part of.

"Tell me that you and Gavin had a nice ride until this man intruded," Winnie said.

Lexie swallowed down her distress the same way she'd choked down her father's callous behavior for years. "The ride was lovely."

Betty returned with the water and handed the glass to Lexie. "Now drink up and, once you're up to it, you can tell us what happened."

She settled on the sofa next to Lexie, who caught a

hint of the rosemary Betty had used on the fresh focaccia bread she'd made to go with the lemon chicken for dinner.

Lexie drank the water and took a few breaths before telling the women about the night. Not the intimate time at the pond or how she'd felt being with Gavin again, but about their mad dash across the property.

"The horses." She jumped up. "I need to take care of them after such a hard run."

"I don't think it's a good idea to go outside."

Jed poked his head into the room. "This guy has likely skedaddled. Especially after hearing Walt's sirens."

"Still, I don't think Walt or Gavin would appreciate Lexie going outside," Winnie said. "I can take care of the horses."

Lexie shook her head. "Working with them will help me calm down."

"But—"

"I'll go out with her," Jed interrupted, lifting his rifle. "She'll be fine."

Winnie opened her mouth to say something, but Lexie marched to the door before she continued to argue. Still, Lexie wasn't foolhardy, so she waited for Jed to join her on the porch before descending the stairs and taking Beauty's reins from the fence rail. She approached Lightning with caution, letting him smell her before touching his nose. He whinnied his acceptance, and she was glad he remembered her and would let her lead him to the stable.

Jed crossed his rifle over his chest while letting his gaze rove the area as they walked. "You've had quite a few days of it, haven't you?"

She nodded. "I'm thankful for your family's support."

"It's nothing. Only wish I was out there with the others tracking this guy."

"I'm glad you're here, or I'd be stuck inside instead of spending time with the horses." She opened the corral gate and led the horses into the stable.

"I'd help out, but it's best for me to stand watch at the door."

"No worries." Lexie moved deeper into the stable. She should walk the horses after the hard run, but Jed wouldn't allow her to spend time outside. The walking would have to wait for the men, if they got back before the horses cooled off.

She started the grooming process by loosening the girth then removing the bridle and replacing it with a halter and lead shank for each horse. She would have to rinse off the bits, wipe off sweat and dirt from the saddle and girth and put the tack away, but first she wanted to give the horses water, so she led them to the trough.

Lexie stroked Beauty's nose before she dipped it into the cool water. "Thank you for bringing me safely home, girl."

"You and Tessa are a lot alike," Jed called out. "Give her a horse to talk to and she's happy as a lark."

Lexie couldn't disagree. Misty had been with her for years. Her companion, allowing her to unload all her feelings after Gavin left. She wanted to unload now, too, but not with Jed within hearing distance, so she waited until Beauty drank her fill then rested her head against Beauty's neck and stroked her soft head. She loved the feel of her, and how she simply stood and let Lexie absorb comfort.

As much as Lexie wanted to stand there, she needed

to examine the horses for any problems from the ride. By the time she'd checked for rubs and chafing from the saddle and tack, and the legs for cuts, bumps and bruises, she heard a car rumbling up the driveway.

"The men are back," Jed said. "I'll tell Gavin you're here."

Lexie nodded, but she was afraid to hear what he'd discovered.

Jed yelled to Gavin and then she heard a single set of footsteps. She looked out the window to see Gavin headed their way and Walt marching up to the house.

Gavin crossed over to her. "You don't have to take care of the horses. I can do it."

"I'm glad to. Besides, it took my mind off the man."

"Any luck?" Jed asked.

"He was long gone by the time we got there," Gavin said disgustedly. "But Dad called Tessa to the overlook, and she may have found a lead."

"A good one?" Jed asked.

Gavin shrugged. "She lifted an oily footprint and another substance she couldn't identify from where the car was parked. The oil appears fresh. It might mean nothing, but it could also tie the mechanic we'll be questioning in the morning to the scene. She collected samples and will send them to the nearest lab for processing."

"How long does evidence processing like this take nowadays?" Jed asked.

"Depending on the lab's priorities and backlog, it could be days—even weeks—but Dad will use his influence to get the tests moved up the calendar. Still, it will most likely take three days or so before we hear anything."

"Three days," Lexie muttered and hoped that it

wouldn't be that long because with Gavin standing close, his scent firing her senses, she didn't know how long she could continue to keep him at arm's length.

Gavin stood by the fireplace, presumably to warm his hands, but Lexie's warning to reconcile with his dad before it was too late continued to plague him. His gaze went to his father as he sat in his big leather chair and talked to Lexie. Her respect for him was evident in her look. A respect Gavin had once been blessed to have.

He glanced at his parents and grandparents. Such a strong family unit that he'd once thought couldn't be cracked. Until he'd taken off and left behind a wide fissure. He missed each of them for different reasons. His mom and nana for their unreserved love. His granddad for companionship. No one made a better fishing buddy. His dad—for what? An admirable role model to emulate most of the time, as well as a strong leader of his family and men. All of them for the way they let their faith guide them. Something he'd completely ignored for years.

He needed to admit it once and for all. He wanted to come back here. But it wasn't possible. Not with his father's reaction when he'd learned of the man at the lookout. His dad had jumped up to take charge, claiming territory and barreling over Gavin's plan. Gavin's gut had cried out to take lead so nothing could go wrong, and it had been on the tip of his tongue to tell his dad to back off. But it wasn't just his dad he would have fended off. Shockingly, since Emily had been shot, he didn't trust anyone to help him. Not even a family member.

Lexie stood. "It's a school night, and I need to get Adam over to the cabin."

Gavin crossed his arms and widened his stance in preparation for the battle he knew was coming. "I'm staying at the cabin with you and Adam."

She lifted her chin. "No."

As much as he hated arguing with her, he found her stance cute and nearly irresistible. "It's nonnegotiable."

"It's a solid plan," Walt said.

She opened her mouth, likely to argue, when Adam joined them. "I think Gavin should stay with us, too."

Lexie's mouth dropped open. Gavin's almost did, too. With Adam so mad, asking Gavin to stay at the cabin meant he had to be seriously afraid.

"Okay, then." Lexie gave in, sounding defeated in more ways than one.

Gavin had to ignore her pain and move on before she changed her mind. "Give me a minute to grab a few things."

He gathered only a couple of items he'd need for the night from his room, as he planned to come back here to shower and change in the morning. He picked up his computer and a few files, and hurried to escort the pair down the stairs and into the snow.

Adam held out a hand. "I'll carry your bag for you."

Gavin didn't need the help, but he saw the offer for what was intended and handed over the bag. "Thanks, man. Mind helping me keep an eye out as we walk over there?"

Adam nodded and shouldered the bag. Gavin turned to discover Lexie watching them. He couldn't read her eyes in the shadowed night, but he hoped she would be happy that Adam was feeling less hostile toward him.

They walked in silence, their footfalls barely audible in the snow. They passed six small cabins, a fire pit blazing with a roaring fire and ringed by wide stumps where several guests roasted marshmallows. Another couple tossed snowballs and shrieked as they ran from them. The kind of picture-perfect scene that would make a great advertisement for the dude ranch.

He unlocked the largest cabin's door, ushered the pair inside, then checked every inch of the four-room building. "You two go ahead and get settled while I step out to talk to the guests by the campfire in case they saw anything odd tonight."

Lexie paused in taking off her jacket. "But the trail is nowhere near here."

"True, but I won't leave any possible lead unexplored."

"Keep an eye on her while I'm gone, okay?" he said to Adam as he passed.

Adam nodded, and Gavin was thankful that, for now, the teen didn't cast a hateful look his way.

Gavin stepped up to the roaring fire. Two men and one woman looked up. One man sat off to the side, and Gavin knew from looking at the guest list that he was alone and the other two were a couple, as was the pair frolicking in the snow.

"Evening," Gavin said. "Mind if I join you?"

"Please," the single guy said.

Gavin gave his first name and learned this guy was Dean, the woman Anita, and her husband, Randy. All names matched the guest register.

"You staying at the big cabin?" Dean asked.

"Just settling in." Gavin took a seat on the far side of the fire to keep the cabin in view. "Nice night even if it's cold and snowy."

"That's what the fire is for." Dean chuckled.

"With that pile of red-hot embers, it looks like you all have been out here for a while."

"Started the fire right at sundown."

"What about the other guests?" Gavin asked, though he knew that, other than the couple in the snow, no other guests were registered. "Any of them join you?"

"What others?" Randy laughed. "Not too many people foolish enough to rough it in the cold like this and right before Christmas."

"Really, no other guests?" Gavin asked. "I thought I saw a guy hanging out at the overlook a couple of hours ago."

"Now, that's just plain nuts," Anita said. "It would be crazy cold without a fire." She slid her arm around Randy's shoulders. "Or love to keep you warm."

She laughed, and Randy joined in, but Dean looked like he might be sick.

Gavin moved on, mixing small talk with tossed-out questions he thought they'd find innocuous. It soon became clear that they hadn't seen anything, so he excused himself and returned to the cabin. On the way, he received a text update from his father.

Inside, he found Lexie sitting on the sofa and a light spilling out from the bedroom where Adam poked his head out. Gavin exchanged a nod with the boy telling him everything was okay, and he stepped back into his room. Gavin took a seat next to Lexie, careful to put a safe zone between them.

"I've been thinking about the car you saw," she said. "Can't you track it?"

"All I caught was that it was a small Honda. Likely an Accord, which is too common of a make and model to begin searching by that criteria alone. And Dad just texted to say none of the men on our suspect list own a Honda."

"Maybe it's the mechanic, and he borrowed one of the cars in for repair."

"I'll ask him about it in the morning." He pointed to her tablet. "What are you up to?"

"Returning an email from the funeral home. They told me that the ME hasn't released Dad's body yet."

"That's not unusual in a murder investigation."

"Just hearing you say that dumbfounds me." She sighed. "I mean, how did my life come to this? To a murder investigation, the loss of my father. Much less having someone trying to abduct me and ransack my home and truck."

"I know it's a shock, Lex. To me, too. Especially around here. You know if I could change things for you, I would."

She nodded but didn't speak.

"Have you thought any more about talking to your dad's lawyer?"

"I've thought about it, but I still don't see the point."

He leaned toward her and captured her gaze. "What if he left money for Adam? Won't be long before he goes to college and could need the money."

"I've set aside enough money for him," she insisted.

"That's good but—"

She held up a hand. "I don't want to talk about it, Gavin. Not now. Not ever. So promise you won't bring it up again."

"See, here's the thing," he said, wishing he could just let it alone, but he felt a deep-seated need to speak. "You want me to reconcile with my dad, but even in death you haven't reconciled with yours."

She snapped back. "It's not the same."

"Isn't it?"

She jumped up and glared at him. "Maybe it is, but I said I don't want to talk about it. Especially not with you. And I mean it." She marched into the other bedroom and closed the door with great force.

After her intensity at the pond, begging him to fix things with his dad, this was the last response he expected from her. But with such a visceral reaction on her part, he'd honor her wishes in this matter going forward.

Well, unless it conflicted with the investigation. Then he'd have to do what he thought best. Even if it pushed an even bigger wedge between them.

Chapter Twelve

As the morning sun climbed into the sky and sparkled off the snow, Gavin wasn't sure if he could bring himself to walk out of the house and leave Lexie behind. She sat at the small kitchen table with Adam, his mother and Matt, and it was easy to see she was still shaken up from last night.

"We don't have all day, Gavin." His dad's voice rang from the foyer.

"You probably don't want to keep Dad waiting," Matt said.

Gavin met his brother's gaze. "You'll call me if the slightest thing happens, or if you hear anything from Kendall at the school."

"Do you think something will happen to Adam?" Lexie's worried expression tugged at him to stay. But he knew she was safe with Matt and Granddad, and Gavin could gain valuable intel by going to the interview.

He smiled for Lexie's sake. "Adam will be fine. I'm just being cautious."

"Something you've become in spades," Matt muttered, drawing Lexie and his mother's attention.

But Gavin ignored his brother's comment and kept his focus on Lexie. "If anything seems out of the ordinary, you call me, too."

She nodded, but her expression said she was unlikely to turn to him unless the situation was dire. After the way they'd left things last night, he wasn't surprised at her response, but her unwillingness to rely on him still stung.

"Especially if the burner phone rings," he added.

She nodded again and gave him a pointed look that he took to mean she didn't want to discuss that phone in front of Adam.

"Last chance, Gavin," his father bellowed.

Gritting his teeth, he headed for the door only to discover his father had already gone outside and was settling into his car. The moment Gavin hit the passenger seat, his dad shoved the gear into Drive and took off.

Just like last night, his father didn't give a care about Gavin's thoughts or his feelings. Not that his dad would even admit to having feelings. Okay, fine, Gavin might not admit to them much, either, but that wasn't the point. The point was that his dad clearly hadn't changed, and it didn't bode well for their time together.

He merged onto the road. "I called the lab. They're moving the evidence up, but don't hold your breath." He shook his head. "When I first started out in law enforcement, we didn't depend on forensic evaluation as much. But then, we didn't have the levels of crime that we have today."

That piqued Gavin's interest. "The crime rate going up in Lake County?"

"I hate to admit it, but yeah. We've seen an influx of people from the city, and not all of them are law-abiding. So I don't know the people the way I used to. Means I have to depend on forensics more to solve even the smallest of cases."

Surprised at his stance, Gavin peered at his father. "Thought you didn't much like depending on something you couldn't explain."

"That was shortsighted." He glanced at Gavin. "I might be getting old, but I can still change."

Gavin gaped at his father, but he'd already turned his focus back to the road. While the miles disappeared beneath them, Gavin sat back to think. A spark of hope that his father may have changed in other areas took purchase, but he quickly tamped it down. Despite Lexie's valid points about reconciling, it took two people to repair the damage and that meant Gavin had to change, as well, if he wanted to get along with his dad and trust him to have his best interest at heart again.

Was he letting the constant worry from Emily's near death extend to places it shouldn't, like to his siblings? He'd once fully trusted them and happily worked alongside them. But looking back on the last few days, he'd really given them a run for the money. Especially Matt, who was fully competent.

It was one thing not to trust outsiders, but his brother and sisters? He'd sunk way low if he couldn't work with them. He may not be able to do anything else, but that he *could* change. If it extended to his father, then that would be a bonus, and maybe it would help him at work, too.

They hit the outskirts of Lost Creek and his dad pulled into Clem's Garage, with its two gas pumps, an old wrecker and an equally old whitewashed building with a rusty metal awning. The snow was the only fresh-looking thing on the property.

Hoping to see the Honda, Gavin got out to look around, but found only a pickup and minivan parked in the spaces reserved for repair service.

"I'll take lead," his dad called out as he passed Gavin.

He thought to argue, but his promise to try to reconcile came to mind and he bit his tongue.

His dad looked back and arched his bushy eyebrow. "What? No response?"

"Nope." Gavin trailed his dumbfounded father into the shop. The small, grease-stained waiting area was empty, so they pushed through the swinging doors to the repair area holding two bays.

Earl Clark wore dirty denim coveralls that hung on his body. He looked up and ran the back of his hand over a scraggly beard, leaving an oil stain on his cheek.

"Sheriff." Earl switched his focus to Gavin. "Oh, looky what we have here. Heard you come back home… Mr. Big Shot FBI Agent all dressed up in a suit."

Gavin left the guy's barb alone, as it served no purpose in responding.

"You here to harass me like you used to do when you was a deputy?"

"Guess we don't remember things the same way," Gavin said. "You were chopping up hot cars for parts and I was just doing my job."

"*Allegedly* hot cars." Earl crossed his arms. "Never proved that, now, did you?"

"That's water under the bridge," Gavin's father said and Gavin stood back to let his dad do his thing. "I was hoping you could tell us where you were last night around nine."

"Home. Watching TV."

"Can anyone vouch for that?"

"Maybe you should tell me why I need vouching for."

"What about two nights ago? Where were you about the same time and the next morning?"

"That's when that plane exploded and Doc was killed, right?" Earl pulled off a stained Texas Rangers ball cap worn backward and ran a hand through his thinning hair. "You think I had something to do with his death. Unbelievable."

"Clem said you called in sick the next morning."

"That don't mean I killed someone."

"No, it doesn't, but you do have the skills to build a bomb."

A sly grin crossed his mouth. "I do at that. But again, doesn't mean I did it."

"Just tell us where you were," Gavin snapped.

Earl smirked.

"Don't make me haul you in for formal questioning, Earl," Gavin's dad warned.

Gavin hated that his father was keeping his cool when he'd lost it. And he hated that this conversation was going nowhere, so he pulled out his phone and faked checking a text, but turned it on to record Earl's voice for Lexie. Sure, if he confessed to something, the audio wouldn't hold up in court, but Gavin didn't plan to use it in an official capacity.

"Fine," Earl grumbled. "If you must know…it was payday, and I tied one on the night before and was sleeping it off. Again. I was alone."

"Might you have a Honda that you're working on?"

"Not at the moment, no."

"You have one here recently?" Gavin asked.

Earl shrugged.

"If you can't be more specific, I'd like to take a look at your records," Gavin said.

"And I'd like a million bucks." Earl grinned.

"We can get a warrant," Gavin's father said. "Or just ask Clem for the files."

"Clem's not about to give up the records any more than I am."

"Are you sure about that?" Gavin asked. "He willingly told us you called in sick."

A buzzer chimed from the reception area.

"Gotta see to this customer. What with Clem being mad at me for calling in sick an' all, don't want to peeve him off more." That sly grin returned as he walked away.

Gavin followed him and had to fight the urge not to make some smart-alecky comment. It likely wouldn't faze Earl, and if Gavin spouted off in front of a customer, it could only serve to hurt Clem's business.

"That didn't go so well," Gavin said after settling back in the patrol car.

"You liking him for this?" his dad asked.

"He doesn't have a verifiable alibi. He fits the size and build of Lexie's almost abductor, too. So I won't rule him out."

"Agreed, but none of that's enough for me to arrest him." His dad shoved the key into the ignition. "Plus we don't have any obvious motive."

"From what I know about Earl, he doesn't really need a motive to break the law, but killing Dr. Grant and the near abduction took some planning."

"And Earl isn't real big on the planning skills," his father finished for him.

For once Gavin agreed with his dad when he wished

he didn't. Because that meant they weren't any closer to finding a suspect and, in his opinion, time was just ticking down until the killer ramped up his efforts to find the information he obviously thought Lexie possessed.

From her spot on the sofa, Lexie heard the front door close and Gavin in the hallway talking with his father. They stepped into the room, both of their gazes tight. She didn't know if it was because they'd struck out or because they hadn't gotten along.

Gavin marched straight over to her and held out his phone. "I recorded Earl's voice for you. Take a listen and let us know if he's the guy at the airport."

She held her breath as he tapped his screen to get the audio going. Despite her desire to see the killer caught, she was relieved when the man's voice wasn't familiar. "It's not him."

"We didn't think so," Gavin said.

She opened her mouth to respond when the burner phone in her pocket rang. She jumped. "It's the phone from my truck."

"Answer and let me listen in." Gavin sat next to her and, once she lifted the phone to her ear, leaned so close she nearly fumbled the phone.

"Hello?" she answered breathlessly.

"Who is this?" the scrambled voice asked.

"Lexie Grant. Who is this?" she demanded.

Gavin shot her a look that said to cool it.

"You will leave the files in Lost Creek Park," the voice said.

"I don't have any files. You took them."

"Took them? I have no idea what you're talking

about, lady. I've looked everywhere. Found nothing. You must have them."

Why was he playing dumb?

"I don't have a clue what information you're looking for," she said.

"Fine. Lie to me. It doesn't matter. You'll bring the files to the park at eleven o'clock. Come alone. No cops. Drop them in the garbage bin at the bench by the swing set. Then leave. I'll be watching. If you don't do what I say, you'll die."

"But I—" she started to say when the call disconnected. She dropped the phone like a burning log on the couch.

Gavin grabbed it and tapped the screen a few times. "We can get records for the caller's phone number, but I imagine it'll lead to another burner phone."

"Trace?" his father asked.

"Call was too short."

Walt widened his stance. "Then we need to do as he says and set up a dummy file for the drop."

Gavin eyed his father. "Lexie's not going anywhere near the park."

"We'll scout it out and go in plain clothes to protect her."

"The caller sounds familiar with the town and could recognize all of us." Gavin scowled at his father. "Even your other deputies."

"Then I'll get deputies from Cypress County."

Gavin jumped up and puffed out his chest as he crossed over to Walt. "They can't protect her from a gunshot."

The sheriff took a matching stance. "She can wear a vest under her jacket."

"And her head?"

"A ballistic helmet under the hood."

"No," Gavin said, his hands curling in fists. "She's not going."

"Listen, son. We need her to do this."

"Will you two stop it," Lexie blurted out. "This is my decision to make."

They both turned to look at her as if they'd forgotten she was in the room.

"And before I make it, I have one question," she added.

"Go ahead," Walt said.

"If this guy has the envelope, why is he asking me for information?"

"Good question," Walt replied.

"Two people could be looking for the information," Gavin said. "One of them is looking and doesn't know the other one has already gotten his hands on it."

"You thinking partners who've turned on each other?" Walt asked, his eyes lighting up with interest.

"Could be, or the information is just so valuable that more than one person wants it."

Lexie couldn't believe what she was going to suggest, but she had to do it. "Then if this is ever to come to an end, it's even more important for me to go to the park. I admit I'm afraid, but I'll do it so Adam isn't living in fear all the time." She met Gavin's hard gaze. "With the protection your father has offered, that is."

"I'll put the plans into place." Walt charged out of the room.

Gavin watched him go for a moment then dropped back on the sofa and clutched her hands. "Don't do this, Lexie. Please."

She should pull her hands free, but she honestly liked

his touch. "Do you disagree that making the drop is the best chance we've had so far to capture the killer?"

"No, it's a great opportunity, but I won't risk your life."

"Would you be on board with this plan if it involved someone other than me?"

"It would depend on the circumstances, but yes, I likely would." He tightened his grip. "But it *is* you, sugar, and I still care about you. I can't stand the thought of you getting hurt."

She reveled for a moment in his caring. In thinking that he might still love her. But it was precisely for that reason that she pulled free and went to look out the window to put distance between them. "If there's any chance that this will keep Adam safe, then I'm willing to take that chance."

"And what about a chance that you could die? How will that help Adam?"

She spun. "What are the odds that this person would shoot me before determining that I left him the correct information?"

"Not very good."

"Couple that with the vest and helmet, and I'm guessing it's extremely unlikely that I will die." She lifted her shoulders into a firm line. "I'm going, Gavin, and nothing you say will stop me."

Chapter Thirteen

Nerves near the breaking point, Lexie watched the bustle of activity from the sheriff's conference room. Walt had two deputies from Cypress County under his watchful eye as he instructed them on his expectations, while Matt hustled down the hallway carrying a vest and helmet. Gavin snatched the items from his brother's hands and gave them a thorough going-over.

Matt frowned, but walked away without commenting. Lexie was impressed that Matt was able to let Gavin take over like this without speaking out.

Gavin entered the room and placed the items on the table. "I don't like this. Not one bit. We haven't had enough time to strategize. What if there are loopholes in the plan? And I wasn't able to vet the deputies Dad's putting in place. How can I know if they're qualified?"

By the time he finished talking, his voice held rare panic that scared her. She'd never seen him like this. Never. Not even when she'd said no to a long-distance relationship. He'd changed in far more ways than his clothing. This extreme cautiousness and unease, when he had always been decisive and strong, broke her heart.

"Houston has changed you," she said.

He fisted his hands. "Why does everyone keep telling me that when it's not important?"

"Maybe because it's true. You're bordering on obsessive about taking care of every single detail."

"Well, you're wrong. It's not Houston. It's..." He clamped his mouth closed.

"It's what?"

He took a breath. Blew it out. Seemed to weigh his thoughts, then closed the door. "It's because of my big mistake here. With Dad. When I shot Emily. I can't let that happen again. Can't injure someone or let someone be injured on my watch. It'll..." He shook his head and his eyes filled with anguish so deep that Lexie's breath stilled.

She'd been wrong. Way wrong. If he was this distraught even three years after leaving his deputy job, he really had needed to quit working with his dad and step away. "I had no idea how deeply this affected you. And I only made things worse by getting angry at you for leaving town."

He watched her carefully. "I'm trying to get control of it. Trying to let down my guard and work with others, but when it comes to your safety..." He rubbed a hand over his face. "Man, it's worse than ever."

She laid a hand on his arm. "But here's the thing, Gavin. You've let your feelings sway you and moved to the other extreme. Might it keep you from acting when needed? Keep you from making a necessary decision for the right reasons?"

He grimaced. "You have a point."

"Then do an honest risk assessment here to decide if I should go."

He seemed to weigh it over. "You'll keep your head down to prevent a direct shot to areas not protected by the ballistic helmet?"

"Yes."

"And you'll listen to me in your earbuds and react as I tell you? If I say abort, you'll abort."

"Yes," she promised.

"You won't linger."

"I'll do everything you've briefed me to do."

"Okay, then," he said, reluctance lingering in his tone. "I won't stand in your way."

She squeezed his arm, but he suddenly jerked her close and folded his strong arms around her. She rested her head against his broad chest and listened to his fast heartbeat. Felt the warmth of his arms. Remembered so many times when he'd held her in the past.

Then everything became clear—her hopes, her dreams, coming to the surface. She hadn't realized until now that she still hoped he would come home and they'd get back together. But now that she knew he needed to stay away from Lost Creek for his sanity, she had to let that dream go and forget about ever being with him.

She gently freed herself from his arms, the loss immediately carving out fresh pain in her heart. His gaze remained locked on her, even when Walt, carrying a communications system, opened the door. She took a step back.

Walt placed the items on the table. "Everything okay in here?"

She nodded.

"Then let's get you dressed."

"I'll do it." Gavin picked up the earbuds before his dad had a chance.

Walt nodded. "I'll double-check that we're ready on our end."

Lexie gaped at him.

"What's wrong?"

"For the first time since I've seen the two of you together again, you didn't argue with Gavin."

He glanced at Gavin and then back at her. "Seemed natural, I guess."

Gavin opened his mouth to speak then closed it and nodded instead. Walt offered a similar nod and left the room. They didn't say a word, but Lexie could tell the unspoken communication was a huge breakthrough.

Are You behind this, Father? she wondered, a flash of the faith she'd once clung to giving her hope.

Her heart sang for the progress. For both of them. For Winnie and Gavin's entire family. For herself, too?

Let it go. You know Gavin is never coming home.

"This is how you use the comms device." Gavin demonstrated, and she listened carefully to his directions.

Once the earbuds and cords were secured in place, he helped her with the vest, each touch of his fingers as he adjusted the Velcro giving her a fresh awareness of him.

She obviously still had feelings for him. Crazy, right? He might have had to leave town, but he'd still abandoned her. Exactly like her father's retreat after her mother died. That was a betrayal she'd never gotten over, and she likely wouldn't get over the same treatment from Gavin.

He settled the helmet on her head and reached for the straps, but she couldn't let him touch her any longer, so she stepped back to adjust them herself. He didn't seem to notice the change in her, just held out her jacket.

She quickly slipped her arms inside and moved away from him. She knew she was overreacting, but she couldn't let herself fall for him again. She couldn't take another abandonment. Just couldn't.

Gavin glanced at his watch. "We've got just enough time to test out the audio and get the deputies in place. Then you'll drive over to the park in my car. We'll be a short distance away in the van, monitoring you. Got it?"

She nodded.

"Then let's go." He turned for the door then suddenly spun and grabbed her in another fierce hug. She could barely keep from lifting her face and asking him to kiss her, but she reminded herself that this hug was all about him gaining control of his concerns, not a demonstration of his love.

He let her go as quickly as he'd taken her into his arms and marched from the room. Outside, he climbed in the van to conduct audio tests. Then suddenly it was time for Lexie to step out on her own. She settled in his SUV and felt so alone. She'd claimed such confidence, but her hands shook as she cranked the engine and started down the road.

Keep it together. You're doing this for Adam.

She swallowed down the fear and drove to the park. Under overcast gray skies and a biting wind that kept most people indoors, she clutched the envelope tight and crossed the park. Her knees shook and sweat peppered her forehead. If the man was watching her, which she assumed he was, he had to see her protective gear. That also meant he'd know she'd reported the call to the sheriff. Could it have made him mad enough to shoot her? She wanted to look for him, but kept her head down as Gavin had instructed.

At the bin, she dropped the envelope inside. A sense of relief mixed with her fear, but she'd succeeded in her job, so she turned and hurried toward the exit.

On the sidewalk, the burner phone rang. She quickly answered, as she was sure the caller would praise her for following instructions.

"So you thought you could pull the wool over my eyes," the scrambled voice said.

What? "I don't know what you mean."

"I told you to come alone."

"I am alone."

"Please—do you think I'm stupid? That I wouldn't recognize Deputy Ulstad?"

"Deputy who?" she asked since she couldn't very well admit to not following his directions.

"You're ticking me off."

"Sorry." She did her best to sound like she meant it.

"Lucky for you, I'm giving you another chance. I'll contact you tomorrow and set up another drop. If you don't come alone, you'll pay with your life."

She stifled a gasp.

"And I suggest you retrieve the envelope before anyone finds it." He disconnected the call.

"Did you hear that?" she asked Gavin.

"Yes."

"Do I go back for the envelope?"

"I'll have Ulstad pick it up. You go straight to the car and back to Dad's office."

"On my way." She'd really angered the killer. Though he was giving her another chance, retaliation was a strong possibility, and the only thing she might have accomplished today was to put herself in even more danger.

As Gavin took the highway exit for the city of Cumberland to watch for Silas Ross, he glanced at Lexie in the passenger seat. She'd stared out the window in silence since they'd climbed into his SUV. A good thing or he might say something he shouldn't.

The minute he'd reached his dad's office to see her sitting with her arms wrapped around her waist and her beautiful blue eyes filled with fear, he'd had to fight from drawing her into his arms and never letting go. He'd already held her twice today. What message did that send? Was she thinking he wanted to get back together? Was he leading her on? Totally not fair to her and he needed to do a better job at keeping his distance.

"Do you really think Silas Ross could be our killer?" she asked.

"The caller recognized Ulstad, so that would suggest he lives in Cypress County, which—"

"Which is where Silas lives," she finished for him. "I wish we had more time to figure out the connection, but a second drop tomorrow doesn't leave much time."

"Dad and his team are working on it. If anyone can find the connection, they will," he said without thinking. Did he really feel that way or was it just a platitude to make her feel better?

She watched him as if she, too, saw the significance of his statement.

"If you're worried about tomorrow," he said, "the agents I called in to monitor the drop are very capable."

"Sounds like you have more confidence in them than you had in Deputy Ulstad."

"Not that Ulstad isn't capable, but I don't know him. I've worked with these agents for three years and know they're top-notch."

He parked in front of the clinic and sat back to wait for Ross to show up.

Gavin kept looking at his watch, the time ticking by

slowly, but he wasn't about to start up a conversation and get distracted. About an hour after they arrived, Ross strolled down the street.

"There he is," he said.

Lexie sat forward, her hands clutched together in what looked like a death grip.

In his late twenties, the guy wore faded blue jeans and a black T-shirt under a leather bomber jacket. His hair was long, and when he entered the building, Gavin saw that it curled up in the back.

"Could he be the guy from the airstrip?" Gavin asked.

"He's the right size, and he has a similar confident strut."

"Then we'll wait for him to come out and have a chat with him so you can hear his voice."

If Gavin thought time had moved slowly before, it crept by at a snail's pace now. Just as he thought he'd crawl out of his skin, the door opened and Ross stepped out carrying a brown paper bag.

"Let's go." Gavin jumped out. He'd been worried that Ross would run when he saw him, but he didn't even notice them as he ripped open the bag to pull out a pill bottle. His hands shook as he tried to get it open.

"Silas Ross," Gavin said.

The guy's head popped up and surprise lit his face.

Either he was shocked that Gavin had caught on to him, or he was simply surprised to see Gavin back in the area.

Ross shoved the bottle into his pocket. "You back in town, McKade?"

He nodded and glanced at Lexie to see if she recognized the voice. She gave a shake of her head and

Gavin's hope that Ross was their killer fizzled, but he could still provide a vital link to the Medicaid fraud.

Ross eyed him. "Doesn't look like you're a deputy."

"No. I work for the FBI." Gavin displayed his credentials. "That's why I'm here."

"To talk to me?" His voice squeaked high.

"I saw you come out of the doctor's office with those pills."

"So?"

"So I was wondering what they were for."

Ross eyed him. "That's none of your business."

Gavin held up his hands. "Hey, relax. You're not in any trouble. I'm interested in what the doctor is dispensing, that's all."

"Then you'll have to ask him." Ross backed away, watching Gavin as if waiting to be stopped.

Gavin had no probable cause to arrest Ross and had to let him go. He turned and bolted for his truck.

Gavin knew Ross would pop a pill as soon as possible and the lawman in him wanted to stop him from driving off. He might not be able to do anything, but others could. Gavin grabbed his phone to dial 9-1-1 to report a man potentially under the influence and provide Ross's license plate. He hung up and it took but a moment to realize that with Ross disappearing, so did another lead.

"Enough messing around. I'm going to go straight to the source." He jerked open the door and stepped back for Lexie to enter. He displayed his credentials and demanded to see Dr. Lowell immediately. The receptionist cringed, but got up and disappeared down a hallway.

Gavin wasn't going to let her warn Lowell and have him run out the back door.

"C'mon." He grabbed Lexie's hand and slipped through the door to a hallway.

Down the hall, he spotted Lowell talking to the receptionist. He wore thick glasses and a worried expression, which could mean something or could simply mean he was concerned that the FBI had come looking for him. Not unusual when people learned an agent wanted to talk to them.

Gavin didn't give the doctor a chance to go back into the room, but displayed his credentials and introduced them. "I need to ask you a few questions in private. Now."

Lowell nodded. "Follow me."

They went to a nicely appointed office and took seats around the desk.

Lowell leaned back in his chair. "What's this about?"

"Medicaid and drug fraud."

He blanched. "I don't know what you're talking about."

"That's not what Silas Ross just told us."

"Silas? I'm not sure—"

"C'mon, Doc. Don't give me the runaround. Silas just left your office, and he couldn't wait to take the narcotics you gave him then get in his truck and drive. Maybe injuring someone while under the influence. We have to stop him."

"He… I…" Lowell shoved his hand through his short gray hair. "I don't know what to say."

"How about telling me what's going on, and I'll make sure the DA knows you cooperated."

"Fine. I had financial issues, okay?" He shook his head. "My wife died suddenly. Heart attack. Let's just say I took it hard. Engaged in some pretty risky behavior to drown my sorrows. Racked up a big gambling debt that I couldn't pay and was going to lose the house. Maybe the practice. Then I remembered hearing about a doctor who'd bought a list of names to bill Medicaid. Got myself a list and my debt paid off."

He paused and snapped his chair forward. "I was going to stop billing then. I swear. But the hacker who sold me the list worked for a drug syndicate. They smuggled narcotics in from Mexico and distributed them through doctors. They threatened to expose the Medicaid thing if I didn't peddle their drugs."

"Wouldn't that just expose them?" Gavin asked.

His head shook with vehemence. "They had it set up so the two couldn't be connected."

If they were dealing with a drug syndicate out of Mexico, the danger to Lexie was even greater. Her worried expression said she understood that, too.

"How exactly does the program work?" he asked calmly to keep his rising concerns hidden.

"I'm given a list of patients who make an appointment. I set them up under one of the phony Medicaid names. I create a diagnosis that will keep them coming back on a regular basis and hand them the pills. They fork over the cash and I give it to the syndicate."

"How long has this been going on?" Gavin demanded.

"About two years, if you can believe that. Not that I didn't try to get out a few times, but they said they'd rather see me dead than let me walk around with knowledge of their operation."

Gavin didn't doubt that. "Who exactly are they?"

"I was never given names of syndicate members. I simply get calls via a burner phone, and I'm told where to pick up the drugs and leave the money. The location always varies. Each time I pick up the drugs, there's another phone waiting for me, and I destroy the current phone."

"How often do you meet?"

"Every few weeks, but it's not regular. It's their way of keeping me from planning anything. I'm due for one soon. Maybe this week, but I can never be sure."

Gavin couldn't sit back and wait for a potential drop to find the killer, but this was just the lead he needed in the fraud investigation. He pulled out his card. "I want you to call me the minute you receive the drop call. Got that?"

Lowell nodded. "Are you going to turn me in?"

"Not at this point if you listen and call me."

"You better believe I will."

Gavin stood. "I caution you not to mention this conversation to your contact. If they're as dangerous as you say, they'll kill you for meeting with me."

Lowell's color faded even more and Lexie's followed suit.

Gavin thought to warn Lowell, but his warning about the syndicate being extremely dangerous applied to Lexie, too, and there was no way to sugarcoat it for her.

Chapter Fourteen

Lexie washed the flour from her hands in the kitchen sink and stared out the window. She couldn't put the conversation with Dr. Lowell out of her mind. Had her father been involved with this drug syndicate, too? How could she reconcile that? Worse yet, how did she even move forward with such dangerous men after her? Did they think she was trying to bring them down? If so, when she couldn't produce this evidence, she and Adam would be in very grave danger. She'd asked Gavin about it in the car, but he'd simply said he had to process the news and then clammed up.

"Your mind has been somewhere else all afternoon," Betty said, interrupting Lexie's musings. "Is there anything I can help with?"

"Thank you—no." Lexie dried her hands. "Only Gavin can help."

"If it's about your relationship," Betty said matter-of-factly, "I hope the two of you have had a chance to talk it out. We'd all dearly love to see you as part of our family." She smiled, her wrinkly cheeks lifting and the skin tightening.

"Don't get your hopes up," Lexie cautioned. "Seems like Gavin isn't any closer to moving back here."

"But if he did, would you have him back?"

Lexie wasn't over his abandonment and couldn't pretend all was well with them, so she shook her head.

Betty frowned and placed her hands on Lexie's shoulders. "Life's too short to waste time. If you still love my grandson, I urge you to work things out with him." She took a long look into Lexie's eyes then drew her close for a hug. She smelled of cinnamon from the snickerdoodles they'd been baking, and the familiar scent of Gavin's favorite cookies brought tears to Lexie's eyes.

She loved this woman. All of the McKades. But was that enough to let go of the deep ache she still felt over Gavin deserting her? After all, with her father gone, no one was stopping her from moving to Houston if Adam was agreeable to such a move. But could she trust Gavin not to leave her over something else?

Betty stepped back. "I've said my piece, and I won't interfere again. I'm leaving it in God's hands and I know He has big things planned for you both."

"Thank you for caring," Lexie said, wishing she thought the same thing, as she didn't think God had plans for her at all.

Betty squeezed Lexie's hand. "You go find Gavin, and I'll finish up the cookies."

"Are you sure?"

She nodded. "Might want to bring a plate of cookies to him, though."

Lexie filled a plate and went to the office where he was reviewing files to see if he could find any connection between Dr. Lowell and her father.

He looked up from behind his computer and smiled,

looking heart-stoppingly handsome. "Please tell me those are snickerdoodles."

Speechless over the return of the good-natured Gavin, she nodded and set the plate next to him.

He snatched up a cookie, his smile disappearing as he chomped a bite and moaned with joy.

She loved seeing him as carefree as he'd been before the shooting. Oh, how she wished he could let go of his past to find this kind of contentment again. Not for her. But for him. To find the peace he needed to be whole again.

He swallowed. "I know these aren't traditional Christmas cookies, but you've gotta love Nana for adding them to her Christmas baking list because she knows I love them."

"She spoils all of you so much." Lexie sat before she did something dumb like lean over the desk and kiss him.

"She says that's what nanas are for." His silly boyish grin that Lexie had seen in many of his family portraits crossed his face.

Lexie understood his emotions. She'd once been spoiled by Betty, too. Even after she and Gavin had broken up, Betty had dropped by with freshly baked goodies until Lexie told her it was too hard to see her. She wished she'd known her grandparents, but they'd all passed and she could hardly remember them.

"So are you trying to butter me up for something with these cookies?" He took another one.

"No. I was on my way to talk to you about Dr. Lowell, and Betty told me to bring them to you."

His smile disappeared. "What about Lowell?"

"If my dad was involved in the Medicaid fraud, might he have escalated to dealing illegal drugs, too?"

"Seems quite possible."

"What if he'd tried to get out from under their control like Dr. Lowell, and they threatened to kill him? Perhaps the very reason he turned the three patients away when he did."

"Sounds plausible and could also be the reason he disappeared," Gavin said. "But there's a difference in that Lowell didn't have a family where your dad did."

"Family? I don't see how that would make a difference."

"Your dad was worth more alive and peddling their drugs than dead, so it's likely they'd threaten to kill you and Adam first."

"But when Dad took off, wouldn't they have approached us?"

"I could be wrong, or maybe when he disappeared they didn't see any point in threatening you until your dad came back to town."

"So maybe Dad didn't try to get out. Or he might not have been involved in the same syndicate and this is about something else entirely." She thought for a moment. "One thing is certain… Dad's killer said he was involved in a syndicate, and he was going to meet with the leader. But what about?"

"I suppose he could have found a way to collect information on them, and they left him alone because he could turn them in."

"And Dad put the information in the envelope. He'd said it was my insurance, so that makes sense."

"This all sounds plausible, but they were so careful to avoid giving Lowell any information. Your dad would have had to be crafty to gather anything on them."

"Well, Dad was a crafty guy. He could have followed the guy with the phone, or even paid someone to follow him. I could totally see him doing that if these men were putting pressure on him. He had such a big ego, he didn't back down from anyone, maybe not even these guys."

"You could be right, but at this point we have no proof."

Lexie's phone rang but she didn't recognize the number. Thinking it could have to do with her father's funeral arrangements, she answered.

"Ms. Grant, this is Dr. Thomas. Medical examiner."

"Yes, Dr. Thomas, how can I help you?" she asked, but wasn't sure she wanted to hear what he had to report.

"I've completed your father's autopsy and thought you might be interested in my findings. You likely already know this, but I discovered a mass in his brain. Cancerous and inoperable. If he hadn't been shot, he would've had a month or so left."

"Cancer. Dad?" She let the news settle in. "Is it possible that he wouldn't have known about it?"

"Not likely. At the cancer's advanced stage, he couldn't have explained away the symptoms. Especially with his medical knowledge."

Lexie's heart clenched and she couldn't think of a single word in response. Even when her father knew he was dying, he hadn't wanted to spend his last days with her. With Adam. Her heart creased and tears pricked her eyes.

"Also," the ME continued, "the body's been released, and you can now arrange for the funeral home to transport him."

"Thank you, Dr. Thomas." She ended the call.

"What is it?" Gavin asked.

She managed to tell him about the call before her tears took her to a place she didn't want to go.

Gavin came around the desk and knelt at her feet. He took her hands.

"How could he not want to be with me in his final days? Am I that horrible? Unlovable?" She didn't care if Gavin saw her distress, but let her tears fall, her body heaving with the pain. She freed her hands and wrapped her arms around her body to rock in place.

"Look at me, sugar," Gavin demanded.

His sharp tone snapped her from her reverie and she peered at him.

He gently pried her arms free and held her hands, the warmth of his touch comforting. "You're an amazing woman, Lex. He was a fool if he didn't love you enough to spend his last days with you."

She thought to mention that Gavin had done the same thing in leaving her, but she couldn't battle that pain now, too, so she kept her mouth shut.

"You know," he said, "maybe he left because he loved you."

"How's that even possible?"

"What if he feared the syndicate was coming after him, and he left so they'd hunt him down and leave you and Adam alone?"

Was that possible? "But wouldn't they still come after us to see if we knew where he was?"

"I suppose they might have. Maybe he explained all of this in his will, and you should consider reading it."

"I'll think about it," she said and freed her hands to wipe away her tears.

Could she honestly handle it if her father didn't mention her at all? If he hadn't said goodbye and had left because he just didn't love her?

Gavin tried to sleep on the lumpy sofa in the cabin, but he couldn't let go of his conversation with Lexie that afternoon. His heart ached for Lexie. How could she not realize what an amazing woman she was?

He wished she'd agree to get her father's will. Even if she was right and her father hadn't wanted to be with her in his dying days, it was better to know about it so she could move on.

At least, that was what he'd want to do if it was his dad. Man, thinking about his dad dying was a kick in the teeth. Would he really want to know his father resented him until his last breath? That they hadn't reconciled. How could Gavin live with that? But this wasn't about him and how he would feel if he lost his father.

It wasn't even about reconciling so he could come back home and be with Lexie. It was about now. Today. About how he and his dad couldn't talk to one another. Couldn't comfortably be in the same room together. And it was also about his mom, the whole family, in the middle of their feud, suffering.

They'd made a bit of progress today, if his dad's earlier nod when readying Lexie for the meet meant what Gavin had thought it meant. So was it the right time to approach him to try to work this out?

Gavin just didn't know. He sighed and turned over. Forced his mind to still and listen to the whistling wind. He fell into an uneasy sleep until a noise woke him.

Shivering, he lurched forward and discovered the room was freezing cold. Had the noise been in his dreams or had something happened to the heater? He got to his feet and slipped into his boots before grabbing his holster and clipping it on his belt. He took a few steps when the strong smell of propane gas stopped him dead in his tracks.

Propane powered the stove and heater, which seemed

to be out. He raced across the room to the stove, the smell growing stronger as he approached the kitchen.

The knobs were all turned off, but the smell came from behind the stove.

No! Oh, no. He's trying to poison her.

Gavin bolted for the bedrooms and pounded on the doors. "Get up! Gas! The place could explode!"

He heard movement behind Lexie's door but not Adam's. Gavin shoved the door open and jerked earbuds out of the kid's ears. "Get up. There's a propane leak. We have to leave."

He stumbled out of bed.

"Meet me at the door." Gavin ran back to the living area, where Lexie hurried to the front door and was slipping into her boots. Adam joined them. With one swipe of his hand, Gavin pulled all of their jackets from the hooks and tossed theirs to them.

"Stay here for a moment while I take a look outside." He stepped out to check for a trap. He peered around the vicinity while shrugging into his jacket.

Thinking it was safer outside than in, he turned back to them. "C'mon. Let's move."

The moment Lexie stepped outside he grabbed her hand. "We're going to run all the way to the main house." He looked at Adam. "Can you keep up?"

"Yes."

Gavin started running, but kept checking to make sure the boy was in step with them. His free hand on his sidearm, he led them to the house and unlocked the door.

"What happened, anyway?" Adam asked, his eyes filled with fear.

"A noise woke me, and I smelled propane. It was coming from the stove area."

"But we didn't use the stove."

"Exactly," Gavin said. "Wake Dad up and tell him what's going on and to call 9-1-1."

"Why can't you do that?" she asked.

"I'm going back to the propane tank to turn it off and warn the other guests."

"Isn't it dangerous to go back there?" she asked.

"The tank is a distance from that cabin, so I'll be fine."

Lexie looked like she might cry, but instead she drew him close for a hug. "Be careful."

"Always."

He headed for the stairs and heard Adam ask, "So you're hugging him now? Unbelievable."

Gavin's gut twisted as he ran across the property. He soon reached the large propane tank and turned the lever. He wanted to go into the cabin to confirm the propane source, but he wasn't foolish.

He woke the other guests and evacuated them a safe distance away. By the time sirens sounded from the fire trucks, his dad came barreling down the drive.

"You're okay." He sighed out a breath.

"Fine," he said, his mind now turning to what could have happened if he hadn't woken up. He could have lost Lexie. Adam. His own life. Lexie was right. He didn't have all the time in the world to fix things. Not only with his dad, but with everyone.

God, please. If You're there. Listening. I can't keep hurting my family. Lexie and Adam or myself. This has gone on long enough. Bring it to an end. Please. I'm ready. More than ready.

Gavin heard the fire truck stop nearby and hurried over to update Lieutenant Frazer. Carrying a device to read propane levels, the lieutenant entered the cabin while his men stood at the ready.

Frazer soon stepped outside and, after talking to one of his men, joined Gavin. "The propane levels are high, but the place isn't gonna blow. We'll add fans to suck out the fumes and I'll monitor things. Not that a carbon monoxide detector can pick up propane, but you might want to consider installing a propane alarm."

"We did install them," Gavin's dad said. "In each unit, near the stove."

"Then someone removed it." Frazer frowned. "But your location was spot-on, as the leak came from the stove."

"But I checked it," Gavin insisted. "Everything was turned off."

"True," Frazer replied. "Someone disconnected the main line."

"So this was no accident." Gavin let the deadly implication settle in. "No accident at all."

Chapter Fifteen

Gavin spent the morning getting agents up to speed and in place for the envelope drop while Lexie met with Aunt Ruth, who'd returned from vacation. Now he sat in the van with his father and watched Lexie on the large monitor. She marched up to the new drop location at the post office, and he could hardly sit still. The past few days told him he wasn't over her and that she still meant the world to him. How could he possibly rest easy with her in danger?

"I have to admit this case has me baffled," his dad said. "If our suspect was expecting Lexie to provide the information today, he wouldn't have tried to kill her last night."

"Unless he found the info between the time he called her and bedtime last night, and he no longer needs her."

"But why kill her?"

Gavin wondered the same thing. "He could think she'd read the files and he had to silence her before she told anyone. Like maybe the second guy we suspect is involved. Or maybe he thinks she's double-crossing him to try to catch him, and the attempt on her life is all about revenge."

"That would make sense, but where could he have found the files?" His father frowned. "If we don't apprehend the guy on this drop, I'll head back to Ruth's house to see if anyone's been there since Betty and Winnie cleaned up."

"Sounds like a plan." Gavin shifted his attention to the screen where Lexie tossed the envelope in the trash can and walked away. She soon stepped out of camera range. Gavin wished she could talk to him as she walked to the car and assure him of her safety, but that would alert the guy if he was watching.

Each moment he waited felt like an hour. He counted. Waited. Prayed. Yeah, him. Praying again. Maybe believing a little, too.

"I'm at the car," she finally said. "Any action?"

Gavin sighed heavily, his relief riding on the gust of air. "Not yet. Head back to the office and let me know the second you arrive."

His stress level dropped a notch. He didn't fully relax until the next call from Lexie came in. But just then a man dressed in a parka with the hood up, his head down, moved furtively down the street, grabbing Gavin's attention. The oversize parka seemed too severe even for the cold snap. It was as if he was wearing it to disappear within the huge hood. He paused near the trash can and took out his cell phone. Acting as if he was simply talking on the phone, he leaned over and grabbed the envelope.

"Move in," Gavin instructed his agents.

"You have him?" Lexie asked.

"Looks like it."

The agents slipped out of the shadows and grabbed the man. He resisted arrest, but the agents soon had him on the ground and in cuffs. They jerked him to his feet and pulled off his hood. He had slicked-back hair and a spotty beard, and was generally well-groomed.

Roiling emotions ground through Gavin's gut and he had to restrain himself from leaping out of the truck to tear into the man.

Matt arrived to take the suspect into custody. He pulled a phone from the guy's pocket and then tapped the screen a few times. "It's the phone used to call Lexie," Matt reported over the comms unit. "I'm bringing this jerk in."

"We have him!" Lexie cried out.

"Don't get too excited, Lex," Gavin warned as his father got their van on the road.

They arrived at the office and Lexie met them in the hallway. A male, cursing at the top of his lungs from the back entrance, declared his innocence in the arrest. Lexie's eyes widened and then she clapped a hand over her mouth.

"What's wrong?" Gavin asked, peering worriedly down at her.

"If that's the man you arrested, he's not the man from the airport. Not the man who killed Dad."

"Are you sure?"

She nodded, her eyes going wide. "So this isn't over."

"Let's not jump to conclusions," his father said. "The interview could clear things up."

Gavin nodded. "We'll talk to him right away."

"Will you come back to update me when you finish?" She clutched Gavin's arm.

"Of course." He squeezed her hand then followed his father to the interview room.

"Meet Yancy Vandale," Matt said as he settled the suspect in a chair. "He's the pharmacist at Speedy Pharmacy in Willow."

Eager to figure out how a pharmacist was involved, Gavin gestured for his dad to sit in the chair across the table from Vandale.

He shook his head. "It's all yours, son."

Gavin couldn't hide his surprise, but quickly recovered and took the chair to begin questioning.

Matt departed, and his dad leaned against the wall. If Gavin read him right, he appeared confident in Gavin's ability. Maybe his dad *had* changed, after all.

Gavin turned his attention to the suspect. "You're in a lot of trouble, Mr. Vandale."

He scoffed. "For picking up an envelope out of a trash can. Not hardly."

"Your comment might fly if you weren't carrying the burner phone used to call Ms. Grant and threaten her."

Vandale tried to cross his arms but the cuffs prevented it, so he jutted out his chin in defiance.

Gavin sat higher. "Take that attitude, and you'll soon be going away for murdering Dr. Grant."

His mouth fell open. "I didn't kill the guy. He was alive and kicking when I left him at the airstrip."

His statement almost knocked Gavin off his chair. "So you admit to meeting him at the airstrip?"

"Yeah, I…well…guess I shouldn't have said that. But I didn't kill him."

"So you didn't take the envelope, then?"

He paused for a moment as if searching for the right

answer. "The only envelope I took is the one I picked up today."

"What was your connection to the doctor?"

Vandale sat quietly for a moment then shrugged. "I'm done talking until you cut me a deal."

"The only thing on the table is us telling the DA that you cooperated," Gavin said, but his father would have to arrange it, as Gavin wouldn't give a guy who'd stalked Lexie a break. "And that offer expires in thirty seconds."

"Fine. That'll have to do." Vandale took a breath and let it out slowly. "Dr. Grant wrote Medicaid prescriptions for me. I didn't dispense the meds but billed Medicaid. Was pure profit."

More Medicaid fraud. Unbelievable. "Why would Dr. Grant do that?"

"For a kickback. Said he was going to live like a king in retirement. Then he disappeared and I kinda freaked out. Thought maybe you all were onto him, and he left information about our little side business behind. So I looked for the files."

"Starting with ransacking Dr. Grant's office and home right after he disappeared," Gavin clarified. "And more recently Ms. Grant's truck and Ruth Paulson's house."

"Yeah. I mean, I had to know."

"But you didn't find anything," Gavin prompted.

He shook his head. "And with Grant missing it worried me sick. Then out of the blue the doc calls me. Tells me he's coming back to town to meet with his daughter. Says he wants the money I owe him in cash or he'll hand over proof of my fraud to the authorities."

Odd. "Why would he do that when it would implicate him, too?"

"He was bluffing. He told me at the airstrip that he

was dying and claimed he'd destroyed all the Medicaid information so no one would find it. He just wanted me to show up and give him the money from the last quarter."

"But you were still worried that he didn't destroy the records and Ms. Grant had them."

"Thought she might find something when she went through his stuff. Had to push her to see." Vandale slunk down in his chair.

"Tell me why I should believe you didn't kill the doc."

"I'm not a killer—that's why."

"Or are you just trying to avoid charges even more serious than defrauding our government?"

Vandale sat forward as if suddenly realizing he was in serious trouble. "Look. You have to believe me. For one, I don't even own a gun. And two, I wouldn't have any idea how to blow up a plane. I was as shocked when that happened as you. I mean, the fireball was huge."

"You were still at the airport when it exploded?" Gavin asked.

"Didn't trust Grant. So I hung around to see what he was up to."

"You witnessed the murder, then."

He nodded. "Some dude on a dirt bike. Skinny. Crazy. Hiding behind his face shield." Vandale shook his head. "Could hardly believe what I was seeing. Then you rode up, so I took off. I was going to leave a phone and message for Lexie at her house, but I saw her truck. Figured right after seeing her daddy die, leaving the phone in her truck would scare her even more, so when I contacted her, she'd comply."

Gavin fisted his hands and had to breathe deep to keep his anger in check. "But you saw the killer take the envelope. It could have held your information."

"Could have, but the killer was focused on a syndicate. That had nothing to do with me."

Gavin had heard all he'd needed to hear. This wasn't their killer. Especially since his voice didn't match the man Lexie had heard. He got to his feet.

"Book him," he said. He left his dad to move Vandale into lockup and went to the conference room to update Lexie.

Her eyes lit up when he entered the room. "What did he say?"

Gavin explained his connection to her father.

She took in all the information, her expression tightening with his every word. "Seriously, Dad was involved in prescription fraud, too?"

"Again, we have no proof, but I have no reason to think Vandale is lying."

Her phone rang, snagging her attention. "It's Ruth. I asked her to pick Adam up from school so I could be here, and to call me when they got to Trails End."

Lexie answered, her love for Ruth burning in her eyes. Gavin couldn't help but be reminded of the days when she'd looked at him with such love, too.

She listened for only a moment and her face went deadly pale. "No, no. That's not possible. Are you sure?" She grabbed on to the wall.

"What's wrong?" Gavin asked, his cell ringing in the tone he'd assigned to Deputy Erickson.

"It's Adam." The words came out in a strangled cry. "He's missing."

The room spun. Lexie couldn't breathe. Her brother was missing. Gone. No one knew where. She was hyperventilating and her legs wouldn't hold her, so she slid down the wall and landed on the floor with a bone-jarring thump.

Gavin rushed to her side, took her hand, and she let him hold fast. Walt entered the room and Gavin filled him in on the development.

"How in the world did Erickson lose the kid?" Walt shouted.

"That's what I'd like to know."

"I'll call Erickson." Walt snapped his phone from the belt holder.

Lexie watched him like she was in an out-of-body experience. She felt numb. Lost. Like she couldn't do a thing. But she had to do something to protect her baby brother, right? But what?

"C'mon, sugar. Let's get you to a chair." Gavin helped her across the room, his warm arm around her back thawing a bit of her frozen state.

"Let me get you some water," he said and stepped into the hallway.

As if water could help her. Help Adam. She was a basket case. But she was no good to Adam this way. Ruth had few details to share except that she'd arrived to discover he was gone, and Deputy Erickson hadn't known he was missing. They'd called Adam's cell, but he hadn't answered.

That's it. Maybe he knew he was in trouble and wouldn't answer for them, but might take her call. She grabbed her phone and dialed him.

"C'mon, bud, pick up," she whispered, her heart shattering into tiny pieces as it continued to ring then went to voice mail. She left a frantic message, then stared at the phone in her hand while trying to come up with where he could be.

Gavin returned with the water and gently pried the phone from her hand. "We'll find him."

Would they? She took a sip of the water, but could barely swallow.

Walt hung up and came to sit across from her. "Erickson said he went out for a smoke. Two minutes was all, but he had to step off the property so he didn't violate school rules. He kept the front door in sight, but when he came back, Adam was gone. All-fire stupid thing to do." Walt slammed a fist on the table, sloshing the water. Gavin jerked in response. For all Lexie knew, it reminded him of the way his dad had reacted when Emily was shot.

Gavin stood. "I'll head straight over to the school to look at surveillance videos."

"Don't bother," Walt said. "Budget cuts kept them from installing them."

"Then I'll interview teachers and students."

"I'm going with you." Lexie struggled to her feet.

Gavin opened his mouth, but she wasn't about to let him waste time trying to talk her out of it. "I'm going. Period. No discussion."

"I wasn't going to argue," he said gently. "Let's go."

Walt got up. "I'll be right behind you, and I'll get Matt and Tessa over there, too."

Her legs still felt wobbly, so she let Gavin help her to the SUV. He quickly got them on the road toward the school with sirens and lights running, but despite the noise and flashing lights, it still seemed to take forever to get across town to the school. What if they were too late and something awful had happened to him?

Lexie took several deep breaths, trying to calm her nerves. She had to focus on finding Adam…not jump to the worst-case scenario. "With Vandale in custody, this proved there really are two suspects."

"Vandale could have hired someone to take Adam," he countered.

"But why would he do that if he thought he was getting the information from me today?"

"After we gather facts, I'll question Vandale again." Gavin blew out a breath. "Who knows? We could arrive to find out Adam was just in the bathroom. Or cut class and he's fine."

She shot him a questioning look. "Do you really believe that?"

"I don't know what to believe." He slammed a fist on the steering wheel. "I can't fathom the thought of anything bad happening to the kid. I love him, you know. And this happened on *my* watch."

What? Love? She'd known he'd once loved her little brother, but hearing him say he still did gave her hope she had no business embracing. Even if her heart wanted to go there, she had to let it go until after Adam was found and she could think about it. "This didn't happen on your watch but on Erickson's."

"Don't give me an out, Lexie. I'm in charge of your and Adam's protection."

"Actually, that would be your dad."

"No! Stop! Don't give me an excuse. This is my fault. You can't convince me otherwise." He swung into the parking lot.

Lexie didn't wait for the SUV to stop rocking before bolting outside and starting up the walkway.

"Hold up," Gavin called out, his footfalls pounding

closer. "This could be a trap to get you here, and I want you by my side."

He slid an arm around her waist to draw her close. They moved quickly, bursting through the door to find Deputy Erickson waiting for them.

"Any updates?" Gavin asked.

"I located one of Adam's friends. She said he got a text from Lexie telling him she'd pick him up early and to meet her in the back parking lot."

Lexie stared at the man responsible for her brother's absence. "I didn't text him, and he's a smart kid. He'd know the text didn't come from my phone."

"Supposedly the text said you had to get another phone because yours was tapped. Adam bought the story and was glad to get out of school even a few minutes early, so he readily followed the directions."

"What time did these texts arrive?" Gavin asked.

"The friend said two thirty or so." Erickson worried his lip between his teeth.

Lexie changed her focus to Gavin. "Then Vandale couldn't have sent them."

"Doesn't mean he didn't have someone else do it for him," Gavin replied. "In fact, maybe he planned this in case anything went wrong at the drop. Then he would have leverage to try to get us to release him."

"I'm sorry, Lexie," Erickson said. "This is all my fault. I shouldn't have left the school."

Lexie agreed, but she also knew people were fallible. Like when Emily had been shot. Gavin hadn't meant her any harm. He'd only wanted to help. So had Erickson. "Just help us find him."

Ruth came out from the office, her face pale, her hands shaking. "I don't know what to do. Tell me what to do."

Lexie had never seen her strong aunt shaken like

this, and it upped Lexie's own anxiety. What were they going to do? She didn't know, but calling out for God's help felt like the right thing to do.

Chapter Sixteen

Striking out on any other leads at the school, Gavin drove Lexie back to Trails End. They hung their jackets in the silent house, and he felt his family's absence acutely. While Tessa combed the school for forensic leads, everyone else had hurried into town to help man the phones at his dad's office. They were calling students just in case someone had seen something and could provide additional information on Adam's whereabouts.

Lexie wanted to make calls, too, but Gavin and his father agreed that they needed to slow down, review the investigation and work on a more expansive plan to find Adam. Since Lexie knew him best, they wanted her in on the discussion, too. But lingering in the office and continuing to hear call after call that didn't produce a lead had raised her panic level, so they'd returned to the ranch to talk.

Gavin wished Ruth could be there with Lexie, but they'd sent her home with a deputy to monitor the landline. If Adam had been abducted, and all signs were pointing that way, and the kidnapper wanted to contact Lexie but didn't have her cell number, he would call the house.

His father's phone rang and broke the silence. He answered and dread filled Gavin's gut.

"Hold on, Larry," his dad said. "Nothing about Adam, but I have to take this call." He went down the hall toward his office.

"Let's go in the dining room." Gavin gently took her arm and escorted her into the room.

They settled in chairs and Gavin kept his focus on Lexie. With each passing moment, her distress escalated and he hoped the conversation didn't make things more difficult for her.

She folded her hands on the table. "Do you think Vandale's lying and he hired someone to help him?"

"No way to be sure at this point," Gavin said. "But since kidnapping carries such stiff penalties, it seems pretty aggressive just to cover up a simple white-collar crime. My gut says Vandale's issues are unrelated to the envelope, and we need to keep our focus on the patient billing fraud."

She nodded.

"Still," Gavin said, "it's important to keep the burner phone with you in case the kidnapper is connected to Vandale and he uses that phone."

Lexie dug both phones from her pockets and placed them on the table. "Why doesn't he call already?"

"He could be drawing this out to make you suffer so when he does call, you'll jump to do his bidding and give him the information."

"I can't, though." She grabbed Gavin's arm. "I don't have what he wants, and he'll kill Adam. I can't lose him, too."

"Don't cry, sugar." He rested his hands over hers when all he wanted to do was to lift her into his arms and promise he'd fix this for her. "We'll find Adam."

"How can you be so sure?"

He couldn't, but then, he wouldn't tell her that, either, so he continued to hold her hand and prayed for Adam's safety.

Lexie sat staring out the window for how long, Gavin didn't know. He couldn't sit and do nothing, so he got up. Paced. And thought things through. Grasping for anything they might know to locate Adam. But what? What rock had they left unturned?

The will.

He pivoted to face Lexie. "Your dad's will could contain information to point us in the right direction."

"Wouldn't Mike Alexander bring it to our attention if it did?"

"Confidentiality might keep him from revealing anything. Or if your dad left a sealed envelope for you, Mike wouldn't know what it held."

"You think?" Her face brightened for a moment, and then the hope vanished. "But I can't… I mean hearing… I—"

"What if I read it so you don't have to?" he offered, as he knew where her thoughts were going.

"Yes, that would be perfect."

"Then give Mike a call while I see if Dad will go pick it up."

"Can you go?" she asked. "I feel silly enough about not taking care of this myself, and I don't want to send the sheriff to run an errand for me."

"He cares about you, Lex, and he wouldn't mind."

"Still, I'd feel better if you'd do it."

She wanted something from him. Exactly what he'd been hoping. Maybe not this particular thing, but there was no way he'd say no. He'd be gone for thirty minutes at most, and if a half hour might help repair the rift between them, then it was worth the risk of being gone when the kidnapper called. Besides, if the kidnapper phoned, his dad could immediately notify him.

"You get hold of Mike, and I'll ask Dad if he can stay home long enough for me to pick up the will."

She picked up her phone and Gavin started for the office. It felt weird to be going to ask his father for a favor. Even odder, that he trusted his father to keep Lexie safe. But surprisingly he did. Completely.

His dad was stowing his phone on his belt clip when Gavin stepped through the doorway.

"Something new happen?" he asked.

"No, but I'm wondering if Dr. Grant might have left a letter to Lexie with his will that might explain things."

"Good thinking. You call Mike to bring it out here."

Gavin had let his emotions to help Lexie color his thinking and miss this obvious solution. Still, he wasn't going to back out on telling her he'd go. "Lexie wants me to head into town to pick it up."

"It's not a good idea to take Lexie into town."

"I totally agree, which is why I wanted to ask if you can stay here to keep an eye on her."

"Me? You want me to handle her protection?"

Gavin nodded and their gazes locked. He'd have to be blind to miss the burgeoning look of hope and pride in his father's eyes. Another good reason for Gavin to go to town. He could start repairing the rift with his dad, too.

Emotions raced through Gavin and he cleared his

throat to ward them off. "Unless, of course, you have something else you need to do."

"Of course not. I'll do whatever I can for that little girl. You know that, right?"

Gavin nodded.

"It's none of my business, but you ever think maybe it was a mistake to let her go?"

"I didn't let her go. I wanted to try for a long-distance relationship until Adam went off to college, but she didn't want to have anything to do with me." Gavin couldn't believe he was sharing the details of his breakup with his father, of all people.

"I can see that." He quickly held up a hand. "Not that I'm judging you for your decision, but after the way her daddy hurt her, your leaving had to do a number on her."

"Yeah," he said, but didn't know what else to say.

Fortunately, Lexie poked her head into the room.

His dad smiled at her. "Sounds like you and I are going to hold down the fort for a little while."

"Thank you," she said.

"Hey, no problem." His dad was doing his best to sound cheerful, but a hard edge rode under the tone, giving Gavin reassurance that his father was taking this duty seriously.

"I just need a piece of paper to write out a letter authorizing Gavin to pick up the will," Lexie said.

"Still keep paper in the top drawer?" Gavin asked as memories of coming in to get paper to draw as a kid assaulted him.

"Yep."

Gavin pulled open the drawer and it hit him then how very much he wanted God's help to reconcile with his dad and regain his relationship with his family. It would have to wait until they brought Adam safely home and the killer was behind bars, which he prayed they would do, but wanting the change was half the battle, right?

Lexie couldn't sit there staring at the phones. Walt was in the office taking care of whatever business Larry had called about. The sheriff loved coffee, so she went to the kitchen to brew a pot in thanks for his support. She set the phones on the table and got the coffee brewing. While she waited, she decided to load the dishwasher with baking dishes that Betty had left behind in her rush to leave.

Lexie soon completed her task when her phone chimed. She turned to discover her phone lit up and rushed to the table. She found a new text with a video but no message from a number she didn't recognize. She opened the file. It started loading, a circle spinning on the screen as fast as the thoughts in her head. The video cleared, and at the sight of the image filling the screen, she gasped. Weakness invaded her body and she dropped the phone.

"No, oh, no." She scrambled to pick it up. "Please let it work."

She tapped it and the screen came to life. "Thank you!"

She watched the short video of her brother gagged and handcuffed to a bar on a worn, slatted wall.

Her brother. A captive. Prisoner. She thought she might be sick and dropped to the chair. Panted to catch her breath. To think.

There was no message, sound or request—why? Maybe to torment her more. Was that even possible?

She sat staring. Playing the video over and over, trying to make out the location. Willing the phone to chime again. When it did, she jumped.

Don't tell anyone about this text. Come alone to meet me, and I'll let Adam go. If you're not here in thirty minutes, he dies.

A chill pierced her heart. He was going to kill Adam. Kill him if she didn't join him. Her brother. Her poor little brother. Bound. Gagged. Needing her. Needing her now!

She'd bolt out the door right now if she thought Walt would let her go, but if he heard her, he'd come after her. Just the opposite of the kidnapper's demand, likely ensuring that he would kill Adam.

She thumbed in a response to buy time to think.

Can't get away. The sheriff's being extra vigilant.

Are you sure? I made sure the sheriff and his men are far too busy to notice you.

What in the world did this guy mean? Did he know something she didn't?

She had to check on Walt. She silently crept down the hall.

He paced his office, his phone to his ear. "What do you mean Vickson's old house exploded? Why would someone blow up an abandoned house? Are we looking at a bomb here?"

A bomb. A perfect distraction—and it fit with the profile of the guy who blew up the plane. A guy who now had her brother. Her heart constricted and she glanced at Walt one more time.

He was indeed distracted, and she had to believe the kidnapper had set the explosion for that very reason.

She was free to go to Adam. To save him. She grabbed her jacket from the foyer peg and rushed back to the kitchen to text the kidnapper, asking where she was to meet him.

He provided a rural address not too far away.

On my way, she replied, her fingers trembling so hard she had to use autocorrect to send the simple message.

Calm down, she warned herself. *Adam needs you calm. Not a basket case.*

She pulled in a deep breath. Let it out. Took another and then grabbed the keys for the ranch truck from the holder by the back door. She quietly slipped out of the house and ran for the truck. Near the stable, she paused to lift her face.

God, please. Please let me be doing the right thing and make sure the kidnapper releases Adam as he promised.

She climbed into the truck, and thankfully, it fired on the first try, so maybe Walt hadn't heard it start.

When she made it to the narrow, rutted road leading to her destination and no sirens sounded behind her, she heaved a sigh of relief that she'd gotten away without being detected. She drove for several miles then pulled off the road onto a weed-infested lot. She got out and childhood memories came racing back.

The property owned by an oil company held abandoned drilling equipment. Most notably, an old, wooden oil storage tank that Lexie estimated at twenty feet high. One of her classmates had gotten stuck in it when she was in second grade. The oil company had put a lid on the open tank the next day and removed the ladder. They claimed it was cheaper than cleaning up the oil residue. They'd also fenced the property with barbed wire, but as Lexie approached, she discovered the wire had been cut.

She spotted a Honda Accord parked farther in. It had to be the car Gavin had seen at the overlook. She made her way down a path of knee-high grass flattened from foot traffic. The sound of a generator or pump drew her attention to a small storage shed. The door opened and a man stepped out.

"Where's Adam?" she screamed at him.

He faced her, a gun in his hand. She instantly recognized him from when she'd passed the fire pit at the cabin. He was staying at the dude ranch. He'd been there right under their noses all along. Right next door.

Anger started flowing through her body. "Where's my brother?"

"All in due time."

She gasped. It was him. The man from the airfield. The killer. Standing right in front of her. A murderer, and he had Adam.

"My brother?" she demanded, though fear invaded her every cell.

"Like I said, you'll see him soon."

She had to believe him, as thinking that he could have killed Adam wasn't something she could bear. "Who are you?"

"Name's Dean Wilcox."

Fear fought to take control, but she swallowed hard. "Is your name supposed to mean something to me?"

"Not likely, but it should. I'm your brother."

"Brother? You're nuts. I only have one brother."

"That you know about." He scoffed. "Dear old Dad got my mom pregnant before he married your mother. Left my mother in a lurch. Alone and penniless."

"I don't believe you."

"Figured you'd be just like Dad." He pulled a folded piece of paper from his jacket pocket. "Had to show him the DNA results, too. Not that it mattered. He still didn't care and wouldn't acknowledge me."

Dean handed over the paper and she took a long look at it. He could have faked the document, but he was angry enough for her to believe him. She looked at him then. Really looked at him. Saw her father's aquiline nose. His stance with the uneven shoulders and bowlegs. How had she missed that at the airport? Shock. Fear. So many reasons.

"You look like him," she said.

"Not that I want to resemble that jerk, but yeah, I do."

"How could you kill him? He was our father."

He narrowed his eyes at her. "How do you know I killed him?"

"I was there. In the building shadows. I saw you shoot him, take the envelope that he tried to give me and then ride right past me."

A shock of surprise lit his face. Then his lip curled like an angry dog. "So he *was* planning to betray me that night. I should have known."

"You said he didn't want to have anything to do with you, but obviously you were connected somehow."

"Yeah, because of his stupidity," Dean snarled.

"Explain, please." She tried to sound calm but her heart was racing as fast as Gavin's stallion could move.

"He abandoned Mom, and me, and we had very little to live on, but we got by. Then when I was in high school, she developed a chronic illness. I had to find a way to provide for us. To pay her medical bills. But how? I was just a kid. So I got involved in dealing drugs." He snorted. "Turns out I was good at it. Worked my way up in the organization. Until I called the shots."

Was he part of the drug syndicate? If so, he was a very dangerous man and she had to be careful not to make him mad. "I'm sorry you had to resort to that, but what does this have to do with killing Dad?"

"My mom said if he'd stuck around, our life would have been easier. I begged her to tell me who he was so I could contact him, but she refused to tell me until she was on her deathbed."

"But why?" Lexie asked as she looked around for any hint of Adam. "He could have helped you."

"Ha! He wouldn't have lifted a finger and she knew that. She said he wouldn't have anything to do with me, and she didn't want me to face rejection on top of being abandoned." His voice caught and he fisted his hands.

At his intensity, Lexie's fears rose.

"She brought him up all the time to tell me how horrible he was so I wouldn't pine for him," Dean continued. "And she was right. He said acknowledging me would ruin him. He couldn't tarnish his precious reputation. I hated him."

"Then why did you contact him?"

"*Why?*" He sneered. "Because when she died I was left all alone. With no one to rely on but myself. I had to give him a piece of my mind. But you wouldn't understand. He babied you and your brother."

"You don't know what you're talking about! After my

mom died, we lived with our aunt and he didn't spend much time with us."

"But he acknowledged you!" He spit on the dirt and ground it in. "That's what he thought of me. Told me to my face." He glared at her as if he was staring right through her.

She didn't want to believe her dad could have been so cruel but losing her mother had changed him. A bitter man, he'd lived for his reputation. And also money, as she'd learned in the last few days. This guy had threatened that, so she could see her father rejecting his son.

A car drove by on the road and Dean snapped out of his trance. "Enough talking. Time to act."

"But you didn't tell me about the syndicate."

"Why would I?"

"So I can understand my father."

A slow, snide smile slid across his lips. "No point. Not when you won't be long for this world."

Chapter Seventeen

Gavin wanted to tear open the envelope and read the will, but he set out for the ranch so he wouldn't be gone from Lexie any longer than necessary. Especially with the explosion that had recently occurred on the outskirts of town. His dad would be chomping at the bit to get to the scene, and Gavin didn't blame him.

Eager to see Lexie, he climbed the stairs and pushed open the door. His dad came charging out of the office, his hand on his service weapon. "Good. It's you."

Gavin was thankful his dad was taking Lexie's safety seriously by checking out who was entering the house. Gavin glanced in the family room. Found it empty. "Where's Lexie?"

"She was making coffee and doing the dishes when I last checked on her." He glanced at his watch. "That was about fifteen minutes ago. Been tied up on the phone. I'm sure you've heard about the explosion."

Gavin nodded but his gut felt unsettled. His dad had come running when he'd heard the front door open, but what if someone had come to the door in the kitchen? Would he have heard that from his office?

"I'll just go check on her." Gavin's apprehension got the best of him, so he charged for the kitchen. Found it empty. Spun and returned to the hallway. "She's not in the kitchen."

"Then where...?" His dad's face paled.

"Lexie!" Gavin climbed the stairs two at a time, though he had no reason to suspect she'd be upstairs. "Where are you?"

He glanced into the bathroom then flung open all the bedroom doors. She was nowhere to be found. He bounded back down the stairs. "Not upstairs."

"She could've gone out to the stables," his dad said.

Gavin took off running, calling for her on the way. He heard his father charging after him. Gavin did a quick inventory of horses in the corral. All present and accounted for, and she wasn't anywhere nearby. He fumbled with the latch on the fence and charged into the stable, but quickly determined it was empty.

"Dear God," Gavin prayed in desperation, "where can she be?"

He couldn't stand around to wait for an answer. He raced outside.

"Son?" his father said as he joined him.

Gavin shook his head and couldn't speak aloud the words that Lexie was missing and the killer could have taken her, too.

"Man, oh, man." Looking panic-stricken, his dad started to pace. "How could I have been so *stupid*? I should have been more vigilant. I really let you down."

Gavin opened his mouth to snap at his father as he once would have done, but what good would it do to rail at him? To blame him, when he'd done nothing wrong. Gavin would have let Lexie do the dishes and gone about his own business, too, as the ranch was a secure location. They were all people. Fallible people. This could have happened to any one of them.

He met his dad's distraught gaze. "I'm upset that she's missing, but I understand how it could happen."

Tears filled his dad's eyes. If Lexie wasn't missing, Gavin might say something more, but she was gone. "Pull yourself together, Dad. We have to find her and Adam."

Nodding, his dad squared his shoulders and then clapped him on the back. "We'll find them together, son. You have my word."

"Together," Gavin said, but had no clue where to start.

Gun at her back, Lexie moved deeper onto the property. She needed more information from Dean. Like why he wanted to kill her. Hopefully asking more questions would also distract him long enough to figure out how to get away and free Adam.

"While we walk," she said, "you can at least tell me how my father got involved in the syndicate."

"Our father," he snapped.

She stopped to look back at him. He shoved her and her feet tangled in the long grass. She lost her balance and hit the ground hard. Dean stood over her, sneering, but she wouldn't say a word. She simply got up and straightened her clothes.

"*Our* father," she said. "How did he get involved with the syndicate?"

"Started with him treating me like dirt. Less than dirt. Pond scum. So he had to pay." He gestured with his gun for her to keep moving.

She'd rather watch his face to see his emotional state, but she stared off slowly. "You wanted him dead."

"Not back then, but I did want to see him ruined. To shred the reputation he thought more of than me."

"So you planned to release the DNA results?"

"Are you kidding? That wasn't enough. I wanted him to beg me to help him first. So I had a colleague sucker him into our Medicaid fraud scheme. He had no idea I was behind it all, and he took the bait. Figured he would, what with his love of money."

"And then you blackmailed him, so he had to peddle your drugs."

Dean laughed. "I wasn't quite ready to reveal myself, but yes, that's exactly what my associate did. Once dear old Dad was in too deep to get out, I made sure he knew I was behind it all. That I now had control over 'his royal highness.'"

He stopped talking and she glanced over her shoulder to see him frowning.

He caught her gaze then pushed her forward as if taking out his anger at their dad on her. How odd it was to think "their dad" and mean someone other than her and Adam. Totally surreal.

"But then Dad took off," she said to keep Dean talking while she looked around for a way to get the drop on him. She caught sight of the old oil tank in the distance, the top removed and a tall ladder on the side. That had to be where he was keeping Adam. She frantically searched for a weapon to use to take Dean out.

"I had to admit I didn't see that happening," he continued on his own, and she listened while surveying the area. "I could never have predicted that he would get a tumor and not have long to live. That he'd want to go somewhere and lick his wounds to die."

So Dad had indeed known he was dying and hadn't told her. "You knew about the cancer?"

"He tried to use it to bargain with me to leave him alone. Didn't believe him until he produced proof. But then he tried to burn me with the syndicate."

"How?" she asked.

"He made me feel like such a loser that I got stupid. Thought if he realized how resourceful and successful I was that I could change his opinion of me. So I bragged about outsmarting the syndicate and skimming money from them. He recorded our conversations and was going to meet with them the day he came back to turn the file over to them."

"Why didn't he do it before he took off? Why wait?"

"He thought if he held on to the tapes that he could control me by threatening to turn me in to the police." Dean's voice vibrated with anger. "He knew I already had two strikes against me and another arrest would put me in prison for a long time. I wasn't going back there."

"It worked, though, didn't it?" She was surprised that she sounded proud of her father's skills when she was beginning to see what a truly unethical man he'd been.

"Until I put all of the syndicate's resources to work and found him." An evil grin slid over his mouth.

"So this envelope contained tapes?" she said, hoping to get all of her questions answered.

"Among other things. Like a mushy letter to you and Adam explaining what he wanted you to do with the tapes."

"Which was what exactly?"

"He admitted that he never was going to turn me in to the police. That would tarnish his reputation. He only wanted to see me pay and figured the syndicate would take care of that." A muscle ticked in Dean's jaw. "So he hired an investigator to follow our delivery mules and figure out my superior's identity."

Just like Lexie suspected. "And did he?"

"Yeah, but he was worried that after he handed over the files, the syndicate would turn on him since he knew their identity, too. And he also thought they might still go after you and Adam."

"But they didn't."

"Only because when he learned he was going to die, he wanted to live out his last months on his own terms, not looking over his shoulder and ending up some syndicate hit. So he held on to the information until nearer his death. Came back to town to give you a copy for leverage against the syndicate."

"I would have turned it over to the police," she said.

"He was banking on your love for Adam to stop you from giving up your insurance and putting his life in jeopardy."

She hadn't thought of that. That was probably what she would have done. Either way, she was thankful she hadn't had to make that decision. Still, it had put her in this situation. Endangered their lives. But why had Dean targeted her?

She stopped walking and faced him. "None of this explains why you abducted me and Adam."

"Why? You want to know why?" His voice rose, stirring birds into flight. "Because even in death he found a way to cheat me out of my rights as his son."

"How?"

"His stinkin' will, that's how. I'm surprised you haven't heard about it yet."

"I don't want his money or things, so I haven't asked to see his will, but how do you know what's in it?"

"He included a copy in the envelope with another stupid explanation for you. Of course he left everything to you and Adam, but he wasn't taking any chances that the syndicate might not get rid of me." Resentment darkened Dean's tone. "He was afraid if I was alive, I could use DNA to prove my parentage and contest the will. So he named your aunt as the estate executor with instructions on how to handle the money. If at any point you could prove I died, the money would be disbursed to you."

She didn't know how to respond, so she said nothing.

He glared at her. "Everything was your fault. If he didn't dote on you so much, he would have spent time with me. He might be dead, but I'm still going to get my revenge."

"How exactly?" she asked.

"You're so stupid you have to ask? How could he have loved you? I'm the superior one. I'm the one he should have loved." He bared his teeth in a snarl. "No matter. You will die today, and I will have the last laugh. Now, get moving before I shoot you without letting you talk to your precious little brother."

"What are you going to do about Adam?" she asked, afraid to hear the answer. If Dean wanted the inheritance, he couldn't possibly leave Adam alive.

"It's not about the money, you know," he said as if reading her thoughts. "It was never about the money. I have plenty. Our snooty father despised Adam as much as me, so I have a soft spot for the kid."

Lexie doubted he had a soft spot for anyone or anything.

"So I don't care what happens to Adam. I didn't let him see my face and didn't tell him my name. Means I can let him go." Dean fixed his gaze on her then fingered one of her curls. "But you, my dear sister, won't make it through the day."

Chapter Eighteen

❧

Gavin needed to be in the last place Lexie had been seen. He had no idea why, but he settled in the kitchen and ripped Dr. Grant's will from his pocket to see if it did, in fact, hold a lead.

His dad bustled in the door. "I noticed the truck was gone, so I called your brothers and sisters. None of them took it. Means Lexie must have grabbed the keys from the hook."

"So you think she left of her own volition?"

"Either that or the truck was stolen. Not a likely scenario."

"But why would she leave?" Gavin asked.

"No clue, but I've got Matt requesting a warrant for her phone records. I have to warn you, son, without any sign of a struggle here, we may not get it." He stepped to the back wall and ran his fingers over the key rings dangling on the pegs.

"Keys are gone, all right." His father shook his head. "I should never have let your mother hang them up here. I'm the sheriff, for pity's sake, and know criminals can smash a window and grab them. But with Dad around all the time…" He shrugged. "Still, it's my fault."

"Remember we're not playing the blame game," Gavin said. "Let's tear into Dr. Grant's will." Letting the envelope flutter to the floor, he started reading, his dad standing behind and peering over his shoulder.

"No way." Gavin pointed at a long clause. "Lexie has a half brother."

"Give me that." Walt grabbed the paper. "Guy's name is Dean Wilcox. Never heard of him."

"Say that again," Gavin said before his mouth dropped open.

"Dean Wilcox. You know the guy?"

"He's one of the cabin guests."

"Here? On my property?" His dad slammed the paper on the table. "How'd I let that happen right under my nose?"

"How could you have known he was a killer?"

"Couldn't have, but still—"

Gavin jumped to his feet. "We need to get over to the cabin. See what we can find."

"I'll grab a set of keys from my office, and I'm right behind you."

At the base of the oil tank, Lexie called out, "Adam, are you in there?"

She thought she heard moaning and reached for the ladder.

"Hold it right there, Lexie," Dean warned. "Your brother's waiting for you, but we need to get you ready first."

She spun. "If he's in there, why didn't he answer?"

"Duct tape. Couldn't have him screaming and alerting anyone who might be brave enough to venture onto the property." He pulled shiny metal handcuffs from his pocket and crossed over to her. "Take off your jacket."

"But why?"

"Just do what I say or I won't release Adam."

She shed her jacket and let it fall to the ground, the cold instantly chilling her body.

"Now, hold out your left wrist."

She complied and he clamped a cuff tight enough to cut off her circulation and bite into her tender flesh. She wanted to cry out, but pressed her lips together so he couldn't see he'd hurt her.

He pulled a ski mask from his pocket and slipped it on. Good. If he continued to hide his face, she'd be seeing Adam soon, and Dean would still let him go.

"Now climb up the ladder and down the one inside." He met her gaze. "Mention my name to Adam and the boy will die right beside you."

Eager to see Adam, she moved fast. She crested the rim and spotted him in good condition minus the tape on his mouth. Her heart soared at seeing him alive and peering up at her, but fell when she noticed his wrists were cuffed to a metal rod that looked something like a towel bar bolted to the wall on both ends.

"Adam," she cried out.

He tried to speak but the tape muffled his words.

She didn't know why he didn't simply slide his hands up the bar to remove the tape. "Take the tape off so I can understand you."

His eyes widened in fear and he shook his head.

"I told him I'd kill you if he did." Dean chuckled as he climbed the ladder.

Adam slid his hands up the pole as if reaching out to her. She hated seeing his desperation. He may be as tall as a full-grown man, but he was still a boy inside.

When she got out of this situation, and she would, she'd make sure Dean paid for hurting her brother.

"Get moving, *sis*," Dean said.

She ignored his mocking endearment and maneuvered over the top to the other ladder. On the ground, she grabbed Adam in a hug and kissed his cheek over and over, her helplessness in not being able to free him almost more than she could bear.

"I'm here, bud," she said, making sure she sounded confident. "And I'm going to get us out of this."

"Ha!" Dean peered over the top. "Good luck with that. I've thought of everything." He laughed, the sound reverberating off the walls. "Now, Adam, be a good boy and secure your sister's cuffs to the bar. Make sure it's nice and tight, as I'm going to come down there to check, and if you don't do as I say, she dies."

Tears glistened in Adam's eyes. She didn't want him to have to suffer even more by securing her, so she arranged her hands above his to allow him to easily close the cuff. "It's okay. Do as he says. We'll still find a way out of here."

Adam clamped the cuff, a tear dropping from his cheek onto her arm.

Her anger at Dean mounted. Turned to rage.

She swallowed it down and jerked on her cuffs to show Dean that Adam had followed through. "Ready for your inspection."

He stowed his gun and moved into the tank. Once on the ground, he checked her cuffs.

"What are you going to do with me?" she asked.

"Simple. I'll be filling the tank with water." He backed toward the ladder.

Water? No. He couldn't possibly do that, could he?

"Why go to all this trouble?" she asked. "You've got a gun. Why not just shoot me?"

"Payback. My mother died from lung disease. She struggled to get her breath all the time. I watched her at the end. Her chest convulsing with the need for air. You're going to see what that feels like." His gaze locked on Lexie, hatred and bitterness oozing from his every pore.

"By why this tank?" she asked, hoping to keep him talking to buy time for Gavin to realize she was missing and find her. "It must have taken a long time to make this watertight when a bathtub or lake would have done the same thing."

"You can thank dear old Dad and Grant Oil for that." He sneered. "When Mom told me his name, I couldn't believe it. One of his wells was pumping away on our rental property. Right in the backyard. Day and night, the pump jack's swishing noise nearly drove me crazy."

Nearly?

"Even worse—" he shook his head "—my mother wanted to feel the sun on her face, so we moved her bed by the window. As she suffered, I sat with her and looked out at that pump jack. At the sign boasting Grant Oil. Day after day. Even as she took her last breath, I imagined how wonderful it would be to have the good doctor die in a situation where he couldn't breathe. So I prepared the tank. But he's gone now. My fault. I couldn't control my temper. No matter. You're the sacrificial lamb, and you'll bear the burden of his sins."

Gun in hand, Gavin pushed the door open. Scanned the one-room cabin.

"He's not here." He shoved his gun into the holster and started to enter, but his dad grabbed his arm.

"Let me get gloves and booties from the car so we don't contaminate any evidence."

As much as Gavin wanted to tear the room apart to find a lead, a few seconds to take protective measures for evidence that could help them find Lexie was well worth it.

He snapped on the booties and started prowling the room. "No suitcase or clothes."

"He's taken off."

"Could mean he has Lexie and has no need to come back here."

His dad's jaw clenched. "I'll get Tessa out here to process the space. Maybe she'll find evidence we're missing."

As he called her, Gavin inched through the room, looking for any lead. He spotted a piece of paper in the wastebasket by a small desk and flattened it on the desktop.

"Tessa will be here in less than five," his dad said. "What's that?"

"A receipt. For waterproof caulk. Ten tubes. Bought it at the hardware store in Cumberland five days ago. Paid cash."

"What could he be using all that caulk for?"

Gavin shrugged. "Sealing something. But what?"

"He might own property around here. Let me get Matt to run a background check on Wilcox and see what we can find out about him."

Gavin nodded and returned to his search. He had to find something. Anything to lead them to Lexie. Dear, sweet Lexie. In a killer's hands.

Gavin's heart constricted and he could hardly breathe. Time ticked past. One minute. Two. Five.

Hurry. Hurry. Find something. But what?

Nervous sweat beaded along his neck even in the cold. He heard a car drive up and saw Tessa through the window. He raced to greet her but a drop of liquid near the front door stilled his feet. He squatted to figure out what he was looking at, but his mind was a jumbled mess of fear and panic and he couldn't make sense of the liquid.

"What do you think it is?" his dad asked.

"Looks like oil. But, if so, it's dirty. Like it came from used oil."

"Or crude," Tessa said at the door.

He shot her a look. "If you can tell that from up there, you're better than I thought."

"I wish," she replied. "I got a text on the way over. The oil from the overlook wasn't refined, but crude oil."

A flash of hope took hold in Gavin's heart. "Wilcox could be employed by an oil company. That could be the lead we needed."

His dad shifted his hat. "Makes sense. Those jobs turn over fast, and I can't keep up with the workers coming and going in the county."

Gavin peered at Tessa as he came to his feet. "We found a receipt for ten tubes of waterproof caulk. So where would caulk and crude oil come together?"

"An oil well, I suppose, but surely not with that quantity of caulk."

"Unless he performed maintenance on a large number of wells." Gavin's mind raced over the facts, lighting on them, then spitting them until one held. "You think he took Lexie to a well?"

"If so, we're looking at hundreds of wells in Lake County alone. Not to mention the surrounding counties."

Panic raced along Gavin's nerves and he sought any answer to find her. "These wells just sit out in the open. He'd keep Lexie and Adam in a secluded location."

"Got enough abandoned shacks around here, too," Tessa reminded him.

"Like wells, these shacks are a dime a dozen," his dad said.

"Too many for us to check out in a timely manner." Gavin kicked the doorjamb and thought about slamming a fist into it, as well. He was powerless to help.

How could he have let this happen? How?

His father rested a hand on his shoulder. "That's what family and friends are for, son. We can split up the work and have Lexie home in no time."

Gavin nodded, but they had nearly five hundred square miles of county to cover. How could they possibly do so in a timely basis?

Lexie heard Adam quietly sobbing and could hardly bear his anguish. At least when Dean's task was done, he would let Adam climb out of the tank.

"What good little listeners you are." Dean laughed.

Lexie looked up at him. "Now let Adam go."

He narrowed his eyes. "Um, about that. On second thought, he stays."

"What?" she shouted. "No. You promised."

"I did, didn't I," he said. "But then I saw the torment you felt when you saw him tied up. How much pain will you feel if I leave him behind, too?"

Chuckling, he went for the ladder.

"No! No! Come back here."

He didn't listen but kept moving and cleared the rim. She soon heard water rushing from a three-inch pipe in the wall. At this rate, it wouldn't take long before water covered their heads.

Dear God. Please. I'm begging. If You're there, send Gavin to help us.

Chapter Nineteen

Gavin pressed out a county patrol map on the dining table. He was surrounded by his family minus Matt and Kendall, who were on their way to join everyone at the ranch.

"My deputies know their districts better than we do, so I've already got them looking," his father said. "We'll help search the quadrants that are sparsely populated and too large for one deputy to search."

He picked up a marker and Gavin was thankful for his dad's level head. Gavin wished he was thinking as clearly, but nerves had his hands trembling.

The door opened and he spun to find Matt and Kendall stepping inside.

"Any new info on Wilcox?" Gavin demanded.

"A few things actually," Matt replied.

A tight smile crossed Kendall's mouth. "I got access to Wilcox's credit card account. He's been buying caulk for months from various locations around the area."

His father arched a brow. "I don't want to know how you did that, young lady, but thankfully you did."

"And," Matt added, "Wilcox doesn't work for an oil

company. In fact, he has no known source of income, but he's been arrested for possession and intent to sell narcotics."

"Syndicate. Drugs…" Gavin muttered to himself to process. "So why's he tracking crude around on his shoes?"

"That, we don't know."

"He'd have to be stepping all over in it to still be carrying even a trace on his shoes by the time he hit the cabin," Tessa said.

"Probably has rubber mats in the vehicle," Matt said. "If this still has to do with pump jacks, I doubt he'd pick up much near them, as the oil companies are doing a much better job in preventing contamination these days."

"An oil tank," Gavin said.

"You think he has her in a storage tank." Tessa's face paled. "The fumes would—"

"Not a modern metal tank," Gavin interrupted. "But remember that old wooden one that looked like a big wine barrel?"

"The one we wanted to play in when we were kids." Kendall grinned. "And that kid got stuck in the sludge in the bottom."

His dad frowned. "We had to rescue him."

"Is it still standing?" Gavin asked.

"Not sure. I do know the oil company covered it, and we've had no incidents since then."

"It's a perfect place to hide Lexie and Adam, and it could also explain the caulk." Tessa's eyes narrowed. "He could be caulking the slats to make it watertight."

"Because?" Gavin asked, but the answer quickly became clear.

If Gavin didn't get to the tank in time, Wilcox would fill it with water and end Lexie's life.

Cold water lapped around Lexie's knees and she shivered. How were they going to make it out of the tank alive?

Dean's head poked over the top of the tank. "Good. I see the water is flowing well."

"Please don't do this," Lexie said, her teeth chattering. "At least not to Adam."

"The more you ask me to let him go, the more I want to leave him with you." Dean clapped his hands. "Now, I must go. Your big, bad FBI agent is likely looking for you by now and I don't want to run into any roadblocks."

He disappeared and Adam ripped the tape from his mouth.

"Have you been here all night?" she asked.

He shook his head. "He kept me in some old house with him. So who is he, anyway?"

She quickly explained.

Adam shook his head. "A brother. *Our* brother? Totally freaky."

"We need to let that go for now and get out of here."

"How?"

"Let's start by trying to pull these bars free." She wrapped her hand around a bar so shiny that it had to be newly installed.

"I tried all morning. No luck." Adam held up his wrists covered in angry cuts and bruises.

"I'm so sorry, buddy."

"For what? You didn't do this. It was totally Dad's fault." He sighed and leaned against the wall. "I might still be mad at Gavin, but I would give anything for him to find us."

"You know he has to be searching for us by now."

"Do I?"

"Look," she said and kept trying to wobble the bar holding them captive. "I get it now. He had to leave here or he would die inside." She explained what she'd seen in Gavin and his behavior. "If he'd stayed, he would have been miserable and so would we."

"Fine, but that doesn't mean he couldn't have come back to hang out with me."

"I think he wanted to, but it was too painful for him." She stopped tugging on the bar. "Remember when you and Shelly broke up and how hard it was to see her every day after that. It would have been easier if she'd moved away, right?"

He nodded.

"Well, imagine that when you're all grown up and truly in love. How painful that would be." She peered around the space, looking for a way out while hiding her panic rising as fast as the water.

"Yeah," he said grudgingly.

"Maybe now would be a good time to forgive him," she said not only for Adam but for herself, as well.

"Because we're not getting out of here, you mean?"

"No, because carrying the pain around hurts."

"Sounds like you still love him?"

Did she? She just didn't know. "I'm not sure how I feel about him. Would you hate it if I did love him?"

"I don't know, either," he said. "But I'll think about forgiving him."

She nodded. "Now, how about helping me figure a way out of here?"

"Our only hope is the ladder and we can't even reach that."

He was right. Dean had thought of everything.

"We can pray." She took his hands and offered a prayer, her eyes filling with tears that she blinked away before Adam saw them.

"God will help, right?" he asked.

She nodded, but one thing she knew for sure. God's help didn't always come in the form you hoped for. If it did, Gavin would be beating a path to them right now.

Come on, Gavin. Please hurry. I need you.

Did it matter that she needed him? Could he get here and free them before the water took her down, or before the cold did them both in?

She jerked on her cuffs again. Shook the bar and started screaming for help until she was hoarse. Adam took over and called out, but the water kept coming. Rising higher. Her thighs. Hips. Waist. Nothing to stop it. She was shorter than Adam, and it reached her chest first. Her heart beat furiously.

"You can float and hook a leg over my shoulder for support," Adam said.

"Just worry about yourself."

"No," he snapped. "I might only be fourteen, but I'm strong and can help you."

"Okay." She hated the thought of him standing in the water alone, but when it hit her chin, she let her body float up to the surface. Lying back, she closed her eyes and prayed again.

"Put your leg over my shoulder," he said.

Lexie didn't want to, as it would hold him down, but it would give him something to concentrate on, so she did. She talked about the future and all the things they had to look forward to to give him hope. He responded, but when the water reached his chest, he stopped talking.

The water would soon reach his mouth, but her hands were fastened above his, so she didn't know if he could float high enough to get his head out of the water. Worse, if she couldn't keep her position she'd drop onto him, and he'd completely sink below the water. And there was no way to change that. No matter how much she loved him and would give her life for him, she couldn't.

She could only trust God now. With the way He didn't seem to hear her, that thought brought little comfort.

Gavin careened the ranch's open-air Jeep around a curve on the narrow road. He and Matt might be safer in his bigger SUV, but the Jeep was a cross-country edition and they'd taken a shortcut to reach the rutted road.

"Careful, bro," Matt said from the passenger seat. "You won't do Lexie any good if you can't get to her."

Panic had his foot pressed to the floor on the straightaway, but Gavin eased up before the next curve. He rounded the bend and a car barreled toward them.

"Watch out!" Matt shouted.

Gavin jerked the wheel to avoid the other vehicle. The Jeep plunged off the road and slammed into a tree. Gavin somehow managed not to hit his head on the dash or windshield.

He shook off the shock. "Are you okay, Matt?"

"Yeah, but no thanks to your lame driving." He unhooked his seat belt and rubbed his chest before climbing out.

Gavin got his belt off, too, and scrambled out of the Jeep and after Matt, who was crossing over to the other vehicle that had run off the road and flipped.

"It's Wilcox," Matt called out.

Gavin's feet stilled. "Is he alive?"

"Yeah, but unconscious, so I can't ask about Lexie and Adam."

"We must have the right location, otherwise why would he be out here?"

"Go after her. But grab the ranch toolbox."

Gavin didn't want to waste time jogging back to the Jeep, but he also didn't want to show up at the oil tank without equipment he might need to rescue them. He clawed through weeds to locate and grab the wayward toolbox. He held it to his chest, allowing him the freedom to run. The weight slowed him down, but he kept going until the oil tank was in view.

"Lexie!" he shouted.

"Gavin!" Her voice came from far off. Had he actually heard it or was it the whistling wind?

He dropped the toolbox and raced for a tall ladder lying on the ground. He heard the hum of a pump in the distance and water running.

"Lexie," he yelled again as he leaned the ladder against the tank.

"In here. We're in here," Adam cried out.

The boy was alive, but what about Lexie? Fear squeezed Gavin's chest as he leaned the ladder against the tank then took the rungs two at a time.

He peered over the top and thought his heart might stop. Adam was cuffed to a long bar and Lexie floated nearby. Her leg hung over Adam's shoulder, the water nearing the teen's chin.

"I'll get you both out of there," Gavin promised. "Just hang on."

She opened her mouth to speak but water threatened and she clamped it closed.

"I'll grab a bolt cutter from the toolbox," Gavin said. "Hold her up, Adam. Please hold her up."

"I've got her."

It took everything Gavin was made of to turn his back on Lexie, but he leaped from the ladder. He hit the ground hard and ran toward a rickety shed where he heard a motor running. He located the water pump near a covered well, going full force, and turned it off to stop the rise of water.

He charged to the toolbox, prayed it held bolt cutters and fought with the rusty old latch. He jerked it open and dumped out the contents, revealing bolt cutters he'd used for years working on the ranch. Back he went toward the tank, pausing to shove his phone into his jacket pocket and shed the coat next to Lexie's, as they would need the warmth once he freed them.

He sped up the ladder. Lexie was sinking. Water lapping at her mouth, her eyes closed.

"Hurry," Adam called.

"Lift her higher," Gavin demanded.

"I can't. I can't." Adam started sobbing, his mouth barely above water.

Gavin wanted to lunge into the water, but he'd create a wave and further swamp them. So he eased down the ladder and into the icy liquid. The cold seeped into his bones and took his breath. They both had to be freezing.

"I turned off the water pump," he said to assure Adam, then felt around for Lexie's wrist. She stirred.

"I've got you, sugar. Cutting off the cuff now."

"Adam first," she mumbled and got a mouth full of water.

She started coughing.

"I'll help Adam next." Gavin found Lexie's handcuff. Sliced through the chain. "Can you put your arms around my neck and hold on while I cut Adam free?"

She tried to lift her arms but was unable to manage. Gavin hated to do it, but he had to let her go to clip Adam's cuffs. He worked fast, but she sank under the water. The moment Adam was free, Gavin reached for her and pushed her head above water.

She coughed and gagged.

"Go," Adam said, his teeth chattering. "Take her out. I'm fine."

Gavin didn't know if the chattering was from the cold or from fear, but in either case, he was right. Gavin had to move Lexie now.

"Get to the ladder and I'll be right back to help you."

"Just make sure Lexie's all right. Okay?"

"You're a good brother, Adam." Gavin made his way to the ladder and shifted her over his shoulder. As he climbed the rungs, he heard her breathing, and his heart sang at the sound. It took him longer than he'd hoped to clear the top and get down to the ground. He gently laid her down and ran for her jacket to drape it over her.

"Adam," she gasped.

"I'm going back for him now." Gavin returned to the tank to find Adam clinging to the ladder.

"Hold your breath," Gavin shouted and plunged from the top.

He got behind Adam and lifted.

Adam started pulling himself up.

"That's it," Gavin encouraged. "You're quite a kid, you know that? You save your sister's life, and you still have something left to climb out of here."

Adam glanced back, pride lighting his face. When he started moving again, he seemed to have more energy, and in short order, they were back on the ground.

Adam glanced around. "Your car. Where is it?"

"I crashed the Jeep about a mile from here. Let's take shelter in the shed, and I'll call for backup. Grab my jacket and put it on."

He scooped Lexie up into his arms and trudged to the dilapidated building that would at least keep them out of the wind. He sat and cradled her on his lap then turned to Adam. "Sit as close to me as possible so we can share body heat."

Adam's whole body trembled as he lowered himself next to Gavin.

Gavin fished his phone from his jacket pocket and dialed Matt to fill him in and request an ambulance.

"Already called one," Matt said. "Dad should be here ASAP, too."

"Wilcox alive?"

"Yeah."

"Good," Gavin said. He wanted the man to live so he could spend the rest of his life behind bars to pay for his crimes.

Gavin stowed his phone and slung his arm around Adam. He pulled both of them closer and offered a prayer of thanks. God had been there. With him all this time. He got that now and understood that, no matter how many times he'd asked God to change his circumstances since Emily had been shot, the point was for God to leave him in his mess to work through his own problems and change him along the way. He was changed now. For good. His priorities were finally straight.

"I made a big mistake when I left both of you," he said fervently. "Can you forgive me?"

"I can," Adam said.

Gavin knuckled his head and peered at him. "Thanks, bud. You know I love you, don't you?"

"Yeah," he said, now sounding embarrassed.

Gavin turned his attention to Lexie. She was looking at him, but her gaze seemed far away. He pressed a kiss to her forehead and stroked her cheek. "Did you hear me, sugar?"

"Yes," she said, but then closed her eyes and didn't continue speaking.

Gavin's heart split. Had he waited too long to realize he couldn't live without her and now she was unable to forgive him? If so, he'd do everything he could to change her mind.

"I'm never leaving the two of you again." He tightened his hold on them. "I'll find a way to make things work with us," he promised, but Lexie's eyes remained closed.

He had no idea if she'd even heard him, much less wanted a future with him, but he wouldn't give up.

Epilogue

Lexie unloaded the dishwasher in Ruth's kitchen and glanced at the clock. Eleven fifty-five. In precisely five minutes, the doorbell would ring and, as much as she wanted to avoid it, her heart clutched at the thought of seeing her daily visitor.

She dried her hands and went to the foyer, where she'd placed a small wooden storage box with twelve slots. Eleven slots held Christmas tree ornaments depicting the Twelve Days of Christmas. For the last eleven days at precisely twelve o'clock, Gavin rang the doorbell to pick Adam up to take him on a fun outing. Gavin also gave her an ornament and reminded her that she was his one and only true love, and he was one day closer to living in Lost Creek.

He'd reconciled with his father, but didn't think they should work together, so he'd left the FBI to take a job with the Texas Rangers' division of the Texas Department of Public Safety in Austin, which was within commuting distance to Lost Creek. He also offered the promise that he would never give up on their being together. And each day that he arrived with an ornament and proclaimed his love, her heart let go of a bit of the hurt his abandonment had caused. With today being Christmas Eve and day twelve of his ritual, she had no idea what he planned next. She had to admit she was eager to see.

The bell chimed and her heart lurched in anticipation. She opened the door and her eyes drank in the sight of him looking so ruggedly handsome in his jeans, boots and cowboy hat. He held out his hand, revealing a delicate glass figurine of a drummer in a red uniform with a silver drum. She took the ornament and held her breath in wait for his next words.

"As of this moment, I am no longer an FBI agent, and I have submitted my change of address to the Lost Creek post office," he said. "Means we're neighbors again, sugar, but I'd like it to be much more."

"Gavin, I—"

He tipped her chin up with one finger and stared deep into her eyes. "I love you, Lexie, and I hope you'll consider giving me a second chance."

Her heart told her to trust him. To throw herself into his arms. But her brain warned her that he'd once promised a future with her and then left her behind.

What was it going to take to convince her to give him a chance? Could she even do so?

"I want to but…" She felt the urging to give in but she held her ground.

His smile vanished. "What's it going to take for you to trust me again?"

'I don't know."

"But you do think you'll get there, right?"

"I don't know that, either."

He took a long breath and blew it out, his gaze filled with angst that tore at her heart.

"You know I'll never give up until you, me and Adam are a family, don't you?"

"I know that's what you want now, but will you still want it tomorrow? Or next year."

He pressed his forehead against hers and she was powerless to move.

"I have never known anything was more right in my life and I will never leave you again. Never. You hear me, Lex. Never."

She wanted to melt closer. Fall into his arms. The pain of his abandonment was gone, but the fear of him going again had a strong grip on her and she couldn't say yes.

Adam stepped into the foyer, holding a basketball and keeping her from having to answer.

He glanced between them. "She said no again, huh?"

"Basically," Gavin said, disappointment crowning in his voice. "But I still want to invite the two of you and Ruth to come to church with us tonight and then have a late supper with my family."

Adam faced her. "Can we go? Please?"

She may not be ready to commit to Gavin, but Adam wanted Gavin in his life and she didn't want to stand in his way. "I'll think about it."

His happy expression fell and she almost caved on the spot, but she really did have to think about whether she was ready to be a part of the McKade family if only for a night.

"C'mon, bud." Gavin knuckled Adam's head. "Time for me to skunk you in b-ball."

They departed, and as tears flooded Lexie's eyes, she settled the ornament in the case. She ran her fingers over each one, thinking about what it meant to be someone's true love. Gavin was hers. She knew that and wanted nothing more than to be with him forever. But…

She closed the box and felt as if she was closing the door on their relationship. Tears started falling in earnest now. She heard footsteps behind her and turned to find Ruth.

"The last ornament?" she asked.

Lexie nodded.

"And now you're crying." Ruth shook her head. "You know I've stayed out of this, but I can't any longer. I understand your pain, and see how you can't trust him. He hurt you, and you've gone through so much to get your life back. But, honestly, I don't think you ever made it back to normal. You've been reliving the pain over and over, right?"

Lexie nodded.

"Then let me tell you what my daddy once told me. Bad things happen to good people. It's a given. But it takes a smart person to know when and how to let it go. You're smart, Lex. You have to see how Adam has blossomed with Gavin back in his life, and I know you can, too. Trust God. Let this go."

Her words hit Lexie in a way she hadn't experienced so far. Even if she forgave Gavin, and he left her in torment again, she was already in torment without him, so why not give him a chance? Why not blossom as Ruth had said? Trust God to have her back in this. He'd been there for her at the oil tank. Saved her and put Dean behind bars to stand trial. God could handle this, too.

"Gavin invited the three of us to go to church and have dinner with his family tonight. I'd like for us to go."

"Of course, sweetheart." Ruth gathered Lexie in a hug. "I can think of no better way to spend Christmas Eve."

A huge burden lifted from Lexie's shoulders and, later in the day, her heart filled to brimming when she told Adam they were going. She made him promise not to tell Gavin, as she wanted it to be a surprise. She spent the rest of the day choosing an outfit, taking a long bath and then dressing for the night.

When they arrived at the small white church on a hill in the country, she was nearly breathless with excitement. The air still held a nip and her bare legs beneath the flowing skirt of her red dress were chilled, so she hurried up the steps.

The pastor greeted them at the door and she eagerly stepped inside the foyer to inhale the fragrance of pine from strung garland and a towering tree with white decorations. She quickly spotted the McKade family settling into their usual pew at the front. Gavin, still standing, glanced back and caught sight of her, stilling in place.

They stood there unmoving, locked in each other's gazes. For how long, she didn't know, but when his family members all turned to stare at her, she came to her senses. His mother reached up and clutched his arm, a wide smile crossing her face.

He started down the aisle toward Lexie, but she couldn't move.

Ruth cleared her throat. "Adam and I'll take a seat."

Gavin passed them in the aisle, his smile lighting up as he gave Adam a playful punch. Adam threw his arms around Gavin and hugged him.

Tears came to Lexie's eyes. Glorious, happy tears.

They parted and Adam continued down the aisle.

"You came," he said gruffly.

She nodded.

"Does this mean—?"

"I forgive you and want us to be together. Yes, that's exactly what it means."

"I love you, Lexie." He pulled her into his arms and twirled.

"I love you, Gavin," she whispered. "You're my one true love, too."

He suddenly stopped and lowered his head. She knew he was going to kiss her, but then he tipped his head at his family. "We have quite the audience."

"I suspect we're going to have the same audience in this very place when you kiss me on our big day."

"Yes, but I want privacy for this." He clutched her hand and led her outside and around the building.

His lips pressed against hers, the kiss urgent and fraught with emotion. She flung her arms around his neck to draw him closer and deepen the kiss, her heart bursting with happiness.

Peace settled over her. God's peace and peace in her core for the first time since her mother had died. Today was the beginning of a new life. She had her brother and Ruth, and now the entire McKade clan, to call family. What could be more right?

Gavin lifted his head, his boyish grin on his face. "I can assure you that no matter the plans you, Ruth, Nana and Mom get up to, I'm putting my foot down now. Our big day won't be in the distant future. Not distant at all."

"No worries, cowboy." She ran her fingers over the solid planes of his face. "I've thought about our wedding so many times, I can plan it in my sleep and I'll have you down that aisle before you know what hit you."

* * * * *

Get 4 FREE REWARDS!

We'll send you 2 FREE Books plus 2 FREE Mystery Gifts.

FREE
Value Over
$20

Both the **Love Inspired®** and **Love Inspired®** Suspense series feature compelling novels filled with inspirational romance, faith, forgiveness, and hope.

YES! Please send me 2 FREE novels from the Love Inspired or Love Inspired Suspense series and my 2 FREE gifts (gifts are worth about $10 retail). After receiving them, if I don't wish to receive any more books, I can return the shipping statement marked "cancel." If I don't cancel, I will receive 6 brand-new Love Inspired Larger-Print books or Love Inspired Suspense Larger-Print books every month and be billed just $6.24 each in the U.S. or $6.49 each in Canada. That is a savings of at least 17% off the cover price. It's quite a bargain! Shipping and handling is just 50¢ per book in the U.S. and $1.25 per book in Canada.* I understand that accepting the 2 free books and gifts places me under no obligation to buy anything. I can always return a shipment and cancel at any time by calling the number below. The free books and gifts are mine to keep no matter what I decide.

Choose one: ☐ **Love Inspired**   ☐ **Love Inspired Suspense**
 Larger-Print   **Larger-Print**
 (122/322 IDN GRDF)   (107/307 IDN GRDF)

Name (please print)

Address   Apt. #

City   State/Province   Zip/Postal Code

Email: Please check this box ☐ if you would like to receive newsletters and promotional emails from Harlequin Enterprises ULC and its affiliates. You can unsubscribe anytime.

Mail to the **Harlequin Reader Service:**
IN U.S.A.: P.O. Box 1341, Buffalo, NY 14240-8531
IN CANADA: P.O. Box 603, Fort Erie, Ontario L2A 5X3

Want to try 2 free books from another series! Call 1-800-873-8635 or visit www.ReaderService.com.

*Terms and prices subject to change without notice. Prices do not include sales taxes, which will be charged (if applicable) based on your state or country of residence. Canadian residents will be charged applicable taxes. Offer not valid in Quebec. This offer is limited to one order per household. Books received may not be as shown. Not valid for current subscribers to the Love Inspired or Love Inspired Suspense series. All orders subject to approval. Credit or debit balances in a customer's account(s) may be offset by any other outstanding balance owed by or to the customer. Please allow 4 to 6 weeks for delivery. Offer available while quantities last.

Your Privacy—Your information is being collected by Harlequin Enterprises ULC, operating as Harlequin Reader Service. For a complete summary of the information we collect, how we use this information and to whom it is disclosed, please visit our privacy notice located at corporate.harlequin.com/privacy-notice. From time to time we may also exchange your personal information with reputable third parties. If you wish to opt out of this sharing of your personal information, please visit readerservice.com/consumerschoice or call 1-800-873-8635. **Notice to California Residents**—Under California law, you have specific rights to control and access your data. For more information on these rights and how to exercise them, visit corporate.harlequin.com/california-privacy.

LIRLIS22R2

HARLEQUIN
PLUS

Announcing a **BRAND-NEW**
multimedia subscription service
for romance fans like you!

Read, Watch and Play.

Experience the easiest way to get
the romance content you crave.

Start your **FREE 7 DAY TRIAL** at
<u>www.harlequinplus.com/freetrial</u>.

SPECIAL EXCERPT FROM

LOVE INSPIRED SUSPENSE
INSPIRATIONAL ROMANCE

An undercover agent must break her cover to save someone she doesn't trust.

Read on for a sneak preview of
Blown Cover *by Jodie Bailey,*
available November 2022 from Love Inspired Suspense.

Darkness lurked in the shadows of Christmas tree lights. Sinister. Deadly.

Special agent Makenzie Fuller could almost feel it.

The bride and groom twirled beneath the raw-beam ceiling of the ballroom at Hunter's Ridge Castle.

The air seemed to buzz with danger.

Makenzie had felt this kind of hum against her skin in the past, shortly before her first partner was found dead.

Shortly before her second partner, Ian Andrews, vanished in a hail of accusations.

Makenzie took in a deep breath and exhaled. If she looked as ill at ease as she felt, her nerves could unravel almost a year's worth of undercover work. It had taken months to earn Robert Butler's trust.

"We have a problem." The voice at her elbow nearly made her jump.

She dipped her chin to the side, bringing her ear closer to Robert Butler, who'd slipped up beside her. "What can I do?" She kept her voice low, playing the part of his protector.

"There's a traitor in the room." The only agency investigating Robert Butler was her military investigative unit.

She was the only undercover agent on the case. *Traitor* would certainly apply.

She managed not to tense.

Makenzie furrowed her brows and reset her thinking into character. Her life depended on it. "Point him out and I'll handle it." That was her "job," after all. She could take the person into custody and get him out of harm's way without blowing her cover. Her team might even be able to offer a deal for testimony against Butler or his *associate*. "I'll—"

"No. This one's personal. It's been a while since I got my hands dirty. You stay and make sure no one disrupts Emma's wedding."

It would mean standing by while he killed a man.

She couldn't do that.

Slipping through the crowd, Makenzie trailed Butler.

Butler put his arm around the shoulder of the man he'd approached.

As they passed the window, the man stumbled, and his blue eyes met hers through the glass.

Familiar eyes.

Ian Andrews's eyes.

Don't miss
Blown Cover *by Jodie Bailey,*
available wherever Love Inspired Suspense books
and ebooks are sold.

LoveInspired.com

LOVE INSPIRED

Stories to uplift and inspire

Fall in love with Love Inspired—
inspirational and uplifting stories of faith
and hope. Find strength and comfort in
the bonds of friendship and community.
Revel in the warmth of possibility and the
promise of new beginnings.

Sign up for the Love Inspired newsletter
at **LoveInspired.com** to be the first
to find out about upcoming titles,
special promotions and exclusive content.

CONNECT WITH US AT:

  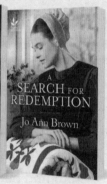